T5-ASP-187

I hope you feel
the love in
every page!

HELLO FAKE BOYFRIEND

KELSIE HOSS

kh

Copyright © 2022 by Kelsie Hoss

All rights reserved.

No part of this book may be reproduced in any form or by any electronic
or mechanical means, including information storage and retrieval
systems, without written permission from the author, except for the use
of brief quotations in a book review.

This is a work of fiction. Names, characters, businesses, places, events,
locales, and incidents are either the products of the author's imagination
or used in a fictitious manner. Any resemblance to actual persons, living
or dead, or actual events is purely coincidental.

Editing by Tricia Harden of Emerald Eyes Editing.

Cover design by Najla Qamber of Najla Qamber Designs.

Have questions? Email kelsie@kelsiehoss.com.

**For info on sensitive content, visit https://kelsiehoss.com/
pages/sensitive-content.**

This book was previously titled Confessions of a Smutty Romance Author.

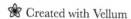 Created with Vellum

For my boys.

CONTENTS

A QUICK NOTE FROM THE AUTHOR

Dear Reader,

This book is full of humor, romance, and sexy scenes. Readers 18+ only, please!

Love,
Kelsie Hoss

I love men.

I love short facial hair, especially when it's artfully shaved and delightfully rough.

And god, do I love a good dick. The soft skin, the ridges of veins, and how responsive they are to my touch.

Men.

They're great to look at. To write about. To talk to (sometimes).

To fall in love with? Not so much.

- Mara Taylor

1

MARA

Confession: I'm a romance writer, but I don't believe in love.

I WOKE UP TO SNORING. Not my own. The bed wasn't mine either.

Hayden's arm rested over my middle, and I gently peeled it off of me, not disturbing his snoring even for a moment.

I rolled out of the bed, landing on my knees, and peeked at him, the better half of his body covered in his mismatched bachelor sheets and blankets. He was good-looking, with his muscles visible even in his relaxed state. And when I tell you he had a package that made up for the snoring...

My phone vibrated from under my clothing, and I lifted up my dress from the night before to see a group call from my best friends, Birdie and Henrietta. "Hello?" I whispered.

"Why are you whispering?" Birdie asked. "Do you have someone over?"

"No, I'm leaving Hayden's."

"Now?" Hen asked, stunned. "You have to get ready!"

I pulled the phone back, glancing at the time. "I have plenty of time. My girl at Sephora said she'd do my hair and makeup for the show."

"Nice," Birdie said. "I take it Hayden won't be coming along to support you."

I slipped my dress over my head. "Ha ha." I snagged my heels and tiptoed out of his room. As the snoring continued, I slipped on the heels and walked out the front door, locking the handle behind me.

"So how are you feeling?" Henrietta asked. "Nervous?"

"Not really." Warm summer wind wrapped around my body, lifting my hair and the edges of my dress. The sun was bright, and the whole world felt full of my energy. "It feels like my whole life has been leading up to this moment."

I could hear a smile in Henrietta's voice. "I love your confidence. I'm not so sure I'd be that brave on stage."

"Well, I wouldn't be so brave working with a bunch of high schoolers or managing a bunch of crazy renters. We all have our talents."

They laughed and Birdie said, "True."

"I wish I could be there," Henrietta said. "You're going to be amazing."

"No big deal. You can always catch the replay online. They said they're streaming it live." I reached my pickup and opened the door to get in. The car salesman I bought it from had tried to sell me on something smaller and sleeker. *Perhaps something to fit car seats in later,* he'd said. All I'd done was laugh. I loved sitting behind the wheel of my *single cab* truck, feeling like I owned the road. Plus, between the bed and the long seat, I had plenty of room to do whatever *and whomever* I wanted.

It easily fired up, and I asked Birdie, "How did Cohen feel about cutting the honeymoon short so you could make it back in time? You didn't have to do that, by the way."

"Girl, please, we're going to be married forever. We'll have plenty of chances to take all-inclusive vacations in Cancun. My best friend only goes live on television to talk about her first movie deal once."

"True," I admitted, driving down the now familiar roads of Brentwood, California, toward my favorite Sephora. I'd been so lucky to get this deal, and even luckier that the studio was already in talks for a sequel. "I know it's crazy to say for someone who doesn't even have a GED, but I feel like I was made for this." I wanted every girl who grew up like I did, being told she was too sexy or promiscuous or too much in general, to know that she deserves to live life the way she wants. "It's like my life's purpose is finally coming true, even if it took me thirty years to get here."

"Some people never find that," Birdie said. "We're so lucky."

I grinned. "I'm lucky to have you both." I pulled into the Sephora parking lot and stopped the truck. "I've got to get beautified, but I'll see you at the studio, Birdie?"

"I'll be there," she promised.

Henrietta added, "We can all celebrate how great it went tonight."

We hung up, and I went inside, ready for the transformation of a lifetime. Kell, the girl who'd managed to sell me hundreds of dollars of just-right products greeted me with a hug and a kiss and a "tsk tsk tsk." Okay, so maybe staying up late with Hayden hadn't done my under-eye any favors.

She got to work, barely pausing to talk as she cleaned my face and washed my hair and balanced my skin tone and curled away until I looked as good as I ever had in my life.

"Oh my gosh." I gently fluffed the waves in my hair. "It looks amazing."

Kell smirked. "Better than that topknot."

"Hey." I pointed at her. "No knocking the topknot. It's a vital part of my uniform."

"You work from home."

"Exactly." I grinned. "My boss is such a hard-ass."

She shook her head at me, laughing. "Good luck today. The girls and I are going to watch it on my phone. It's the first time one of us has styled someone for TV."

"You did amazing," I said, giving her a hug. I was still wearing my dress from the night before, so I hurried home, changed, and started the drive to the television studio on the outskirts of LA. It was about a forty-five-minute drive, which gave me plenty of time to go over the talking points in my head.

My publicist, Charlotte Cado, had written them for me in case I got nervous. At this point, they were just as ingrained as how to give a good hand job.

- Swipe Right *is a sexy romance showing the good, bad, and ugly of online dating in your thirties.*

- *Swiping right makes it seem so easy! But that's when the real work begins.*
- *Have you ever texted with a man? It makes you wonder about the last time they took a spelling class!*
- *When you find the one, you always have to be careful! If it's too good to be true, it probably smells like catfish in real life!*

My GPS guided me toward the studio entrance, blockaded by a red and white security gate. Once I told the guard who I was, he lifted the gate, telling me where to park.

As I followed his directions to the back parking lot, I couldn't help but think the outside of the building wasn't glamorous at all—dirty and smelly, just like any other part of LA.

But there were three shining spots there in that parking lot. Birdie, my agent, Jenny Nash, and my publicist, Charlotte Cado.

Birdie was already out of her car, leaning on the tailgate, looking fabulously tan and blissfully happy. Jenny stood next to her in a sleek black suit that was all business. They couldn't have been more opposite. Charlotte, on the other hand, was still in her Range Rover, the windows so tinted no one could even hope to see inside...

(Mental note: Get window tinting for pickup. Immediately.)

As soon as I got out of the pickup, Birdie rushed me, giving me a big hug. Jenny followed her, saying hello, and Charlotte got out of her vehicle, placing expensive sunglasses atop her head.

Charlotte looked absolutely horrified. "What are you *wearing?*"

I glanced down at my green dress. What was she talking about? This thing had been tailored to the hilt to keep the girls in, not to mention it would have cost an entire month's rent at my first apartment in LA. "Do I have a spot somewhere?"

"It's green!" she cried. "Didn't I send you a dressing guide?"

"You said jewel tones," I replied. "Last I knew, emerald is a jewel."

She covered her face with her hands. "You're going to be in front of a green screen. You'll just disappear!"

Shit. "My first debut on television cannot be as a floating head!" I cried. "I don't have time to go back home!"

Charlotte paced back and forth, somehow staying steady on the asphalt in her little kitten heels. "We don't have time to change." Then she stopped, looking between Birdie and me. "Are you the same size?"

"I'm a twenty-two," I said. "That's four sizes bigger than her."

Birdie glanced down at her bright yellow dress. It looked like an oversized Hawaiian shirt, which was adorable on her, but for me?

"You have to," Charlotte said. "I'd give you the clothes off my back but..."

"They won't fit," I finished, clenching my teeth. "Let us in your car."

Charlotte popped the trunk, and Birdie and I climbed in the pristine back. As soon as it closed behind us, I muttered, "Not my favorite reason to get undressed in the back seat."

Birdie giggled. "This *has* to go in a book."

"You know it will," I said, handing over my dress. "You know, once enough time has passed that it's actually funny and not devastating."

"I know my clothes aren't your style. I wish I would have thought to wear something cooler, but I got it on vacation and I—"

"Zip it," I said, turning my back to her so she could zip up the back of her dress I was now wearing. "You are beautiful, and I love your style, and I'm just glad you didn't wear green too. We were always accidentally matching when we were roommates."

"Oh my gosh, I remember that." She adjusted the collar of my dress. "Let's get inside?"

"Absolutely," I said with a grin. We walked toward the entrance and Charlotte said, "We'll see if they can focus the cameras on your face."

That was code for *yellow is not your color*. Noted.

The second we got through the doors and Charlotte told the receptionist who we were, everything seemed to speed up. Or at least that's how I saw it with all the stars in my eyes. Before I even knew it, I was standing on the wings in my friend's gaudy yellow dress and trying to take deep breaths.

Birdie rubbed my shoulders. "You're going to do amazing."

Jenny nodded. "Your books are going to fly off the shelves."

Charlotte was all business. "Just stick to the talking points we went over, and you'll do fine."

A producer wired up in a way that couldn't be fun outside of the bedroom approached us and said, "You're on in sixty."

My pulse quickened. It all felt so real, standing here in the wings, waiting to be interviewed, to announce a movie being made about my books. Something I'd created in my own mind. The premiere was only six months away, and it still didn't feel real. My dad used to tell me I was worthless. That I'd never amount to anything.

"You're on," the producer said.

My dad was wrong.

The studio audience cheered for me as I walked toward the open seat across from Mia Parker, television host and my ticket to the daytime spotlight.

"Hi, Mia!" I said, going to give her a hug.

She wrapped her slender arms around me, then stepped back and took me in. "I love the dress! Are we the last stop before the beach?"

"Nothing like drinking mai tais in the sand, right?"

She laughed. "Count me in." Gesturing toward the open chair, she said, "Sit, let's chat!"

I did as she asked, carefully crossing my legs so nothing would be videoed through the slit in the oversized Hawaiian shirt.

Mia leaned toward the audience like I might lean in toward Birdie and Henrietta at Wednesday morning breakfasts. "We have the fabulous Mara Taylor here today to talk about her book, *Swipe Right*, which is being turned into a movie!"

The audience applauded me, and I soaked it all in. The spotlight felt like a hot stone massage on my skin. Never had I ever felt so glamourous in my life, and that included the girls' trip Birdie and I took to Tulum after my first five-figure month as an author, where we had spa days and sat on the beach getting margaritas delivered every hour on the hour.

"Tell us about the book, Mara," Mia said.

I grinned into the camera, spouting a talking point I'd practiced on the way. "*Swipe Right* is a sexy romance showing the good, bad, and ugly of online dating in your thirties."

"Lord help us," Mia said, doing the sign of the cross over her chest. "Dating in your thirties is like a minefield, isn't it?"

I laughed. "I haven't been thirty long, but so far, there's been plenty to enjoy, if you know what I mean."

Mia rocked back, clapping her hands together. "So that's what we can expect from your stories? Good sex and a happily ever after?"

"And a few laughs in between," I added with a smile.

"How much of your fiction is inspired by your life?" Mia asked.

This was so fun, like talking to a friend. So I shared maybe a little more than I should have. "The good sex part? Very similar. The happily ever afters? Not a chance."

Mia's eyebrows rose. "What? A romance writer who hasn't had her own happily ever after?"

"My version of an HEA is walking out of a store with a pair of Jimmy Choos paid in full."

The audience laughed, but Mia narrowed in. "Now, Mara, how are we supposed to read about romance from a woman who doesn't believe in love?"

I didn't like that insinuation, that my fiction was

somehow less valid because of my personal life. "The book's fiction, Mia, it's not a memoir."

"But you must believe in love. I know you're single now, but hasn't there ever been anyone you could see yourself spending forever with?"

"What I believe in, really believe in, is a woman's right to unapologetically chase after whatever she wants, whether it's sexual pleasure or a career or lifelong friendship. Love is a nice concept to think about and dream of, but the reality is it doesn't happen for everyone."

Mia rocked back, then clapped her hands together and faced the audience. "There you have it, folks, a romance author who doesn't believe in love, cashing in on women's dreams. I'll see you after this commercial break."

I opened my mouth to argue, but it was already too late. Mia was getting off her chair, walking off the stage. "What was that, Mia?" I demanded, following her.

She turned toward me, disappointment in her eyes. "I've been reading your books for the last five years... Finding out that you don't believe in what you wrote... it's like finding out Santa isn't real all over again."

It wasn't my fault she was holding on to false promises sold to her by greeting card companies. "So you admit, believing in love is like believing in Santa Claus."

She shook her head slowly and walked away.

I watched her go until Charlotte grabbed my shoulder and said, "Mara, we have a problem."

"What?" I asked, dread filling every pore of my body.

"The studio canned talks for a second movie."

2

MARA

Confession: My career is the love of my life.

BIRDIE DROVE me back to her house because I was a complete and utter mess. Every bit of backup we had was invited, including Henrietta, my agent, and my publicist. I didn't even know how I made it inside. All I knew was I was lying on the couch, cradled in Birdie's lap, tears still streaming down my cheeks. This was worse than any breakup.

On the opposite side, Henrietta sat on the recliner, providing moral support. As soon as she heard the interview, she faked a stomach ache and dodged work.

"It's over," I cried into Birdie's lap.

Cohen, her husband, set a steaming mug of cider on the coffee table and said, "This should help."

I couldn't bring myself to get out of the fetal position, much less drink anything, even if it smelled as amazing as the cider did.

Birdie ran her hand over my hair. "Surely you can convince them to get the deal for a second movie going again. They were interested in it once; they can be again."

Jenny, who looked just as distraught as me (probably at the loss of potential income), stood by Ralphie's cage. He was a white bird I'd known just as long as I'd known Birdie, and he was studying Jenny suspiciously.

Charlotte stood near the door, staring at her phone, like she was ready to leave. "It's going to take a miracle to spin that interview around. We'd have to say Mara got nervous in front of the camera and have some very real evidence that Mara isn't a sex-crazed porn fanatic like the media's already making her out to be."

Okay, that got me sitting up. "What exactly are they saying about me?"

Charlotte flipped her screen to face us and played a video for me.

"Hi, I'm Jeanie Walters, and I'm here with Georgia Pflumm, head of the WAP, Women Against Pornography, a California-based nonprofit that shares information about the dangers of porn both in visual and literary form. Georgia, I'd love to get your take on today's interview with prominent 'romance' author, Mara Taylor."

"Air quotes?" I muttered.

Georgia sat up straighter, her puffy sleeves so crisp they barely moved. "Jeanie, I'm glad you asked. This interview is a perfect example of the dangers of the romance novel. Women justify their reading habits by saying it's all make-believe, but all the while they're being indoctrinated on pleasure before purpose, sex before love.

Is that the kind of message we want being spread in the world?"

Birdie groaned. "Turn it off."

Charlotte obliged but added, "There's more where that came from. There are memes and hashtags and videos..."

"But you said we could turn it around," I said, a desperate energy quickly working its way through my nervous system. We *had* to turn it around. If this deal went down so negatively, no other studio would want to touch me.

Jenny looked solemnly at Ralphie. "We'd have to prove that you were somehow in a serious relationship, and no one would buy that."

"Unless..." Charlotte tapped her chin. "We could say you were playing it cool on TV so he wouldn't think you were being too clingy. You would have to make a public appearance with him... whoever *he* is. And it couldn't be some rando either. It would have to be someone that your community could believe you've been dating in secret. And with your history as a—"

I gave her a warning look.

"—a woman of the world, we're going to be very hard pressed to make a relationship look like anything other than a publicity stunt."

We were all quiet for a moment until Birdie said, "What about Hayden? Would he be up to something more... permanent?"

"More permanent than his semen living inside me for the next five to seven days? Not a chance." I leaned over my lap, rubbing my temples. Why had I opened my big fat mouth? Couldn't I have just stuck to the robotic talking points and moved along with my life?

Mia was not my friend, and I should have known that. The way I grew up, that was one of the biggest lessons I'd learned: People were always out for number one. And my "gotcha" interview with Mia had to be sending her ratings through the roof.

From the archway between the living room and the dining room, Cohen asked, "What about Jonas?"

We all swiveled our heads toward him, seeking an explanation.

"What about Jonas?" Birdie asked.

Cohen shrugged, folding his arms across his chest. "I mean, Mara's around him quite a bit since we're all in the same friend group. It wouldn't be that far of a reach to think that you two could be together."

"But *Jonas*?" I asked.

Seeming defensive, Cohen said, "What's wrong with Jonas? He's a nice guy."

I glanced at Birdie, then Hen. "He's an accountant."

Cohen laughed. "And?"

"Who would buy that we were together? He's completely the opposite of my type! I bet he wears white socks with khakis. I bet he likes missionary position, and his favorite part of sex is cuddling. I bet, I bet he sleeps with a mouth guard in because he grinds his teeth. I bet he dreams about balance sheets. I bet he wakes up excited to go to the office and eats egg white omelets on wheat toast every day for breakfast—"

"We get it," Cohen said. "You think accountants are boring, but I don't see any other options here."

Charlotte nodded. "Plus, it gives you a good reason for keeping it secret."

Henrietta set down her cup of cider and said, "They make a good point. It would be super easy to fake a relationship with him, just until the movie premieres and the sequel gets rolling so you wouldn't burn any bridges in Hollywood. Have they scheduled the premiere?"

"Six months from today," Charlotte answered, giving me a look. "Half a year's a long time to fake a relationship with an *accountant*."

Birdie nodded. "And you wouldn't be able to see other guys during that time..."

Six months without sex. That thought hadn't even struck me yet, but now that it was there... "I'd do it, if I had to," I decided out loud. "I need to save my career."

The wheels were clearly spinning in Jenny's head. "I could call the studio owner. He's a bit of a hothead, but if he's had some time to cool down, maybe I could convince him this was just a little blip and we'll do more practicing before the next interview, if there is one."

Birdie put her hand on my leg. "What do you think? It could be a good way to turn this around."

Hen said, "What's six months out of a lifetime of success?"

A little *jois de vivre* back in her features, Jenny said, "I'll set a meeting with the studio owner in person. Bring him a box full of those chocolate-covered cherries he likes for god knows what reason."

"Wait!" I said, making everyone turn and stare at me.

"What?" Charlotte asked. "This is the best-case scenario."

"Don't we have to ask Jonas first?" I said. "He'd have to say yes too."

Cohen cracked a smile. "I'll call him now."

"Hurry," Charlotte said. "The sooner Jenny gets things patched up with the studio, the sooner I can do damage control on this whole mess."

The room went quiet as Cohen lifted his phone. Even Ralphie stayed perfectly still, his black eyes taking in the crowd in his living room.

"Put it on speaker," Birdie asked.

Cohen obliged, and ringing emanated from his phone speaker.

"Yello?" Jonas said.

I cringed.

Birdie hit my side and whispered, "Beggars can't be choosers."

True.

"Hey, Jonas," Cohen said. "I'm in kind of a tight spot, and I was wondering if I could ask you a favor."

"Yeah, what's going on?" Jonas asked.

Birdie whispered, "He really is a good guy."

Cohen held his fingers to his lips and said, "You know Mara? She got in a bit of trouble today and she's needing a boyfriend—a fake boyfriend just to make appearances with her until her movie airs in six months."

"Cohen, I—"

"Don't make a decision yet. Go out to lunch with her, talk about the details. I'm sure there's a way you both can get some good out of the situation."

Jonas was quiet for a long moment.

"It would be a real favor to me," Cohen said.

The silence drew out until finally Jonas said, "Just lunch."

"Great! She'll meet you at Waldo's Diner. Say around one?"

I nodded quickly. I'd take what I could get.

"Make it one thirty," Jonas replied. "See you later."

Cohen hung up and gave a hopeful shrug. "That's good news, right? At least he'll meet with you about it."

"Now I have to convince an accountant to go out with me. Just when I thought I couldn't get any lower." I put my head in my hands, and Birdie rubbed my back.

"He's going to love you," she said.

Charlotte leveled her gaze at me. "You better make sure he does, or your career's over before it even began."

3

JONAS

I didn't really have time to go to lunch, but for Cohen, I would. Mara was Birdie's friend, and from what I knew of her, my exact opposite. She was a writer, and she worked whatever hours she wanted whenever she wanted. She was always either drinking a cocktail or a coffee, and that was basically her two personalities, as far as I knew. But Cohen said she needed help. And for my friend, I'd at least hear the girl out.

With tax season coming up soon, I had to make sure all my clients were caught up from the year before. I went through their books, making sure it was all up to date and emailing my bookkeeper, Charlie, for anything that was missing. My boss was retiring at the end of April, and I wanted to make sure I was at least considered for the job.

I'd been working at ESR Accounting for ten years and had moved my way up from staff accountant to senior accountant, and I knew the promotion would be down to me and one other person.

If I craned my neck just right, I could look through

my office window and see his office across the open space with half-height cubicles for all the extra seasonal help.

Ronnie Jenkins was his name. He had a wife and six kids, but I never saw them except at the company barbecue each summer. He also had a houseboat somewhere up in Washington, where they went for two weeks every year after tax season.

Me, on the other hand? Work was my life, aside from my family and Wednesday poker nights with the guys.

For the next hour, I got in as much work as I could and then closed down my computer. I turned my phone off do not disturb just to make sure Mara hadn't backed out of this crazy idea. She seemed like the kind of girl who'd change her mind.

Unlike Tracey.

I scrolled down my text messages, seeing the last one I'd received from her.

Tracey: I haven't forgotten about you. I just need some more time to think it over.

This coming a month after I'd asked her on a date.

Tracey was my sister Tess's best friend, and she seemed like the girl I could spend forever with. My family already liked her. She was beautiful, with blonde hair and a big smile that made you feel like you hung the moon. Plus, she had her own business working as a virtual assistant, so she was successful, and her schedule was always flexible.

Unfortunately, I had a feeling I was just waiting on a no.

I put my phone back in my pocket and walked out of my office. Before I even hit the parking lot, my phone began ringing. Half hoping Mara had canceled so I could go back to work, I pulled it back out to check the name.

My sister was calling. "Hold on, Tess, I'm getting in my car," I said to my sister as I fumbled with my key fob. I unlocked it and got into my Mercury, and the call connected to the car's system. "You there?"

"I'm here. Are you going to be free Friday morning to bring Mom to dialysis?"

I winced as I pulled onto the road, wishing we could talk about anything other than our mother's failing kidneys. Mom had never been weak or frail or sickly in my life—she'd always been the type of woman up at five in the morning to drink her coffee or waiting up at the table until I got home from hanging out with friends just to make sure I was okay. But now it was our turn to be there for her, no matter the inconvenience. "I am. I just wish I could stay with her. I feel guilty every time I drive away."

"I wish we could hire someone to do it at their house," Tess said. "I'm pretty sure Dad's job is the only thing keeping him sane, and I can't afford to close the store anymore."

"No way would Mom let a stranger come into the house," I said, wishing I could do it myself. She'd done so much for me throughout my life, from changing diapers to helping paint my first home; I owed her this.

"Mom might not have a choice. Tax season is in two months. We barely saw you last year."

I didn't want to think about it, much less talk about it.

"She needs to let us hire someone to help her more permanently, Jonas. She's not getting better, and if we're lucky, we have years of this ahead of us. Maybe over time she'll be more comfortable with them."

"Nursing services like that are notorious for the turnover," I said. "It would just put her through even more stress."

"I'm putting a job listing up right now. I'm sure we'll find someone perfect," she replied happily.

"No, absolutely not," I said.

"I can't miss any more work. If I'm not at the store, I'm not selling product. And do you really want to miss out on a life-changing promotion because Mom's uncomfortable for a few weeks?"

I didn't like either option. "Just give me some time to think about it. There has to be something we haven't considered."

"Fine. But if you don't have an idea by Monday, it's going up," she said, her mouse clicking away. "Why are you in the car, by the way? Playing hookie?"

"I wish," I said. "Late lunch."

"Okay, I have a customer coming into the store. I'll talk to you later. Love you."

"You too," I said, pushing the button to hang up.

Waldo's Diner came into view, and I parked near the door. I'd come here more since Cohen married Birdie, the owner's granddaughter. For the first time, though, I was nervous to go inside.

Mara was... a firecracker wrapped in dynamite. The kind of girl you knew you could love if it didn't tear you apart. I pushed through the front door, looking around for her. She sat sideways in a booth toward the back of the restaurant, her heeled feet hanging over the edge. She waved her hand at me, her smile big and thankful.

She *did* have a nice smile.

But that was beside the point.

I didn't have time for games at this stage in my life. My sister's wedding was coming up, my mom was sick, and I had to work harder than ever to be named partner at work. A fake relationship for the media circus didn't fit into that equation.

When I got a few feet away from Mara, she stood up and said, "Thanks so much for agreeing to this, Jonas. It means a lot."

I had a hard time keeping my eyes off her body in that green dress. It hugged her curves and displayed her cleavage, and damn, her legs looked good in those heels. I reminded myself why I was here and said, "I haven't agreed to anything yet."

"I meant thanks for coming to lunch," she quickly clarified. Which made me feel like an asshole. She was a friend—or at least friend adjacent. We could have lunch together without it being weird.

"Sorry," I said. "I am hungry."

"Good," she said, sitting down and sliding a menu toward me. "Betty told me they have a new dessert on the menu named after her. Apple Brown Betty. With ice cream. It sounds amazing." She kissed her fingers with such delight I couldn't help but smile.

"That does sound good, although don't tell Betty that was already a dessert name."

Mara giggled, the sound happy and tinkling.

Betty herself came to our table, offering us both a smile. "Can I get you anything to drink? Maybe a coffee like Mara?"

"Water's fine, thanks," I said, glancing back at my

menu. I tried to stop with the caffeine after noon. "Can I get a cheeseburger with fries? No onion."

"Sure thing, sweetie," Betty said. "What about you, Mara?"

"Can I have that dessert you mentioned? I'll decide on food later."

"Of course," Betty replied, walking away with our orders while I sat in stunned silence.

"What?" Mara asked.

"You're eating dessert first?"

Mara laughed. "It's all going to sit in my stomach together anyway. Why does it matter what order I eat it in?"

She had a good point. A point that would have horrified my eat-your-vegetables-first mother. "Fair enough."

"So." She leaned across the table. "I know Cohen talked to you a bit about what's going on."

"What is going on?" I asked. "All he said was that you needed a fake boyfriend until your movie premiere? Is it for some reality show?"

Mara laughed, and I found myself both slightly embarrassed and slightly liking the sound. "I wish," she said. "No, I made an ass of myself on television this morning and ruined my chances at a second movie deal."

My eyebrows drew together. "What did you say?"

"Basically, I said I don't believe in love, and the producers heard it and now talks of a second movie are completely off the table. So now I need to prove somehow that I was only saying those things to save face with a boyfriend I didn't want to scare away."

I didn't know what shocked me more. What she'd said on TV or the ridiculous proposition. I decided to start with the part that made the least sense. "Wait, you don't believe in love?"

"No, so—"

"Hold on. You write romance, and you... haven't fallen in love yet for yourself?"

"No. I think it's a sham. Less common than a lightning strike."

I rubbed my face. "I don't understand." How could she be saying this when her best friend and mine had just experienced their own whirlwind romance?

She leaned forward, her long brown hair falling over her shoulders in a distracting way. "What is there to understand? The divorce rate in America is higher than fifty percent, right?"

"That's the statistic." My parents would have blamed it on a failure in moral character or a lack of willpower. Probably both.

"And you acknowledge that sometimes marriage is advantageous for reasons other than love?" she continued.

"Okay..." Where was she taking this?

"So, some people stay together not because they love each other but because they're benefiting in some way. Either in income or status or childcare or—"

"Okay, I get it," I said. "What's your point? That all marriages are a sham? Because I can't get behind that."

She shrugged, sitting back in her seat. "If marriage fails fifty percent of the time, and plenty of people who stay together are miserable... it seems like an archaic, patriarchal contractual obligation based on hormones, money, and a desire for disease-free sex. I'm not great at math, but that means the chance of a real, loving marriage that lasts 'til-death-do-us-part' is pretty slim."

If Betty had brought my water out any earlier, I would have been sputtering it all over the table. "Tell me again why you write romance novels?"

"There's more than one kind of happily ever after," she replied with a wink.

Betty brought my water, and I thanked her before taking a cautious sip. After I had safely swallowed, I said, "You're talking about sex?"

"I'm talking about sex, yes, and a woman finding herself, finding friendships, finding pleasure, creating the kind of life she deserves. Of course, that can be with a partner, if she chooses. And, I suppose part of me loves romance because it's the ultimate dig."

"A dig? At who?"

"At men who think they should give a woman anything less than what she deserves."

I sat back, laughing. A literal *romance writer* had taken something I'd been working toward my whole life and simplified it to a societal construct—and a bad one at that. And hell, half of me believed her. If only it weren't so ironic.

"What's so funny?" she asked.

I shook my head. "A romance writer who doesn't believe in marriage and hates men?"

She frowned, spinning her coffee cup around her hands. "Well, apparently you're not the only one who's put off by my opinions because unless I can show the studio that I actually do believe in love, this could be my last chance to make it *big* with my writing. I don't want to be one and done."

"How bad was the interview?" I asked. Surely she could recover without me.

Pressing her lips together, she got out her phone, pressed play, and slid it across the table. I watched in horrifying detail as she confessed her feelings on national TV. "And there's more where that came from," she said. "Everyone's talking about it."

"Can't you just say it was a misspeak?" I asked, knowing already that was impossible. Mara had been pretty blunt about her beliefs.

"I know it's a lot to ask, but it would just be until the movie comes out in six months, so it doesn't look like I'm with you just to sign the deal for the sequel, then you would be in the clear."

"I don't know, Mara," I said, shaking my head slowly. I didn't like lying... and turning down a chance with anyone else to pretend-date someone who didn't even believe in love...

Betty came with a plate full of dessert and put it in front of Mara. Mara thanked her, but she didn't move her fork. "Please," she whispered, her eyes shining. "My career is *everything* to me."

I wish I would have turned Cohen down on the phone for this reason. I couldn't say no to Mara. Not with her jaw trembling and moisture shining in her eyes. But I couldn't say yes either. As lame as it may have sounded, I wanted the real thing. I wanted the kind of love my parents had. And as my mom liked to remind me, I wasn't getting any younger. If I spent half a year or more being Mara's pretend boyfriend, it would be more time of missing out on something real.

"Look, Jonas," she said. "I'm willing to do whatever it takes. I'll clean your house and do your laundry and make every single meal for you if it'll help you say yes. *Please.*"

I looked down at the boomerang pattern on the laminate tabletop, trying to think of a way to let her down easy. But then it clicked.

"There is something you could do for me," I said slowly.

"Anything, Jonas. I mean it." Her brown eyes were wide and earnest. They looked almost like my mother's.

I took a deep breath, knowing my mom was worth it. Every single time, she'd be worth it. "My mom has to have dialysis three days a week for four hours at a time. We want to do it at home, but we all work, and we don't want just anyone to be there with her..."

"I'll do it!" she said, smiling so wide it lit her eyes from the inside out. "My schedule's flexible, and I can always write while it's happening or after—"

"Hold on," I replied, a sinking feeling in my stomach. I didn't want to give her false hope. "My mom is nervous around new people. If she doesn't like you, it's not going to work."

"She's going to love me! I know she will." Mara clapped her hands together. "Thank you so much, Jonas. You're not going to regret this, I promise."

God, I hoped she was right. "Come to supper at my parents' house tomorrow night. If Mom likes you, we have a deal."

4

MARA

Confession: Reverse cowgirl is my favorite position. Yee haw!

I HELD UP MY PHONE, staring at my friends' faces on the screen. "I'm freaking out. This could be my last night to have sex for half a *year*."

Hen raised her eyebrows. "Who's saying you won't have sex with Jonas?"

I pointed my finger in my mouth. "He's an *accountant*." Not that he was bad looking. In fact, he was kind of hot, but missionary wasn't exactly my speed.

Birdie snort-laughed. "So because he's an accountant, that means he's bad in bed? Is there a list of approved professions?"

"Of course," I replied, using my fingers to count. "Lumberjack, firefighter, police officer—basically any of your public service, man-in-uniform types—cabana boys—"

"Prostitutes," Henrietta added, laughing. "They are professionals, after all."

I stuck my tongue out at her. "It's not that I can't live without good sex... It's just really fun."

"Who says you have to stop hooking up when you're fake dating Jonas?" Birdie asked. "Maybe you can just do it on the down-low, you know, if he's okay with it?"

I shook my head, already knowing my answer. "I'm not going to go hang out with the guy's mom while banging some other guy. Even I have boundaries."

Birdie and Henrietta were quiet for a moment, and then Birdie said, "Guess you better call the cowboy for one last rodeo."

I laughed. "He works at Petco."

"Close enough," she teased, then kissed her hand and waved. "I've gotta go. Cohen's taking me on a date tonight."

"Gah," Hen said. "Where can I get one of him?"

"Go scratch some lottery tickets. Your chances of winning are higher," I said, then blew a kiss. "Love you guys."

We hung up, and Hayden was my first call. Or text, rather.

Mara: Want me to come over?

Within minutes, he replied.

Hayden: Bring the whipped cream.

He didn't need to ask me twice, especially since this night was my last hurrah. I went to my room and put on the sexiest lingerie I had, a bright red silk set with too many straps that did nothing to cover what underwear was meant to. Then I slipped on a long silk robe and cinched it around my waist. It could pass for a dress. In the dark. Maybe.

Then I went to my fridge, grabbed the whipped cream I kept on hand for coffee and... other activities, and ran to my truck.

I had one night left, one night of sexual freedom, and I was going to make it count.

Hayden's place was about twenty minutes away from mine, but I preferred going over there to him staying at my place. Having him over regularly just felt too... intimate. It was easier going there and making sure to never leave anything at his place. No muss, no fuss.

I pulled up to his place and glanced around the neighborhood, knowing it would be the last time I saw it for a while. The houses were smaller here than in my part of Brentwood, but they were spaced far apart with big lawns and massive trees giving the hint of privacy.

I parked beside a sycamore and got out, walking in my furry boots to his front door. I knocked, and as soon as he cracked the door open, a crooked grin formed on his face.

Hayden was good-looking in the way ex-boy band members are good-looking. More pretty than chiseled and a floppy haircut that would never fly in a C-suite. But at Petco, he had all the approval he needed from desperate (read: horny) pet owners.

In fact, that was how we'd met. Birdie needed me to pick something up for her bird, Ralphie. A few questions later, Hayden was escorting me to the break room, indulging me in services he only offered *special* customers.

It had been the beginning of a beautiful, open, *casual* relationship. The other women he slept with didn't bother me, because right now, his blue eyes were on me. On the dip where the lapels of my silky robe met.

"I didn't order pizza," he said, biting down on his bottom lip.

I pulled my robe to the side, giving him a preview of the lingerie and everything underneath.

"I did order that." He opened the screen door and pulled me inside.

With the door closed, he gripped my wrist and lifted my arm above my head, kissing my neck, drawing away my robe and biting down on my shoulder.

God, I was going to miss this.

I fisted my free hand in his shirt until my knuckles grazed his solid abs, and I pulled him close to me. The length of his hard cock pressed into my hip, and I moaned.

Did I mention I was going to miss this?

"Take off the robe," he ordered, and I let go of him to slip it over my shoulders. He kept his house cool, and the air raised goosebumps on my skin, contrasting with the heat of his lips moving down my body.

His teeth teased aside a strap of my bra, and he caught a nipple in his mouth, sucking and playing while he thumbed the other one.

I closed my eyes, letting my head fall back against the wall. I loved this about sex, the ability to let my mind go and get lost in the sensations of my body.

He rubbed the heel of his hand against my clit, and I moaned, biting my bottom lip.

"I want you in my room," he said. "Now."

I started walking that way, but he caught my hand. "Get on all fours. I want to see that ass."

I grinned at him, shaking my head. "You're a fucking freak."

His eyes darkened. "Hands. And knees."

I left my robe on the floor and bent down, arching my back so he could see my hips, my ass, on full display. Glancing over my shoulder, I asked, "Like this?"

His eyes were hazy as he nodded.

I crawled, slowly, across the wood floors, feeling his eyes watch every shift of my body. I felt so heady with power, with sexiness, that the simple shape of my body did this to him. Fuck, it was hot.

As soon as I reached his bedroom, he ordered, "On the bed. Face down."

I did as he instructed and heard the sharp sound of his zipper cracking open, the slide of denim against his skin until it fell to the floor. Then the yank of softer cotton as he pulled off his shirt, all while cool air teased my skin.

The hiss of the whipped cream can sounded, and I felt cool cream slide along the crease where my legs met my ass. My pussy tightened as his tongue lapped up the cream, coming so close to my center but missing it all together.

I gripped the sheets, already feeling wet. Already wishing his cock, his fingers, his tongue could relieve the pressure.

The next strip of whipped cream formed over my ass crack, dangerously close to my pussy. "If you go any further, you'll get a different kind of cream," I said.

"I'm fucking counting on it," he said, his voice husky before licking my ass clean. His tongue danced around me, and then he yanked on my hips, pulling my ass to his face.

His tongue slid along my slit, making me quiver, before he began licking and sucking and softly blowing until my hips were shaking. "Fuck, Hayden," I moaned.

He flipped me over, spreading my legs over his shoulders so he could eat me more thoroughly, and I came around his tongue, releasing all the cream he could ever want.

When he rose up, my eyes landed on his cock. Long, hard, with veins threading from his balls to the smooth, pink tip.

I was going to miss this cock. I got off the bed, kneeling in front of him, and took it in my mouth, tasting the salt of his precum, feeling the ridge where his shaft connected to his head. I danced my tongue around it, memorizing every fucking feeling.

His fingers threaded through the hair behind my bun and he gripped my head, shoving his dick deeper down my throat, like we both liked. I moaned against his cock, and his knees buckled.

"Fuck, Mara, not yet."

I backed out, moving away from his tip, and sucked on his balls. First one, then the other, letting my nose graze the length of his dick.

"Fuuuck," he moaned.

"Lie down," I ordered.

He followed my command, and I found the whipped cream can discarded on the floor. I put some whipped cream on the tip of my tongue before lifting his heavy sack and pressing the nozzle to lay a strip of cream along his seam. I licked it, pressing my tongue hard into his perineum.

He fisted his hand in my hair, moaning, "You're a fucking goddess."

I knew it. It was good to hear it.

I licked down the length of his cock again, taking it in my mouth and bobbing up and down until the salty, bitter taste grew stronger, contrasting the leftover sweetness of the whipped cream.

"Get on top of me," he demanded, and I was quick to oblige.

I turned my back to him and straddled his legs, slowly guiding his tip into my opening. I stayed there, just the tip, until he raised his hips and I pulled back.

"Don't fuckin' tease," he growled, grabbing my hips and slamming me down onto him. The length of him filled me, spreading me, easing my tension in the best possible way.

"Shit," I moaned, slowly gliding my hips up and down. His hands fisted in the thickness of my thighs. I knew he loved this. Loved seeing my ass spread in front of him, loved the weight of my body on his.

And that made me love it even more.

I lifted my hands and released my hair from its bun, playing with it and then dropping my head back so the ends danced over his abs.

He fisted my hair, yanking, making my scalp explode with the most delicious pain. I licked my fingers and rubbed my clit, edging myself closer and closer to oblivion.

"I can feel you getting tighter," he said. "You're going to come with me."

"When?" I panted.

"Five," he said, thrusting himself deeper inside me.

"Four." My fingers circled faster.

"Three." He gripped my hips tighter.

"Two," I moaned, barely holding back.

"Now," he let out, wave after wave of pleasure coming across me as I milked his cock for everything he had inside.

I slowly lifted my hips off his and rolled to the side, our panting breaths mingling in the cool air.

"Fuck," he said, kissing me roughly, then rolling back. "*Fuck.*"

I grinned, seconds from giggling. "Fuck."

We lay there for a while on our backs, staring at the circling ceiling fan, and soon came Hayden's soft snores. He was worthless after sex, always falling asleep so quickly.

I slipped out of bed and went to his bathroom, showering off the day, but using his soap to keep his scent on me.

It wasn't that I loved Hayden. He was just... the most consistent man in my life. Any time I needed a booty call, he was there. Any time I didn't need him, he wasn't. He worshipped my body like I was a goddess and ate me out like it was a god damn commandment.

But it was over between us now.

Fun could only be fun for so long until it wasn't anymore.

I got out of the shower, toweled off, and went to the living room for my robe. I slipped it over my shoulders, tying the belt around my waist. I'd leave the lingerie though, for him to remember me by.

He was still snoring when I went to his room, but I nudged him awake.

"You heading out?" he mumbled sleepily.

"Yeah," I said. "Early morning." Lies.

"Sure. Come here." He gripped the back of my neck and drew me to his lips. He still smelled like me. "Bye, baby. Drive safe."

"I will," I promised. Then I walked out the door and saw.... exactly the last person I'd been expecting to see.

5

JONAS

"Mara?" I asked, looking between her, her truck, and the house she was parked in front of.

She tightened her silk dress around herself and smoothed her hair. "Jonas... what are you doing here?"

I pointed my thumb over my shoulder. "My parents' house is across the street there." I noted the flush in her face, then the house... That guy who worked at Petco lived here. My eyebrows rose.

"Shut up," she said.

"I didn't say anything," I replied.

Her cheeks were growing redder by the second. It was kind of adorable, honestly.

"I do have a question, though," I said, crossing the street to stand closer to her.

"What?" She glanced at her pickup like she'd rather be behind the wheel heading far away from here.

"Why do you need me to be your fake boyfriend when you could ask him?" I nodded toward the house.

She lifted her chin, challenging me. "You sound jealous."

"I'm not jealous." But I was a little irritated. Was she really hooking up with another guy the same day she asked me to fake date her?

"Hayden and I have never been anywhere in public together. There's no proof. And..." She hesitated, looking down at her feet. She was wearing these brown furry boots with a stain on the toes. It looked like something Tess would have made.

"And what?" I prompted.

"I don't want him to get the wrong idea."

I glanced back toward the house where she'd clearly just been having sex with him. "What wrong idea?"

"That our relationship is anything more than physical. I don't do long-term commitments."

I shook my head as if that would help me understand. This woman was a fucking unicorn. I could think of so many guys who would have loved that arrangement, but I couldn't help thinking of the one she made between her and me. "And our relationship?"

"Mutually beneficial. All the best ones are." She glanced across the street from where I came. "Do you live in this neighborhood, or were you having a last hurrah too?"

"No," I said. "My parents do." He glanced back at the house directly across the street with a limestone rock out front that had Moore etched into the stone.

"Your last name is Moore?" she asked.

I scrubbed my face. "Oh my gosh." This really was a bad idea.

"What?"

"What? We've been friends for a year now and you don't know my last name?"

"I mean, we're not exactly friends..."

I stared at her. "Your name is Mara Taylor. You write romance for adult women. You live in a bungalow in Brentwood, less than ten minutes from the beach because your favorite place to be is the water. You drink coffee all hours of the day, unless you're at a bar where you order mojitos or, on rare occasion, a dirty martini. You don't have any pets, but your favorite animal is a giraffe. Oh, and you eat dessert before regular food when the mood strikes. Does that about cover it?"

Her mouth gaped open and closed. "Wh—how did you know that?"

"Because I pay attention when you speak!" I let out a breath. Why was she making me so crazy already? "We've been in the same friend group for two years, and what do you know about me?"

She opened her mouth.

"Other than the fact I'm an accountant."

She closed her mouth. "I'm sorry. I'm not used to people staying in my life."

The way she said it, the way she wouldn't quite meet my eyes... it made my chest ache. But I had more important things to worry about. Especially now that I knew she'd been fucking my parents' neighbor. "You know my parents have seen your truck in front of Hayden's house before."

"And?" she asked.

"And? They might wonder why their son's theoretically serious girlfriend is at some other guy's house all the time."

"Shit," she mumbled. "*Shit*. What am I supposed to do? I can't exactly get rid of my truck."

"You're going to have to get to my parents' house somehow, if Mom agrees, and you can't bring that truck."

She looked longingly at her pickup. "Bertha's the first brand-new vehicle I ever bought."

I would have had a little more sympathy if I wasn't currently standing outside her booty call's house. "There'll be more brand-new vehicles. If you get another movie deal."

I knew I'd won the second that realization crossed her face. With that, I turned to walk back toward my car parked across the street. "See you tomorrow for supper," I called over my shoulder.

"I hate you," she called back. "But thank you," she added.

I couldn't help but smile despite the feeling in my gut that this was a terrible, *terrible* idea.

6

MARA

Confession: Family isn't my thing.

HENRIETTA TOOK off work to go car shopping with me. I couldn't bring myself to get rid of Bertha, but I did have it in my budget for a payment on a decent used car. Birdie offered to ask Cohen to come along so we wouldn't get stiffed, but I had dealt with so many bullshitters over the years that used car salesmen were nothing new.

We went to the lot near my house and parked up front. Pretty soon, a guy maybe five years younger than us walked up. My eyes immediately traveled to the tattoo of a phoenix decorating his muscular forearm.

"Hi, ladies," he said, his voice as smooth as honey. "Looking for something particular today?"

I nodded, drawing my eyes away from his muscles and back to his honey-brown eyes. "I want a four-door sedan, less than fifty thousand miles, and newer than five years old. Nissan's my preference, but I like Hyundai too."

He nodded, his lips curling into a sultry smile. "I like a girl who knows what she wants. Let me go see what we have. You two can come in and grab some coffee while you wait?"

"We just met and you're already taking me out to coffee?" I teased, laughing.

"Next time it'll be drinks." He winked.

We followed him into the building toward the plushy seating area with a coffee machine, sodas, and even snacks.

"Help yourselves, ladies," he said.

As soon as he walked away, Hen hit my side. "Keep it in your pants, woman!"

I bit my lip. "I can't help it!"

"Well give some of that mojo to me," she said.

I frowned. "Did that guy from the coffee shop not call you back?"

"Nope." She grabbed a foam cup and pressed the button to dispense coffee. "I don't know what happened. I gave him my card, and he said he'd call me sometime. It's been a week and nothing."

"Ugh." I groaned. "That's the worst."

"Uh huh. My parents are going crazy, saying I'll never get married or be happy. I wouldn't be surprised if they put up a countdown—days left until Henrietta's eggs go bad."

I snorted. "You could just tell them you don't need to worry about an expensive wedding or an even pricier divorce."

"I'd rather get the divorce," she said. "Then at least they'd be off my back for a little while."

I laughed, taking a sip of my coffee. I couldn't relate

to Henrietta, but I felt for her. My mom had left when I was young, and I'd ran away from home at sixteen, so I didn't exactly have blood relatives invested in me and my well-being. She and Birdie were as close as it got.

"Great news," the hottie salesman said, coming back and jingling a few keys. "We have some good options to test drive."

I clapped my hands together. "My hero."

He laughed and said, "Come with me."

Oh, how I wished I could.

♥•♥•♥•♥

I STEPPED out of the bathroom and walked to my living room, where Birdie and Hen were on the couch. Partially to drink some Cupcake wine before my dinner with Jonas's family, mostly for moral support.

"What about this dress?" I asked, smoothing the skirt over my legs. "Does it scream 'let me clean your blood'?"

Hen snorted, spitting her wine back in her glass. "I should know better than to drink around you."

Birdie agreed, "It's an acquired skill."

"Come on, guys, tonight has to go well. Charlotte already scheduled a press conference for tomorrow after-noon, and all the major local outlets will be there. If I show up without Jonas, that's it."

Hen stood up from the couch, set her wine glass on the coffee table, and walked around me slowly. "The dress is great, but I'd grab a cardigan or something to go over it. Some old people are weird about bare shoulders."

I raised my eyebrows, looking to Birdie for confirma-tion. Was shoulders really where they drew the line?

She nodded. "Especially if they're more conservative."

"Well, he's an accountant, so... better go cover up my *scandalous* shoulders." I walked back to my room, digging through my closet. I basically lived in tank tops and leggings during the summer, and leggings and sweaters during the winter, but I found something that went with my dress.

I knew I was being a brat, but I hated this whole situation. A woman shouldn't have to believe in love to write about it. After all, men wrote about aliens shooting each other and we all knew that wasn't real.

I put the cardigan over my shoulders and walked back out to the living room. Birdie covered her chest with her hands and said, "If my son wasn't gay and seventeen, I'd marry him off to you."

I laughed out loud. "Gee, thanks, Bird."

A horn went off outside, and I glowered at the windows. "Seriously? He won't even text me to let me know he's here or walk to the door? No wonder he's single."

Birdie shrugged. "Maybe the charade doesn't begin until you get to his parents' house."

Hen added, "You might want to remember that he's doing you a favor, babe."

She had a good point. And that was humbling. I hated needing people. But needing Jonas was kind of my only option right now.

I did another spin in front of my friends and asked, "You're sure I look good enough to meet his mom?"

"Of course you do," Hen said. "She's going to love you just like we do."

I took a deep breath. I could do this. Six months would go by faster than I knew. Hell, it seemed like only yesterday Birdie and I were splitting rent on a tiny apartment. That had been almost ten years ago.

"Lock up after you guys leave?" I asked.

Hen raised her glass of Cupcake wine. "We got you, boo."

I laughed through the tightness in my chest and said, "See you later."

Jonas's car waited in the driveway, and as I approached, I saw him holding his phone to his ear. Maybe that was why he hadn't texted or come to the door. As he saw me, he waved, then reached across the seat and opened the door for me.

That was kind of nice.

I got in, setting my purse between my feet and buckling up. He gave me a smile, then continued talking on the phone.

"If you get their books done, I can look over their last year's return in the morning and see if we need to file an amendment," he said into the phone. "I appreciate it... Great, see you tomorrow."

He hung up and gave me an apologetic smile. "Sorry, normally I wouldn't honk, but I had to work something out with my bookkeeper, and I don't want us to be late."

"It's totally fine," I said with a smile. Anxious flutters danced in my stomach. "Maybe it was better I had a second to prepare."

He put his car in drive, then glanced my way. I couldn't help but notice the way his eyes lingered on my chest, even when it was half-covered by a cardigan. "Having second thoughts?" he asked.

"Not at all," I lied.

He kept both his hands on the wheel, at ten and two like he was still strictly following rules from a driver's ed course he took in high school. I'd learned how to drive at twelve, taking my drunk dad home from whatever bar he'd landed at during closing time, so it was amusing and endearing to see him being so cautious.

"So there's something I need to tell you about my mom," he said, his eyes trained on the road.

My eyebrows drew together. "What is it? I know you said she was nervous around new people."

"It's related to that..." He was quiet for a long moment, and he let out a heavy sigh before turning down a side street and parking along the curb.

Those nerves in my stomach spread across my whole body. This felt like bad news, and I wondered what on earth I'd gotten myself into.

He released the wheel, putting his hands in his lap, and turned toward me. I didn't think I'd ever been this close to him all by myself, but now I noticed things I hadn't before, like the Cupid's bow of his lips shaped almost exactly like a v. Or how his nose curved slightly out in the middle. It made me want to sit at my keyboard and write, to fill pages describing his features.

But I realized I was daydreaming again, lost in a story when I should have been focused on the current chapter of my life. I refocused my attention on him, listening carefully.

"About sixteen years ago, my mom went to visit her parents in Toronto. One of their friends had passed, and Mom wanted to be there for them while they were struggling." He tipped his head down, as if not speaking the next part could keep it from happening. "They lived in an old house, the wiring was outdated..." He swallowed, his Adam's apple sinking and rising. "Her parents died, and she nearly died trying to save them. She barely made it out alive, and she still has scars. Both the kind you can see, and the kind you can't."

I covered my mouth, horrified for him, for his mom and grandparents. "How old were you when it happened?"

"Fourteen. She was in the hospital there all throughout the summer, and my sister and I stayed with Dad's sister in Toronto so we could keep visiting her after Dad had to go back to work. It was hard for all of us, but of course, Mom's been different ever since."

"Of course she has," I breathed. Trauma, I understood. I knew first-hand how it could mold and shape you. How it made the world look different, even years after the fact.

"After she got home from the hospital, she tried to go back to normal life, but it was hard. Kids would stare at her when we went out and ask their parents what was wrong with her. People thought she was contagious and would always stay feet away from her. After a while, I think it just got easier for her to stay home or not meet new people who didn't understand or love her like we did."

I pressed my hand over my heart, feeling the ache for her. I might not have been a burn victim, but as a plus-size woman, I was used to the judgement. To the strange looks and people wanting to stay away as if standing too close to me would somehow make them obese.

I'd grown a thick skin to give those types of people the

middle finger. But Jonas's mom... It broke my heart that she felt like she had to hide away because she looked different.

"The house is a little... cluttered. I feel like since everything was lost in the fire, she has a hard time letting anything go. Dad makes sure it's not a hoarder situation or anything, but there are stacks of books everywhere and photos on every inch of the walls. She pretty much spends her time reading and gardening."

I nodded, wishing I knew Jonas well enough to cover his hand with mine. "I'm sorry that happened. And thank you, for letting me know."

"She's excited to meet you," he said quickly. He shook his head with a pained smile. "Apparently my sister's wedding coming up has her thinking I should probably get the ball rolling too."

I smiled slightly, trying to hide my painful envy at this whole life he had. A mom who loved him despite her demons, a dad who stuck with her, a sister looking forward to her happily ever after... He'd won the lottery. I wondered if he knew it. "Why don't you date?" I asked instead. "Since it seems like you believe in love and all."

He studied me for a moment. "Despite my involvement in this... shenanigan, I take love seriously. Once I'm in, I'm in."

7

JONAS

My gut worked itself in knots as we approached my family home. The one where I'd grown up and made mistakes and had way too many baby pictures hanging on the walls. The one where my parents and sister waited to meet my new "girlfriend."

I'd never lied to my mom before.

Scratch that.

I'd lied to her once as a seventeen-year-old in high school. She'd asked me if I used protection sleeping with my girlfriend and I said yes. There must have been a tell in my expression because she slapped me in the face and made me come to the store with her for the morning-after pill. Mom had looked me in the eye and said, "Conceiving and caring for a baby never happens alone. You're *just as responsible* for every single step in the process as she is. You can choose whether you want to be responsible for preventing pregnancy or caring for one."

The next day, when my girlfriend came over, we had

the world's most uncomfortable conversation, in front of my parents and giggling sister.

Needless to say, I wore a condom from then on out, and now I asked my adult girlfriends if they needed help paying for their birth control since my mom was absolutely right. It shouldn't just be on one person.

That was the kind of woman my mother was. She was smart and strong and loving and wouldn't hesitate to tell you if you were royally fucking up.

I just hoped this wouldn't be one of those times.

We parked in the carport in front of my old bedroom, and I stared at the navy-blue curtains in the window. Mom and Dad had converted the garage to my bedroom when I was twelve and Tess was ten and sharing a bedroom with my little sister just wouldn't do anymore.

"Ready?" I asked Mara.

She only nodded.

"Wait in your seat." I got out of the car and walked around to her side to open the door. If I didn't, my dad would be out here making damn sure I knew how to treat a woman.

Mara stepped out, giving me an annoyed smile. "I can work the handle perfectly fine myself."

"Not relevant," I replied with a smirk. "Not when you're with me."

Her smile was contagious. I extended my elbow for her and she slid her hands through the gap, linking her fingers in the crook of my arm. The warming of my skin under hers felt natural. I wondered if it was because she was so comfortable with men. Or if she was just easy to be around in general.

Before I even reached the door, Dad was pulling it

open and smiling wider than I'd ever seen at the girl on my arm. "You must be Mara!" he said, stepping aside. "Come on in, sweetheart."

It was clear how ecstatic he was for me to have a woman with me. Tess, on the other hand, gave us a tight smile from where she sat on the couch in between our mom and her fiancé, Derek.

Tess had been more than a little suspicious at my all-to-convenient revelation of a girlfriend who'd be willing to help with Mom's dialysis. Between her and Mom, I had about a one in a million chance of pulling this off. But Mara was already working magic with my family.

She released my arm to shake Dad's hand. "Mr. Moore, I see where Jonas gets his good looks from."

She had that fifty-year-old man blushing like a teenage boy. "Call me Cade," he said.

"Cade," she corrected. "It's nice to meet you."

Dad gestured toward the couch where everyone was now standing up. "This is my daughter, Tess the Mess, my soon-to-be son-in-law, Derek, and"—he wrapped his arm around my mom—"the love of my life."

Mom smiled, her scarred skin creasing. "You can call me Mariah."

"Nice to meet you," Mara said, shaking her hand, then smiling at Tess and Derek.

Paws scrabbled over the floor in another room, and we all swung our gazes around to see our scruffy, ugly dog running toward us, only seconds from jumping up on Mara and ruining her pretty dress. I extended my hand in the sign we'd learned to calm Oaklynn down.

Oaklynn danced on her feet, her claws clacking on

the hardwood, and I chuckled, bending to scratch her ears. "Mara, this is Oaklynn. We call her Oak for short."

She smiled at the speckled brown dog, bending to pet her scruffy, wiry hair. Oaklyn snorted, her teeth sticking out of her mouth at odd angles. "Hi, sweet girl," Mara cooed.

"She has a *great* personality," Derek said, to which Tess responded by smacking him in the stomach.

"She's a *beautiful* girl," Tess said.

Behind her, Derek spun his finger around his ear.

I chuckled. No one could tell Tess, but Oak was the ugliest damn dog I'd ever seen. Mara immediately sided with Tess. "You are beautiful, aren't you, Oaklynn?"

"Exactly," Tess said. "You both need to have your eyes checked." She glared at Derek and me. Tess would die on this hill a million times over.

Mara grinned at Tess and said, "So do you prefer Tess the Mess or should I just call you Tess?"

I snorted, earning a glare from Tess.

"So what if I'm a little clumsy?" she said.

Derek sniggered. "A little?"

She hit his waist.

With an amused smile, Mom clapped her hands together. "Now that everyone's been introduced, who feels like roast?"

"You made roast?" Mara asked. "That's my *favorite*."

Mom smiled happily. "You can't go wrong with a good pot roast. Meat, potatoes, vegetables, broth, something for everyone."

"Exactly," Mara said, following her through the living room toward our eat-in kitchen with stacks of books in all the corners. The same table I'd grown up with sat in the middle, already set with dishes and silverware.

"Can I help?" Mara asked.

Mom grinned at me. "I like her." Then she said to Mara, "Do you want to pour the lemonade? It's in the refrigerator."

"Absolutely," Mara said, walking toward the white fridge in the corner of the room.

Tess and I exchanged a surprised look. Mom hardly ever got on this well with anyone. It made me give Mara a second look to see what my mother saw.

And from here, I got a great view of Mara's ass. Even though the dress wasn't tight, I could see the way her bottom curved under the fabric, and damn if I wasn't having completely inappropriate thoughts in front of my entire family. I sat at the table, thankful to have a shield for the movement happening in my pants.

What the fuck was wrong with me? I wasn't a teenager anymore. It had been a while though.... This would be a long celibate six months if we went through with this.

Mara came back with a pitcher of lemonade and bent over the table to pour my dad's glass.

Good fucking Christ, her cleavage.

I looked away, focusing on Derek. "How's closing on the new house going? Looking like it'll come through?"

He nodded. "Oh yeah. Should be able to get all our stuff moved in when we come back from the honeymoon. Although we might not have anything left if Tess helps carry it in."

She rolled her eyes at him while Dad and I exchanged a look. Our wedding gift to them was going to be to move in most of their stuff while they were honeymooning in Montana so they would have less to do when they got back.

Mara asked, "You're buying a house? That's amazing."

Tess grinned. That house was her pride and joy. "It's a three-two on the west side of Emerson. Beautiful back-yard, tire swing in the front." She rested her head against Derek's shoulder for a moment. "Perfect for little ones someday."

"I love it," Mara said, bending over to pour my drink. Her breast brushed my shoulder, and whatever blood was left in my head was suddenly redirected.

I quickly reached for the drink, knocking it over, and she moved to get the glass, pressing her body even more tightly against mine.

Good fucking Christ.

Mom laughed as though nothing were amiss, bringing a big kitchen towel to me. "You haven't spilled glasses since you hit that growth spurt as a teenager." As I wiped up the spill, she said to Mara, "He grew six inches in a summer, and his arms were so long he didn't know what to do with them."

Mara laughed. "I ran into things with my butt for an entire year for the same reason."

That had Mom and Dad and Tess laughing.

I was thankful. She'd quickly deflected from my embarrassment, laughing it off. That was nice. Really.

I stood to place the rag in the sink, but Mara offered to take it, bringing it back with her. She put the lemonade in the fridge covered in magnets and photos and receipts, then rinsed out the rag just like she belonged here.

Maybe she did.

I immediately recoiled from the thought. Was my dick that desperate that I was already forgetting this arrangement was fake? Mutually beneficial, but ultimately shallow?

I shook my head as if that could clear it and took the platter of sliced meat being passed to me. The table was quiet for a moment as we began loading up our plates and took those first delicious bites of Mom's cooking.

"Mariah, you have to give me this recipe," Mara said, wiping at her full lips with a paper napkin. "It's so good."

Mom grinned proudly, her eyes crinkling at the corners. "Most people add cream of mushroom, but I add French onion soup to the broth. It flavors the meat and the vegetables so well, then you can use the broth for a really good gravy the next day."

"Ooh, I love that idea," Mara said. "How did you come up with that?"

"When you have two kids and limited ingredients around, you get creative. You'll understand when you have littles of your own."

Mara's face fell slightly, but she took a bite to mask it.

Dad said, "Tell us about yourself, Mara."

She swallowed and gave him an amicable smile. "What do you want to know?"

Dad shrugged. "Where do you come from? Any siblings? What do you do for a living?"

Mara glanced down at the table, her brown eyes hidden by a thick fringe of lashes. "My family's from a small town outside of LA, but we don't really keep in touch anymore."

Dad frowned. "I'm sorry."

"It's for the best, really," Mara said, flashing him a reassuring smile. "And I'm a romance author."

My mom's mouth fell open. "No. Way. What's your last name?"

"Taylor," Mara said.

Mom's face split into a grin, and she pushed up from the table, hurrying to one of the stacks of books in the living room. She pulled off the top ten or so, then grabbed a paperback that had been very well-loved.

"*Swipe Right* by Mara Taylor," Mom said, grabbing a pen from the coffee table. "You have to sign it for me."

Mara smiled, her cheeks filling with color. "I can't believe you have one of my books!"

"I loved it," Mom said. "I'm so excited it's being made into a movie! Jonas, you didn't tell us you were dating someone famous."

I shrugged. "I like to keep her humble."

Mara rolled her eyes at me, taking the pen and book and signing it on her lap. "Here you go!"

Mom held it to her chest. "My new favorite copy." She walked it to the living room and set it atop the mantle, covering our latest family photo.

Tess said, "I see how I rank."

"Hush," Mom said, laughing. "Tell us, where do you get ideas for your books?"

Mara smirked. "Be careful what you say. Everything is fodder for fiction." She laughed, and it was contagious, making everyone around the table crack a smile of their own.

"If you want stories," Mom said, pointing a fork at me, "I have plenty about Jonas in his young and wild days."

"That's hardly necessary," I grunted. The last thing I needed was to relive my stupid teenage years. "No need to write about the young and dumb."

Mara laughed. "I have plenty of material of my own to go off of in that category."

We ate the rest of the meal, and then Mom got out her classic chocolate pudding dessert. It had a graham cracker layer on the bottom, chocolate pudding, a layer of crunched walnuts, then whipped cream and chocolate shavings on top. Before the fire, we used to go to a lot of potlucks, and everyone always requested the dessert from Mom. It was her specialty.

"You're going to love this," I promised Mara, giving her a slice.

She took a bite and moaned.

And damn if my dick didn't listen.

"Can you just come home with me, Riah?" Mara asked. "You're so amazing in the kitchen!"

"Riah?" Mom said.

"Is it okay that I gave you a nickname?" Mara asked.

Mom smiled, glancing side to side as if mulling over the moniker. "Riah. I like it."

"Good," Mara replied. "Because people might get Mar and Mara confused."

They bantered back and forth until it was time to wash the dishes, and Mara insisted she help. She and Mom stood at the sink, washing and drying as if they'd been doing it for years.

Mara must have really cared about her career to be trying this hard with my family. I tried not to think what it would do to Mom and Dad when we broke up.

Dad pulled me aside in the living room, saying quietly, "She's a good one, Jonas. I like her."

Tess nodded. "Me too. Why'd you keep her secret for so long? If it's because of her size, I'll—"

"My god, Tess," I said. "She's hot as hell. Why would I keep her hidden away?"

Tess flushed, and I shook my head, saying, "I'm just glad Mom likes her."

"Me too," Tess whispered. "When are we going to tell Mom about the dialysis? Surely she'd be happy to have Mara around."

"Dialysis?" Dad said.

"I'm going to ask her tomorrow morning on the way to the appointment if she'll be okay with Mara doing it here at the house," I said. Dad was being oddly quiet, so I turned to him and said, "You think that's okay, right?" I'd thought he would be overjoyed.

He was still quiet.

"Dad," Tess admonished. "You can keep a secret for one night, can't you?"

Dad held up his hands in surrender. "I'm shit at keeping secrets from her. You know that."

I shook my head at him. Some things never changed.

Mara and Mom came into the living room, laughing about something. I smiled between the two of them. The woman I looked up to and the woman who was quickly stealing her heart.

"Ready to go?" I asked Mara.

She nodded, coming and looping her arm through mine. "It was great to meet you all. I'm so thankful you had me over."

"Come back any time," Mom said. "I've never had someone so complimentary of my cooking."

Dad chuckled, "We're all used to the greatness."

"Uh huh," Mom said. She came and gave both of us a hug. "See you in the morning, sweetie."

"See you," I said.

Then Mara and I walked out the door, toward my car. Once inside, she looked over and said, "So? Do you think it's going to work?"

Knowing it was a terrible idea, I nodded anyway. "You've got yourself a deal."

8

MARA

Confession: I didn't expect fireworks.

JONAS WAS quiet for a little while on the drive to my house, which was probably a good thing. I needed time to sort through my thoughts too.

I should have been thrilled he'd agreed to go along with the plan, but there was a tightness in my chest more intense than it had been in a long time. Seeing Jonas's family, all of them so loving toward each other... it reminded me of that missing piece within myself.

I hadn't talked to my mother since I was twelve years old. Hadn't seen my dad since I was sixteen. I couldn't help but stew on the fact that they were existing in the world, living their lives without me.

We'd never have family dinners like that where my mom shared pot roast recipes. My dad would never worry over her or shake hands with my boyfriend. There would be no jokes about my growth spurt at fifteen or shenanigans I pulled as a teen thinking my parents weren't watching.

They hadn't been watching long before Mom left, long before I followed in her footsteps.

Jonas broke the silence, asking, "Do you really put people from real life in your romance novels?"

I smiled at the question. "Only bits and pieces."

"What do you mean? Only noses and toes?"

I laughed, finding it easier with him than most people. "Not exactly. I take moments. Little things that draw my attention..." Like your lips earlier, I didn't say. "Earlier, when your dad smiled at your mom. His eyes crinkled around the corners and his gums were showing... He looked at her like she was his reason. That's the kind of thing I describe."

Jonas smiled slightly. "I used to think it was gross, how affectionate they were toward each other."

"And now?" I asked.

He lifted a corner of his lips. "After the fire, it all made more sense. Things always seem more special when you realize you could lose them at any moment."

He was right.

We drew near my street, and he turned, slowing to park in my driveway behind my new used car.

I unclipped my seatbelt to get out and tell him good-bye, but then I heard the click of his buckle. He was opening his door and getting out of the car.

Was he walking me to my door?

I pushed the door open and stepped out, seeing Jonas waiting for me on the sidewalk leading to my house.

It looked beautiful at night with little solar lights illu-minating the walk and a vintage sconce lighting the front entrance. Even in the dark, the light yellow paint seemed bright and cheery.

Kind of like Jonas's house. All the pictures on the wall, the books stacked chest high... they were signs of love. Of life. Of light.

"You don't have to walk me to my door," I said to Jonas.

He smiled slightly. "Had to make up for not ringing the bell earlier." He paused on the elevated concrete pad of my front porch. "And I wanted to say thank you. Mom really loved you."

Something in my heart twisted painfully. Like how could this complete stranger come to like me when my own mother had been so eager to leave? "I liked her too," I admitted. "She's sweet. But..."

Jonas seemed concerned. "But what?"

"I feel a little guilty. Lying to her about us." More than I ever thought I would.

His frown deepened, only emphasized by the shadows outside. "Life is full of shades of gray. Our decision doesn't have to be all good for it to be the right thing in the moment."

He made a good point. "You think it will help her? To be able to do dialysis at home?"

"You have no idea. She gets so tense every time we have to walk into that building, and Dad's been feeling so guilty he can't afford to stay home and do it with her before he can retire next year. You're really helping us out, Mara."

That thought brought a smile to my lips. "I'm glad to do it, really."

"Thanks." He hooked his thumbs in his pockets. "So what do we have to do tomorrow for your thing?"

Back to business. For the reason we were both here. "We have a press conference at five. I'll be sending my publicist photos of us from Birdie and Cohen's wedding, things like that, to prove we've been together. But we'll have to act... familiar with each other at the press conference."

"What do you mean?" he asked, seeming skeptical.

"Charlotte said some hand holding, maybe a kiss or two should do it." I was almost worried about telling him, afraid of how he'd react, but Jonas didn't balk at all.

"Do you think we should practice?" he asked.

I laughed. "Practice holding hands?"

"Or kissing," he said, not a hint of humor or flirtation on his face. Which, I supposed I should have expected from an accountant. "I don't want to get there and mess it up for you. Or my mom."

That twisting sensation in my heart was back. He was willing to do anything for her. Even kiss a person he clearly had no interest in at all.

"Kissing is easy," I said. "Just press your lips together for a moment and there you go."

"I don't think so," Jonas said, his brown eyes even darker at night. "They're going to be scrutinizing you, looking for any hint that you're putting on an act."

My eyes instantly traveled to his lips. I was going to kiss an accountant. "Are you sure?" I asked.

Those lips I'd spent way too long examining earlier spread into a gentle smile. But he didn't speak. Instead he reached out, gently weaving his fingers through the curls at the back of my head. Second by second, he came closer. Tentatively, he looked into my eyes, as if making sure I was still alright. If I wanted this.

His consideration of me was new... and sweet.

I nodded slightly, his eyes drifting shut, his black lashes forming an intricate fringe. And then his lips were on mine.

His touch was soft, careful, gentle...

Consuming.

I tilted my head to the side, exploring the way his full lips molded to mine, the pressure of his hand at the back of my head, the gentle flutter of his breath over my skin.

I'd thought it would be a simple, feelingless kiss—one peck and done.

I'd been wrong.

His lips parted slightly, and his tongue danced around my lips, begging entrance. A swoop of excitement rushed through my stomach, and I opened my mouth, deepening our kiss.

It had been a long time since I'd just made out with a guy so patiently with no end goal in mind, but Jonas was in no hurry. Tasting my kiss, feeling my hair, my lips, my tongue. His hand slid down my shoulder to my waist, pulling me closer, and my hands instinctively linked behind his muscled shoulders.

His body shifted in response, his chest pressing against mine. My heart beat quicker, heat already pooling between my legs. But he slowly retracted his tongue, pressing his lips to mine once more before pulling back.

He was only inches from me now, his dark eyes heated and his lips slightly parted. "Do you think that will convince them?" he asked.

Still dazed, I asked, "Convince who?"

The crease between his brows deepened slightly. "The media?"

Right. This kiss had been an experiment. Practice. I needed to remember that. "I think it'll be fine. Thanks, Jonas."

Before he could say anything more, I had my key in the door and said goodbye.

Inside, I pressed my back to the door, closing my eyes. What had just happened?

Jonas had kissed me. Not like a chore. Not like a boring accountant. But like... someone who knew what he was doing.

The sound of his car turning on reached my ears, and headlights panned through the curtains as he drove away. I smiled, biting my bottom lip.

Maybe this wouldn't be so bad after all.

9

JONAS

At half past seven the next morning, I pulled up to my parents' house to pick Mom up for dialysis. As soon as I parked, Dad was walking her out the door, one hand gripping hers. They held hands often, something I didn't notice most couples doing.

When he reached my car, he pulled open the door and said, "Take good care of my woman, will you?"

Mom chuckled at him. "Get out of here."

I shook my head at the pair. "Have a good day at work, Dad. Tell Hank I said hi."

Dad nodded. "Will do."

He walked toward his truck he'd been driving for the last twenty years while Mom and I pulled away from the house. It took her less than two seconds to bring up Mara.

"Everyone around here's quite taken with Mara," she said.

I smiled. "I'm glad you think that, because she's up to start being with you at the house when you do dialysis."

Mom clasped her hands together as if in prayer, shaking them at the sky. "Thank you, God."

I laughed. "That's what I was thinking."

"So when were you planning on telling me your relationship with her is fake?" Mom asked. "After I got all attached to her or before?"

I flinched. "Wh-what are you talking about?"

She scoffed, adjusting her books in her lap. "You think I don't know how to use Google?"

"I—"

"You've never mentioned the girl and all of a sudden you bring her over the day after she's in hot water over that interview."

I shook my head. Of course my parents had Googled my fake girlfriend. "Did you run a police report too, detective?"

"Results pending."

I smiled over at her. No matter how annoying this was, it felt good to know she still cared about me to look out, even though I'd rounded thirty. "We both needed something. I wanted a good person to be with you to do dialysis at home, and she needs a boyfriend to save her second movie deal. Easy peasy. But please don't tell Dad if you haven't already. He's the *worst* at keeping secrets."

"Just from me," Mom said. "Marriages don't have room for secrets."

I nodded, knowing that was true. Dad was as loyal as they came when it came to our family.

Mom studied me skeptically. "You know, I'd be more worried about the arrangement, but I saw the way you looked at her all night."

Now I had to take my eyes off the road to ask her.

"What do you mean?"

Mom laughed as if I were being daft. "I remember your father giving me that look when we were only twenty. That's how you were conceived."

And now I was blushing. "*Mom.*"

She chuckled. "You looked like a thirsty man in the desert and she was your oasis."

Mom wasn't wrong. I'd gotten caught off guard last night, seeing Mara in that dress, watching her get along with my family. And then that kiss.

Damn. That kiss.

Mara was too damn good at pretending this wasn't fake.

"She's a beautiful woman," I said finally.

"Absolutely," Mom agreed. "I used to wish I had curves like that."

"You did?" Mom had always been small and petite, and I'd never heard her complain about her size before. She didn't even complain about her scarred skin. She just faded into the background. Stopped showing up, going out.

She nodded. "They had these water bras that you could wear to make it look like you had big boobs. They were great as long as you didn't run into anything sharp."

"Okay, I've heard enough." I laughed.

She smiled. "I'm glad you're happy. You have a little extra bounce in your step."

"It's probably nerves," I replied, turning toward the dialysis center. "I'm doing a press conference with her today to help salvage the movie deal."

"What channel will it be on?"

"Why don't you google it?" I retorted.

She gave me the side-eye, and I smiled back as I parked in front of the center. We walked inside together, Mom's shoulders tightening the closer we got to seeing people. I handled most of the talking as we checked in at the reception desk, and a nurse took us back to the row of chairs. There were a few people already in, so I asked for a chair farther away "so she could focus on her book."

Mom squeezed my arm in thanks and then sat in the chair, the nurse connecting the machine to her port. When Mom had first been diagnosed with partial kidney failure a year ago, I'd been so terrified of losing her. All those feelings from the fire came flooding back. But now that I knew more (and was prepared to donate a kidney if needed), this was mostly just business as usual.

They got her set up in no time, the machine whirring with the rest of them. She got out her book, cracked the spine, and started reading, while I propped my laptop across my legs and started working on client emails. I could stay with her, for a little while at least.

"Oh my word," Mom sputtered. I looked up, worried she was hurt, to see her cheeks turning bright red and her hand covering her mouth.

"What?" I asked.

She giggled silently. "I'm reading one of Mara's books and—"

"And what?" I asked nervously. "Is it bad?"

She shook her head quickly and passed the book to me. "Three paragraphs down."

Not sure what to expect, I closed my laptop and looked at the page, counting down three paragraphs.

He laid me back on the bed and spread my legs wider than they'd ever been. I didn't care about the pain. Only the pleasure I knew would be coming from his perfect, thick pink cock. As soon as he pressed into me, I knew I'd been right. He filled me like I'd never been filled before. Satisfied me like I'd never been satisfied before.

Mom laughed even harder. "You should see your face!"

Thank god she was looking at my face and didn't have X-ray vision to see through the laptop covering my lap, because damn, Mara had painted a mental image like none other. "How long have you been reading this?" I asked her, handing back the book.

"This is only the first chapter!" She giggled. "Your father is going to be so happy tonight."

"*Sheesh*, Mom, I don't need to hear about this."

She was already staring at the book again, giggling, and I adjusted myself, then got up. "I'm going for a walk."

"Mhmm," she said, already completely distracted.

I hung my suit jacket over the chair and stepped outside with my phone. I dialed Mara's number as I walked down the sidewalk. It was a warm day for January, and the morning sun felt good against my back.

After a few rings, Mara picked up. She must have had me on speaker because I could hear the gurgle of an old coffee pot in the background. "Hello? Did I forget something in your car?"

"Not at all. I just thought I'd call to let you know you have a new fan."

"And who would that be?" Just from the tone of her voice I could imagine a smile on her face.

"Me. Thanks to my mother. She's reading your book and completely ignoring me now."

"Oh my gosh, which book is she reading? Some of

my older books are a little rough."

Her nerves made me laugh because she had no reason to be nervous. That scene had painted a plenty clear picture. "I didn't see the title, but she may have shown me a passage."

"Oh no."

"Oh yes," I said, chuckling. "It was quite... descriptive."

"Well now I'm blushing."

"That must be a first, making you blush." I paused at the corner, waiting on a car so I could cross the road. "It was hot. The bit that I read."

"Tell me about it," she said.

I cleared my throat. "I better not, standing in broad daylight with no laptop to cover me up."

She giggled gleefully. "Jonas Moore, are you saying you were turned on by my writing?"

"Don't get too full of yourself," I said. "It's been a while." I instantly regretted saying it, embarrassment heating my ears just as thoroughly as the sun. "Are you ready for tonight?"

She paused for a moment, the sound of the coffee pot now silent. "I think so. Charlotte should have emailed you talking points to go over. It would be great if you practiced them. I wouldn't be in this mess if I had stuck to my own damn talking points."

"I got them. I'll be sure to memorize them before this afternoon."

"Great," she said. "Do you want to ride with me? There might be limited parking, so..."

"Sure," I said.

"Meet me at my house. We're taking my truck."

10

MARA

Confession: The only person I'm afraid of is my father.

I WISHED Birdie and Hen didn't have to work a regular eight-to-five schedule, but they did, so I got ready for the press conference on my own. (Aside from the video call I made to Charlotte to confirm my blue dress was appropriate. She said it was.)

I had just finished curling my hair when the doorbell rang.

That had to be Jonas. Fifteen minutes early. Nervous flutters kicked in, and I wished he wasn't so damn punctual so I had more time to make my home, and myself, more presentable.

Why did I feel nervous to have him see my home? See me? Probably just because this press conference was such a big deal. I was projecting on him for no reason.

I hurriedly finished applying my mascara, then went

to let him in. I swung open the door and my jaw dropped. "Jonas. You..."

He looked down at his suit, which fit him better than a suit should fit an accountant. It had to be expensive and tailored. "Is it too flashy?"

I shook my head, stepping back so he could come inside. "You look great." The dark blue material complimented his naturally tanned skin, and his chocolate-brown eyes seemed to dance with mystery.

"Good." He smoothed his hands over the lapels. "I know this is important to you. And my mom. She's so excited to be doing dialysis at home."

Right. This wasn't for me. It was for his mom. *Get it through your stinking head, Mara.*

"Do you want a cocktail?" I asked. "Maybe a martini to take the edge off?"

"I'll have one after it all goes well," he said.

"A nightcap it is." I smiled. "Let me grab my purse from my room and I'll be right back."

I left him standing in my living room and walked down the hallway to my room. The blanket was messy on the bed, and I had to pull it aside to find my Chanel bag. It was one of the first splurges I'd made when I started doing well.

When I came into the living room, I saw him looking at a photo I had framed on the wall over my plushy recliner where I did a lot of my writing.

"Who is this?" he asked, noticing me.

My cheeks instantly warmed. "Me." It was the only childhood photo I had of myself. My parents hadn't taken many, and I hadn't thought to grab the few there were before I left the house. This one had been tucked into my favorite book as a bookmark. "My therapist said I should hang it there to talk to my inner child."

I instantly knew I'd said too much at the confused look on his face. Of course Jonas didn't know what inner child work was. He'd had a great childhood that didn't require hours that turned into years of therapy.

"My therapist says it's supposed to help heal things that happened to me when I was younger," I explained. "And if I can re-parent myself, I'll be able to accept what I deserve more easily."

Jonas nodded, stepping back from the picture. "I think I've heard of that."

"Ready to go?" I asked, eager to have him away from the photo. Away from the feelings that were still so raw and vulnerable, even a decade and a half later.

"I am." He followed me out of the house, waiting beside me as I locked the front door. He walked with me to Bertha, my pride and joy. Her white paint gleamed as if even she were showing off for the night.

I hit the unlock button on my key fob, and we both climbed in.

Jonas laughed as he looked over the dash through the windshield. "I feel like a big man in your truck."

I laughed with him. "That or a golden retriever in the passenger seat."

"Hey," he said, humor in his eyes.

With a smile, I tapped directions to Charlotte's PR office into my phone, then turned on the vehicle and pulled out of my driveway. We had a forty-five-minute drive, and I couldn't help but wonder what the hell we would talk about for that long, not to mention the drive back.

"How did Tess and Derek meet?" I decided to ask. At least then I could maybe pick up an idea or two for a story.

"It's kind of cute but super embarrassing," he said. "Perfectly describes Tess the Mess."

"Okay, I have to hear this," I said, already smiling.

"Tess owns a boutique that sells baby clothes and furniture, and Derek came in looking for a gift for his brother- and sister-in-law. He sat on one of the rockers, not realizing it was display only, and the whole thing kind of shattered."

I laughed out loud. "No! That must have been so embarrassing!"

"Oh, it was, especially when one of the pieces went up his... Well, let's say Tess was closing down the store and taking him to the emergency room."

I covered my mouth with my hand. "You're kidding."

"Derek wishes I was," Jonas said. "So she locks up the store and takes him to the ER, but he can't sit down in her car, so she opens the trunk and has *him lie inside face first*. And it's not a big car, so the trunk's open and his feet dangle over the edge."

I laughed so hard my stomach was shaking. "Oh god no."

"Yes! And Tess drives two miles an hour to the hospital with her window rolled down so she can hear him if he screams—it's only a mile away from her store."

"Shut up," I laugh, picturing the whole thing in my head.

"So when they get there, the nurses rush out with a gurney and take him back, this chair rod sticking out of his... well, you know, and Tess stays with him because that's just Tess."

"Of course," I said. "Naturally."

"She in the waiting room for hours while they do all these tests to make sure he's okay. And then his mom and his brother- and sister-in-law and their preacher come to the hospital."

"Poor Derek," I said, still shaking with laughter.

"Poor Tess because the second they figure out it was her store where he got injured, they start threatening to sue her and questioning her on why she would have a chair set up that you couldn't actually sit on, which, fair."

"Right," I said.

"She's in tears by the time the doctor comes out and says Derek's going to be completely fine. The tear was really small, and they were able to sew it together with an endoscope. The stitches will dissolve after a couple weeks, and he has to take antibiotics and stool softeners for a while to, you know, protect the area."

"I think I'm going to be sick," I said.

"Well, Tess was," Jonas said. "She threw up, right on the doctor's shoes."

"You're kidding," I said, cringing. Even I couldn't make up something so embarrassing.

"Nope. Then she ran away to the store and was just waiting for a lawyer to call and tell her she's being sued for everything she has. But instead, Derek walks into the store that evening, and he has a deal for her. She's so nervous she apologizes over and over and says she'll do anything to make it up to him as long as he doesn't try to destroy the store."

"What did he say?" I asked, desperate to know.

Jonas shook his head, smiling. "He said his parents wanted to sue, but he'd drop the suit on three conditions..."

"Which were?"

"One, she let him set up all furniture in the store."

I laughed. "Naturally. And two?"

"She picked out a gift for his new nephew. He had no idea what to get them."

"Cute," I said.

"And three, she let him take her out to dinner." Jonas smile, the love and amusement clear in his eyes. "She said yes to all his conditions, purchased liability insurance, and now we have *the best* story to tell during speeches at the wedding."

"That's the best worst meet cute I've ever heard."

"What's a meet cute?" he asked.

"It's the part in the story where a couple meets for the first time. Usually it's adorable, like a guy and a girl bumping into each other on a sidewalk and dropping all their books," I explained. "They start picking up their things and slowly rise, looking into each other's eyes for the first time."

He gave me a wry smile. "So ours would be a girl begging a guy to be her fake boyfriend so she can keep her movie deal?"

I laughed. "Something like that. I really am thankful you agreed to this."

He smiled over at me, his teeth shining white in the afternoon sun pouring through the windshield. "You don't get to fake date someone famous just any time."

"Famous," I said slowly. I used to dream of fame, of being someone big. Changing lives. And it was happening. Really happening. And Jonas was helping make sure it wouldn't slip through my fingertips. I could kiss him again just for that.

My GPS directed me the rest of the way to Charlotte's office, and we parked in a garage.

"I hate these things," I muttered, walking away from my beloved truck.

"Why?" he asked, keeping pace beside me.

"Maybe it's something about having twenty-thousand pounds of concrete and vehicles over my head."

"Have you ever heard of a parking garage collapsing?"

"No, but that doesn't matter," I said, staring at the news vans parked near the elevators. This was real, and I was terrified of messing up again.

Jonas followed my gaze and said, "You're going to do great."

"How do you know?"

"Because if my mom likes you, you can win anyone over."

I looked up at him, searching for a lie in his eyes. When you grow up with an alcoholic for a parent, you learn to catch them in every word. But all I saw was the truth. "I hope you're right."

Jonas pushed the elevator button, and we rode up together in silence. Despite the nerves emanating from every single one of my pores, Jonas was calm amongst the eye of a hurricane. I'd never admit it to him, but having him here made me feel better.

The door opened into the office space, and Charlotte's assistant met us by the doors. She had been waiting for us.

"I'm so glad you're here," she said, handing me a bottle of water. "Take a sip so your throat's not dry." I did as she asked and then Jonas did the same. She stopped outside of Charlotte's office, and through the open door, Charlotte asked, "Are you ready?"

"I have to be," I replied.

She looked to Jonas, as if for confirmation, and he nodded.

"Great," she said. "Jenny called me earlier. The studio is open to resuming production on the second movie, if today goes well."

I let out a sigh of relief. "That's amazing!"

Jonas nodded in agreement.

"I think so too," Charlotte said with a wink. "Now, hold each other's hands. We're going in."

We walked back with her down a hallway and through the door into a massive conference room. Chairs six rows deep were filled with reporters holding cameras and notepads, and there was a podium up front with at least ten microphones attached.

This was big.

Charlotte gestured toward the chairs on stage, and Jonas and I sat next to each other. I squeezed onto his hand, and he gently squeezed mine back. "I'm here for you," he whispered.

My nerves stilled, if only for a moment.

Charlotte cleared her throat and said, "Welcome to our press conferences about the *Swipe Right* series. I'm excited to have Mara here, the fabulous author of the story, and her boyfriend, Jonas."

Muttering broke out around the room.

"Before you ask questions," Charlotte said, "Mara would like to make a statement."

I nodded and pulled the notecards out of my purse before getting up. My hand felt empty without Jonas's, but I knew what it was like to walk alone. I was enough, all by myself.

I stepped up to the podium, took a deep breath and began talking, reading directly from the cards Charlotte and I had worked on together.

"I've dreamed of becoming a writer since I was five years old. See, I didn't have the greatest home life, and a lot of times the only place I could escape to was my imagination. Over the years, writing has become so much more to me. It's sharing happy moments with friends, letting those closest to me know how much I love them, and showing women that they are worthy of everything they desire in life, regardless of what anyone thinks. Even me." I smiled slightly. "The truth is, it's hard for me to believe in love because of how my parents lived their life, but I'm learning every day that real love, happy families heading toward happily ever after, exist. My boyfriend, Jonas, has been showing me just how true that is." I smiled toward him where he sat in the folding chair, and he gave me an encouraging nod. "We met when our friends began dating, and the two of us have been together for just shy of three months. I didn't want to go on live television and act like he's my forever, because frankly, it scares the hell out of me."

The audience chuckled politely.

"But Jonas is an incredible man. Kind, giving, selfless, and you should see the way he treats his mom." More laughter as I smiled back at Jonas. "I'm lucky to have him by my side today. Now, if you have any questions, I'd be happy to answer them."

A man I hadn't seen in fifteen years stood up, his dull brown eyes boring into mine. "Would you be willing to answer a question from your father?"

11

JONAS

As soon as that man stood up, I knew I needed to be at Mara's side. Her shoulders tensed, her jaw shut tight, and she seemed to close in on herself, making herself as small as she could possibly get.

It was horrifying, painful to watch, and completely wrong. I'd only ever been on the periphery of her life up until now, but I'd never seen Mara be anything but confident, funny, and kind. This man, who claimed to be her father, deserved nothing but the title of scum.

Mara's silence did nothing to deter him. He stood there, waiting for her answer.

Mara's breath was jagged, so I spoke for her. "I assume you know there's a reason she hasn't spoken to you for more than a decade."

His jaw clenched, and a ruddy red color filled his cheeks.

"Perhaps it's because you're abusive," I continued. "Or perhaps it's because of the fact you'd show up to an important press conference for her career and attempt to derail it with family drama." I scanned the room, looking for Charlotte, who was already speaking quickly into her phone. "Security is on the way, and unless you'd like to make a very publicly recorded scene, I suggest you leave."

I could see his meaty fists clenching at his sides, and if he was acting this way in public, I could only imagine the way he'd acted behind closed doors when Mara was a much younger and less powerful woman.

He walked out of the room, pausing in the doorway to give Mara a lingering look, and then left. Murmurs broke out amongst the people in attendance. I turned to Mara, seeing she was pale, shaking.

I took her face in my hands if only to warm her up. Her skin felt so cold. "Are you okay?"

She let out a strangled sound somewhere between a laugh and a cry. "Family reunions don't always go the way you think they will, do they?"

I shook my head and brushed my thumb over her cheek to clear away a tear. "He showed his true colors. And you showed yours. There's nothing to worry about."

She nodded quickly, turning tearfully back to the audience. "Sorry about that. Now you know where the inspiration for my villains comes from."

They gave her a polite chuckle, maybe as thankful for the drop in tension as I was.

One of the reporters stood and said, "What did you think of Jonas when you first met him?"

Mara smiled at me for a moment. "I thought he was just a boring accountant."

"Hey," I said chuckling.

Her smile grew wider. "And I was right."

The entire audience was laughing with her, and okay, maybe I was too.

"But he's boring in the best possible way," she said. "He's dependable, kind, and his family knows they can always count on him for whatever they need. Any girl would be lucky to have a guy like that."

Her words were doing strange things to my heart, tying my stomach in knots. I knew it was all for show, and maybe that's what had me out of sorts. I wanted it to be real—I wanted a woman who would look at me and appreciate me the way Mara just had—for real.

Another reporter stood and said, "This question is for Jonas. Do you ever help Mara with book *research*?"

My neck got hot, and I quickly pulled out a line Charlotte had written in bold on my list of talking points. "No comment."

The group chuckled.

Someone else stood and cheered, "Just kiss her already!"

I knew this moment was coming. That's why I kissed her the night before. Partially.

Partially because she looked so beautiful standing across from me on the porch and I wasn't ready to say goodbye. Partially because she'd gotten along so well with my mom, and I'd always dreamed of being with someone who would just become part of the family. Partially because I couldn't think of a reason not to kiss her.

She looked up at me, her brown eyes wide and shining. This close, I could see the scar on the side of her jaw. The dimple on her left cheek. The sweep of her hair across her forehead.

Her full lips that so easily stretched into smiles that lit a room better than any bulb.

I slid my hand over her cheek, weaving my fingers through her hair, and drew her closer.

She responded so easily to me, her head tilting back to meet my height, her lips parting slightly.

I took a last breath, taking in the mix of her shampoo and whatever perfume she wore that smelled like a field of wildflowers, and pressed my lips to hers.

My eyes closed, but I didn't need to do that because the whole room fell away the second her body was pressed to mine. Just like the night before, my pulse quickened, my brain slowed. Instinct took over as I slid my tongue against her lips, desperate to taste her sweet mouth, to feel the slide of her tongue against mine.

This might have been fake for Mara, but the way my body responded to hers... it was real.

All too soon, Mara pulled back, resting her forehead against mine for a moment before stepping back completely. My body felt cool without hers, empty. But I shoved that feeling down, realizing just how publicly I'd let myself get carried away.

The reporters were cheering and Charlotte was stepping up to the podium, speaking into the microphones.

"That is the end of our time! Thank you, everyone, for coming," she said. "Please feel free to grab a flash drive from the table by the door with our media kit. Have a great day!"

The reporters began shuffling out of the room, and I couldn't help the sigh of relief that escaped my chest.

My mom was really going to be able to do her dialysis at home. Mara would get the movie deal back on track.

Charlotte turned to us and said, "Hey, will you two head to my office? I'll be there when we get everyone out."

"Sure thing," Mara said. She easily slipped her hand through mine and began leading me off the stage.

As we walked toward the door, a few reporters tried asking her questions, but she simply smiled and said to speak with Charlotte. She had so much poise and grace, it was almost impossible to believe that weathered old man calling himself her father had such a strong effect on her.

We reached the office with Charlotte's nameplate on the door and let ourselves in. Mara locked the door, saying, "Just in case."

"Do you think he actually left?" I asked. We both knew who I was talking about.

She shook her head. "Dad doesn't give up that easily. And he definitely doesn't like being made a fool."

Just the word "dad" coming out of her mouth seemed so wrong. When I thought of "dad," I pictured my own father, getting up at six thirty in the morning to feed the dog and make coffee for Mom. He always added cream and sugar, then brought it to her in bed so she could wake up just right.

I thought of Dad wearing his denim jeans and work shirt with his nametag stitched into the material. I thought of the special soap Mom kept by the sink so he could wash the oil off his hands when he walked through the door.

The person making Mara scared enough to lock the door, even in my presence, didn't deserve that word.

"What do you think he wanted?" I asked.

"Money, probably." She looked down at her lap,

twisting her lips to the side. "We'll probably need to have security walk us to my truck." She let out a sigh. "And I need to get a security system installed at my house, just in case."

My eyes widened. "Do you think he'd come to your house?"

"It's not like it would be that hard. I bought it and he knows my legal name now."

"Did you have it changed?" I asked.

She nodded. "I thought it would be better when I became an author to go with a different name, and my financial planner helped me make it official. I never thought he would find my new name, but now could find me on the county register now that he knows who to search."

I hated the idea of Mara going home to that house alone, even with a security system. A tight knot of worry was already forming in my gut.

A knock sounded on the door, and Mara jerked, physically reacting to the adrenaline in her body.

"It's Charlotte," her publicist called from outside the door.

Mara got up, unlocking the door to let Charlotte in.

She had a big smile on her face, oblivious to the turmoil stirring in the room. "You two did great! I just got off a call with Jenny and the producers, and the second movie is back on! They want you to sign papers next week!"

She clapped her hands together giddily, but Mara still seemed to be in shock.

"Seriously?" Mara asked.

Charlotte nodded. "They want to start casting next

month, and they'll start promo at the 'Swipe Right' premiere!"

Mara's eyes filled with tears, and they quickly spilled over her cheeks. She hunched over, face in her hands, sobbing.

Charlotte's eyes were wide, and she was frozen in place, giving me a what-the-heck-is-going-on look.

I knelt on the floor in front of Mara, gently rubbing her knee through her dress.

"Sorry," she said through a sob and attempted to wipe her dripping eyes. "I'm just really happy. I thought it wasn't going to happen and I—" She broke down in tears again.

"It's okay," I said, gently moving her hair away from her wet cheeks. "That would have been enough to stress out anyone." Not to mention her estranged father showing up without warning.

She nodded, sniffing.

Charlotte found her voice, saying, "It's been a long day, honey. Why don't you head home and get some sleep?"

Mara nodded again, and I stood up, putting my arm around her to help her stand.

"Can you send security to walk us down?" I asked. "Just in case." Not that we needed it. If that man so much as said a word to Mara, I'd rip out his asshole and shove it down his throat.

"Absolutely," Charlotte said.

Within minutes, there were two burly men at the door who escorted us, incident free, to the parking garage.

At her pickup, I said, "I'll drive."

Mara looked between me and the vehicle. "No one has ever driven Bertha except for me."

"Bertha?"

"Big Bertha, to be exact," Mara said.

I couldn't help but smile. "Time to pop that cherry."

She laughed out loud, the most beautiful sound, and passed me the keys. "Just once."

I winked. "That's what they all say."

Shaking her head, she got into the passenger side, and I climbed into the driver's seat. I had a feeling Mara was used to taking care of herself.

Tonight, that was going to change.

12

MARA

Confession: I don't have many—any guy friends.

"ARE YOU HUNGRY?" Jonas asked me before we got to my house.

I nodded. "Starving, actually." I'd been planning on ordering pizza and pouring myself a triple martini the second we got home.

"Let's grab something."

The way he said that was almost as sexy as the way he drove my truck. He was more relaxed now, with one hand on the steering wheel, the other elbow rested where the door met the window. His suit jacket was curled up in between us. And even though it had been several hours since he first arrived, I could still smell the faint hint of whatever intoxicating cologne he'd put on earlier in the day.

Maybe I was so turned on because of the way he'd been there for me at the press conference. Or maybe it was because he was offering me food, and that was definitely the way to my heart.

I tried to breathe through this strange desire I was feeling, reminding myself that he was doing all of this to help his mom. But that only made me like him more, so I sat quietly, texting Birdie and Henrietta to let them know it had gone okay. That the second movie was back on. They were probably already asleep at this point, so I'd talk to them in the morning about my dad's surprise appearance and what that could mean.

I was already going to call a lawyer to see how I could get my name off the house altogether so he would have no way of surprising me when there weren't security guards and dozens of reporters there to protect me.

Jonas steered Bertha into the parking lot of Waldo's Diner, and no place had ever seemed so close to home. I'd spent hours here with Birdie and now Henrietta. Whether it was Wednesday morning pancake breakfasts or Saturday night milkshakes, this place was a home away from home.

We got out of the truck, and he held the door open for me. I half expected to see Chester sitting in one of the booths, giving Jonas the nod of approval, but it was late. He was probably already at home with his sweetheart, Karen. They were another one of those rare couples who won the love lottery.

"Where do you want to sit?" Jonas asked.

Still feeling a little jumpy, I picked an empty booth toward the back where I could see everyone coming in and no one would be able to see us through the windows.

A waitress I didn't recognize came and asked us what we wanted to eat, and I ordered without even looking at the menu. "Can I have a chicken bacon ranch sandwich with fries and a chocolate shake?"

She nodded. "Absolutely, sweetheart. How about you?" she asked Jonas.

"That sounds great," he said, "but can you make the shake strawberry for me?"

I scrunched up my nose, and after the waitress walked away, he said, "What?"

"Strawberry? It has to be the worst flavor of milkshake."

He laughed. "You're judging my ice cream choices?"

"Of course. I happen to be an expert in this area."

Shaking his head, he said, "Is that so?"

I nodded. "I've tried every flavor here with Birdie, and I can say, hands down, that chocolate is the best."

He chuckled. "I have been here way more often since she and Cohen got together."

"Lucky you," I said.

He looked me straight in the eyes. "I am lucky."

My stomach did a swoop without consulting my brain. I hastily changed the subject. "I'm curious about something... How does one decide they want to be an accountant?"

He laughed. "This again?"

"I just don't understand. It seems so..." I cut myself off, realizing I was being rude.

"Boring," he finished anyway.

"Well..."

Chuckling, he said, "When I was growing up, my parents weren't the 'chase your dreams' kind of people. They were the 'get a good job and provide for your family' kind of people. So, when I was looking for jobs, I looked for something that paid well, had decent hours at least most of the year, and was fairly secure. So it was pretty much between being an accountant or a mortician."

"Death and taxes, huh?"

He shrugged. "And it's really not that bad. I've been promoted several times in the last ten years, and I get to help entrepreneurs like you save money on their taxes. I meet lots of different people and learn something new all the time."

I smiled, shaking my head.

"What?" he asked.

"I'm just trying to picture an eighteen-year-old Jonas planning how to support a family."

"What were you doing at eighteen?" he asked. "Writing raunchy romance and smoking cigarettes?"

"You have half of it right," I replied.

"The writing part?"

I shook my head and scooted sideways on the booth so I could stick my legs out and lean my back against the wall. "I was waiting tables and trying to keep myself off the streets."

His dark eyebrows drew together, and when he did that, I couldn't help but notice how much he looked like his dad. "What do you mean?" he asked. "Weren't you busy with high school?"

"I couldn't keep up with school when I ran away from home. My whole childhood was about survival, in one form or another."

His brown eyes seemed to grow even darker, and I hated to admit it felt good that he cared enough to be even a little sad for me. People in my position were supposed to hate pity, but I could never find it in myself to push it away. Pity was the natural reaction—no one should have had to grow up the way I did. In a lot of ways, I pitied that ballsy, broken teenage girl just as much as I admired her for getting away.

"How did you learn how to write then?" he asked. "Did you go back to college?"

I laughed. "College? I didn't even get my GED. I learned how to write by being really crappy at it and scrounging together tips to hire editors who could fix it."

"That's amazing," he said. "Really."

"Thank you." I gave him a small smile. "It almost seems like a different life looking back on it now."

The waitress came back with our food, and I was way too hungry to keep talking. I pulled the milkshake toward me and started eating it with my French fries. And when I looked up, I saw Jonas doing the same thing.

"You're eating your dessert first?" I asked, half stunned, half impressed. "I thought that went against your code of ethics."

He gave me an exasperated smile. "Someone told me it all goes to the same place."

Laughing, I picked up the silver milkshake tin and held it out. "To eating dessert first."

Meeting my eyes, he lifted his cup too. "And to strong girls who become daring women."

If my heart didn't melt right along with the ice cream. "Cheers."

♥·♥·♥·♥

I TOLD Jonas I could drive to my house, but he said it didn't count for Bertha if they didn't cross home plate with him behind the wheel. I rolled my eyes and let him drive.

It was nice actually, being able to relax while someone else took care of the road. I checked my phone for new messages. Birdie nor Hen had replied to my text, so it was safe to assume they both were asleep. Charlotte had texted me, though, and said the media was going wild about my dad's appearance at the press conference and the way Jonas had stepped in for me.

No matter how shitty it felt to see that man again, he'd helped me in a big way by making me sympathetic to the public. But it did feel shitty. My heart was racing with old anxiety knowing I would be alone tonight. Any other night, I would have stayed with Birdie or gone to the bar to find a warm body to keep me safe overnight.

I didn't have that option. Birdie was married, and I was still skating on thin ice with the studio.

So, I held my head high and walked to my front door like I wasn't completely fucking panicked at the idea that my home address was just a google search away for someone like my dad. Maybe I'd just pack a bag and book a hotel for a while...

Jonas walked me to the door, and just like the night before, I turned on my doorstep to tell him goodnight. Was it bad that part of me wanted to "practice" kissing him some more... see if we could practice something else to draw my mind away from this building sense of panic?

He didn't kiss me, though. Instead, he said, "I can wait out here while you pack a bag."

My eyebrows came together, and I searched his face

for some type of explanation. Finding none, I asked, "What are you talking about?"

"You're not staying here until you have a security system in place."

"But Birdie's asleep. I can't just show up at her place."

"You'll stay with me." He said it like it was the most obvious thing in the world. Like I never should have thought of another option.

My lips parted, but no words came out. The invite was a godsend, so why was something in my gut telling me it was a terrible idea to stay at his house? To need him, even if it was only for a night?

"I'll be okay, Jonas, really. I have a baseball bat and pepper spray and—"

"If you don't want to stay at my place for your own safety, do it for me? I don't want to be up all night worrying about you." His brown eyes were full of honesty, not even a hint of innuendo in any of his features.

I studied him a moment longer, not believing my ears. Men didn't do anything without expecting a favor in return. "Are you sure? I don't want to put you out."

He let out an exasperated sigh and went into my house. "I'll pack a bag for you myself."

The fighter in me came out, and I said, "Pack all the bags you want. I know you won't be able to carry me to your car."

He turned abruptly, and I nearly ran into him. We were barely an inch apart, but I didn't back down. His eyes trailed up and down my body. Slowly. Hungrily. "I can handle you."

And just the way he said those words made me want to see him try. But I knew I needed things between us to remain uncomplicated for our arrangement to work. Jonas was the kind of guy who'd been preparing for a family since he was a child, and I was the kind of person who'd been running from family for just as long. He couldn't come anywhere near my bedroom. More specifically, he shouldn't be coming anywhere near my heart.

But I still heard myself saying, "I'll go get my bag. Wait here."

I stepped out of the charged space surrounding us and went to my room. I packed the granny panties I saved exclusively for day one of my cycle, a pair of old Christmas pajamas I'd gotten on sale, and a couple pairs of leggings and sweaters. I didn't even bother grabbing makeup, just some shampoo and conditioner.

There was no need to tempt fate, or myself.

After I brought my bag out, I convinced Jonas that I could drive myself to his place, and I took my car just in case his parents dropped by and saw me there.

On the way, my phone began ringing, and I eagerly picked it up, desperate to talk to Birdie or Hen, whoever was calling.

Instead, I read Jonas's name on the screen.

"Hello?" I asked, half expecting him to say he'd changed his mind.

"I just realized... you never told me what you named your car."

13

JONAS

Her laugh through the speakers was music to my ears. I couldn't believe I was already missing her, already worried about her, and we'd only been apart a handful of minutes.

"What do you think I should name it?" she asked. "I haven't come up with anything yet."

I pretended to think it over, but I already had the answer. "I think you should call it Trouble."

"Trouble?"

"Because you're using it to get out of trouble."

"That's confusing then," she teased. "I'm using trouble to get out of trouble?"

"It has a double meaning, because whenever you show up in it, I'll know trouble's arrived." As soon as I said it, I could *feel* her rolling her eyes.

"What's your car named?" she asked.

I shook my head, even though she couldn't see me. "Grown men don't name their vehicles. Unless it's a boat, then it can be named, but only after the woman you love."

"So we should name it after your mom?" she teased.

"Hardee har har," I said. Although, she made a good point.

"Maybe I shouldn't name this car," she said, "because I don't want to get too attached. It would be like cheating on Bertha."

The sincere way she said it had me laughing. "Bertha doesn't have feelings, Mara."

"Shh," she said as if the pickup could hear her from miles away.

I turned down the street, seeing her headlights follow behind me.

"I love this neighborhood," she said. "My realtor even took me to a showing down the street. Do you live here?"

"Yeah. Just around the corner here." I slowed my car and parked in front of the mid-century modern home I'd purchased just a couple years ago. I'd saved for years to be able to afford the down payment on it.

I didn't really need a house this nice just for me, but when I'd been searching, I couldn't help but wonder what a woman would think about my home. I wanted whoever I stayed with long term to love my home as much as she loved me.

"This is me," I said on the phone and switched off my car.

I waited until Mara had gotten out of Trouble (alright, so I was already claiming the name) to hang up.

She looked between me and the house. "Why did I picture you living in a two-story farmhouse with white siding and blue shutters?"

"Like in *The Notebook*?" I asked, *instantly* regretting it.

Mara's smile was bigger than I'd seen it all night. "You've seen *The Notebook*?"

"Mom and Tess made me," I said quickly. "It wasn't my choice."

"Uh huh." She eyed me closely. "Look at me without smiling and tell me you didn't cry at the end." My goddamn lips flinched, and she shouted, "Ha!"

"Come on," I said, walking toward my front door. "You're a romance author. You can't say you don't appreciate a man who likes romantic movies."

"That's a double negative," she said. Then, "I like your wreath."

I couldn't tell if she was teasing me about the flower door ornament or not, but just in case, I said, "Mom and Tess do these virtual crafting nights, and something *always* finds its way to my house."

She laughed. "That sounds so fun. Birdie and I keep meaning to do one of those wine and paint nights."

"Tell my mom. I'm sure she'd love to have you both over."

She smiled for a moment, but it seemed to fall so quickly. I tried not to think about why as I unlocked my door and swung it open for her. She stepped into the dark hallway, but I flicked on the light, showing the front entrance with stone floors and art carefully selected by Tess, my self-appointed interior designer.

Mara stepped farther inside, holding her backpack straps, looking around. I watched her closely, trying to tell what she thought. If she liked it.

She reached out and gently touched a cracked glass

vase filled with stems and artificial flowers. "This is pretty."

"Tess," I said in explanation.

I led her farther into the house, showing her the living room on the way to the kitchen.

Mara's lips pressed together at my living room, and I asked, "What?"

She gestured at the couch Tess had helped me find. "How are you supposed to watch movies on this couch? It doesn't look squishy at all."

"It's not bad," I defended. I sat on it, sinking in only an inch.

"Uh huh." She sat beside me and gave me a look, putting her hand on my shoulder. "Jonas. If you're going to watch movies like *The Notebook*, you have to have a cushy couch to do it on."

I laughed off my bruised pride. "I'll keep that in mind."

"Good." She smiled. "Where's your guest room?"

"Oh shit."

Her eyebrows drew together. "What?"

"I have a mattress for it. It's one of those fancy ones that comes in the box, but I haven't bought a frame yet and I haven't taken it out of the box, and you're supposed to let those things air out for twenty-four hours."

She gave me an amused smile. "And, of course, your couch isn't at all comfortable to sleep on."

I pulled at my collar. It really was time to get out of these clothes and hide my embarrassment. "I mean, I can handle the couch for a night. My neck might not be okay, but..."

She shook her head. "You sly dog."

"What?" I asked, raising my hands in defense. I didn't know what I was defending against, but I already felt guilty.

"It's a classic trope."

Now my eyebrows were raising too. "Trope?"

"It's like a common staple of a bunch of stories. Like every spy movie has to have a sexy girl with a gun. It's a trope."

"Okay... but what does that have to do with my lack of a guest bed?"

She laughed out loud, handing me her backpack. "It's called 'only one bed.' A guy and a girl who aren't supposed to be together share a bed. Of course, it would be silly for one of them to sleep on the floor or in the bathtub or an *insanely uncomfortable couch*." She gestured toward my sofa. "So, they agree to share the bed, but they both promise to keep their hands to themselves. Of course, they both secretly want to have sex with each other. They fall asleep, and the girl always wakes up first with the guy spooning her with a hard-on."

God, my ears were hot now. "I didn't realize I was such a cliché."

She laughed. "They're clichés for a reason. So where's your room?"

Without waiting for my answer, she began walking down the hall. She first peered into the guestroom, where a big box with an indigo mattress sat in the corner, along with a few other boxes I'd never managed to unpack.

"You weren't lying," she said, then continued down the hallway. "A home office? Are you a workaholic?"

"Are you saying that to me when you can bring your work with you literally anywhere?" I asked.

"Touché." She paused at the end of the hallway looking into my bedroom.

I was proud of this room, really. My parents had forever slept on a full-size mattress and shared the house's single bathroom with my sister and me. And no matter how many times Tess and I offered to help them buy a bigger house or renovate, they always turned us down. They loved their home.

Just like I loved mine.

The room was big enough for a king-sized mattress. In the space next to a big window looking over the back yard, I had set up two comfortable chairs and a table for reading in the morning.

"Oh my gosh," Mara breathed, stepping inside. "You live in a spa."

The compliment brought a smile to my face. "Wait until you see the bathtub."

She walked farther into the room, going through a door on the right, and said, "Shut up!"

There were two walk-in closets and a bathroom that could put any hotel's to shame, with a soaking tub and glassed-in tiled shower. "It's nice, right?"

She grinned at me. "So, um, how about I live here, and you take my house?"

I laughed. "It would defeat the purpose of the *trope*."

"True." She gently brushed her fingers over the glass shower door, taking it in. "But we're adults, right?"

"Right," I said. "And now that I know about the trope, I'll try not to be such a cliché."

"Good," she replied. "Now hand me my bag? I'm going to take some bathroom time."

The thought of her in my bathroom, naked, wasn't

one I'd been prepared for. And fuck, I couldn't get the thought of her tits freed from the dress out of my head. My eyes were going to give me away if my semi didn't.

I turned away from her and reached for the bag I'd set on my bed. "Here you are. Will you let me know when you're finished?"

"Oh, I will." She bit her lip, and my mind went crazy all over again.

Why did everything she do send all my blood to my dick? There wasn't enough left over for thinking the kind of thoughts I should have.

"I'll be awhile," she said. "I want to enjoy this."

I laughed, the sound coming out strangled. "Have fun." Before I could betray her trust and make her think I'd only invited her over for sex, I left the bedroom and started down the hall.

I didn't even know how I got to the living room, but I sat on the couch, my dick hard and desperate. It had been too damn long, and the idea of six months of this waiting... fuck.

I had to do something to distract myself. To make this pulsing longing go the fuck away, because I couldn't act on it now. Not with Mara Taylor naked in my bathroom.

Holy fucking shit.

I could hear the water running from here, the scattering of the drops as it hit her body and landed on the tile floor, and that had to mean...

I bit down on my knuckles, hard, trying to take away the pain in my groin, but it did nothing. My dick pressed painfully against the zipper in my pants, and this wasn't the kind of hard-on that was going away.

Fuck.

I was supposed to sleep with her in the same bed tonight and not wake up with my boner pressed into her backside.

The only way to keep that from happening...

I pushed myself off the couch, reached into my pants and adjusted my dick so I could walk. Then I want to the guest room and began tearing at the cardboard box holding that stupid fucking mattress that I should have fucking taken apart a fucking month ago.

When I got through the box, though, there was a thick plastic sheet I couldn't rip apart no matter how hard I tried.

The kitchen was too far, so I walked to the foyer, still hard as fuck, and grabbed my keys. Inside the room, I ripped through the plastic, shoved it aside to let the mattress air out.

And then I unzipped my pants and took my throbbing dick in my hands. I pumped once and groaned. Shit, I needed to come.

I didn't know how much time I had, so I spit in my hand and started rubbing my shaft, slowly moving back and forth. Images of Mara in the shower instantly came to mind, of the water flowing off her hair, over her face, dropping from her full tits to the floor. She would tilt her head back, that long mane tickling her voluptuous ass.

I moaned quietly at the thought of squeezing her ass. Of pumping deep inside of her and filling her like no man had before.

Of *claiming* her.

Because in real life, I could never hold on to a girl like Mara. She was wild in all the ways I was not. But in my fantasies, she was *mine*.

14

MARA

Confession: I may have been wrong about accountants...

EVERY TIME I closed my eyes, I saw Jonas in his suit. Jonas holding my face in his hands. I could feel the memory of his lips on mine and how it stirred something unbidden and powerful inside me.

I wanted to fuck him tonight. To get out of this shower, completely naked and dripping wet, and wait for him in his bed until he came and found me there, ready for him.

I wanted him to use those strong arms to hook around my hips and drive himself deep inside me.

I wanted him to fuck away every messed-up thing that had happened today until we were both panting and gasping for air, satisfied in every sense of the word.

No matter how lame my pajamas or underwear were, they'd match his marble floors just fine.

I crossed my legs, trying to ease the pressure there.

Any other night, I would have called up Hayden or George or some other guy to distract me, but that wasn't a possibility now.

So, I pulled the showerhead from its slot and lowered it to hit my most sensitive spot.

My head instantly dropped back, and I stifled a moan.

The thought of Jonas showering in here later, standing in the same place where I'd fucked myself just thinking of him... Shit, it got me hot.

With my free hand, I cupped my right breast and thumbed the nipple before moving to the other one. If I closed my eyes, I could picture the way he'd look, sucking on my tits, tasting them and teasing them with his gorgeous white teeth. The way his dark brown eyes would haze over with lust.

I bit back a moan, getting closer and closer to the edge with the pressure of the water and the idea of what Jonas could do with me. If the way my heart raced with his hands on my knees, toying with the edge of my dress, was any indication, he could do plenty.

I wondered if he was thinking of me too. If the idea of me being naked sent him wild. What he would do if he saw me. How his touch would feel. I was fucking desperate for it.

I bit down on my bottom lip as I came, letting the shudders take over my body.

With weak hands, I put the showerhead back in the rack and lowered myself to the floor, taking in every sensation. The aftershocks of my orgasm, the steam rising around me, the hardness of the floor and tile lines under my ass.

Part of me wished I could act out those fantasies with

Jonas, but I knew better. This was strictly business; our hearts or bodies had no need getting involved past what was required to trick the media into thinking our relationship was legit.

Besides, he was too nice for me. No guy I'd ever been with would have been so adamant about me staying at his house for my safety. His pleasure? Sure. But never when he wouldn't get anything out of the deal.

Maybe Jonas could be a friend instead of simply an acquaintance I knew through my friend's husband. He would make a good friend with how loyal and thoughtful he clearly was. The thought should have brought a smile to my face.

It didn't.

The water was cooling, so I pushed myself up and turned off the shower. I pulled down the towel I'd hung over the glass shower door and wiped off my face, going to the mirror. After wiping off the steam, I took myself in. The ruddy color in my cheeks and chest. The way my hair looked nearly black when it was wet. My full lips and even fuller stomach and hips.

I tilted my head to the side, wondering what Jonas thought of me. I knew I was sexy, knew I could please a man. But did he know that?

I let out a sigh—it was best not to worry about things that couldn't ever come true.

I finished toweling off my body and hair, then applied my favorite apricot lotion to my body. It made my skin so soft and the smell was heavenly. As soon as I was done, I twisted my wet hair into a bun and pulled on my Christmas pajamas.

Now I was smiling in the mirror. The red shirt said

Santa Loves Curvy Girls, and the pants were red with white Santa hats printed on them.

After putting the last of my things back in my bag, I stepped out of the shower, shivering as the air-conditioned air hit my still-damp skin. I listened for the TV, but when I couldn't hear it, I walked down the hall, calling, "Jonas?"

There was a bumping sound from the guest room, and he called back, "In here."

I slowly went to the door and cracked it open. The top few buttons of his dress shirt were undone, and his pants were rumpled, surely from a long day. But then I caught sight of a giant mattress where there used to be none.

"You're airing out the bed?" I asked.

"I'm assuming the security company won't be able to come set up at your house until at least Monday, and I'd hate to be a cliché with the only-one-bed thing." His smile was so endearing, especially with the extra color in his cheeks. His eyes slid over my body, and he chuckled. "I like your shirt."

"I don't have many pajamas since I normally sleep naked," I lied, just to see his reaction. His cheeks gained even more color, and I laughed, pointing at him. "Got you!"

He shook his head at me. "Ha ha. I'm going to shower. Feel free to help yourself to anything in the house. I had groceries delivered a couple days ago, so there should still be plenty in there."

"Thanks," I said with a smile.

He pushed off the wall and walked past me, his shoulder brushing mine. Goosebumps erupted on my skin. I rubbed my arm and waited until he was safely in his own bedroom to venture farther out.

I heard the shower come on, and I was thankful I'd stifled my own sounds while I'd been in there. I felt a little embarrassed now; I'd been in there touching myself and thinking of him while he'd been doing what he could to get me out of his bed.

I tried not to think about it as I went to his kitchen, to look around if nothing else. The cabinets were a sleek white, and when I looked inside, I was impressed to find he actually had matching sets of dishes, unlike me. I saved cups from every restaurant that would let me have them and bought most of my dishes second-hand.

Even though I'd been supporting myself comfortably for years, I still had a hard time spending money on things like that. I'd rather see money sitting in my bank account than in my cabinets.

I switched from his cabinets to the pantry and was even more impressed. Each of the boxes were lined up neatly, and there was some organization going on too with wire baskets. I wondered if that had been Tess's doing as well.

And then I found the refrigerator with French doors. In the freezer side, there was a tub of ice cream—a brand I actually liked—some meat and bags of vegetables. Pretty standard. The refrigerator side didn't even look like a bachelor's fridge. Sure, there was beer and salsa, but he had bread stored, sandwich fixings, a few bagged salads. Even a tub of hummus, which I got out to have with some of the pita chips I saw in his pantry.

It was more than late, so I only ate a few before packing it back up and putting it away.

As I walked back down the hallway toward Jonas's room, I saw him stepping out of the bedroom. I'd half expected him to wear an old-man pajama set to bed, but his snug-fitting white T-shirt and gray sweatpants caught me more than a little off guard.

And if he looked like that without a hard-on... Fuck.

My eyes had strayed down south for a little too long, so I quickly looked back up at him and said, "I'm tired."

"Me too. I'm going to grab a glass of water and go to bed. Do you want anything?"

I wasn't used to people taking care of me, so the gesture, even if it was small, felt big to me. My therapist said I needed to get used to accepting help from others, so I nodded and said, "That would be nice. Thank you."

"Of course." He seemed genuinely pleased to be able to get me a glass of water.

I tried to settle my nerves as I went to his bed. If growing up in my family home had taught me anything, it was that good things never came without strings attached.

But that wasn't my life. Not anymore. I wasn't a little girl trying to navigate the world, taking on beliefs my parents had given me about myself.

I got to choose.

So I chose to walk into Jonas's bedroom, set my phone on the bedside table, and get underneath the covers. They smelled like fresh laundry detergent. I pulled them up to my chin, taking in the softness and fresh scent, thinking Jonas really did live in a spa.

"Here you go," he said, walking through the door, carrying two glasses of water. I shifted up, resting my back against the upholstered headboard, and took a glass from him. The cube inside was large, bigger than a golf ball.

"You have fancy ice cubes too?" I asked, staring at it.

He laughed. "They keep the water colder longer, so if I wake up in the middle of the night wanting a drink, it's still cold."

"The untold brilliance of Jonas Moore." I took a sip, feeling the heavy ice cube—ice ball?—against my lips.

I set it on the table next to my phone and lay down again.

Jonas did too, and we were quiet for a moment.

I'd never slept next to a man without *sleeping* with him. I felt like Ricky Bobby in *Talladega Nights*. I didn't know what to do with my hands. "This is awkward, right?" I asked, turning on my side and resting my head in my hand.

He laughed, doing the same. The room was dim, sans our bedside lamps, but his eyes seemed brighter than ever. "I'm glad it's not just me."

"Can I ask you a question?"

He nodded.

"Why aren't you married yet?" He seemed like the dream guy for every girl who wanted to settle down with a house full of kids.

He let out a humorless laugh and rolled to his back. Then, looking over at me, he asked, "Do you want the real story?"

I nodded.

"I was married."

My eyes nearly bugged out of my head. "What?"

He nodded slowly. "I married my high school sweetheart a week after graduation, and we went to college together."

"What happened?" I asked. I couldn't even imagine Jonas being divorced. That had to be a dirty word in the house he grew up in, even if he was still a child when he made that commitment.

His eyes were trained on the ceiling as he spoke. "We were young and dumb. Being married wasn't as fun as we thought it would be, especially surrounded by eligible singles. We fought all the time. I nearly dropped out of college and came home to work at the shop with Dad. But after the last semester of college, she packed her bags and told me she was transferring to another college out of state and that she never wanted to see me again."

I covered my mouth with my hands. When I was eighteen, I was focusing on surviving, making my rent and utility payments. Jonas had another whole human, an entire marriage, to worry about. "That sounds awful."

"It was. But I learned a lot and focused on my studies." He kind of shrugged, as well as a person could shrug while lying down.

"Do you ever think about getting married again?" I asked.

"Yeah," he said without hesitation. "But this one is going to stick."

I laughed slightly. "Flip a coin. You've got a fifty-fifty chance."

"I forgot you don't believe in that kind of thing."

"That's not it," I said.

He rolled his head to the side, looking at me with those deep brown eyes. "What is it then?"

"I just have no doubt you'll make it work with

whoever she is. Especially if your bathroom continues being that nice."

He gave me a teasing grin. "High praise from *the* Mara Taylor."

"It is," I agreed, letting out an involuntary yawn. The day had worn on me, and it was late, well past midnight at this point.

"You've had a big day," Jonas said. "Why don't you get some rest?"

I smiled sleepily, lying back down. "Sounds good." I tucked my arm under the pillow. "Just don't spoon me in the morning. The only-one-bed trope only works if you wake up spooning."

"Got it." He smiled at me. "Goodnight, Mara."

"Goodnight, Jonas."

15

JONAS

I didn't spoon Mara.

No matter how much I wanted to feel her back pressed into my front.

No matter how many hours I stayed awake listening to the sweet sounds of her gentle snoring.

No matter how much the curve of her hips under my blanket turned me on.

But when I woke up, she was spooning me.

Her arm draped over my middle, and her warm chest was pressed to my back. Her knees curled into the crook of my legs, and her breath softly played against the back of my neck.

And shit if I didn't have morning wood.

Every part of me wanted to roll over, kiss her awake, and then give her the morning sex of a lifetime.

But I couldn't.

So, I lay there, reveling in the feeling of having someone close. Of having *her* close.

Mara's phone began vibrating on the bedside table,

and I hurriedly untangled myself from her embrace, hoping I could silence it before she woke up. After the kind of day she had yesterday, she deserved every ounce of slumber she got.

I pressed the lock button to silent the phone, then saw it was Birdie calling. I wasn't sure what Mara had told her yesterday, but I figured it would be best to fill her in so she could be gentle with Mara. I swiped to answer and quickly padded out of the room, glancing back once to make sure Mara's eyes were still closed.

They were, so I shut the door and swiped the screen to answer, whispering, "Hey, Birdie, it's Jonas."

"Jonas?" She seemed confused. "Where's Mara? Is she okay?"

"She's sleeping," I said, feeling instantly guilty even though we hadn't done anything wrong. "I asked her to stay over after what happened yesterday."

"I saw the news," Birdie said, concern plain in her voice. "How'd she handle it?"

I reached the living room and dropped onto my couch. Mara was right—it was fucking unbearable. "She was like a different person, Birdie. The second she saw him, it was like she made herself as small as she possibly could."

"Oh gosh," Birdie breathed. "Poor Mara."

"I know. Security took him out, and we didn't see him in the parking lot or anything, but she's been worried that he's going to look up her address and find her in private this time. And I can't blame her. He was very agitated at the press conference, and he was surrounded by fifty people."

"I'm glad you had her over. I worry about her living alone sometimes."

We were both quiet for a moment. A ping sounded in my ear, and I looked at the screen to see a low battery notification.

"Did anything... happen?" Birdie asked.

The heat to my cheeks, neck, and ears was instant. "Nothing at all." Besides me fucking myself while your best friend was in the shower.

"Will you have her give me a call when she wakes up?"

"Sure thing."

We hung up, and I went to the kitchen to grab an extra phone charger from the junk drawer. Once I found it, I plugged the cord into the wall and set her phone up to charge.

The screen flashed at me, and I couldn't help but see two text messages.

Hayden: Can't stop thinking about the way my cum looked on your tits. Come over?

George: Lonely tonight. Call me.

I quickly set her phone face down, my stomach souring. Why the fuck was I reading her text messages? And why was I so damn upset to see two guys in her phone?

She had an active sex life before our arrangement, and she'd have one after. I knew that—she wasn't shy about it. But the image of her being fucked by another man, his cum shining on her naked tits, made me want to punch something more than I'd ever wanted to in my life.

What the fuck was wrong with me?

I was her friend. Her *fake* boyfriend. We'd slept together in a bed and done nothing. If she stayed the night again, I'd be in the guest room. I was helping her. That's what friends did.

But that fucking image wouldn't get out of my mind, so I got to work making Dad's scratch pancake recipe. When I was younger, Mom always cooked throughout the week, but Dad went all-out breakfast on weekend mornings. He squeezed oranges for fresh juice, made scrambled eggs with extra cheese, and always had the best buttery toast to go with it. But my favorite was always the pancakes.

I had the recipe memorized by now, so I got to work, mixing together the flour, baking soda, and salt in one bowl before getting the wet ingredients together.

I had bacon in the fridge too, so I laid it flat on a baking sheet and put it in the oven before mixing together the pancakes and cooking them on a griddle.

Even though I normally waited until I was at the office for a cup of coffee, I had a coffee pot at home. I got it down from the cabinets and rinsed it out to start a pot with grounds I kept in the freezer. All the smells of the kitchen brought me back to my childhood, waking up to the smell of bacon and the gurgling sound of a brewing coffee pot.

I was so lucky for my childhood. I never wanted to take it for granted.

I got my own phone out of my sweatpants pocket and sent my parents a text in our family group chat.

Jonas: Just wanted you to know how thankful I am for you, Mom and Dad. You were the best parents a kid could have. Still are. Love you both.

I set my phone down, but the notification quickly chimed.

Dad: Well now your mother's crying.

Mom: He's lying. Your dad's tearing up over here.

Tess: Jonas is a suck-up. As usual.

Tess: But also, he's right. You're the best. Love you both so much.

In a separate, private text, Mom sent me a message.

Mom: Hey, is Mara doing okay? She looked so shaken up after her dad showed up.

Jonas: She's okay, I think. She's strong.

Mom: Will you check on her today?

Jonas: Um...

Mom: You dirty dog.

Jonas: It's not like that.

Mom: Sure it's not. Be sure to make Dad's famous pancakes for her.

Jonas: Already on it.

I smiled at my phone before setting it back down and getting to the pancakes. No way was Mara waking up to the smell of burned pancakes.

They were nearly finished when I heard the sound of her shuffling footsteps over the floor. She was walking toward me, rubbing her eyes in the most adorable sleeping way. "Good morning."

"Good morning," I replied, holding up a pancake on my spatula. "I hope you like pancakes."

"Love them." Her eyes widened at the coffee pot. "Coffee!"

I set the pancake down and reached for a mug from the cabinet. "Enjoy," I said, pouring her a cup.

Her smile made me feel way better than I should have. I focused on the cooking food as she doctored her coffee with sugar and milk from the fridge. Then she leaned back against the granite countertop, holding the cup with both hands and taking a careful first sip.

It was like she belonged here, the way she so naturally fit in my space.

"Can I help?" she asked.

"Not at all. Why don't you sit at the table? I'll bring you a plate."

She rewarded me with another one of those smiles. "I feel like a queen."

"You *are* famous," I retorted, reaching for a plate from the cabinet. I set it on the counter, then pulled the bacon from the oven.

"I must be famous to get bacon and pancakes for breakfast," she replied, pulling a chair back across the stone floor.

I used a few paper towels to get the grease off her strips and added them to her plate, along with pancakes and a cube of butter sliced off the stick. My parents never used margarine, so it sort of stuck.

When I brought the plate to the table with a bottle of Canadian maple syrup, Mara said, "This looks amazing, Jonas. You didn't have to do all this for me."

"I wanted to," I replied honestly.

She took a bite of the food and moaned, sending a jolt of lightning straight to my dick. This was so not the way I wanted to make her moan. I wanted to make her *scream*.

I turned away to clear my head and made a plate for myself. As I sat across from her and took my first bite, I thought how funny it was. Having her in my dining room, seeing the midmorning sun filter through the sheer curtains and bounce off her brown hair, making it shine every hue of brown I didn't know existed. I hadn't planned to have her here... but I liked it.

"Hey," she said, "do you know where my phone is? I thought I set it by the bed, but I didn't see it there when I woke up."

"Oh, yeah," I said, quickly getting up to grab it. "Birdie called, and I didn't want it to wake you, so I answered. I hope that's okay. She said to give her a call when you got up."

I handed the phone to her, and she looked at the screen. I watched carefully to see her reaction to the notifications. She either had the world's best poker face or didn't care about having those guys text her like that. I hated that I didn't know which it was.

"Did you sleep alright?" I asked.

She set her phone face down on the table and said, "I slept great. And I can't believe you didn't wake me up with your boner in my back."

I nearly choked on my pancakes. Recovering, I asked, "I couldn't be a cliché, now could I?"

"If you're a cliché for anything, it's 'nice guy.' Really, Jonas, I can't tell you how thankful I am you had me over here. It would have been a long night at my house."

"No problem," I said, trying to ignore the part of me that bristled at being called a "nice guy." It was a compliment. Especially coming from someone like Mara. But that's not the only way I wanted her to see me.

How exactly did I want her to see me... I still wasn't sure.

She finished the last of her food, then held up her phone. "I better call Birdie."

I nodded, continuing to slowly work my way through

my breakfast while she went back to the bedroom. I could hear the muffled sound of Mara's voice from the table. I wondered what she was telling her friend. If she thought I was too forward by asking her to stay. If she couldn't wait to get out of my house.

But when she came back to the kitchen, she didn't say any of those things.

No, she surprised me by saying, "We're going to Collie's tonight."

I drew my eyebrows together. She wanted us to go to Cohen's bar tonight? "Why?"

She smiled. "We're all going to celebrate the success of our fake relationship."

16

MARA

Confession: Tequila is my sexy drink.

JONAS PULLED his car into Collie's crowded parking lot. I looked around at all the full spaces, the people walking inside, thinking it had been too damn long since I'd dressed up and gone out to the bar. And this was the first time that I'd arrived with the guy I intended to go home with.

To be fair, Jonas looked like the kind of guy I would go home with if I didn't know he was an accountant. If I wasn't fake dating him. He was fit, and the jeans he'd put on looked damn good on his ass. Not to mention he had on this navy-blue T-shirt that hugged his body in all the right ways.

I felt good too. Birdie had a stretchy body con dress that she let me borrow, and I loved the way it hugged my curves and showed just a hint of cleavage. It would be perfect for dancing.

We'd gone over there to get ready instead of chancing it back at my place. Jonas was adamant I would stay with him until the security system was installed, running, and *tested* at my house. He'd even set up the guest bed with freshly washed sheets and pillows. Too bad I didn't want to sleep in it.

Even if we hadn't done anything, it had been oddly comforting to sleep next to him and know he was there.

And when I woke up? He'd been right. The water was still cold from that ridiculous ice cube.

He held the door to the club open for me, and the bouncer, a college kid named Stanley, let us in without a cover. "Hey, Jonas, Mara," he added with a wink.

Always trying to punch above his weight.

I gave him a flirty wave and followed Jonas to the bar, where Cohen and Birdie were standing together. Birdie was sitting on the chair, and Cohen stood in between her legs, whispering something into her ear.

They were so happy and completely in their own world. Cohen had given Birdie everything she'd dreamed of—a good home for her and her bird, Ralphie, a stepson she loved just as dearly as if he were her own flesh and blood, and plenty of romance she could count on.

I could feel my belief start to crumble, if only a little. If Cohen was a good guy... maybe there were more out there like him.

And yet again, he could be a unicorn, giving false hope to girls like me.

I followed Jonas toward the two of them, and they smiled at us. Cohen already had a beer for Jonas and a mojito for me to match Birdie's signature happy drink.

She'd been drinking less and less of her sad drinks ever since she met him.

I took a sip, and my eyes widened. "Cohen, you have to keep the bartender. This drink is so good!"

"Right?" Birdie said excitedly.

Cohen rolled his eyes and hit Jonas's chest. "They just want me to keep him because he's hot."

I looked around to see what Cohen was talking about and *damn*. This guy had to be newly twenty-one with that fresh face and biceps that showed his extra enthusiasm at the gym.

Birdie giggled and said, "Mara didn't even know what he looked like!"

"Oh, so it's just you," Cohen said dryly.

She smiled and kissed him.

Jonas and I exchanged an awkward smile. Even though there were four of us, I still felt like a third wheel sometimes after having Birdie to myself for so many years.

"Hey!" Henrietta cried, and we turned to see her coming toward us. She looked adorable in a flowy green dress.

I kissed her cheek. "Working late?"

She gestured at her dress. "Meeting with the big boss to discuss my future with the company." She held up crossed fingers. "Hoping for a promotion sometime soon!"

"That's awesome!" Birdie said. We turned toward her, one big group again. "Have you seen the new bartender yet?" Birdie asked Henrietta, pointing down the bar.

"Damn," Henrietta said, fanning herself. "Is he available?"

Steve, Cohen's bar manager who was more like a best friend, came over and said, "What do you ladies think of the drinks? I'm trying to decide if Jackson's actually a good bartender or if all the girls are flocking to the bar because he's hot."

I laughed. "Who cares if he's bringing in business?"

Steve shook his head and was about to say something when Birdie's favorite group dance song, "Wobble," came on. She squealed, and I squealed right along with her.

"Watch our drinks?" she asked Cohen and, without waiting for an answer, took my hand, along with Henrietta's, and practically dragged us onto the dance floor.

I laughed the entire way, loving this for us. No matter how old we got, I couldn't imagine not getting on the dance floor for "Wobble" with my best friends.

People all around us were shimmying to the music, and I let the sound waves roll over my body, easily moving with them. Dancing was something that came naturally to me. I loved that I could let go of the day or my worries and get lost in rhythm. I loved the way guys responded when they saw my body move. It was freeing and empowering all at the same time.

Birdie, on the other hand, was adorable when she danced. She was all big toothy smiles and moves from awkward teenage dances. Going out with her had always been so much *fun*.

Henrietta made it even better, the perfect mix between our two extremes. She was like a slow-moving river, constant and steady and always there when you needed her, in good times and bad.

We danced through the song, and when we hit the end, Birdie was grinning ear to ear. That song always made her day. The three of us stayed on the dance floor for the next song, rocking back and forth to the music.

In our tight little dancing circle, Henrietta asked, "What's going on with you and Jonas? Is that chemistry I'm seeing?"

"Only if you consider oil and water not mixing chemistry," I replied, dancing alongside her.

Birdie moved her arm like a sprinkler and danced in a circle. "That's the literal definition of chemistry! But it looked like you two were mixing just fine."

I shimmied to the right again. "Okay, maybe there is something... but I don't think Jonas wants to be with a girl like me. He wants something serious, a family and marriage, and I just want to enjoy my life."

Henrietta gave me a wry smile. "Who says you can't do both?"

I shook my head. "I'm not that kind of girl."

"Maybe you could be," Birdie said. "You just need the right guy."

I gave a noncommittal answer and focused on dancing. The truth was that I couldn't fall in love. Not with Jonas. Not with the first guy who seemed actually concerned with my well-being. Not with someone who was only doing this for his mom.

Because happily ever afters didn't exist in real life.

Not for girls like me.

After a couple of songs, Birdie, Hen, and I went back to the bar where Cohen and Jonas were still talking. Cohen went back to make Henrietta a drink while I picked up my mojito from earlier, took a sip despite most of the ice being melted. I needed to find that pretty bartender again, but he was farther down the bar and completely swarmed by college girls.

Jonas asked, "Want to dance?"

The question caught me so off guard, I looked between Hen and Birdie just to confirm I'd heard him correctly. Birdie nodded back toward Jonas, and I realized he was still waiting for an answer.

I nodded, and Jonas took my drink, handing it to Birdie. "Watch this, will you?" It was kind of sexy, the way he just... handled it.

"Of course," she smiled.

Jonas clasped my hand in his, and I loved the way he took charge, leading me toward the dance floor. I tried to think back if I ever remembered Jonas dancing, but I couldn't. As he took me into the mesh of bodies and began moving, I couldn't believe I didn't remember.

Damn he had moves. And not just boring accountant rocking side to side moves.

His hands were on my hips, swaying to the music as the strobe lights reflected all hues in his brown eyes. Getting used to this side of Jonas, I danced with him, running my hands through my hair, letting the sound carry me away like it always did.

By the end of the song, my breath was coming heavy, and I was warm, sweating along my hairline. And then a slow country song came on. I turned, ready to walk back to the bar with our friends, but he took my hand, spinning me to his chest.

I looked up at him in surprise. "I didn't know you liked dancing so much."

He smiled down at me. "It's fun with you. Besides, the bar photographer is going to have great photos for proof."

"Proof?" I said. Then I instantly remembered. This was fake. At least to him. And it should have been to me. "Right. That's a great idea."

He nodded, then spun me back and then to him again, taking my breath away.

"Where did you learn to dance?" I asked.

"I could ask the same of you. You've always drawn my eyes on the dance floor," he said.

A flush formed on my cheeks. He'd been watching me. "I like to go out. I guess I've had a lot of practice."

"My dad taught me. My parents thought a man should know how to dance."

"They're right," I said. People always said you could tell how a man made love by the way he danced, and in my experience, that was a hundred percent true. But I needed to stop thinking about Jonas that way. Especially since I was staying the night at his house. Especially since I'd be spending hours with his mom on Monday for her dialysis.

"You know," he said, "it's been great getting to know you a little better."

I looked into his eyes, searching for some hint of a lie, but all I found was the truth. "Me too," I said, and that surprised no one more than it did me.

Another song started, and Birdie, Cohen, and Henrietta came to the edge of the dance floor. Henrietta held up two shot glasses filled with clear liquid and yelled, "Come here!"

"What on earth!" I yelled, walking toward them with Jonas. I hadn't done shots in a *long-ass* time.

We met them at the railing, and Hen handed me a shot glass while Cohen gave Jonas one. I sniffed the liquid, and my mouth fell open. "Tequila?" Birdie and Hen both knew this was my sexy drink. What the hell were they trying to do?

"Drink up!" Hen yelled with a suggestive smile.

I glared at her but still took a drink. I could handle my liquor.

Or at least, I thought so.

17

JONAS

Somewhere between shots two and four, Mara insisted we keep dancing, and fuck was she hot on the dance floor. The way her body rolled to the beat, the sultry look in her eyes, and how she looked as she ran her fingers through her long brown hair. *Damn.* I wanted to take her to the bathroom and fuck her right there.

But that would have ended poorly for both of us. So instead, we danced, and we drank, and we danced some more, and then we drank some more, and I realized I was actually having fun. Not worrying about Tess's wedding or my mom's dialysis or how this was all supposed to be fake.

No, I was focused on Mara, our friends dancing with us. So much so that I didn't realize how late it was until the pretty-boy bartender yelled, "Last call!"

Mara and I looked at each other in shock, and I raised my voice over the music to ask, "How is it that late?"

"I have no idea!" she said back.

Next to us, Cohen said, "We're gonna feel it in the morning."

"Speak for yourself, old man," Birdie teased.

He gave her an annoyed grin, and Birdie said, "I better get this old man home." Then, not so quietly, she added, "I *looove* sloppy drunk sex."

"Come on," Cohen said. "I'll call a ride."

Henrietta nodded slowly. "I'm calling one too. Hopefully my parents are asleep." She groaned. "I've *got* to move out."

Laughing, I said, "I'll get one for Mara and me."

Within fifteen minutes, Mara and I were away from our friends in the semi-privacy of our Uber driver's back seat. Mara had her legs crossed and her dress was riding up, and fuck if I didn't want to pull her leg over my lap and kiss her until we were both gasping for air.

She rolled her head to the side, an adorable drunken smile on her face. "That was a good time, huh?"

I nodded. "Definitely."

"I didn't know accountants could have fun," she said with a wry smile.

"You'd be surprised what accountants can do," I returned, my voice husky. I could smell her sweat mixed with apricot, and damn, I wanted to lick every sweet and salty inch of her. I looked out the window as if that would protect my thoughts. The second we got home, I was getting into the world's coldest shower.

"What are you thinking about?" she asked.

I looked away from the window and back toward her. "You don't want to know."

I swear I saw her tits rise as her breath caught in her chest. "Why not?"

"It wouldn't be appropriate."

Her smile grew, and she licked her lips in the sexiest possible way. "Those are my *favorite* kinds of thoughts."

"They're the kind of thoughts that would get us in trouble," I retorted.

The car stopped, and I looked out the window to see my house, illuminated by the front porch light.

Thank fuck I'd prepared that extra bed. If I was left alone with Mara tonight, there was no way her Christmas pajamas would make it through the night.

I got out of the car and opened the door for her, then began walking up the sidewalk. After sitting for a while and now stepping into the cool evening air, I could feel the alcohol slogging up my brain, fogging it with thoughts of her body and what I wanted to do with it.

I fumbled for far too long with my keys, and she came up behind me, resting her chin on my shoulder. "A little drunk, are you?"

I gave her a look. "Me? How many mojitos did you get from the pretty boy?"

Her lips spread into an evil grin. "Are you *jealous*?"

"Maybe," I huffed, finally jerking the key into the lock. The truth was I wanted to punch him in the face every fucking time he looked at Mara. Not a thought I'd *ever* had before, several tequila shots deep or not. "What's it to you?"

She stepped through the open door. "It's cute, you being jealous."

"Cute?" I growled, shutting the door. I didn't want to be fucking cute. I wanted to be fucking her.

She dropped her purse on the floor and turned toward me. "What?"

My eyes slowly slid to her cleavage and back to her face. "You're sexy. I'm cute. That's what."

I was sober enough to know I shouldn't be admitting things like that to her or getting all fucking pouty, but drunk enough not to care. My dick hurt, and I liked her, and I just wanted the games to stop already so I could take her on a fucking date. Why was everything so *complicated*?

"You're hard," she breathed, looking at my pants.

She licked her lips again, and I groaned. "You've got to stop doing that."

"What?" She was still looking at my dick.

"Stop licking your lips."

She stepped closer.

She did it again.

"Fuck," I groaned.

She stepped closer yet, lowering herself to her knees, and before I could even think to object, she had my zipper between her fingers, had my jeans open, giving her a better view of my cock straining against my gray boxers.

Her face this close made my cock twitch, and she smiled up at me before peeling back my underwear and freeing my shaft.

Her eyes went wide. "I knew you'd be big, but..."

I waited for her to say but what, but her lips were on the tip of my dick and my nerves were going crazy. I moaned hard, my attempt at begging for more. I wanted to feel the back of her throat, the swirl of her tongue, the tightness of her soft lips over my shaft.

But there was something else in my mind. A small fucking annoying voice that told me if we continued, I'd regret it.

She opened her lips farther, taking me deeper in her mouth, and I groaned, hitting the wall before stepping back and buttoning up my pants, angling my cock so the blue balls of the century wouldn't eat me alive.

"What?" She looked upset. Confused.

"We can't do this," I said, despite the fact that my dick was protesting otherwise. "We're drunk."

"And?" Mara replied, standing up. "Didn't you hear Birdie say that sloppy drunk sex is fun?"

"I don't want to have fun," I said, walking past her. "Not with you." Before I reached the guest room, I said, "You take the main bedroom. I'll see you in the morning."

I locked myself in the guest room. Literally, I locked the door. Not because I didn't trust her, but because I didn't trust myself.

I'd been staring at her all night. Not just thinking about her body, but about *her*. Mara was already so much more than I imagined her to be, and we'd barely started getting closer.

I'd admitted to Cohen I wanted to date her while she and Birdie were dancing, no matter how impossible it seemed that someone like her, so sexually free and fun and uninhibited, could be interested in someone like me.

He'd put his hand on my shoulder and said, "Mara's been hurt. It's going to take a lot to show her that it's safe to give more than just her body to you."

And those words had been going through my mind all night. Especially when I pulled away from her.

When I heard the bedroom door shut, I let out a sigh of relief. Instead of leaving to get fresh clothes from the laundry room, I stripped into my boxers and lay in the bed. It really was soft. But I still couldn't help but wish I was sleeping beside her instead.

MARA

Confession: Cake is an excellent motivator.

I SLEPT ALONE in Jonas's bed, and when I woke up, I felt like shit. Not just because of the tequila. (Although that certainly didn't help.) But because of the way I'd come onto him in his own house when we'd both been drunk out of our minds.

It wasn't fair to him. He'd invited me here to keep me safe when he didn't have to. He'd agreed to be my pretend boyfriend when he didn't have to. And now he had the weight of keeping the lines from blurring while my mouth was on his dick?

Either I was losing my touch or Jonas Moore had the self-control of a Navy SEAL.

I wasn't ready to face him yet, so I went into the bathroom and turned the hot water on over the big soaker tub. It was made of white porcelain and had luxurious hardware. There was even a window overhead, letting diffused light drift into the bathroom.

As soon as the water was halfway up the sides, I dipped my toe in, feeling the burn of the water. Slowly, I eased my way in, the water rising around me. Usually I didn't enjoy baths, since most tubs weren't big enough for the water to cover my body, but this one was the perfect size. There was even room in here for two.

I closed my eyes against the activities I imagined Jonas and me doing. I had a problem. Especially since he made it very clear he wasn't interested in having sex with me.

I dried my hands off on a towel next to the tub and texted my friends group chat.

Mara: I have a problem.

Henrietta: What happened?

Mara: I may or may not have attempted to give Jonas a blow job last night.

Henrietta: Attempted?

Birdie: Did he have whiskey dick?

Mara: No, he was perfectly hard. He told me to stop!

Mara: God, I'm so mortified. I can't even come out of the room to face him and apologize.

Henrietta: Wait. Don't guys love blow jobs?

Birdie: That's an understatement.

Henrietta: Why did he turn you down?

Birdie: Did you do it wrong?

Mara: Did I do it wrong???? I don't want to toot my own horn (pun intended) but I have it on good authority that I am VERY good at blow jobs.

Henrietta: What did he say when he asked you to stop?

I closed my eyes, trying to think back to last night. It was fuzzy, and my brain was moving slower than I liked.

When I remembered, my eyes popped open.

Mara: I said something about drunk sex being fun and he said, AND I QUOTE, "I don't want to have fun. Not with you."

Mara: WHAT DOES THAT MEAN?

Henrietta: You're the romance writer! You don't know?

Birdie: Do you think he meant he wants sex with you to mean something? That's what it sounds like to me.

I didn't know how to feel about the swoop that went through my stomach at that idea.

Henrietta: That makes sense to me. In my LIMITED experience.

Mara: What would he want it to mean?

Birdie: Something real.

Mara: But this is all fake so I can help his mom. It'll be over as soon as the movie premieres.

Henrietta: Do you want it to be over?

I let out a sigh and put my phone back on the ground.

A knock sounded on the door, and I jumped, sending water over the edges of the tub. I hurriedly grabbed my phone, drying it on the towel, and said, "Sorry, do you need the bathroom?"

"No, I'm going to a cake tasting with Tess and Derek, and I was wondering if you wanted to come along?"

I scrunched my eyebrows together. He wanted me to come with him and spend time with his sister after everything that happened the night before? That didn't make sense. "Hold on," I said.

I hurriedly picked up my phone and texted the girls.

Mara: HE WANTS ME TO GO TO A CAKE TASTING WITH HIM FOR HIS SISTER'S WEDDING. WHAT DO I DO?!?!

Come on. Reply. Please.

Birdie: GO WITH HIM!

I stepped out of the tub and wrapped one of his big bath towels around my body. I tried not to think about how much I liked the fact that all his towels matched and that they were big enough to fit me. It was almost like he'd been planning to have someone like me here before he even knew me.

I reached the door and took a deep breath, steeling myself to see him. But when I opened the door, nothing could have prepared me for how good he looked, freshly showered, in dark jeans and a light blue button-up shirt that brought out the tan in his skin.

He seemed surprised by me too, but I pushed out the words because I had to.

"I'm sorry about last night," I said quickly. "I'm so embarrassed, and I never should have put you in that situation."

"No worries." He gave me a gracious smile. "Tequila's trouble."

He had just brushed off the whole encounter so easily, but my cheeks were still hot. "Well, um, thank you. It won't happen again," I promised.

He seemed uncomfortable, but he quickly regrouped. "Did you want to go to the tasting with me? I know you're the ice cream connoisseur, but I assume that also translates to cakes."

I laughed. "I do have a great judgement for buttercream frosting."

His smile came easily. "So you'll come with? I always feel like such a third wheel at these things."

"I'm impressed you're going," I said.

He scratched his neck, looking down at the floor. "I'm helping them pay for the wedding, so they want me to be there."

If I didn't need to hold up my towel, my hand would be over my heart. That was so sweet of him, to give to his sister, and then to be shy about taking credit... "How much time do I have to get ready?"

He glanced at his watch. "Thirty minutes." When he looked back up at me, he said, "What?"

I nodded toward his silver accessory. "Who still wears watches? Everyone can see the time on their phone."

Giving me an exasperated smile, he said, "Get ready."

With a smile growing on my own face, I stepped back, closing the door, and went back to the bathtub with butterflies dancing in my chest. I didn't want to think about why going to this cake tasting with him meant so much to me, but it did. Maybe just because things wouldn't be awkward between us forever.

Even if I'd never forget a cock like his.

I wasn't shy about the number of names in my "little black book", but this one was hands down the best I'd ever seen. Perfectly pink, veined along the shaft. The tip was thick around the edges. And his sack was perfectly proportioned.

It was beautiful. I'd be using it for writing inspiration for years to come.

I drained the bathtub and started getting ready. Since I hadn't thought to bring a hair dryer, I did the best I could with a twisted bun and got dressed in some clothes I'd borrowed from Birdie.

When I walked out of the bedroom, I found Jonas sitting in the living room, flipping through a magazine.

"What are you reading?" I asked.

He flipped it over, showing *The Economist* on the cover.

"Lame," I said.

He rolled his eyes. "Let's get out of here."

We walked down the sidewalk together and got into my car, since his was still at the club.

"Where are we going?" I asked after we had buckled up.

"Seaton Bakery. Do you know where it is?"

My eyes widened with glee. "Birdie and I go there all the time! I *adore* Chris and Gayle. Are they making Tess and Derek's cake?"

He nodded, a smile in his eyes. "I think Chris does most of the baking though, and he has a few flavors he wants us to try out."

"Well, that's easy," I said, putting my car into gear. "All three. We don't even need to taste them."

Jonas chuckled. "Try telling Tess that. She's loving all the wedding planning stuff."

"And Derek?"

"Somehow enjoying it even more than Tess?" he said.

I laughed. "Is that so?"

"Don't be sexist," he teased. "Guys can enjoy wedding planning too."

"Especially when they get a babe like your sister," I said. "She's so pretty."

A look of pride crossed his face. I recognized it from

all the other times he spoke of his family. "She's a great girl. Especially now that she's grown into her teeth."

I laughed out loud. "I'm telling her you said that."

"You wouldn't dare."

I glanced over to him, raising an eyebrow. "Try me."

He shook his head. "You, Mara Taylor, will be the death of me."

I couldn't help but think it was the other way around.

19

JONAS

After the way things got off track with Mara last night, I had to find a way to make it right, and maybe, selfishly, I wanted to spend a little extra time with Mara too. Sitting next to her in her car, I couldn't help but take her in. She was so adorable in her shirt and her hair in a pile atop her head. Her nose was especially cute from this angle.

"Is there something on my face?" she asked me, wiping at her cheek.

I laughed. "No, I was just admiring you from over here."

She gave me an exasperating look. "You're still drunk."

"It's possible." I laughed again. It seemed like with Mara I laughed more than I ever had with another woman. Hell, I couldn't remember the last time I'd laughed so much at work or playing poker with the guys. I was glad she'd agreed to come along with me today. Wedding prep would be so much more bearable with her at my side.

We arrived at Seaton Bakery and walked inside together. Gayle came around the counter, wrapping her slender arms around Mara's body. "I didn't know you were coming!" Gayle said. "It's so great to see you! We've been following all the news, and we're so excited for your movie to come out." She yelled over her shoulder, "Aren't we, Chris?"

A tall, thin man with a receding hairline and a big smile came out of the kitchen, wiping his hands on an old white apron. "So excited."

Grinning, Mara gestured at me. "You remember Cohen's friend Jonas."

Gayle turned her smile on me. "Of course we do. But he's more than Cohen's friend, isn't he?"

Mara's expression was blank for a second, before I stepped forward and said, "It wasn't easy pinning this one down."

Gayle laughed, one arm still around Mara's shoulders. "Of course not. She deserves the best."

"I couldn't agree more."

Chris said, "Tess and Derek aren't here yet, but I set up the cakes on that corner table back there if you want to give them a look."

I followed his thumb to see three single-tiered cakes beautifully frosted sitting on the table. One had fluffy white frosting, another rich chocolate, and yet another a mocha color in between.

"These are beautiful, and I know they're going to be delicious," I said. "Tess is going to have a hard time deciding."

Gayle said, "His head just grew three sizes."

Just then, the bell over the door rang, and Tess and

Derek came inside. They looked adorable together, holding hands. It made me think back to when I was a dumb teenager getting married after my high school graduation to the girl I thought would be my forever.

We'd picked up a plain cake from the grocer and a topper from the dollar store because we couldn't afford a fancy wedding, and my parents thought if I was old enough to get married, I was old enough to pay for it myself. It had been a hard lesson to learn, because I hadn't been ready. Not even close.

This wedding was going to be everything Tess dreamed of and everything I hoped I could have someday down the road.

Tess and Derek joined us, and Chris launched into a more detailed explanation about the cakes. One was chocolate with chocolate cream cheese frosting. Another vanilla with vanilla buttercream. And then the last one was a mocha cake with white chocolate frosting and mini milk chocolate chips all throughout. My mouth was already watering.

We sat together at the table, and I loved the way Mara's arm brushed against mine. Something about having her close was comforting. Especially after last night. I was so worried we'd messed everything up, but the way she just fit right in at my side... it was right.

Tess grinned across the table at us. "I'm so happy you could come, Mara. Jonas is always bored out of his skull at these things."

Mara smiled over at me and said, "I'm happy to be here."

Gayle came back to the table with four plates, forks, and a serving knife to dish up pieces of cake for all of us.

Just when I thought it couldn't get better than the vanilla cake, we tried the chocolate one, and then the coffee one knocked us off our feet.

Tess looked forlorn at the half-eaten cakes. "How in the world are we supposed to decide?"

Mara replied, "I don't think we can go wrong. They're all so good."

Derek joked, "Why don't we just get all three?"

Seeming excited, Tess looked at Gayle. "Is that even an option?"

"Absolutely," Gayle said. "Anything for your wedding day, sweetie."

"Sold," Tess said. Then she glanced at me. "Sold, right?"

"Absolutely," I replied.

Gayle laughed. "That's the easiest cake sale I've ever had in my life."

Tess and Derek went to the front of the store with Gayle, setting up the details for their wedding date just a month after Mara's movie premiere.

It made me sad to think that Mara would be here for all the preparations, but she wouldn't be at the wedding. Not as a friend and not as my date. Mom would be heart-broken. So would Tess. And maybe I would be too.

I stifled a sigh. I was definitely reaching.

Once all their arrangements were made, Mara asked, "Do you guys want to go to the beach? There's a great corn dog stand there."

"Sorry," Derek said. "We already promised my mom we would come over for lunch. She was horrified we missed church this morning."

Tess shot me a frown behind his back. Even though

Tess had forgiven his family for the whole 'trying to sue her and destroy her store' thing, relations were still a little tense with the in-laws.

"I have time," I offered.

Mara smiled and said, "Sounds great."

We got back in her car and drove the few minutes toward Seaton Pier, listening to music on my radio. It was one of those beautiful early February days that almost felt like spring but still had the briskness of winter. Wind fluttered through the open window, releasing small strands from Mara's bun. She looked perfectly at home behind the wheel. Beautiful, really.

We got out of the car and walked toward the corn dog stand I'd been to a half a dozen times with Cohen. The owner's name was Carl, and every time I came, the corn dogs were just as good as Carl's personality.

He welcomed us with a toothy smile, complimented Mara, and handed us four corn dogs. We each held two as we walked down the wooden pier, farther out over the ocean waves.

"Thanks for coming out here with me," Mara said. "I haven't been to the beach as much as I'd like lately."

I smiled over at her. "Of course."

Mara said, "So what do you think about the cakes? Did they make the right decision?"

"Absolutely."

There was an awkward silence between us as we reached the end and looked out over the ocean. I rested my elbows on the railing, wondering what the hell to say.

So much had changed in such a short period of time, but we still had to carry on with this agreement for a fake relationship. The dialysis machine had already been delivered to Mom and Dad's house. The dialysis technician would be there tomorrow morning to show Mara how to use the machine. Mom was excited to be at home, even if Mara wasn't my "real" girlfriend.

I glanced at Mara, and the sight of her eating a corn dog nearly had me doubled over, especially after the night before. Damn, I really was a fucking teenager right now.

Deciding to change the subject to something less sexy, I asked, "Are you ready for tomorrow?"

She swallowed her bite and said, "I'm more worried about waking up early than I am about helping with dialysis." She let out a little laugh. "I'm not exactly a morning person, if you haven't been able to tell. Although, if you make those pancakes every day, I could be."

If Mara stuck with me, I'd make pancakes every damn day of the year. But I couldn't say that out loud. The lines were already becoming blurred. And even though I liked her, I didn't want her to feel like I was just using her since I couldn't have sex with anyone else.

"What about you?" she asked.

"What?"

"Are you excited to have me out of your hair?"

"Out of my hair?"

"Yeah," she said. "I'm calling the security company tomorrow, and I'm hoping I can throw enough money at them for them to do a same-day install."

I shook my head. "You can stay with me as long as you'd like."

She bit her lip, looking out over the ocean. "I'm sorry, Jonas. I'm just not great at being friends with guys."

The words both hurt and made me worry. Why did it feel like she was breaking up with me already? "What do you mean?"

"Any time a man has done something for me, there were always strings attached." At the crease in my eyebrows, she added, "Like if a guy bought me a drink at a bar, it was only because he wanted to take me home. Or if someone let me crash on their couch, they did it because they wanted to have sex on hand at any time." *Or when a guy agreed to fake date her, he did it so his mom could have dialysis at home.*

She let out a sigh and turned, resting her back against the railing. "Eventually, I think I just found safety in my girlfriends and physical pleasure out of guys. And I know that sounds terrible, but it's just the truth." She met my eyes now, lifting her chin as if challenging me to fault her. I didn't. "So, I'm really sorry if I made you feel uncomfortable last night, but all of this is new to me."

I shook my head, not wanting her to feel an ounce of guilt or shame over her past. "I think you're better at being a friend than you think you are."

"How so?" she asked.

"You came to Seaton Bakery with me to try out wedding cakes for my sister's wedding. That's definitely a friend thing."

She smiled slightly.

"And we went to Waldo's Diner together, where you told me I have crappy taste in milkshakes. If we were dating, you'd definitely try to agree with me more."

She laughed. "I can't argue with that." Then she looked over at me, her smile sincere. "It is nice to have a friend."

I smiled and agreed, even though part of me wished we could be so much more.

20

MARA

Confession: I still miss my mom.

JONAS OFFERED to go with me to his parents' house the next morning, but I waved him off and told him I would be fine. And it was the truth. His parents were some of the kindest people I'd ever met.

So I got in my car and drove to their house, remembering the way there because it was so close to Hayden's house. Luckily, his car wasn't outside when I drove by because that would have been an *awkward* conversation.

As soon as I parked, Cade came out wearing his work uniform with his name stitched in red thread above his breast pocket. He grinned big, saying, "It's great to see you, Mara!"

I smiled back at him, stifling a yawn. "How can you be so cheery in the morning?"

"Years of practice." He chuckled. "I have to get to work, but I left breakfast for you two on the table. The technician should be here in half an hour. If you have any problems, my number's on the fridge. Just call and I'll be here in fifteen minutes flat."

I put my hand on his shoulder. "We've got this. Have a good day at work, okay? No need to worry about us."

He gave me a bashful smile and admitted, "I have been a bit worried."

"Totally understandable."

He nodded. "Have we mentioned how lucky we are that Jonas met you?"

I let out a laugh. "I've been feeling the same way lately."

Glancing at his watch, he said, "I better go," and walked toward his truck.

I waved before going to the front door and knocking.

"Come in!" Mariah called.

I did as she asked and found her sitting at the kitchen table, sipping a cup of orange juice. There was a stack of pancakes on a platter, along with a plate full of crispy bacon and another of scrambled eggs. Now I knew where Jonas had learned to make breakfast.

"Hi, honey," Mariah said. "How was your weekend? We watched you two on the news, and you both did so great."

My cheeks warmed at the thought of her seeing me kiss her son. I wasn't a prude by any stretch, but there was a time and place for everything. "Thank you."

She passed me an empty plate and said, "Eat up. Cade will be heartbroken if he sees too many leftovers in the fridge."

"You don't have to tell me twice." I poured myself a cup of coffee from the pot and then walked back to the table, filling my plate with food. "How was your weekend? Did you do anything fun?"

"Unless giving Oaklynn a bath counts as fun, it was same ol' same ol'."

I chewed over my food, thinking. "What do you typically do in a day?"

She shrugged. "I like to read, so I do that quite a bit now that the kids are gone. Sometimes I take Oaklynn to the beach in the morning and go on walks. I like to cook meals and drop them off at the local foster care agency for new foster parents. Nothing big. And a lot of my time has been sucked up by dialysis now. Twelve hours a week might not seem like much, but it sure does feel like a lot."

"I totally get it," I said. "I don't have kids or family and I still feel like I'm always behind with work."

A knock sounded on the door, and she set her silverware down. "That must be the tech."

She left me at the table, eating the last of my food, and returned with an adorable guy in scrubs. He must have been a year or two younger than me, but he had tattoos all up and down his arms, and I was trying to keep from drooling.

I couldn't help but feel like Mariah was getting the short end of the stick by having me and not him.

"This is Mara," Mariah said. "She'll be here helping me out."

The guy grinned at me, and despite myself, I melted, just a little bit. "I'm Jake. Looks like your day's off to a good start."

"It definitely is," I said, then I realized I needed to turn the flirt dial *way* down. Mariah was my "boyfriend's" mom, after all. "My boyfriend's dad made this amazing breakfast, and now I get to spend time with this dime piece!"

Riah chuckled, waving her hand at me. "She is full of it."

Smiling, Jake said, "If you two are ready, we can get to it?"

We both nodded and went to the sunroom off the kitchen. I'd never been back here before, but it was a cute room with green carpet, mismatched chairs, and a wall full of windows. In one corner, there was a coat tree with their jackets hanging, and a shoe rack rested against the wall.

"I thought it would be nice to get some sun while I do this," Mariah said.

"Great idea," I agreed.

Jake walked to the machine and began programming it, then walked me through each step to get her set up. Soon, the machine was running, and Mariah was settled in her own chair with her Kindle in her lap.

I walked with Jake toward the front door to let him out, while he walked me through last-minute information. "If you have any issues at all, our company has a nurse-on-call line, so you can always get through no matter the time of day. But..." He stopped by the door, getting a pen out of his pocket. "If you want to reach me personally, I live about twenty minutes from here. And I can make time for you." He winked, then handed me the paper with his phone number on it.

"I'll keep that in mind," I said, glancing toward the floor and trying not to pay too much attention to his tattoos or wonder how much of his body they covered.

As soon as he was out the door, I walked back to the

sunroom with my laptop bag and sat in the chair next to Mariah's. "How's it going?" I asked her. "Is it better being here for dialysis?"

She rolled her head toward me. "You have no idea. I *hated* going to that place. It was so sterile, and I felt like everyone was staring at me."

"I get it," I said. "I know it's not the same, but when you're a big girl, especially at the beach in a swimsuit, people like to stare."

"Stupid."

"Agreed." I got out my laptop and opened it on my lap.

"What are you working on?" Mariah asked. "Please tell me it's Liza and Reid's story."

I grinned. "You read Jennika and Martin's book, didn't you? Jonas said you were reading one, but I couldn't really tell from what he gave me."

Mariah laughed. "I think I scarred him for life with that sex scene."

I chuckled, remembering his phone call. "I feel like every guy should read a romance at some point."

"Especially Jennika's." She let out a happy sigh. "Seeing her overcome her eating disorder and make love to Martin, with whipped cream. Oh my god, I didn't think anything could be so sweet and meaningful and *hot*, all at the same time."

Now my cheeks were getting warm. I didn't usually get a chance to talk to readers like this. "Thank you. That means a lot."

"So, what about Liza and Reid? How did they get together?"

"It's a marriage of convenience," I said. "Reid needs

to be married as a term of his trust fund, and Liza's willing to marry him if he'll help her buy back her family's dairy farm. They're total opposites, of course, her waking up every day at four in the morning to milk cows while he's having maids deliver breakfast in bed. They hate each other at first."

Mariah clapped her hands together. "Ooh, I can't wait to read it!"

I grinned. "I can hook you up with an advanced copy, if you want it."

"Um, yes please."

I signed into my laptop and went to one of the sticky notes I kept open all the time. "I'm writing it down right now. What's your email?" She spelled it out for me, and I said, "Got it... Can I ask you something?"

"Anything, honey."

The way she called me honey... it melted my heart. My own mom had left when I was twelve, and she wasn't the affectionate kind. I wondered what it must have been like for Tess and Jonas to grow up with her as a mom. And I realized I wanted her to like me, maybe even more than I wanted Jonas to.

It took me a second to work up the courage to ask. "How do you feel about your son dating a sex writer? I mean, doesn't it make you uncomfortable to know the things I write about and my... history?"

One corner of her thin lips drew down. "I feel like romance is misunderstood. People think it's all about getting off or indulging yourself. That's not what I see when I read your stories. When I see your life."

"What do you see?" I asked, desperate for her answer. To be truly seen by this incredible woman.

She reached across the gap between our chairs and took my hand in hers. "When I look at you, I see someone who needed an escape. You could have picked anything—drugs, violence, alcohol... But you chose one filled with love, and you've shared that love with so many readers. I think you're incredible, Mara."

My eyes stung with unshed tears. I'd never felt so understood before in my life. So un-judged for my past or for my career. "You're going to make me cry."

"Remember what Jennika said in your book? 'Tears are pain's way out, and the emptiness they leave are love's way in.'"

21

JONAS

"Are you okay?" my bookkeeper, Karen, asked me after she had to repeat her question for the third time. She was nearly fifty years old and had worked in this place longer than I had. She had the same big blond hair, rosy cheeks, and penciled-in eyebrows that she'd had when I met her on my first day at ESR Accounting.

I rubbed my temples and sat back in my chair. "Sorry. My mom's doing at-home dialysis for the first time, and I think I'm a little nervous."

"Oh, sugar," she said, in only the way an older woman could. "I'm sure your momma's fine. Those machines have gotten so good they practically run themselves."

"I know," I said. "I should be focusing on that promotion up for grabs, but I'm having a hard time."

She shook her head. "Best not let Mr. Rusk see you waffling. You know how he is. One wrong move and..." She drew her finger across her neck.

I nodded, doubling down on the work. "Now ask me that question again."

Only three hours left until I could break for lunch with the guys and talk to Mom about how her morning went.

❤·❤·❤·❤

I CALLED my mom as I drove to Waldo's Diner to meet Steve and Cohen, and she answered within a few rings. "Hi, honey."

I smiled at her standard greeting. "Hey, Mom, how'd it go?"

"It was great. Mara and I had a grand time, the technician was cute, and we're all set to do it again Wednesday morning."

"Wait," I said, slowing at a stop light. "What was that about the technician?"

"He was cute!" She laughed. "Jealous?"

"No," I said, far too quickly.

"Good, then it won't bother you that he left his phone number for Mara."

"He what?"

"Oh, honey," she said. "Mara didn't give him or the number a second glance."

My chest puffed just enough to completely embarrass me. Was I really going to walk around jealous of every guy who found Mara attractive? I'd be jealous all the damn time.

"Do you want to come by for lunch on Wednesday?" Mom asked. "I could put something in the slow cooker and the three of us can have a meal together?"

"Sure," I said, not thinking twice. "I just pulled into Waldo's, so I should probably let you go."

"Love you," she said.

I said it back and then hung up, going into the diner.

Cohen and Steve were already sitting in a booth with Chester, Birdie's grandpa, who owned the diner. I slid into the seat next to Chester, and Cohen gave me a curious look.

"How'd it go with Mara this weekend?"

"Did you..." Steve raised and lowered his eyebrows.

Chester only chuckled like an old man amused by the immaturity of the boys around him.

"We almost..." I raised and lowered my eyebrows. "But I couldn't go through with it."

"What?" Steve asked. "Why not? You couldn't get your eyes off of her at Collie's. If I didn't know you two were together, I'd be worried about you murdering her."

Cohen laughed so hard he nearly choked on his coffee, and Chester's shoulders shook with mirth. Meanwhile, my cheeks were just as hot as the steam rising from Cohen's mug.

"I can't do that with her when she thinks we're just together so I can get my mom dialysis."

Chester's thick eyebrows drew together. "You made a deal with Mara?"

I nodded. "She needed a boyfriend for public appearances, and I needed someone to give my mom dialysis at home, so we swapped." I let out a sigh. "Now my parents are in love with her, and I'm not too far behind."

Chester shook his head. "There are two kinds of people you shouldn't make agreements with."

"Who's that?" Steve asked.

"Pretty girls and the devil."

Cohen and Steve laughed, but I didn't. I was already in over my head.

"I have to wait, right?" I said. "Wait until her movie comes out and then ask her out for real? I don't want her to just think I'm doing it for the sake of a handshake agreement."

Chester waved his hand. "It's the way of youth to make everything so damn complicated. Just ask her out."

"Ask her out," I echoed.

"Exactly. Take her out to a nice restaurant. Like La Belle. Buy her the fanciest dish on the menu, order up some red wine, and tell her you think the stars shine in her eyes."

"And if it goes badly?" I asked. "We have an awkward six months, and she ditches me as soon as humanly possible. And then my mom..."

Chester waved his hand. "Karen can sit with your mom. She volunteers for stuff like that all the time."

I raised my eyebrows. "Seriously?"

He nodded. "You have nothing to lose."

"Exactly," Steve agreed. "The only thing you'll be losing is our next poker game." Now that Cohen and I both had homes, we alternated between our two places for a weekly poker game. We never played with money and spent more time drinking beer than actually playing, but it was a ritual I never wanted to end.

We sat and bullshitted for the remainder of my lunch break. But even when our lunch was done, I couldn't get the idea of taking Mara on a date out of my head. Would it be a terrible mistake or the best decision of my life? I wouldn't know unless I tried.

On my way back to the office, I called Mara, and she answered within a few rings. "Hello?"

"Hey," I said, already smiling at the sound of her voice. "How did today go?"

"It was great. Your mom and I talked about books, and she even helped me get through a plot hole I'd been worrying about."

The fact that she didn't bring up the technician made me far too happy. Time to bring myself down to earth. "Did you get in touch with the security company?"

"About that..." She let out a sigh. "No amount of sweet talking or bribery will get them to my house until the end of next week. Which means I either need to buy a gun or ask Birdie and Cohen if I can stay with them. Or maybe I could ask Henrietta. She lives with her parents, but maybe she wouldn't mind sharing a bed for a little while..."

"Why would you stay with them? You're more than welcome to stay with me."

"Jonas..."

"Seriously. I don't mind having you at all."

"Really," she said. "You've already done so much for me."

My chest felt tight at the thought of losing her already. I knew I would miss her the second I couldn't smell her on my sheets. "I haven't done nearly as much as what you've done for me and my family. You should have heard Mom when I called her earlier. She was so happy and said she had a great time with you."

"That may have something to do with the hot technician," Mara said. "We were both a little smitten."

My laugh came out strangled. "Is that so?"

"He was a little forward, leaving me his number even though we clearly said I was Riah's son's girlfriend." She made a tsking sound. "He obviously doesn't know I'm a committed woman."

She was joking, but I wished it were true. I just needed to come out and say it. Stop making things complicated, like Chester had advised. "Stay with me."

She was quiet for a moment. "Okay. But can you come by my house with me to get my things?"

"Of course. I can come by after work and then let's go out to eat?"

"Like at Waldo's?"

I adjusted my grip on the steering wheel. "I was thinking La Belle."

"I've been missing their tiramisu!"

Well, she wasn't exactly saying yes to me so much as dessert, but I'd take it. "Meet you at my house at six?"

"It's a date."

22

MARA

Confession: Sometimes I like a man to take control.

I'D BEEN HAVING such a good day until the security company told me they wouldn't be able to come until late the following week.

I hated needing people, but I knew if I stayed at my house my anxiety would be out of control. The thought of my dad just showing up unannounced in the middle of the night made me want to run away from here and start a new life somewhere he could *never* find me.

I used to think he didn't care enough to ever come after me, but clearly I had been wrong.

No matter how hard it was to admit, I felt better being at Jonas's house, under his wing, with his front door video camera and the sign in the yard that said *Protected by Stonewall.* But it wasn't just that. Jonas had such a calming presence. When I was around him, everything felt *easier.* Even if it was so much more complicated.

Since I didn't have anywhere to go until our date, I went to Halfway Café in downtown Emerson and sat with my laptop by a window. I'd been so busy, I hadn't gotten a chance to check in with my virtual assistant, so I dialed her number.

"Hey, girl, hey," Rebecca said with a smile in her voice. "What's the 4-1-1?"

I loved working with her. She was so bubbly and fun. "So. Stinking. Much. Charlotte's been sending you updated statements, right?"

"Yes! They've changed like three times over the weekend."

I laughed, because she was right. "It's been a wild few days."

"And Jonas?" she asked. "PLEASE tell me it's real. I mean, the statement says it is, but...."

"It looks fake," I said.

"Actually, it looked convincing on the news."

"That's good." I chewed the inside of my cheek for a moment. "TBD."

She squealed.

"I wanted to check in and see if you've gotten any strange emails or want to go over anything before I get logged in?" I asked. I could chat for hours with Rebecca, but I really needed to get some words in.

"There was an email from Duncan Schwarz. Is that..."

"My dad," I finished. I couldn't deal with this right now. Not that I had a choice. "Was it threatening?"

"Um, no, I don't think so."

"Then file it," I said. "I don't want to deal with it." Even if my curiosity would eventually get the best of me.

"Absolutely. Anything else?" she asked.

"Nope. Just keep replying to emails and stay on top of social. I want some good focus on Liza and Reid."

"Swoon. Talk soon, Mar."

"Talk soon," I replied.

I set my phone down and took a few deep breaths. My dad had found my website. Was using my assistant's time for whatever he wanted. She said it wasn't threatening, and I didn't have the headspace to deal with it.

So I did what I did best. I opened my computer, and I got to work.

I loved writing with a big creamy latte and a few people passing by outside. All the voices in the coffee shop turned into a dull hum while I got lost in the story, in the characters, in the fabric of their lives. Sometimes it felt like I was pulling and weaving threads, and other times I could watch it unfold. It was the closest thing to magic I knew.

Hours had passed without me knowing when my phone began ringing. I had expected to see Birdie or Hen's name on the screen. Instead, I saw Jonas.

"Hello?" I said, already packing up my computer. It was only half an hour until six.

"Hey, I was on my way home from work and I saw your car outside Halfway Café. At least I think it's your car. And if you were there, I thought maybe we could ride to the restaurant together?"

I laughed, looking out the window for Jonas. His car was parked just in view from where I sat. "Stalker much?"

"My mom calls me 'observant.'"

"Uh huh." I lifted my laptop bag and put it over my shoulder. "I don't mind riding with you." I actually liked not having to be behind the wheel. But I didn't tell him that.

Instead, I walked outside to find him leaning against the hood of his car waiting for me. With his sleeves rolled up and his tie hanging loosely around his neck, he didn't just look good. He looked *hot*.

My watering mouth had nothing to do with the food we were about to consume.

"Hey," he said, getting up. "Have a good day?"

"It got a little off track in the middle, but overall really good," I replied. I didn't typically spend my day around people—that was just the nature of my career—but hanging out with his mom had been great. "Is it bad that I'm already looking forward to Wednesday?"

The brightness of his smile rivaled the sun. "Not at all." He opened the door for me, and I got in.

It was nice being treated like this, but when he got in the car, I said, "You don't have to open doors for me. I don't think anyone's watching."

"I am," he replied. And that was that. He rolled down his sleeves and tightened his tie and began driving.

La Belle wasn't too far away, and soon we were leaving his car with the valet driver and walking through the heavy glass doors. He put his hand low on my back as we walked in, sending shivers up my spine.

Jonas greeted the hostess and said, "I have a reservation for six o'clock under Moore."

She smiled warmly at him and scratched her pen across a page. "I have you down. Please follow me." She led us to a private table in the back corner of the restaurant, and I had to wonder whether it was coincidence or if Jonas had specifically requested privacy.

How would I feel either way?

Jonas held my chair out for me, the perfect gentleman, and then walked to his side of the table. "It's been forever since I've eaten here."

"Me too. I'm excited."

Our waiter came to the table, and I did a double take. My jaw dropped flat on the floor. *Hayden* was our waiter?

I knew he worked at the pet store, but he must have picked up another job. And while I stared in shock at him in his waiter's uniform, he was looking equally stunned between Jonas and me.

"So I guess this is why I haven't heard from you," he said, setting our menus in front of us.

I hadn't replied to any of his messages in the last several days, partially because we wouldn't be seeing each other anymore. And also because we weren't a couple—I didn't owe him a response, just like he didn't owe me one. But mostly, I hadn't texted him back because of the man sitting across from me, the one who was looking more and more uncomfortable by the second.

"Um, Hayden," I said, "this is Jonas. My boyfriend."

Jonas stood and extended his hand. "Nice to meet you."

"Wow." Hayden rocked back, ignoring Jonas completely. "*Wow.* I thought you 'weren't the relationship type.'"

I smiled and shrugged, trying to ignore how tense my shoulders, and the rest of my body, were.

"I see how it is," Hayden said, sucking his teeth and then looking between Jonas and me. "This has to be your first boyfriend, right? When it doesn't last, because it won't..." He shrugged. "Give me a call. We'll use the rest of that whipped cream." He winked.

I didn't embarrass easily, but let me tell you, I was *mortified*. "Hayden!" I hissed.

A manager approached us and said, "Is there a problem here?"

"No," Hayden quickly said.

Jonas said, "It's fine. We just needed to check on something, in the bathroom. We'll be right back, *Hayden*."

Hayden's expression hardened while the manager looked surprised. Before they had a chance to recover, Jonas was leading me away from our table, past staring diners, and back toward the women's bathroom.

As soon as we were away from the table, I began apologizing. "Jonas, I am so sorry. I didn't know he worked here, and I had no idea he would say that kind of thing, especially in front of you. I'm beyond embarrassed, and I'm sure you are too. But I want you to know I haven't seen him since we began our.... arrangement. No way would I disrespect you like that."

But he didn't speak. He only opened the bathroom door, checked to make sure no one was there, and then pulled me into the large corner stall.

"Jonas, what are you..." I asked, but he silenced me with a kiss.

It was fucking sexy, him taking control like this. And his kiss... it sent heat pooling between my legs. He moved from my lips to my neck, trailing rough kisses along my sensitive skin.

"Jonas," I gasped. "What is this?"

He rose from my collarbone, looking me straight in

the eyes. "I hated the thought of that fucker being the last person to touch you."

"He did more than kiss me," I breathed. I knew I was playing with fire. But Jonas was hot, and damn was I horny.

He continued kissing down my neck, into my cleavage, and worked his hand into my pants. He rubbed a slow circle around my clit that made me moan.

His fingers slid along my slit, and then he plunged one in, two.

The door to the bathroom opened, and someone walked in, but he didn't stop. He covered my mouth with his free hand. My eyes rolled back in my head. God, had I wanted this.

He rubbed the heel of his hand against my clit, and my pussy tightened around his fingers.

But instead of pushing me over the edge, he drew his fingers out and slowly put them in his mouth, licking me off of him.

I closed my eyes, shuddering from my want. From my *need*.

The toilet next to us flushed, breaking the spell, but only for a bit. We were silent until the door shut behind whoever she was, and Jonas said, "Dessert first, right?"

I couldn't help the smile that came to my lips.

He opened the stall, put his hand on my lower back, and said, "Let's go eat."

We walked back to our table and sat down again. When Hayden came back, I knew my face was flushed from what had happened. He didn't make eye contact with us at all as we ordered our drinks.

But throughout the whole meal, I couldn't help thinking about the *dessert* that would come after.

23

JONAS

What the fuck had come over me?

I'd gone fucking feral, hearing that guy talk about Mara and realizing he was the last one to touch her in all the ways I wanted to. I spent the rest of dinner thinking about how fucking good she tasted on my fingers and how I should apologize to her for practically assaulting her in the bathroom.

Unfortunately, by the time we got to my house, I still hadn't come up with any apology ideas. We hardly spoke on the ride home, and once we got inside, Mara said, "So, about earlier..."

"I'm so sorry," I began. "I should have asked your permission, and I didn't." I met her beautiful brown eyes, hoping she could see how apologetic I was.

But instead of saying something like it's okay or punching me in my junk like I deserved, she said, "Don't apologize. I wanted you to."

"You... wanted me to?"

She nodded, biting her bottom lip, and then there was no more holding myself back.

I pulled her jacket the rest of the way off and kissed her, hard. I didn't want this to be over fast, but damn I was already hard for her.

We walked, stumbled, fell into my bed. She looked perfect there, her dark locks splayed around her on the white comforter. Before I could tell her how hot she was, she was pulling me down, kissing me with her soft lips and reaching for my dick with her fingertips.

She undid my pants and then reached into my underwear, taking my cock in her hand. She knew what she was doing, that much was clear.

I slid my hand under her shirt, feeling underneath her bra. I ran the pad of my thumb over her hardened nipple, desperate for her to take her shirt off. To see her in all her glory.

So I did just that, began pulling up on her shirt. She took her hand out of my pants, lifting herself up to help me. As soon as her shirt was off, she unclipped her bra. My imagination hadn't even come close to the perfect tits splayed before me. They were full, round, heavy, and so fucking sexy.

I pushed her back down, parting her legs with my knee and taking one hard nipple in my mouth, teasing it with my tongue.

Her back arched underneath my weight, and I moaned against her breast before moving to the next one.

"Fuck, Jonas," she said. "You have no idea how long I've been imagining this."

I pulled back, looking into her hazy eyes. "You have?"

"That first night I took a shower...." She reached for

my cock again, stroking it. "I got myself off thinking about you fucking me against the shower wall."

Her words sent a fresh rush of desire straight to my dick in her capable hands. "You weren't the only one."

"What?"

"I didn't want to set up that fucking bed. I needed to go somewhere else and beat myself off so I wouldn't have a fucking wet dream with you in bed."

The full sound of her laughter was music to my ears. "Maybe we shouldn't have waited this long then." She pushed me back, trading positions with me so I was lying down and she was on top.

Taking her time, she pulled my pants and underwear down, and when they were off, I quickly took off my shirt. When I fucked her, I wanted to feel every inch of her soft skin against mine.

But Mara had other things in mind. She looked at my cock like it was the most amazing thing she'd ever seen and said, "I'm going to finish what I started the other night."

I closed my eyes, thinking about how hard it had been to walk away from her that night. How I'd fucked myself raw and still ached for her mouth. Her pussy.

She kissed my tip, then slowly slid her plush lips down my shaft.

I opened my eyes and watched her slow descent, the cascade of her wavy brown hair around her face. Felt her tits press into my thighs. Fuck, I was in trouble. There was no way I'd hang on long enough if she kept at this.

But I allowed myself the indulgence, moaning as she cupped my balls, as her tongue swirled around my shaft, as she took me deeper and deeper until my tip hit the back of her throat and she moaned, making the sexiest fucking sound.

If she ever thought she was fucking anyone else like this ever again, she was so fucking wrong. Mara was *mine*, and I was going to prove it to her.

I pulled her up to kiss her, hard, then rolled her over, dropping kisses down her neck, her collarbone, between her perfect tits, and down to her carefully trimmed mound. I slid my tongue down the landing strip and along her lips.

She shuddered underneath me, practically writhing to get relief.

I plunged a finger inside her, then two, feeling the wetness that had enthralled me in the restaurant bathroom. The tightness that made me want to break her open until she screamed my name.

Then I added my mouth.

Her fingers gripped my hair, tugging in the sexiest way, and then I pressed my tongue against her clit. She groaned, her pussy tightening around my fingers. I rolled my tongue against her, feeling with each clench, each shift of her hips, that we were both getting closer to exactly what we wanted.

"Fuck, Jonas, fuck."

I loved the way she said my name, loved the way she moved against my mouth, loved the confident way she let loose in the bedroom.

Loved her scream as she came.

"*Fuck,*" she panted as I slid my fingers out of her. "Now it's your turn."

I wiped my face against the blanket before moving up

to kiss her again. She bit my lip, growing more and more forceful with each moment.

"Roll over," she ordered, and who was I to deny her everything she wanted?

I rolled on my back, my dick hard and throbbing, desperate for more of her.

I reached for my bedside table, but she put her mouth on my dick, stopping me in my tracks. "I'm good," she breathed, kissing up my shaft. "I have an IUD, and my tests are clear."

The second she said she was okay with it, I couldn't get the thought of her pussy against my raw dick out of my head.

But instead of getting on, riding me with her tits over my mouth, she turned around and—fuck, I wasn't ready for the sight of her full ass, her hips, as she lowered herself and sheathed her tight pussy over my cock.

She started slow, letting us both savor the feeling of our bodies coming together for the very first time.

Her hair cascaded down her back in messy waves, and I wrapped my fist around it, pulling her head back.

She moaned and her back arched and she sped her pace. I moved my hands from her hair to her hips, helping her move faster and faster over my cock.

"Touch yourself," I said, and she did as I asked. One hand went to her hair, raising it off her back and drawing my eyes to her curves. Her folds. The stretch marks along her sides. Everything about her was sexy.

Her moans grew louder, and her pussy tightened around my cock.

"Come with me," she said. "Come with me!"

It was the easiest command of my life to follow.

I lifted my hips, pumping into her as she screamed and clenched around my cock, milking me for everything I had.

Mara was mine.

And I was hers.

24

MARA

Confession: I had good sex with an accountant.

THE AFTERSHOCKS of my orgasm were still shaking my body as I lifted myself off Jonas and rolled to the bed beside him. He handed me his white undershirt and said, "If you want to clean up."

The gesture was so matter of fact yet thoughtful I almost melted. Or maybe that was all the dopamine running through my body at the hot-as-fire sex I just had with the accountant. I took the shirt and wiped myself off, then he took it back and flung it toward the hamper in front of his closet. He missed completely, and it landed on the floor.

I giggled.

"What?" he asked.

"I think this might be the first time your room has been messy."

He rolled to his side and propped his head in his

hand. My eyes drifted to his arm muscles. I'd been so fascinated with them, but never able to touch, until now. I ran my fingertips over the ridges of his skin curved and shaped by the muscles underneath and then back to his eyes.

They were dancing with his smile. "That was amazing."

I couldn't help but agree. "Who would have thought you'd be so good in bed." I grinned evilly. "Maybe it was beginner's luck?"

He rolled his eyes at me. "I'll take you in the shower right now and prove it wasn't."

I raised my eyebrows and pretended to think it over. "I do need to clean up..."

He grabbed my hand and pulled me toward the bathroom, and I followed him, laughing as I went.

He pressed me against the glass shower wall, silencing my laugh with his kiss. It was playful, sexy, and I loved that I could feel him smiling through it all. Jonas deserved to be happy.

We both did.

He flipped the head and water cascaded to the floor, sending droplets bouncing back up over our feet. As soon as the water warmed, he led me in, letting me stand underneath the stream while he reached for his loofa and soap.

I dipped my head back under the stream, letting the water wash through my hair, not worried about what it had done to my makeup. I watched Jonas's eyes trail the beads of water down my breasts, over my stomach, and down my thighs to the floor. It was hot, the way he watched me without reserve.

I'd been with guys before who tried to look away from my body. They wanted me to fuck them but acted like they could ignore the extra weight I carried. Jonas didn't even try. He took me in, every single inch of me, and worshipped me with his eyes.

I drew my fingers from my hairline, down my neck to the space between my breasts, and his lips parted.

"You have such a beautiful body," he almost whispered.

I took in his form, the ridges of his stomach muscles, not quite a six-pack but clearly strong and firm. And then his dick. Even soft, it was big, tempting. "I could say the same for you."

He gave me a heated smirk. "Turn around. Let me wash you off."

"It's just an excuse to look at my ass," I retorted.

"So what if it is?" He put the soap back in place and began running the loofa in slow circles around my shoulders, my neck, my upper back and slowly my lower back. He took his time, in no rush to cover the extra surface area.

He followed the loofa with his hands, sliding easily over my soapy skin. And then he reached my ass. He lowered to his knees and pressed his hand over my back, urging me to lean forward. The shower stream hit my mid back, dousing both of us as he pressed his nose to my sex.

He ran his fingertips over my hip, along the split of my ass, and then along my slit, front to back. Then he slipped two fingers inside me, stretching my tender pussy.

"Fuck, Jonas," I breathed.

He slid his fingers in and out, saying, "Tell me what

you were imagining that night, in the shower, while you were touching yourself."

I braced one hand against the wall, tugging at my nipples with the other hand. "I was thinking about you," I gasped.

He moved his fingers from my pussy and used the slickness of our cum to tease my clit in slow circles that made my breath come fast. "What about me?"

"I wanted to get out of the shower, soaking wet, and lie in your bed until you found me."

"Fuck," he moaned. He stood up, pressing his body against me; his cock was hard against my ass. With one hand, he cupped my breast, and the other reached around my hip, resuming those slow, tantalizing circles. "What next?"

"I imagined you finding me, tangling your fingers in my wet hair and fucking me senseless," I breathed.

"I would have," he said, his voice rough against my ear. "Just fucking thinking about you in that shower made me so damn hot."

He licked his fingertip, then sped his circles around my clit, pushing me closer to the edge. His other hand roamed my body, my breasts, my stomach, my hips, while his mouth kissed and nibbled at my neck, my shoulders.

"I was thinking about you taking a shower, standing in the same place I came," I said, rolling my head back to rest on his shoulder. Just as I imagined, he tangled his fingers through my wet hair, pulling me back tighter against him.

"I was so fucking pissed when I saw their names on your phone the next morning." He bit my earlobe and said, "I'm going to make you come again, and again, and again, and you're going to forget all about them."

He was right. I couldn't think about anyone else as he pushed me closer and closer to the edge. I came and came and came, and Jonas was the only person on my mind.

25

JONAS

When we got out of the shower, I went to the linen shelves and said, "Come here."

Mara stood in front of me, comfortable in her nakedness, beautiful in her shining wetness. I picked up a towel and ran it over her arms, her legs. Took her hair and pressed the towel around it, soaking all the water. And when I was done, I handed her a new one so it would be perfectly dry and warm.

She took it, pressing the water away from her flushed cheeks. She looked beautiful. And part of me still couldn't believe what we'd just done. That I'd been the one to do it with her.

I got a towel for myself and dried off before walking to the bedroom with her and slipping on some sweatpants.

"You know what sounds amazing?" she said.

I finished pulling up my pants and turned toward her. "What's that?"

"Ice cream," she finished. "And a soapy romance movie. It's my favorite way to end the day."

"Soapy?" I asked, not familiar with the term.

"You know, like soap opera-esque."

"Let's do it," I said with a chuckle. I couldn't think of anything I'd rather be doing than hanging out with Mara doing whatever she wanted to do. Usually in the evenings, I just watched TV since I went to the gym in the mornings. During tax season especially, I didn't have time for much else. "You pick a show and I'll dish us up some bowls?"

"Sounds great." She lifted a pillow off my bed and held it up. "For your uncomfy couch."

I rolled my eyes and let her walk first down the hallway. She was wearing just a long T-shirt and underwear, and damn, did I like the way her hips swayed, the way her shirt showed just the faintest hint of the underside of her ass.

She settled herself on my couch, lying back on the pillow, and grabbed the remote off the coffee table. I gave a last look at her, memorizing what she looked like so comfortable in my home, before going to the kitchen.

I got two bowls out of the cupboard instead of one. Two spoons from the drawer instead of one. After getting the tub of ice cream out, I scooped twice as much. It felt like breathing a sigh of relief, doing this for two people. It felt... right.

I got the chocolate syrup from the fridge, drizzled it over the ice cream, and grabbed a couple lunch-size bags of chips before joining Mara in the living room. She had the opening credits playing to some sappy teen movie Tess made me watch when we were kids.

But I wasn't complaining this time. No, this time, I got to see the smile on Mara's face as I handed her a bowl of ice cream. This time, I got to sit by her feet and lift them into my lap. This time, I got to watch the delight in her eyes as I passed her the bag of potato chips because something sweet always needs something salty.

"This is good ice cream," she said. "I approve."

I laughed, digging a spoonful from my own bowl. "That's good. I'll keep buying it then."

"Good."

We sat quietly, watching the movie. I was about to comment on something lame one of the teachers said, but when I glanced over at Mara, her eyes were closed. Her breathing had slowed, and her hand was still halfway in the small bag of chips.

I stifled my laughter at how adorable she was. She must have fallen asleep mid-bite.

Now, this is the part where most guys would have grabbed the remote and turned off the TV before going to bed, but damn, I was actually into the movie, and I loved being this close to Mara.

Gently, I lifted her hand from the bag and put the bag on the coffee table, then I watched the last thirty minutes of the movie. And no, I didn't fucking cry at the end. Not even a little bit. Nope.

I slid out from under her legs, turned off the TV, and went to my linen closet in search of a blanket. I pulled out one my grandma had given me as a child and brought it back out to the living room. Mara hadn't moved an inch.

I spread the blanket over her and watched her sleep. Just for a little bit. (It wasn't creepy if she was in my own house, right?)

She really was beautiful with her black lashes fanned over her cheeks, her pink lips slightly parted. She didn't have the same guard she put up when she was awake, and damn, it was stunning.

I brushed a stray lock of her hair back behind her ear, and she tilted her head slightly, leaning into my hand.

Something in my heart broke loose. I really liked this girl. And I hoped to hell she could be vulnerable enough to like me too.

26

MARA

Confession: I felt butterflies.

THE NEXT MORNING, I woke up on Jonas's couch, covered in a handmade quilt with diffused light streaming through his living room curtains. My back and neck hurt like hell, probably from the couch, but possibly from all we'd gotten up to the night before.

I still couldn't believe that Jonas and I had sex. Good sex. Like really fucking good sex.

Just thinking about it made me want more.

I sat up and twisted my back, stretched my neck, feeling a few cracks. Out of the corner of my eye, I saw a folded piece of paper on the coffee table. But before I could open it, the doorbell rang.

I walked to the door and stood slightly to the side before answering, since my pajamas didn't cover much. "Hello?"

A guy held up a bag full of takeout boxes. "I have a delivery for Mara Taylor?"

"I didn't order that," I said.

"It's already paid for, by a..." He glanced at the receipt stuck to the bag with a sticker. "Mr. Jonas Moore."

Already smiling, I reached for the bag and said, "Thank you."

After closing the door behind him, I went back to the coffee table and set the bag down, then reached for the note.

Mara, I thought about bringing you to bed, but you looked so peaceful. I hope breakfast makes up for the couch. Jonas

I did something I'd never done—I held his note to my chest and smiled like a dopey teenager. I hadn't even been a dopey teenager when I was in my teens. But this guy...

Maybe it was all his talk about happily ever after that was brainwashing me. Or maybe it was just my love of breakfast food. Either way, I needed to figure out something, and fast, or I'd be heading for heartbreak.

I ran and grabbed my phone from my room and texted Birdie and Hen.

Mara: PLEASE TELL ME YOU CAN EAT LUNCH WITH ME TODAY. I'M FREAKING OUT.

Hen: You know I'm there. Where should we go?

Birdie: I can't leave my office today... but you can come to me? I have a free slot at 1.

Mara: Only if you let me raid the condom jar. ;)

Birdie: You're the worst.

Hen: Want me to grab something on my way? I can pick up something from Seaton Bakery or Waldo's? What are we feeling today?

Mara: This requires sugar and plenty of it.

Hen: Cupcakes it is. <3

Birdie: See you at one.

I sat down at the coffee table and opened the meal. It was full of the things he had made me that first night that I stayed over at his house. There were pancakes and syrup and fresh scrambled eggs and bacon. But the best thing of all was that he had sent it right to me, thought of me, for even a little while.

I picked up my phone again and called his number. He answered within a few rings and said, "Good morning, beautiful."

It brought a smile to my lips. Most guys didn't say "good morning, beautiful." They said, "Want to go again?"

"Good morning," I replied, trying to catch my bearings. "And thank you for the breakfast. That was very sweet of you."

"Of course," he said like there was no other way. "I didn't want to wake you up by banging pans around, so I figured this would be better. Did the doorbell wake you?"

"No, I was already awake when it rang."

"Perfect. So hey, don't make any plans for after work tonight."

"Why is that?" I asked.

"You'll see," he replied. "I'll talk to you later."

I shook my head, smiling to myself. "I'll talk to you later."

Between waking up for breakfast and going to lunch with my friends, I tried to get in as much writing as possible. If I focused for half an hour at a time and pushed myself, I could get some words in and make good progress. I also checked social media, and it seemed like almost every comment about me or my beliefs (or lack thereof) about marriage were gone. I was old news, just the way I liked it.

Around half past noon, I got in my car, Trouble, and drove to the fancy-pants school where Birdie worked. I felt so out of place when I stepped onto the campus full of the children of rich people who thought to get anywhere in life you needed to have an amazing education and an even better wardrobe.

When I was growing up, I went to a really crappy public school with more students than lockers. And I hadn't even lasted there. But that probably had more to do with my family than the school.

I took a deep breath and reminded myself that I've come a long way, not envying these people for all that they had and focusing more on working for what I wanted in life. Then I continued walking toward the big brick building, looking around for Henrietta's car, but I didn't see it.

So instead, I walked up the stairs and through the entry with *Ad Meliora* engraved in the stone archway. I pushed through the heavy double doors and turned right at the principal's office. A woman up front named Marjorie gave me a skeptical look. She probably didn't like the fact that I was wearing leggings at all, much less in this building.

"May I help you?" she said.

"Yes, I have a meeting with Birdie Bardot."

She winced. "Do you know where her office is?"

"I can get there," I replied. I took the visitor name tag, applied it above my chest, and walked down the tiled hallway, looking around. I wondered what it would have been like to be a real kid in this high school, enjoying myself and worrying more about how I looked in my uniform than how I was going to be treated at home.

The truth was, I was never really a kid, even when I was living with my parents. I had too much responsibility and not enough time to be who I really wanted to be. I was lucky to be able to make up for lost time now, as an adult with no supervision and plenty of resources.

I stopped in front of Birdie's door with her new name tag that said Birdie Bardot and smiled. This was just one of the signs of her happily ever after.

As I reached my hand up to knock, I had to wonder why I had spent so long thinking that a lifetime love was out of reach for me. Why had I spent so long shoving everyone away when clearly there were guys like Jonas and Cohen out there who wanted more than just sex?

God, those were exactly the kind of thoughts I needed help with.

I knocked on her door, and Birdie sang, "Come in."

I turned the handle and walked inside, looking between her and her white bird, Ralphie. "Hi there," I said to both of them, then I went to his cage and wiggled my finger at him.

He gently touched his beak to my finger, and I smiled. "How are you doing?"

"Good," Birdie said, coming to stand beside me. "A little nervous because this will be my first year helping Ollie plan his birthday party, but I want to know about *you*. What's going on? Why are you freaking out?"

I closed my eyes and shook my head. "It's probably better if we wait until Hen gets here."

"I'm here," Hen's voice came from the hallway. She walked into Birdie's office carrying multiple bags stamped with the Seaton Bakery logo.

"Girl, you delivered," I said.

She grinned. "A freak-out from Miss Calm And Collected called for it."

I laughed, helping her with the bags while Birdie cleared a space on her extra table for us to eat.

I could only imagine how many uncomfortable conversations had been had around this table. Mine would not be the first or the last.

We spread out sandwiches from the bakery, along with lemonade and, of course, their famous cupcakes. Skipping the sandwich altogether, I went for my cupcake, licking some of the frosting. The sugar instantly soothed me.

"What's going on?" Henrietta asked.

I looked down at my cupcake, wishing I could just eat it instead of talking at all. Instead of facing what I'd done the night before. But I gazed up and looked them in the eyes. "I had sex with Jonas."

I was *expecting* them to freak out like I was internally, but Birdie clapped her hands together and said, "Yay!"

I laughed. "Yay? That's it?" I turned to Henrietta, looking for the more appropriate response, but she was smiling big.

"You guys had some serious chemistry going the other night at the club," Hen said.

"I love science," Birdie said with a wink.

Did they not understand the depravity of the situation? "Guys, he's supposed to be my *fake* boyfriend, and I'm having sex with him! And let me tell you, that orgasm was *definitely* not fake."

Hen pressed her lips together. "Well I don't think sex is the issue. I think feelings are."

Birdie stared between the two of us. "It's not fake anymore, is it?"

I looked down at my hands.

"Oh my god!" Henrietta cried. "It's not fake anymore!"

I blinked quickly, trying to understand what was even going on in my own mind. "I don't know how he feels."

"But..." Birdie said.

"But this is the first time that I've actually felt butter-flies." I covered my face because I felt so lame even as I said it. I wasn't supposed to be that girl who got swept away by emotions and frivolous things like *butterflies*. But Birdie was practically doing a happy dance in her chair.

Hen held up her cupcake. "This is celebratory sugar!"

I shook my head. "This is *bad*."

Birdie and Henrietta exchanged a glance. Birdie asked, "How could this possibly be bad? Jonas is nice, and you deserve to be treated nicely. I never liked how Hayden just called you over when he wanted your body and that was it."

"I didn't mind Hayden calling me over," I said. "What I mind is the fact that my heart's involved with someone who only wants me around to help his mom with dialysis."

Henrietta gave me a look this time. "Do you really think that's the only reason he wants you around?"

My cheeks warmed. "Well, judging by what we did last night..."

Both the girls cheered in delight. I could only imagine what Marjorie would think of the conversation being had in this office.

I shook my head, still in disbelief. "It was crazy! We were out at La Belle to eat, and I thought it was just because he wanted to grab something after work or maybe talk about, like, cleaning his house in exchange for me staying or when he wanted me to leave or something. And then *Hayden was our waiter.*"

"What?" Birdie cried.

"I know!" I said. "He was totally inappropriate, and you know what Jonas did? *He brought me back to the bathroom and said he didn't want Hayden to be the last person who touched me.*"

Henrietta fanned herself. "Who knew he had that in him."

"I didn't," I said, "but I did not mind one bit."

Birdie furrowed her eyebrows. "I still don't understand what's wrong."

"What's wrong," I said, "is that I'm becoming one of *those* girls."

"One of what girls?" Henrietta asked.

"One of those girls who meets a guy and completely loses herself. I've spent my entire life—thirty *years*—believing that love wasn't real, watching dysfunctional relationships, thinking that marriages only lasted because two people settled or won some cosmic lottery, and now I'm here thinking about a guy, *talking* about a guy, wondering if he'll break my heart, wondering if it's for real." I shook my head at myself. "I've never been this girl."

Henrietta said, "People change, Mara. We're not all the same from the day we're born to the day we die."

"No," I agreed, "but I've been the same on this for a long time. One guy's going to change that?"

They were both quiet for a moment, then Birdie reached across the table, putting her hand on top of mine. "You love me, right?"

I nodded.

"You're going to be my friend forever, no matter how many stupid things I do?"

"Of course." There wasn't a doubt in my mind.

"So you do believe that lasting love and partnerships exist," she said. "Maybe... Maybe you were just protecting yourself from falling in love with a man like your father, and Jonas is showing you that you don't have to work so hard to keep yourself safe."

I thought about her words for a minute. My therapist always said, "Every behavior meets a need." And maybe my behavior, my beliefs, weren't about a need for fun but a need for caution. And here Jonas was tearing down all my walls, not with sledgehammers, but with pancakes and kind words.

"What if it's not real for him?" I asked, my chest feeling tight. Just the thought of believing something else, risking my heart for him... it was fucking terrifying.

Henrietta smiled gently. "Then at least you know," she said. "At least you know that your heart is brave enough to ask for what you really want."

Birdie nodded. "And after everything you've been

through, I *know* you'll be strong enough to recover from this, too."

I looked down at my sandwich and my barely touched cupcake. What I really wanted was to enjoy my time with Jonas without all this extra pressure of the movie deal or dialysis or even a relationship. I liked spending time with him. So maybe I should start there.

27

JONAS

I worked through lunch so I could get everything I had to do finished by six. As we neared the end of January, I could feel the pressure building within the office. These would be the last couple weekends we all had off. Not to mention the last couple weeks we wouldn't be working until seven to nine every night.

I walked by Karen's shared office with a couple of the other bookkeepers and noticed all the lights were off. They may have made less money, but their hours were definitely better than the CPAs and other tax preparers.

"Jonas," Mr. Rusk called from inside his office. It was the only one in the building with the light still on. I usually tried not to leave before him—a tip from an old mentor in college—but tonight I had plans with Mara. I didn't want to keep her waiting.

"Yes, sir," I said, stepping into the doorway of his office.

He waved his weathered hand at me and said, "Sit,

sit." He set his reading glasses on his desk and rolled his chair backward. "Want a beer?"

Another rule of thumb? Never say no to a beer from a boss. "Sounds great," I replied.

He reached into the fridge, grabbed a can from a local brewery he liked, and tossed it my way. I caught it, tapped on the lid (did that actually work?) and took a drink of the crisp liquid. Why did beer taste so much better at the end of a long day?

He took a drink from his own can and set it on his desk. "Tax season coming up."

I nodded.

"How do you feel about a little extra responsibility?"

"I'm up for a challenge," I answered, despite the feeling like there was a fish hook in my navel, pulling me toward Mara, away from the office.

"You know the promotion is between you and Jenkins. I want to see how you both perform under pressure. And not just regular tax season pressure, but the kind that comes from employees and clients."

I nodded slowly. Usually, the tax preparers brought their returns to my office for me to look over and sign, since I was a CPA. That alone was a lot of work, but I could take on more for the sake of a promotion that meant I could retire my dad completely. Fully fund a college savings account for my children before they were even born. "Want me to pick up some extra reviews?"

He shook his head. "I want you to manage it front to back. This week, we're transitioning a quarter of the employees from my management to yours, and then another quarter to Jenkins. That means you'll take on far more oversight instead of getting elbows deep in the work. I want to see how you treat our clients and how you keep your employees on top of it."

I nodded, a smile growing on my face. I'd managed bookkeepers before and helped with client acquisition, but I'd never been charged with a team of accountants. Mr. Rusk had been the main person in charge of project management since I started working here, so it would be different, but if he wanted to really retire, this would be the natural next step. "What are you going to do with all your free time?" I asked, taking another swig.

He chuckled. "Watching you and Jenkins like a hawk."

I laughed, but it was more for politeness than actual humor. I needed to step up my game this season and rise to the challenge if I didn't want to get stuck in mid-level management for the rest of my life.

"Where are you off to?" Mr. Rusk asked.

I finished off the rest of my beer. "I have a date."

He winked. "Have fun."

I already knew I would. Waving goodbye, I threw my beer can away and left the office. I sprayed cologne on myself in the car before driving back home to see my girl. Hopefully, she would be excited by the plans that I had. Especially after what we'd done the night before.

I parked in the driveway, leaving my car running. When I reached the door, she was already waiting for me, her patchwork purse over her shoulder.

"Where are we going?" she asked.

"Hi," I said with a teasing smile. "It's good to see you too." I wasn't sure where we were at, but I wanted to kiss her. I couldn't believe how nervous I was after everything we'd done the night before, but I leaned across the space and pressed my lips to hers, my heart pounding. She returned my kiss, making me think maybe we should go straight back to the bedroom. But, first things first.

"You look beautiful, by the way," I added.

She glanced down at herself in her leggings and her oversized shirt and said a surprised, "Thank you." She must have thought I was silly for complimenting her on comfortable clothes, but I liked her like this. She wasn't trying to put on a show for anyone. She was just being herself, and that's what I liked most of all.

"Let's go," I said. As I followed her out the door, I put my hand on her lower back, loving the chance to touch her whenever I could. After locking the door behind us, I walked around to the passenger side of my car to let her in.

She waited for me, and I liked that she was used to me treating her the way she deserved.

I got in my side of the car, then pulled out of the driveway and began driving while she continued her onslaught of questions. "Are we going to do another wedding thing for Tess?" she asked. "Maybe dance lessons? There's always a part in a book or movie where someone can't attend a dance lesson and then someone fills in and they, *of course*, fall in love."

I shook my head. "Like *The Wedding Planner*?"

She gave me an impressed look. "Your sister has taught you well."

I laughed. "Mom would be upset if she didn't get some credit."

"I try to give credit where credit is due," she said with a laugh. "So if it's not a wedding thing, are you taking me to help you pick out clothes?"

I looked down at my dress shirt and slacks. "Is there something wrong with my clothes?"

"No, not at all," she said with a calculating gaze. "In fact, your tailor does great work."

"Who says I have a tailor?" I asked.

Her sultry smile sent blood to all the right places. "Because your clothes fit you way too well not to be made just for you."

My chest puffed up a bit too much at the compliment, but she was looking out the window again, deep in thought.

"So if it's not clothes, and it's not a wedding thing, then you must be taking me to run an errand for your mom."

I snorted. "You're seeing her tomorrow morning. If she needed something from the store, I'd have Dad pick it up after work or you could grab it on the way there."

"Well." She dropped her hands on her lap. "I really have no idea then. What do you even do in your free time besides do taxes?"

I gave an exasperated sigh, having had the same conversation with Tess a million times. "Accountants don't just do taxes."

"Oh, you're right," she said. "What do you do besides taxes *and bookkeeping?*"

I rolled my eyes. "I'll have you know that I do plenty of things, both during and after work."

She gave me a skeptical look.

"I go to the gym, spend time with my family. I play poker with the guys. I grab beers at Cohen's bar from time to time. Plus, Dad always has a project or two that he needs help with. And in the spring, Mom has a garden, so there's plenty of work to do there."

She nodded thoughtfully. "I don't picture myself helping you with any of that except for maybe the beer thing. I could definitely go for a cocktail."

I added that to my mental checklist to grab some drink mixes and maybe ask Cohen for a few tips on how to make a good mojito since that was clearly Mara's drink of choice.

She still hadn't guessed what we were doing when I pulled in front of the furniture store, and she looked from the sign to me, her eyes lighting up with pure glee. "We're getting rid of your couch?!"

"We're getting rid of my couch," I confirmed. "And since I'm clearly terrible at picking out furniture, I thought you could help test them out with me."

She clapped her hands together excitedly. "You have *no idea* the amount of comfort you're going to feel, you know, after the discomfort of the money leaving your checking account."

I shook my head. "It will be the greatest purchase of my life to have you sleeping on a cozy couch when you don't make it to bed."

An expression I didn't quite understand flicked over her face before it was gone and she was smiling at me again. "Let's go inside," she said. "I can't wait to see what they have."

We got out of the car and walked through the glass doors of the furniture store. The showroom was completely massive with tall ceilings and chandeliers and way too many couches. Most of them that looked just the same to me.

A sales associate came over and asked us if we needed help, and Mara said, "I think we're good for now."

As she walked down the aisle, I didn't doubt her one bit. She looked like a little kid in a candy store having so many options and not knowing which to pick. She was so adorable.

I reached for her fingers and held her hand, half expecting her to stop me. Instead, she squeezed back, rewarding me with another one of those smiles.

I smiled back before looking around the store again. In the distance, I could hear a child wailing and the dull chatter of shoppers, but mostly I just focused on Mara.

"So, what are we looking for?" I asked. "I know you said something comfy, but does that mean we have to sit on every chair in here?"

"Well," she said, "since you clearly like leather, I thought maybe we could start in that section. And just stay away from that mid-century modern nonsense. There's never enough cushion on that stuff. What people in the seventies had against lumbar support, I'll never understand."

I shook my head, chuckling quietly at her hatred for that style. "Whatever you say."

We reached a part of the store with a sign that said LEATHER overhead. There was a pretty decent selection in almost every color from light gray to white, rich mahogany brown, and the deepest of espressos.

"I'm staying away from the ones with square arms," Mara explained. "Rounded arms are much more comfortable to sleep on."

"So there's a whole strategy to this," I said.

She nodded emphatically. "It can't be too shallow

either. There has to be plenty of room to spread out." Her eyes lit up, and she ran to a wide sitting chair. "Oh my gosh, I love this!"

I stared at it for a moment. "This isn't even a sofa. If you wanted to sleep on it, your legs would be dangling off the end."

"No," she said, letting go of my hand to sit in the chair. "This would be the *perfect* reading chair. Can you imagine?" She tucked her legs underneath her and sat comfortably. "You could have a little fluffy pillow here to go under your arm, drape a throw blanket over yourself, and have a completely cozy day reading. It would be the best way to spend a rainy day."

I smiled at the picture she painted in my head. I wanted nothing more than to see her do that in my home. "Let's get it," I said.

She stared at me, eyes wide. "That's it? That's all I had to do to sell you? Maybe I should go into furniture sales."

I laughed. "You have no idea how convincing you can be, Mara Taylor."

She's smiled at me and then looked at the couch next to the armchair. "If you're going to buy the set, you should at least sit in it."

"But I want to try it with you." I reached for her hand and pulled her with me onto the couch. She settled into my lap, and the weight of her on top of me was the most comfortable thing I'd ever felt. Screw what was underneath me. All I needed was her to feel right at home.

"I like it," I said.

She smiled down at me. "Really?"

"Absolutely." I reached up, gently pulling her toward

me for a kiss. Her lips moved against mine, and I quickly forgot where we were, who could be seeing us.

Too soon, Mara pulled away. "So you like this one?"

I nodded. "It's the perfect mix of cozy and clean, and I can see it lasting a long time even if I decided to get a dog someday." Or children, I didn't say. One thing that I'd learned in all my years of dating was that children were not something you brought up right after a first date. Not that Mara and I even had an official first date. Accosting her in La Belle didn't exactly count. But that was fine because I wanted to have so many more dates with Mara, sneak away to so many more bathrooms.

A saleswoman in a red shirt approached us. "Is this the one?" she asked.

I glanced up at Mara, looking so beautiful with that smile on her lips. "It is."

28

MARA

Confession: I've never made love.

JONAS ASKED when the couch could be delivered. When the saleswoman said it could be a few weeks until the delivery guy had time to do it, he slipped her a fifty, and the couch was delivered that night. Another fifty had the old couch carried out to his garage until he could find some sucker to sell it to.

As soon as the delivery guy was out of Jonas's house, I fell back on the couch, sinking into the comfortable cushions. "This is amazing! I never would have thought of bribing the delivery guy like that."

"I like to call it *motivation*," he said, coming toward me from the front door. And damn, did he look hot walking toward me with the top few buttons of his white shirt undone and his sleeves rolled just below his elbows. "Plus, I don't know how long you'll be here, and I wanted you to enjoy it."

My heart lurched. Jonas was worried too about how long this would last. But he'd still done what he could to make me comfortable. Just like he did for his mom. Just like he did for his sister.

I reached for his hand, and he laced his fingers through mine, sitting beside me on the couch. Feeling my heart swell for this man who'd so easily taken me in, who'd instinctively fought to keep me safe, I snuggled closer to him until our noses were touching, and then our lips.

Jonas drew his fingertips through my hair, tucked it behind my ear. Held the back of my neck so tenderly I thought my heart would burst. I held the open seam of his shirt in my fist, hanging on to this moment, this feeling, with everything I had.

He teased the edges of my lips with his tongue, deepening our kiss until I could taste him, feel him. And I let myself feel him. This incredible man.

I ran my fingers over his pecs, his shoulders. Held his face in both of my hands, the beginnings of his evening stubble rough against my palms.

Slowly, he pushed me onto my back, kissing down my jaw, my neck. His hands slid under my shirt, caressing the swell of my stomach, teasing along the bottom of my T-shirt bra. He traveled over my breasts, accessing them from the top, running his thumb over my nipple. Bit it through the fabric.

I gripped the back of his shoulders in pleasure, loving the way he made me feel so sexy, so *adored*.

He pulled at the bottom of my oversized T-shirt until he could see me underneath him. I never felt hot at this angle, with my breasts pulling apart, my chin doubling. I wanted to be on top, in power, but he looked at me like I was as sexy as ever.

I reached up, undoing the buttons of his shirt, wanting to feel the warmth of his skin against mine.

His eyes stayed on me the entire time, patiently waiting for me to finish. When I did, he pulled his shirt off himself and went back to kissing me, not in any kind of rush. He nipped at my lips, kissed my neck, slid his tongue along my cleavage.

I could feel the pressure building between my legs, the growing desire I had for him to be even closer. His length was still restrained in his pants, hard against my midsection as he kissed me.

He reached down, pressing his fingers over my sensitive spot, making my need grow even more.

Desperate to be close to him, I reached for his pants, undoing his belt and then his button and zipper. His cock strained against his underwear, leaving a dark wet spot at the tip.

I reached inside his underwear, pulling it free, and running my thumb over the tip. He moaned against my neck. "Baby, that feels good."

"I want to make you feel good," I breathed.

In response, he reached for the waistband of my leggings, pulling them away until all of me was naked underneath him in the bright living room light. There was no hiding. No covering up with his eyes on me like this.

Fear ripped through my chest. He was so close, seeing more of me than anyone ever had. Not just of my body, but of my soul. I could feel it in the way his brown eyes captured mine.

"Do you want to do it from behind?" I asked, my last attempt to protect myself from the edge I was about to fall over into unknown depths below.

"No," Jonas said.

He pressed into me, and I moaned at the fullness of it, the way he stretched and filled me. He slowly pulled back before thrusting into me again, his eyes on mine the entire time.

I closed my eyes, trying to get lost in it all, but he said, "Open your eyes, baby. I want to see you. All of you."

I opened my eyes, afraid of what I'd see, scared of what Jonas would see in me. But his brown eyes were warm as melted chocolate, his touch as gentle as if he held a precious stone. And there was a smile on his lips, a slight one, as if he saw everything he wanted in me. And I fell, deep, deep down into everything Jonas had to offer without me ever asking at all.

I clenched around him, getting closer and closer to the edge. "Jonas," I breathed. His name a question, an answer, everything in between. "Jonas."

"Mara." He thrust again, coming with me as he said my name.

As he rested atop me, tears streamed from my eyes.

We'd done something I'd never done before. Made *love*.

29

JONAS

While Mara slept on the couch, naked and covered only by my blanket, I sat on the chair and watched her. Empty bowls of ice cream rested on the table, and a soapy teen movie played on the TV. I was coming to find she could never stay awake through an entire film at night. It was adorable.

Her dark brown hair was messy and splayed against the cognac leather. Her lips were deep pink from all the kissing we'd done earlier and parted slightly to accommodate her gentle snores. She was the most beautiful thing I'd ever seen.

Something had changed tonight in her, in us. She'd faced me as we made love. Looked me in the eyes. And when it was over, she cried into my chest.

I didn't say anything, because I knew how she felt. What we'd shared was... powerful. More intense than anything I'd experienced before, with her or anyone else. And fuck was I scared to lose it.

Because I knew deep down I could. She didn't need me

to be her fake boyfriend anymore. Jenny had said the studio would have papers for her to sign, sealing the deal for a second movie. The media wasn't following her around to make sure she didn't sleep with someone else. I knew Mara had a roster of other guys waiting for her. Hell, she could probably get out her phone right now and have someone ready within the hour, but she was here. With me.

My phone began ringing, and I carried it away from the living room as to not wake Mara. I answered the call and said, "Hello?"

"Jonas," Cohen said. "Birdie told me the good news."

"She did?" I grinned because I knew what he had to be talking about. And that meant Mara had talked about me to all her friends. That had to mean something.

"Didn't take you long to follow our advice," he replied. "How does it feel?"

I glanced back down the hallway toward the room where I knew Mara was sleeping. "Like I'm on top of the fucking world."

Cohen chuckled. "I'm happy for you."

"I am too..." but I was still scared as shit. How long would it be before the deal was over and Mara didn't need me anymore? How long until she decided she could do better? That our happily ever after would be a happy for now?

"What's going on?" Cohen asked.

"I don't know how to make it last," I admitted.

"I get it." Cohen let out a sigh. "You know Mara and me... we grew up kind of the same way. Part of me thinks that's why Birdie likes me so much. She married her best friend."

I chuckled because I hadn't realized it before, but he was right. Guys didn't really sit around and talk about their feelings very often, but he'd told me enough for me to know that his mom was a user and his dad wasn't in the picture. It couldn't have been great for him growing up. "So what do I do?" I asked, walking into my room and sitting on the bed. "What did Birdie do?"

"Well, she had tits and a vagina, so she has a leg up on you."

I snorted. "Jackass."

"You ever heard about those frogs in the boiling water?" he said.

"What?" I asked, wondering where the hell this conversation was going.

"So there's this parable, and I don't know what twisted motherfucker figured this out, but if you put a frog in boiling water, it'll jump out. But if you put a frog in warm water and slowly turn it up until it's boiling, it'll sit there and overheat to death."

I leaned forward, resting my elbows on my knees. "What does that mean?"

"For people like Mara and me, feeling good is the boiling water. After a lifetime of feeling like shit, anything different scares the crap out of you."

I scrubbed my hand over my face, pissed all over again at her dad. At the person who made her feel like it wasn't safe to be loved.

"So take it slow," Cohen said. "Don't spook her with the boiling water. Just let her get used to the temperature and hope to hell she doesn't jump out."

"Thanks, man," I said.

"Anytime," he replied. "I'll see you at poker tomorrow night?"

"Absolutely."

We hung up, and I tossed my phone aside on the bed.

The last thing I wanted was to take it slow with Mara, but if time was what she needed to feel safe with me, I'd give that to her. I'd give whatever she wanted to hear her say my name again like she had.

30

MARA

Confession: Despite how much I've fought to see my own self-worth, I still stumble sometimes.

THE NEXT MORNING, I told Mariah all about couch shopping with Jonas while we sat in the sunroom doing her dialysis. (I didn't tell her about the sex part, but the twinkle in her eye made me feel like she knew.)

It was only the second day, but it was already much easier to set up. And sitting, drinking coffee with Mariah was like hanging out with an old friend.

After a while, we were done chatting, and she went back to reading her book while I typed away, adding word by word to my story.

"So I have a question," Mariah said, making me look up from my computer.

"I have an answer," I replied.

She smiled. "Tess has a wedding dress fitting later today, and she wanted to know if you'd come with us?"

My eyes widened slightly. "She wants me to come? Are you sure?" Going to a wedding dress fitting felt like a big deal. The only people at Birdie's fitting had been really close friends and family.

Mariah nodded, and her scarred skin was taut against her smile. "We know it hasn't been long, but you're already like family. And we can see the way you feel about Jonas. It's in your eyes."

I suddenly felt just as vulnerable as I'd been the night before. "Jonas is... not like anyone else I've ever met."

"I'm sure he'd say the same about you," she replied.

I chuckled. "I hope that's a good thing."

"You know it is." She tapped her chin, deep in thought. "He needs someone in his life who will add a spark. Pull him away from that office of his."

The thought of Jonas needing a spark brought a smile to my face. Hadn't I insinuated the same thing when I'd judged him as a boring accountant? And to be fair, he was kind of boring, but not in the dull way I'd expected.

He was *dependable*. *Stable*. Someone I could count on.

"So," Mariah said. "Will you come?"

I took a few seconds to think it over. Going to this fitting wasn't just another appointment. It was a commitment. That I'd be there for the wedding. That I'd be there after. "I'd be honored to."

Mariah told me when the fitting was. She said instead of me going off to work, I could hang out at the house while she went on a walk with Oaklynn and grabbed lunch for us and Cade.

So, when she finished her treatment, that's exactly what we did. Riah left the house with Oaklynn dancing happily on the leash. I sat in Cade's recliner with the footrest up while I typed away on my story.

Jonas had acted nervous to have me at the house, around his parents' walls covered in photos and floor space stacked with books, but I felt more at home here than I had almost anywhere else. I loved that Mariah's fingers had touched the pages on each of the books. Loved that Cade's hard-earned money had gone to filling their home with photos of their life together. It was beautiful in the subtlest of ways.

Within an hour, Mariah was back from her walk. She let Oaklynn off the leash, who quickly ran and made a furry puddle on my legs. Giggling, I shooed Oaklynn off my lap, flipped the footrest down, and helped Mariah carry the bags to the table.

"Flanagans is our favorite deli," she said. "Have you ever eaten there?"

"Not yet," I said.

"You're in for a treat."

The front door opened, and Oaklynn went wild, running toward Cade. He held out his hand like Jonas had done that first time I visited, and when she sat down, Cade rubbed behind her ears. He smiled at me and said, "Looks like we have an extra treat for lunch."

Mariah grinned. "I practically begged her to stay. She's going to Tess's dress fitting with us!"

I nodded with a smile. "I still can't believe you want me there."

"Nonsense," Cade said. "You're a ball to have around. Frankly, I'd love for you to come to the car shop sometime and keep me company."

"I wouldn't be much help, but I can definitely bullshit with the best of them," I said with a laugh.

"Just the ticket," he replied, then sat at the table.

The three of us ate together, talking about the food, work, and nothing in particular. It was the most at home I'd felt in ages. And I couldn't help but feel grateful that my big mouth and Jonas's saving graces had brought all this to me.

After lunch, Cade went to work and Mariah and I got into the car, driving to a bridal shop in Brentwood. Tess was already waiting outside, along with Derek's sister, Lottie, and a girl named Tracey she introduced as her best friend.

"I'm so happy you're here," Tess said as we walked inside. "I know it's a little too late to ask you to be one of my bridesmaids, but I still want you to feel like a part of the family!"

I barely managed a smile before she told the saleswoman who she was, and they began walking us toward the back of the store. My brain was still fumbling over her words and what they meant.

A bridesmaid?

A part of the family?

Every part of my brain was screaming *run!* And trust me, you don't get to be my size by having that thought often.

I barely knew what to make of Jonas and me, but his family had already planned for me. Counted me in to events happening months in the future.

I'd never stayed with anyone long enough to make plans like that.

Hell, I'd never even fucked someone long enough to

keep a drawer at their place for fear of losing something and never getting it back!

Thankfully, there was a chair for me around a podium near the back of the store because I needed to sit down and catch my breath, try not to run scared.

Because what Jonas and I had shared the night before... it was beautiful. Life changing. And I didn't want to run away before I had a chance to see what could come.

Tess and Mariah went back to a fitting room while the rest of us sat and waited. Lottie was on her phone, handling a call from work, but Tracey sat next to me, telling me all about the wedding.

"Their colors are deep plum and mint green, which is going to look so beautiful with Tess's complexion. And Flanagans is going to cater, which should be so fun and delicious. Plus, there will be five groomsmen, so you know, plenty of pickings." She giggled. "Not that you'd care. Jonas is such a catch."

"You think so?" I asked with a smile.

"He asked me out not too long before you two started seeing each other." She gave me a wistful smile. "Should have agreed sooner!"

My smile stayed on my face, but out of sheer will alone. "Oh?"

"Yeah." She tilted her head sideways. "You know what they say. You don't know what you have until it's gone."

Tess and Mariah came out of the dressing room, Tess wearing her wedding dress.

"We can talk later," Tracey whispered, giving me a blindingly white smile.

I took slow, deep breaths, trying to fight my panic as Tess stepped onto the podium.

She looked absolutely beautiful in her gown with the lacy sleeves going three quarters of the way down her arms and the delicate tulle skirt flowing behind her.

But I couldn't focus on that.

No, I *felt* the woman beside me. The girl with a narrow waist and bright green eyes and blonde hair. Not to mention the fact that she was wearing an adorable dress with wedge heels while I'd come in leggings and Chucks. She was my opposite in every way. And Jonas had asked her out first. Technically, he hadn't asked me out at all.

I felt something I didn't feel often... *inferior.*

My eyes stung, but I didn't cry. Not in front of Tracey, not during this moment that was supposed to be happy for Jonas's family and their friends.

Tracey went to the podium, hugging her friend. Tears streamed down her cheeks as she told Tess how beautiful she was. She even looked cute when she fucking cried. Not a blubbery mess like I always did when I cried.

I hated the insecure thoughts going through my mind, but I couldn't stop them. It had been so easy to write off Jonas's failed marriage when he told me about it like they were kids. So easy to accept the fact that he was single and waiting for just the right woman. But he'd been serious enough about Tracey to ask her out. That had to mean something, right?

And what did that mean for me? What happened when he saw the two of us standing next to each other? One girl who walked around in pretty dresses, the other girl who exclusively wore holey shirts and leggings while writing about raunchy sex and making an ass out of herself on television?

Mariah turned away from her daughter and waved me over. "What do you think?"

"It's absolutely perfect." Which meant I belonged nowhere near it.

31

JONAS

Around six, most of the employees were packing up or already gone. A few had even stopped in to say goodbye. My first day as a manager had gone pretty well, but it seemed like Jenkins was doing alright too. I looked up from my desk to his office across the way, but I didn't see him through his window like usual. I had half a thought formed wondering where he was. If he'd cut out early.

But then I heard a knock on my door.

I jerked my head back in surprise, then called, "Come in." Someone was on the other side of the window, where I couldn't see them.

The door pushed open, and Jenkins stepped into my office. We didn't really cross paths unless it was at company-wide events. He was ten years older than me, and I got the feeling he didn't like me. I couldn't blame him. If I'd given up as much as he had, working these crazy hours with a family at home, I wouldn't like me either.

"Hey," I said, sitting up. "Wanna sit?" I gestured toward the open chair across from me.

He shook his head, looking around the office. "No pictures on the walls."

I glanced around. The only artwork in here was what had been left behind by the person before me. It was fine. And this was the one space Tess hadn't decorated for me.

"My office has pictures everywhere," he said, still standing, still not meeting my eyes. "Pictures of my kids, my wife, the Little League team I sponsored since I didn't have time to coach."

Where was he going with this?

He folded his arms across his chest. "I've given up camping trips with the Scouts, beauty pageants, school recitals, nights with my wife, to get this promotion." Finally, he met my eyes. "What have you given up?"

I studied him for a moment. "You want me to step aside and let you have it?"

"No, I want you to recognize who's put in more work for it."

Gritting my teeth together, I said, "I've worked hard for this, Ronnie."

"I know," he said lightly, but then he leaned forward, putting his hands on my desk. "But my wife told me you're dating a famous author now. And someday, you'll be holding a tiny little baby, looking into its perfect face that's so much like your own but better at the same time, and you're going to have to leave. You're going to have little hands pulling at your pant leg saying, 'Daddy, don't go.' You're going to have a wife who looks you in the face and says, 'I don't even know you anymore.' And I hope to hell you'll be able to live with the sacrifice you made for people who don't care who does their taxes as long as they get done on time."

I looked down at my desk, then back up. "Are you okay with that sacrifice?"

"I have to be... otherwise it was all worth nothing." He walked away, and my chest felt tight at his words.

I'd spent all this time thinking of financial security for my family, not about the strain it might put on them. Tax season was four months out of the year, and it wasn't our only busy time.

Was I climbing the ladder up the wrong wall?

What if Mara wanted kids and I couldn't be the kind of partner she wanted?

It was all too soon to be thinking about it, but I'd meant it when I told Mara I didn't want to play games with her. She could be the one. And I wanted to be the one for her.

So in an attempt to follow Cohen's advice, I gave Mara some space. Work was the perfect excuse since I had to stay late to accommodate the new responsibilities. Plus, tonight was poker night at his and Birdie's place, where they'd set up the garage with a fully stocked beer fridge and green felt table.

There were plenty of beers, snacks, and an abundance of good times. We'd been at it for so long I couldn't even remember when we'd started meeting for poker nights. Probably around the time Cohen started his bar. He was just getting out of a relationship with his wife where he'd spent all his time on work and had hardly any life outside of that. So when he started his bar and I was his accountant, we hit it off and starting hanging out. Soon after, he hired Steve to manage the bar, and the rest was history. The three of us seemed to get on well, and we just never stopped.

When I arrived, Cohen and Steve were already sitting at the table, open bottles in front of them. As soon as I got out of the car, they started clapping and whooping. And since they didn't normally do that, it was pretty clear why they were doing it now.

"Oh, shut up," I said, despite the shit-eating grin on my face.

Steve patted Cohen's shoulder. "Do you see the way he's walking? It's like Mara took the pole right out of his ass!"

"The only pain in my ass is you," I retorted.

Steve and Cohen guffawed as I went to the fridge and grabbed a beer of my own. Then I sat at the table and began shuffling the deck of cards. "Where's Birdie?" I asked. Her car wasn't in the driveway. I wondered if she was at my place, hanging out with Mara on our new couch. Or maybe they'd gone to get supper together with Henrietta.

Part of me wished I could have gone with them. Or at least been a fly on the wall to hear what they were saying about me. About us.

God, I sounded pathetic, even in my head.

As if he could hear my thoughts, Cohen said, "Sounds like you're doing well with the space thing."

"I mean... Why do you say that?"

"Birdie said she and Hen are helping Mara get settled in at her place again," Cohen said.

My jaw went slack. "They're... what?"

Mara had been at my house that morning, sleeping on *our* couch. She'd been at my mother's house and texted me how good Flanagans was. That we should go there together sometime.

What had happened between then and now?

I got out my phone to see what was going on. Not once, in any of her messages, had she told me she would not be sleeping at my house tonight. Not once had she informed me that the security company had set up and thoroughly tested her system. Or that I wouldn't be seeing her tonight.

Cohen cleared his throat uncomfortably. "Did you... did you not know she was leaving?"

I shook my head quietly.

Steve frowned. "Maybe the call just didn't come through? My wife and I do this weird thing where sometimes we'll call each other at the exact same moment, and both of us will go to voicemail."

The hope in his voice was almost enough to break me in half. "I haven't called her today," I said, leaning forward with my elbows on the table. What the fuck had I done?

This wasn't the time for playing it cool. Now was the time to go all in, while I still had a shot with her.

Despite the knot in my stomach telling me it was already too late, I picked up my phone and dialed Mara's number. Cohen tried to stop me from calling her, but I held my hand up to him. I needed to do this. As it rang, I paced around the opening of the garage, kicking the toes of my dress shoes over the dusty concrete.

I had almost given up when she answered. "Hello?" The greeting may have been normal, but the cool way she delivered it was anything but.

"What's going on?" I strained my ears but couldn't hear anything in the background.

"The security company's going to be at my house first thing tomorrow morning. I'm going to sleep there so I can meet them for the install."

I pinched the bridge of my nose, feeling dizzy. "You're going to sleep at your house without a security system in place?" Without *me*?

"It's just one night. I'll make sure all the doors are locked, and Henrietta brought me some pepper spray. I'll be fine."

"And you're doing this because..." I couldn't think of an answer, unless her reason was wanting to get away from me, then this made perfect sense.

"I'm shit at waking up, and I don't want to sleep through my alarm and have to wait another week for a new appointment."

"You won't be waiting for an appointment if you're fucking dead." My voice shook. Why was she being so careless with herself?

"I'll stay at a hotel then," she said.

"If you're worried about getting up early, I can take the morning off work and go there myself."

"No, Jonas. You have your promotion to worry about."

"Fuck the promotion." I shook my head, looking at the guys, but they were just as clueless as me. "Mara, what's going on? I thought we had a good night, and now?"

"Now what?" she said.

"You're running away!"

"I'm not running away, Jonas. I'm going *home*."

Her words were like a sucker punch to the gut. "Mara, please, just stay the night at our—*my* house and—"

"And what? Have sex and eat ice cream and fall asleep on your couch until I die? I'm not that kind of girl, Jonas. I never have been. I was clear about that from the beginning. I never said I was moving in, and I *never* agreed to forever."

I braced myself on the garage door frame, struggling to stand. "What happened?"

"Nothing that doesn't happen every time a guy and a girl get close," she said quickly. "I'll keep helping your mom with dialysis, but other than that, I think we're good to do a public date maybe once or twice a month. The premiere's just a few months away, and you're off the hook."

She hung up without saying goodbye, and I stared at the phone in my hand.

"What happened?" Steve asked.

Looking between him and Cohen, I said, "The water got too hot."

32

MARA

Confession: I'm an asshole.

I THREW my bags into the trunk of my car, avoiding Birdie's and Henrietta's eyes the entire time. They'd come over and helped me clean Jonas's house from top to bottom, washing the sheets I'd slept on, scrubbing the bathroom floor where we'd had shower sex, taking away every trace of me from his home, where I never should have been.

I had the money. I could have booked a hotel for a couple weeks. I could have rented an Airbnb for the month. But I'd stayed with Jonas, because the truth was, I'd wanted to. I liked being around him. I liked that he'd bought a couch just to make me comfortable. I liked that I could count on him for sweet notes in the morning and a kiss at night.

My friends were already bringing the rest of my things outside, but I left an envelope of cash on the couch to pay him back for the new furniture. I knew money was tight with Tess's wedding and his mom's health issues. It had been selfish to let him buy it, to pretend I could be a relationship girl.

I felt like a piece of shit. Shittier than a piece of shit. I felt like seven pieces of shit, the whole shitty floor of a petting zoo.

But I couldn't keep doing this.

I had been telling Jonas the truth when I said I wasn't that kind of girl, and today just made me remember why. Within moments of meeting Tracey and hearing that Jonas had asked her out, I knew.

It only took seconds for me to start second-guessing myself, picking apart all the "flaws" that I'd worked so hard to love. And not only that, I'd tried to find flaws in her that would make me more worthy. I'd compared myself to another woman, which was the antithesis to everything I tried to do with my writing.

I wanted women to lift each other up. Fix each other's crowns. And most importantly, see themselves for the badass babes they were.

And really, who was I to stick around Jonas's home when I was only playing house? There was a reason I'd made it to thirty without so much as a live-in boyfriend or a broken heart. My father had broken my heart long ago, and there was no fixing it. There was no seeing love another way. Because what had the power to build entire cities, also had the power to destroy nations. And I wasn't giving anyone that kind of power over me. No matter how much it would help my job. No matter how nice he was.

My friends stood by my driver's side door, waiting for me. As I walked closer, Birdie said, "Are you okay?"

I blinked quickly, trying to hold back tears. "Let's just get to the hotel."

Birdie frowned. "Are you sure you don't want to stay with Cohen and me?"

Henrietta said, "You could stay on the couch at our place too if you don't want to be alone."

I shook my head. "I've been imposing on people for too long. It'll be just fine for one night."

They both looked like they wanted to argue with me, but I opened my car door and said, "Thanks for helping me make sure Jonas's house was clean."

Henrietta gave me a hug, a long, hard one that made me want to fall apart in her arms. "You're going to get through this, honey," she said.

I took a shuddering breath before stepping back. "I know I will," I said with tears in my eyes. "I have you two."

They smiled at me, and Birdie brushed my arm with her fingertips. "Call us if you need anything, even someone to clear out the minibar with you."

For the first time that afternoon, I cracked a smile. "I have your numbers."

They walked toward their vehicles, and I got in mine. The automatic headlights came to life with the engine. They panned over Jonas's house, showing the stucco siding, the big windows. From here, I could even see a sliver of the couch in the living room, and I choked back a sob.

Lying on that couch with Jonas, that was closest I'd ever come to believing in happily ever after. But the heartbreak of losing it all? I wasn't strong enough to handle it after everything I'd been through.

I gave the house a final look before backing out of the driveway and starting down the road.

I missed who I was before I knew how amazing Jonas was. I missed being the girl guys were calling to meet their needs. I missed crawling on my hands and knees on Hayden's floor, waiting for him to lick whipped cream off my naked body. Not because I loved him, but because I *didn't*.

I missed when my heart didn't hurt this fucking much and fear didn't constrict my lungs, making it painful to breathe.

The last person who'd touched me was Jonas. He'd looked me in the eyes as he made love to me and whispered my name.

He couldn't be the last one to touch me. I wanted his memory erased, wanted to forget the way he made me feel. Wanted to forget the heartbreak that would come if our relationship ever become something real.

So I did what I did best.

I got out my phone and dialed Hayden's number.

Within fifteen minutes, he was at my hotel room. His lips were on mine. His hands covered my body. And we had sex from behind.

When we were done, I went to the bathroom, turned on the shower, and cried.

33

JONAS

I wanted to find out the hotel where Mara was staying, go there and beg her to be with me, but Cohen convinced me to wait. He said Birdie would be home soon and we could ask her for advice. After all, Birdie was Mara's best friend, one of the rare few Mara let behind her carefully crafted defenses.

I sat at the table, putting cards into the pile, betting money, but my mind was elsewhere, with Mara. I wondered what hotel she was staying at. If she would stay there alone. If she was done with me forever or just for the night. What I could do to earn another chance, to show her I wasn't the kind to break her heart.

Birdie's headlights illuminated the garage as she pulled into the driveway, and my back stiffened, my mouth went dry. I needed to know what had happened. What I'd done.

I rose from my chair, and Steve and Cohen did too. Cohen put a hand on my shoulder as Birdie approached us, an apologetic look in her deep blue eyes.

"What happened?" I managed.

Birdie shook her head, her curly ponytail swinging side to side. "She's afraid."

My heart ached for Mara, for us, for the things she was throwing away. "What can I do?"

"Did I ever tell you how Mara and I met?" Birdie asked.

I exchanged a glance with the guys. "You were roommates, right?"

She nodded. "There was an ad on Craigslist, and the price was right. The apartment barely fit both of us, but I instantly liked Mara. She was so fun and brave and always getting me out of my comfort zone. But when we got too close, when things got too real, she'd run. She'd spend a few days with a guy, take extra shifts at the restaurant, and we wouldn't talk for days or even weeks at a time."

My eyebrows drew together. That didn't seem like their friendship at all. Anywhere I saw Birdie, Mara was almost always there too. "What changed?" I was desperate for advice. Anything that would help get me to a point where Mara would trust me too.

"Time," Birdie said simply. "After a while, she realized I wasn't going to leave, wasn't going to hurt her, and things weren't so hard anymore." She looked down at the gray epoxied garage floor with the white and black speckles. "But you don't have to give that to her, Jonas, if it's not right for you. It's hard to stay with someone who's always running. Especially if she decides not to be lonely tonight."

My throat was tight. Sad for myself. Sad for the woman who thought it wasn't safe to stand still. "I'm not going anywhere."

Birdie smiled at me softly. "I hoped you'd say that." She patted my shoulder and walked inside.

I didn't feel much like playing poker after that. The guys and I finished our beers, and I drove to the last place I wanted to go: my empty home.

I walked inside, half hoping she would be there, waiting for me.

I could feel her absence before I saw it, but walking through my house, it was clear. She was gone.

She and her friends had cleaned the house so thoroughly, there wasn't a trace of Mara left behind. Not a hairpin by the sink, not a single brown hair in the shower drain, not even the smell of her on my sheets.

I still couldn't understand what had happened, what had gone wrong between this morning and now. I knew Birdie said Mara was just scared, but why? The sudden shift didn't make sense. Just the night before, we were laughing, smiling, loving. I'd never experienced lovemaking with anyone that intense. That perfect.

My mom was the only other person who had seen her since this morning, so I called her, hoping for some explanation that would make sense, something that would give me a chance at fixing this.

She answered within a few rings and said, "Hey, honey, how are you?"

"Good, I was just wondering how your day with Mara went? She said you guys got Flanagans?"

"Sure did," Mom said with a smile. I heard a dish in the sink, and I figured she was handwashing dishes like she did every night before reading and going to bed. "We had some lunch with your dad and then went to Tess's wedding dress fitting."

"Fitting?" I asked. "Didn't Tess buy it already?"

Mom chuckled like I was missing something obvious. "She bought it, but they had to make sure it fit right before she brings it home."

"I didn't know that was a thing," I admitted. "And you brought Mara along?"

"It's a big deal. All the bridesmaids typically go along. Mara got to meet Tracey and Derek's sister. She fit right in, chatted up a storm with Trace."

My jaw went slack. She'd talked to Tracey. What had come up in their conversation? Did Tracey tell Mara that I'd asked her out before beginning our fake relationship?

She had to have told her. I wonder what it must have felt like for Mara to know that right before I met her, I was pining for my sister's best friend. God, she probably felt like I was a loser. Or like I didn't really want her. No wonder she'd run away.

"Jonas?" Mom said.

I cleared my throat. "Yeah?"

"I really like Mara. She fits in with us so well, don't you think?"

My smile lasted only a second before faltering. "She does." I didn't want to break Mom's heart, but I had to be honest. "Mom, I don't know how long it's going to last. Mara... she's skittish when it comes to relationships."

Mom was quiet for a moment. "You've told her it's not fake anymore, right? That your feelings are real?"

"Not out loud. But a relationship goes two ways. It doesn't matter how much I like her if she doesn't want to be with me."

"What makes you think she doesn't want to be with you?" Mom asked. "That girl is crazy about you, even if she's afraid to admit it."

I was thirty-two years old, and I still didn't understand how Mom knew all the things she did. I just hoped she was right this time.

"Don't give up on her," Mom said.

"What if she's given up on me?" I asked, my throat tight. "She doesn't even believe love can last."

Mom paused. "It's hard to believe in something you've never seen. But you can be the one to show her. One day, one breakfast, one kiss goodnight at a time."

34

MARA

Confession: The only person who's ever truly scared me was my dad.

HAYDEN WAS asleep when I came out of the bathroom, one foot dangling off the end of the bed, his snores filling the room. His shaggy hair fell over his forehead, and the sheets covered his naked waist.

Jonas wouldn't have fallen asleep first. He would have stayed up with me, watching soapy movies and eating ice cream, and letting my feet rest on his lap.

And I realized, casual sex would never be the same for me. Sex would never be the same without Jonas.

And that realization hurt like hell because I knew I'd just ruined whatever chance I had with Jonas by jumping into bed with Hayden. I hated this situation. Hated my dad for showing me that men weren't safe. Hated myself for showing Jonas that I couldn't be trusted to stick around when things got hard.

With all the pain in my chest, I wrapped myself in the

hotel robe, got out my computer, and sat at the desk, losing myself in a story where the curvy girl got the guy, one where she was brave enough to chase happily ever after without worrying what would happen if it never came.

And I realized that's why I've been writing all this time. Not to escape into another world, but to escape into someone different from myself. These characters in my book, they were so brave. They fought for the people they loved, knowing the entire time that they could face the rejection, the heartbreak of a lifetime.

I'd never been that brave.

Hayden got up around six, slipping on his jeans and shirt, kissing me on the cheek before walking out the door.

I knew before he left it would be the last time. I was done using sex to replace feelings. Because Jonas had shown me that feelings couldn't be replaced, not when you had them for the right person. There was something special in the way Jonas touched me, and I knew I wouldn't find it anywhere else.

A knock sounded on the door, jerking me out of my seat.

I got up from my computer for the first time in hours, ready to tell housekeeping they didn't need to worry about cleaning my room since I'd be checking out later that day. But instead of a housekeeper, there was a girl with a delivery bag stamped with the Seaton Bakery logo.

"I—who," I began, already knowing the answer deep down.

"There's a note stapled to the bag," she said, handing

it to me. "Have a good day." She walked away, and I stood in the doorway, staring at the paper.

You might not believe in happily ever after. But I do. — Jonas

Tears rolled down my cheeks as I realized... it was already too late. I'd messed up too big. I didn't deserve his forgiveness. His love.

My phone rang, and I wiped at my face as I went back to the desk and answered it.

"Hello, is this Mara Taylor?"

"Yes," I said. "How can I help you?"

"We have your security install scheduled from ten to two today. We'll need you to be at the house to let in our technician. If there are pets or children on the premises, please keep them locked up and out of the way."

"Sure, I'll kennel the kids, but I'm not sure where I'll put the dogs..."

"Oh. That was a joke. Right?"

I nodded, pacing the floor. "Right. Apparently I'm better on paper. Yes, I'll be there at ten."

After hanging up, I closed my laptop and got dressed for the day. Not too long ago, I was so excited to be home, but the thought of going back to such an empty place... it didn't feel like an escape or a sanctuary anymore.

I had my friends, but they had lives. Birdie had Cohen, Henrietta lived with her family, and the guys in my contact list wouldn't be there much longer.

In fact... I went through my phone and deleted every name, every number, every casual hookup I'd ever had.

The list of phone numbers left wasn't long. But it included Jonas's name. I couldn't erase him from my phone, just like I couldn't erase him from my heart. But thinking about it, about him, didn't help what had already happened.

Jonas didn't like games, and what I'd done with Hayden last night... he wouldn't like that either. He would want nothing to do with me, despite the note he left.

I let out a sigh and sat at the desk, opening the bag. I could only stare at the breakfast that had been ordered in love. A love I didn't deserve.

♥˙♥˙♥˙♥

THE CLOSER I got to my house, the tighter anxiety squeezed my chest. I took deep breaths, counting to four on the inhale and then four again on the exhale. It didn't help, though. For all I knew, my dad could have thrown bricks through the windows, could be waiting down the block for the payback he probably thought was owed.

But more than that, Jonas's strong and steady presence wouldn't be there to keep me safe. Keep me grounded.

I took a deep breath, reminding myself this was exactly why I had to leave Jonas's house. What happened if I went all in with him? He could die in a car accident. Get drawn into an affair with someone like Tracey. Fall slowly out of love with me as the years went by. And then what? I would be back on my own all over again. Just as weak and powerless and alone as I felt right now.

This was right. This was right. This was right.

No matter how wrong it felt.

I pulled up to my house, and thankfully, the security company was there. No other vehicles aside from my beautiful truck. I missed Bertha so damn much.

I whispered a promise to take her for a drive later as I went to the front door and let in the tech. He talked about as much as the bushes outside, so I just stayed out of the way as he got to work.

My house looked untouched. Even the coffee cups in the sink were just as I'd left them—except with a little extra mold skimming the top.

I realized I hadn't gotten the mail since before I'd hidden out at Jonas's and walked to the mailbox at the end of the driveway. It was packed nearly to the brim, and I pulled it all out. Leaning against Bertha, I flipped through the envelopes until my eyes fell on handwriting I hadn't seen in years.

My dad's.

35

JONAS

I sat across the table from one of our biggest clients, the CEO of SeatonMade, a factory located in Seaton that employed nearly fifty people. She was an older woman with a sharp nose and wrinkles around her lips like she used to smoke.

Mr. Rusk had put me on their account, and the pressure of it was palpable on my shoulders. Or maybe that was just my bad night's sleep. "And these are the Q2 preliminary financial reports?" I asked, flipping through pages in a manila folder.

She nodded. "It should all be there, but if we're missing something, I can call our HR manager to fax them over."

Honestly, it all could have been faxed over, or better yet, emailed, but sometimes people liked doing things the old-fashioned way. And this was part of the job, taking plenty of meetings that could have just been emails.

My phone vibrated in my pocket, and I instantly

grabbed for it, hoping to God it would be Mara. "Sorry," I said, glancing at the screen.

The store owner nodded and said, "Everything okay?"

At the sight of Mara's name, I wasn't so sure. I hoped she wasn't calling me to yell at me for the breakfast or telling me to give up altogether, because I wasn't sure how I would handle it. "I need to take this. Family emergency."

The woman nodded, and I stepped out of my office, swiping the screen to answer. "Mara?" I wanted to hear her voice so badly.

"Jonas?" She sounded completely terrified, and my gut dropped.

"What's going on?" I asked. "Are you okay? Did the security guys try something?" I was already striding toward the parking lot, ready to drive as fast as my car would take me to her house.

"There's a letter from my dad here."

I sped up. "What does it say?"

"I haven't opened it." She let out a hoarse chuckle, trying to be brave. "Do you think there's anthrax in it?"

"I don't know," I answered, getting into my car. "He probably doesn't have access to anthrax."

"Unless he could find it at the bottom of a bottle of whiskey, you're probably right."

"Are you alone?" I asked, just to keep her talking. I needed more information. Needed to keep her *safe* from that man who had instilled such fear in her, even in a room full of people. "There's not a chance he could be there?" I whipped out of the parking lot, taking the roads toward her house as fast as I could. I'd only been there a couple times before, but I knew the way from that first night I picked her up. The first night we kissed.

"I don't see another vehicle around that I don't recognize, and the security tech is here." Her voice shook despite the surety in her words.

"Video call me," I ordered.

"Jonas, I—"

"*Now*," I said. I needed to see her, make sure that she was okay, probably even more than she needed to see me.

A new tone came through my phone, and I glanced down long enough to click the answer button and see her face. My chest instantly relaxed, releasing a breath. Fuck was she beautiful. "You're a sight for sore eyes."

She smiled softly, her lips trembling. "That's one of my favorite phrases."

"Yeah?" I paused at a stop sign to put my phone in the holder my mom had gotten me from one of those ads on TV. This way I could see Mara and the road better. I wouldn't do her any good if I wrecked on the way there.

"Yeah," she said. "It's like seeing the person you care for literally soothes you, heals you."

She was getting lost again, in that world of make believe she had to escape into so often as a child, and I wanted to help her get to the place where she felt comfortable. Where she felt safe. "What are your other favorite phrases to write?"

"I know it's lame, but I love it when a guy and a girl hold hands for the first time and they feel like their hands were made for each other."

"That's not lame."

She smiled again. "It's such a small moment, but I think it's when they first realize that this could go some-

246 HELLO FAKE BOYFRIEND

where. It takes a special person to make you feel butter-flies just by touching their hand."

Mara had done that for me. She didn't even realize it. "What else?" I asked.

"You know that part of the movie where the characters messed up and everyone knows they need to be together, but they have to get their heads out of their asses first?"

"Yeah," I said. "You like that part?"

"I hate it. I hate feeling their pain. But there's always a piece of it, where someone smarter, wiser, more experienced passes on their wisdom. That's the part I love. Everything I know, I learned it from a romance novel. Now that I'm writing, I get to pass it on too. It feels like I'm part of this lineage of women, writing in a genre that everyone underestimates or disregards completely. But they just don't see what we see."

"What is that?" I asked, finally turning down her street.

"That good sex and happily ever after are things worth fighting for."

I reached her house and parked along the curb. As soon as the car was stopped, I jumped out and ran to her where she sat cross legged in front of her pickup. I knelt to the ground beside her and took her into my arms.

She sobbed, shaking into my chest. "I'm so sorry, Jonas. I feel so stupid."

"Shh," I breathed. "Shh. You have nothing to be sorry for."

She pulled back, looking at me with teary, red-rimmed eyes. "But I do."

I drew my brows together. "For taking some space for

yourself? You don't need to worry about that. I know I came on strong, and I talked to my mom about you seeing Tracey. I'm not sure what she said to you, but I'm sure it didn't help."

She shook her head, wiping at her eyes. "It's not that, Jonas. It's what I did after."

My heart constricted all over again, trying to picture what Mara really had to be sorry for. The warning Birdie had given me the night before. "What did you do?"

"I called Hayden."

It hurt worse. Worse than I even imagined.

I stood up, began pacing the driveway trying to process what she'd told me. Trying not to shout or punch something or just collapse and give up.

"Jonas," she breathed.

I held out my hand, telling her to stop. I wasn't ready to talk. I needed to *think*. Mara and I were... what? Dating? Fucking? The only label we'd ever given ourselves was fake boyfriend and girlfriend, and that was only for the sake of her career. I'd never asked her to commit to me, and she hadn't offered. All this time I'd been so against games, but I'd been playing one myself. I had been afraid to ask for what I wanted for fear of pushing her away.

I wanted commitment. I wanted her to be mine and no one else's. I wanted her to sleep in my bed and no one else's. I wanted her to call me when she needed someone, and no one fucking else.

But why wasn't Hayden here? If they'd slept together, if he'd been around, why hadn't she called him?

My heart lifted slightly.

She may have wanted him, but she *needed* me.

"Jonas," she said again. And this time I didn't stop her. I looked at her as she pushed herself up from the cement. She walked to me, cupping my cheeks with both of her hands.

I leaned into her palm, desperate to feel reassured, to know that this wasn't all slipping through my fingers before it really had a chance to begin.

"I need you to understand. You don't have to forgive me, but if you at least know..."

"Know what?" I asked, watching the movement of her lips, hoping her words would bring healing instead of destruction.

"When Tracey told me you had asked her out, I immediately made it about myself. She was skinnier than me, blonder than me, prettier than me. And I assumed that was the kind of girl you wanted. And I didn't like being the girl who had to wonder if she was good enough. So I ran. I tried to distract myself in all the ways I knew how... but in my mind, I kept coming back to you."

I knew there were other guys out there, better looking than me, stronger than me, more exciting and interesting and artistic too. That was okay, as long as I was the one she wanted. The one she came home to. "Mara..."

She shook her head and continued. "I'm shitty at the relationship thing. I've never done it. Never tried. But I want to do it with you. I want to have a chance with you, for real this time. And I'll understand if you just want to give me the middle finger and tell me to fuck off. I'd deserve it. God knows I'd deserve it. But if you give me a chance, if you'd let me be the kind of person I know I could be with you and only you—" Her voice broke off in sobs.

I thumbed away her tears, holding her close and kissing her forehead. "Of course I want to be with you," I said. "Of course I do."

She laughed through her tears. "I have no idea why. I'm a mess."

I kissed the top of her head again, just so thankful to have her in my arms. "I know you said this is your favorite part of the story. You know, the part where everyone's sad and you get to write some kick-ass line... but I'm taking my turn."

She looked up at me, her beautiful brown eyes waiting.

"The only thing being single guarantees you is time alone, but you deserve so much more than that. You deserve someone who will wake up next to you and smile just because they get to see your face. You deserve someone who will worship your body *and* your soul. You deserve someone to sit in the living room with you, reading books on a rainy day. And you deserve to know that you deserve all those things, not because of what you look like or what you do, but because of *who you are*. And who you are is pretty damn incredible to me."

She smiled and hugged me tight, resting her cheek against my chest. "That was pretty 'kick ass.'"

I laughed, finally relaxing enough to breathe in deep. "I'm here for you, Mara. I want you to be mine. Only mine."

She looked up at me, resting her chin on my chest. "I'm yours."

36

MARA

Confession: I want happily ever after with Jonas Moore.

WE HELD each other until the security technician came out and told us the install was complete. I'd almost forgotten about the letter completely until I bent to pick up the mail. My dad's handwriting was staring at me, his letter right on top.

Jonas looked over my shoulder and asked, "Do you want to read it inside?"

I slowly nodded. He held my hand tightly as we walked into the house. I'd never noticed before how perfectly our hands fit together. I set the mail on my table and began brewing a pot of coffee. At this point in the day, it was more for comfort than anything else.

Jonas waited silently while the pot began gurgling.

"I might need something stronger than this," I said, still looking at the coffee pot.

"Agreed," he replied.

I got out a bottle of spiced rum and eyeballed a shot into my coffee cup. I drank it. Then I took another, savoring the burn in my throat, the warming of my insides. Then I filled the cup with coffee and splashed in just a little bit more.

"I need to read the letter," I decided out loud, sitting next to Jonas. "If I don't, I'll be wondering what it says until it eats me alive."

He nodded. "I'm here for you."

I set my cup down with shaky hands and took an even shakier breath. I picked up the envelope, and it felt flimsy in my hands. There was nothing inside except a piece of paper, that much I could tell.

My name was written on the front. Mara Taylor. But that was it. No address, because he'd placed the envelope here himself. He knew where I lived.

I slowly ripped up the flap until I could reach the paper inside. Jonas looked over my shoulder as I read the words.

MARA,

I'd like to speak with you. I know I don't have a right, but if there's any way you can come to 4582 Willow Lane in LA between one and three on Friday the 24th, I'd appreciate it.

THERE WAS no signature to the letter, almost like he couldn't quite decide what to call himself. Dad felt wrong. His first name too familiar. He was a stranger. A villain in a past I tried so hard to forget.

I read it over again, and Jonas spoke my thoughts out loud. "That's today."

I nodded, typing the address into my phone. LA was an hour away from my house, and it was nearly half-past one. My map said if we left now, we could be there in fifty minutes. That would give us about half an hour to talk, but why would we need to?

"Where is it?" Jonas asked.

I zoomed in, thinking it was probably some crummy apartment building. What I saw instead surprised me.

Free Hearts Rehabilitation Facility

Jonas and I exchanged a look.

"I can't drive," I said. "I've already had three shots."

"I can drive you."

"But your work. The promotion." I covered my face with my hands. "I'm so sorry I called you in the middle of the day."

He put his hands on either side of my face, looking into my eyes. "You call me any time you need me. I can always make up the hours later."

"And the house. I haven't tested the system yet."

"Fuck the system. You're staying with me."

"And..."

Jonas looked at me. "If you want an excuse not to go see your dad, there will always be one ready. You don't owe him anything, Mara. The only question is do you want to talk to him?"

For some crazy reason, I said yes.

In a matter of minutes, we were out the door, getting into Jonas's car, and driving toward LA. In moments like these, I appreciated his dependability, the fact that he never let the gas gauge get below a quarter of a tank because time was of the essence.

We held hands as he followed the directions, not talking.

Now it was me who needed to think. I needed to think about what to say to the man who drank away every dime my family had. The man who beat my mom until she left and then turned his anger on me. The man who tore apart a family for a liquid that would never love him back.

Was it crazy to hope for an apology? Illogical to wish he could become that dad I'd always dreamed I could have? Even if I was thirty, I still wanted a father, someone to love and care for me as he should have.

And what would happen if he didn't apologize? If he called me in to blame me for his alcohol addiction and failed marriage and everything else that went wrong in his life? Because he laid plenty of blame on me when I was only a child.

Would the little girl in me survive one more attack? I'd worked so hard in therapy to re-parent and heal my inner child. I didn't want that work to go to waste.

Jonas squeezed my hand, as if to remind me that I wasn't alone. He was right. I had a boyfriend, for the first time in my life. I had friends I could count on. I had my little corner of the world that was mine, and even though my dad took away my childhood, he couldn't take my present.

The map led us to a parking lot in front of a dingy building. There was the sign on front, just like the map had said. Free Hearts Rehabilitation Center.

I looked around, half expecting my dad to be lurking as part of some elaborate scheme, but he wasn't here.

People were walking in and out of the building. Women my age, older couples, parents with small children trailing along.

Then it hit me. Today was visitors' day, and I was here to see my dad.

"Are you sure you want to go in?" Jonas asked, eyeing all the people.

I nodded and unbuckled before I could change my mind. There was only half an hour left, and depending on how this went, it could be too long or barely enough time to say what we needed to say.

We walked into the building, his hand protectively on my lower back, and he led me through the door. There was a short line at the reception desk that moved quickly. When I told the woman behind the glass wall that we were there to see Duncan Taylor, she seemed stunned, but quickly recovered.

She lifted her phone, pressed a button, and said, "Visitors for Duncan Taylor."

"You can go back to the family room," she said, pointing to the right. There was a heavy metal door that said the opposite of family. Family didn't need to be kept behind locked doors. Family didn't need to leave letters because they didn't have phone numbers.

We walked into the room, and it was a family room, of sorts. There were mismatched couches, tables with weathered board game boxes, a TV playing cartoons. Several children looked up at the screens, and I wondered if they knew how lucky they were that their loved ones were getting help now.

I said a quick prayer to whoever was listening that

their parents would be healed, that they'd get the child-hood I didn't have.

And then my eyes landed on him. My dad.

Up close, he was shorter than I remembered him. Thinner. There was gray in his beard to match the steel in his eyes. But something was different too. The lines around his face weren't so deep. His shoulders not so broad and scary.

"Mara," he said.

"Hi." I gripped Jonas's hand even tighter. We walked to the table he stood near and sat down, participating in a choreographed dance no one quite knew the steps to. Dad pulled out a chair, a noticeable shake to his hands as he did.

"Thanks for coming," he said.

I only nodded.

"I'm sorry for leaving a letter like that, but I couldn't get through to you any other way."

Were we already starting with the excuses? They were always there, and apparently, they hadn't gone. "My website is my name."

"I've filled out the form there and emailed you to that address in your books, but I don't know if you saw them."

Then it hit me—Rebecca had said my father had emailed me, and that it wasn't threatening. Maybe he had been trying to reach out all this time. Before I could think on it too long, Dad cleared his throat and leaned forward on the table.

"I wanted you to come here so I could apologize."

"And you couldn't do it in the letter?" I asked, bitter-ness rising in my throat. It had been so long since I'd seen him, but he'd haunted all of my years. Almost all the wounds I had to heal from had been inflicted by him.

Jonas squeezed my hand, giving me comfort. Giving me strength.

Dad took a breath. "It felt wrong not to say it to your face."

"Say what?" I asked, bracing myself for what was to come.

Dad looked me in my eyes, a mirror of his own. "Mara, I took my first drink when I was twelve years old. My dad gave it to me right after picking a fight with me and knocking me out. I was drinking and fighting before I even knew how to properly wipe my own ass. I thought I'd never be like him, but when I got drunk, it came out. And I felt so shitty about what I'd done, I drank some more to help me forget. Soon I didn't know who I was without alcohol, and I didn't like who I was with it." He ran a hand through his graying hair. "I wish I could say I came to this place to get better on my own, but the state ordered me after a car accident a couple months back. It took me losing everything. Your mom. You. My license. My car. My fucking will to live, to come here. And the shrinks, you know, they kind of let me know I had two choices. Drink my liver down the shitter or grow a pair and get sober."

My mind was reeling from all the information, but he kept going.

"How'd you get out of here?" I asked. "Aren't you supposed to stay on site?"

He shook his head. "They let us have outings from time to time. When I heard where you'd be, I asked to go. The worker who took me waited outside."

"But why go to all that trouble to see me? It's been fifteen years, and you didn't look that hard for me when I was just a kid."

He cringed, fighting an internal battle. "This is part of it, recovery, saying sorry to the people you wronged. I couldn't say sorry to your mom, but I'm damn thankful I had a chance to say it to you."

My eyebrows drew together. "Why couldn't you say it to Mom?" Last I heard, Mom was living with some truck driver in Montana. If he could find me, surely he could find her.

The wrinkles around his eyes deepened. "You don't know?"

My throat constricted. "Know what?"

"Your mother, she's dead."

37

JONAS

The words hit me one after the other, then I felt their effects on Mara. The slump of her shoulders. The way her hand went from squeezing me tight to completely slack.

"She what?" Mara breathed.

Duncan nodded. "I found her obituary online. Carbon monoxide poisoning. Apparently, their trailer wasn't well ventilated, and they didn't have an alarm."

Mara's free hand wrapped around her middle, and I tried to read her eyes, understand what she was thinking. How she was feeling.

"I'm sorry you didn't know," Duncan said.

Mara shook her head, blinking quickly. "I hardly knew her."

We were all silent for a moment, and then someone by the heavy metal door called, "Just a few minutes left. Time to say your goodbyes."

Mara and Duncan shared a look that I didn't understand.

Duncan reached into his pocket and got out a card. "I know I don't deserve shit from you, and I wouldn't blame you if you wanted me dead, but I'd like a chance to be the kind of dad you deserve. Make up for lost time."

I couldn't believe what he was saying. Couldn't decide whether to be happy for Mara or outraged for her. I'd seen the way he made her feel at the press conference. Watched the way she so closely guarded her heart because of the wounds he'd inflicted before she ever knew she needed protecting.

She took the card from him and stood up. I followed her lead, putting my hand on her lower back, like that simple touch could let her know I'd do anything for her, protect her however I could.

She held up the card for a moment. "I'll think about it."

He gave her a tearful smile. "Thank you."

We walked out of the room together, quiet amongst all the noise of families leaving around us. I gave her space, let her process something I could never even imagine experiencing, especially after such a big day for the two of us.

I held the car door open for her, and she got in, not meeting my eyes. I shut the door and walked to my side. After I got in, I laced my fingers through hers. "I know that was a lot. Whenever you want to talk, I'm ready."

She smiled for half a second, but it didn't reach her eyes. Instead of speaking, she lifted my hand to her lips and kissed my knuckles.

That was good enough for me. I drove back to Emerson, putting in a call for food to be delivered to my house. I told her I'd have Birdie grab some things from her house, and then I took Mara home. To the place where she belonged.

We walked into my clean house and I led her straight to the couch, the part of this home that was definitely hers. I sat with her on my lap and held her as she cried.

It felt like hours, watching her be in pain, before the tears finally subsided. I ran my hand over her hair, wishing I could take all the pain away. But since I couldn't, I said, "Can I run you a bath?" My mom always drew baths for us kids when we were sick, when we'd gone through heartache. I was home from college, admitting to my failed marriage the last time Mom ran the water for me, adding scented Epsom salts and essential oils.

Mara nodded slowly, accepting my offer. I got up, walking down the hall and through my bedroom to the bathroom. I didn't use the soaking tub much, but it was massive and relaxing. I hoped it would be just what she needed.

I ran the water as hot as it would go, dropped some lavender Epson salts inside, and then reached for the candles stored at the top of my linen closet. I'd bought them on a whim, and they'd gone unused for a couple years, but I was glad they were here.

As soon as I lit all the candles and the tub was full, I turned off the lights and went to get Mara. She was where I'd left her on the couch, her shoulders slumped, like she wanted to make herself smaller. As if she were tiny enough, her pain wouldn't be able to find her.

"Hey," I said gently. "The bath's ready."

She looked up at me and slipped her fingers into my offered hand. We walked back to the bathroom and instead of leaving, I said, "Put your arms over your head."

She did as I asked, the candlelight flickering over her skin, and I slipped the shirt over her head. I did the same with her leggings, pulling them to the floor and asking her to step out of them. Then I unclasped her bra, freeing her breasts. I could see her in the mirror. Beautiful. Stoic.

I dipped my hand in the bathwater, which had cooled just enough to be bearable. "It's ready."

She stepped into the tub, settling in slowly, and looked up at me.

"I'll give you some time," I said, ready to go to the living room and wait for her, even though I wished I could just sit here holding her towel, supporting her until she was ready to get out.

"Jonas?" she asked before I reached the door.

"Yeah?"

"Can you... get in with me?"

I smiled gently. "Of course." She watched as I undressed myself, and then I went to the back side of the tub and said, "Scoot forward."

She did as I asked, and the water rose around us as I sat behind her. The tub was so deep the water came to my chest, still several inches from spilling, and I held her to me, hoping the steady pace of my breath would soothe her.

She rested her head back against my shoulder, and I kissed her temple.

"I haven't talked to my mom since I was twelve years old," she said quietly.

I closed my eyes against the pain I felt for her. The pain I heard in her voice.

"I thought about reaching out to her a few times when I ran away, but I was too afraid she'd never want to see me... I couldn't take the rejection twice."

I kissed her temple again. "You were the child. It wasn't your responsibility."

"I know." She ran her fingers through the water. "But I wondered what she would have been like if we'd met as adults. I hardly remember her. I don't remember much of growing up, really."

"That's common, isn't it?" I asked. "With trauma?"

"Yeah." She reached her fingertips up, running wet paths over my arms. "Do you think it was real?"

"Real?" I asked.

"The apology from my dad... did he mean it?"

I leaned my head forward, resting my lips against her shoulder as I thought. "It seemed sincere, but I don't know him like you do."

"I don't know him at all. Not anymore." She let out a heavy sigh. "I've changed so much in fifteen years. Is it crazy of me to think he has too?"

"It's not crazy," I said.

She was quiet for so long I almost wondered if she'd fallen asleep. But then she said, "Jonas?"

"Mm?"

"Thank you. For being there for me today."

"I wouldn't have had it any other way," I said, and it was the truth. Being with Mara felt natural, right. Some reasons I could list and others I didn't completely under-stand. But Dad had said something similar about Mom soon after she came home from the hospital. He said there wasn't one thing that made him love her. He fell in love with her for all the little pieces that made her who she was.

"I've spent my whole life saying that you can choose your family but..." She let out a quiet laugh. "Maybe a little part of me has always wished that my dad could be my hero. It sounds so pathetic when I say it out loud."

I brushed her hair back, kissing her temple again. "It's not pathetic to want your dad to be the man he should have been all along."

"Isn't that the definition of insanity, though, to do the same thing and expect something different?" she returned.

"It's faith. You always have to believe that things can get better or else they never will be."

She turned in my arms, bringing her lips to mine. "I have faith in us, Jonas."

Her breath was warm on my skin, and her words caught my heart. I kissed her back, hoping I could show that I believed in us, too, with everything I had.

38

MARA

Confession: Sometimes... I need someone.

I TURNED in the bathtub to face him and kissed him deeply. I trailed kisses up his neck, over his strong jaw, until his mouth was on mine, and I kissed him hungrily, wanting all he had to give me. Wanting him to take my mind, my body away from all the pain that I felt in every cell.

He put his arms around my wet body, pulling me close. His erection grew, pressing against the soft flesh of my stomach, and I moaned into his kiss. "Jonas, I need you," I said, turning to lean against the edge of the bathtub so he could take me from behind. "Please."

Wordlessly, he pressed his length against my opening and then shoved himself in.

"Rough," I begged.

He wound my hair around his fist, pulling hard as he thrust against me, bathwater splashing over onto his tiled floor. I didn't care. I just held on to the porcelain, letting him ride me, letting the force of my body slamming into the edge of the tub push me higher and higher, further and further from the pain in my heart.

"I'm going to come unless I slow down," he said.

"Come," I replied. I wasn't even close.

He shuddered against me, coming inside of me and slowly pulling out as the waves from our fucking subsided.

"Come here," he said, pulling me against his chest.

I relaxed into him, tears streaming down my cheeks. He kissed the top of my head, saying, "Let's get you out of here."

He stood, water dripping from his body, and helped me out of the bathtub. Just as gentle as he'd been with me before, he toweled me off and helped me into my pajamas. Wordlessly, he walked me to his bed, pulled back the covers, and then tucked me in.

"I'm going to start a show on my tablet, and then I'll get us some food. How does *How to Lose a Guy in Ten Days* and breakfast for dinner sound?"

My crying only grew stronger. "Jonas, why are you being so nice to me? I took you for granted. I slept with someone else."

He sat on the edge of the bed, brushing my wet hair away from my face. "Just because I believe in happily ever afters doesn't mean I think it'll be easy."

"But what if I mess up again?"

"You will," he said matter-of-factly. "It's what we do with the mistakes that matter. You called me back, you apologized, and I know you won't make the same mistake again. It'll be something new we get to work through and build trust on, every time."

I shook my head, smiling at him. "You're amazing, Jonas Moore."

"I'm amazed by you, Mara Taylor," he said sweetly, dropping a kiss on my forehead.

He got his tablet from the nightstand and started playing the show, but I didn't stay awake long enough to have the food he made or even get to see Kate Hudson interact with Matthew McConaughey.

I drifted to sleep, still feeling the imprint of his lips on my forehead and his love on my heart.

♥·♥·♥·♥

I WOKE up in the morning to the smell of bacon. Jonas wasn't in bed or else I would have rolled over to cuddle with him, one-bed trope long forgotten. Instead, I stumbled out of bed and walked toward the kitchen, ready to kiss him and show him how much I appreciated him for all he'd done the night before.

But before I reached the kitchen, I saw my two best friends sitting in the living room. My mouth fell open at the sight of Birdie and Hen sitting on the couch Jonas and I chose together. "What are you two doing here?"

They turned, stopping their conversation and giving me concerned looks.

Birdie got up first, coming to give me a hug. "Jonas told us what happened. I'm so sorry, honey."

I hugged her back, and then when she let go, Hen was ready to take me next.

"We're here for you," she said.

I smiled at the two of them, then glanced toward the kitchen. I could hear Cohen talking now too with Jonas.

"Jonas has been amazing since everything that's happened."

"Fill us in," Birdie said. "All we know is what he told us."

I sat on the couch with my friends and quickly ran over the details, pressing my hand over my heart when I got to the part about finding out my mom had passed. "All these years, there's been a small part of me hoping my mom would come back and find me, be the kind of mom I wished I had. But now that she's gone, it's like that part died too."

My friends surrounded me, reminding me I wasn't alone, and deep down, I knew that would never change.

"You know," Birdie said, "if I were you, we'd be going to the bar right now to drink it all away."

I laughed out loud. She was right. Going to the bar and forgetting my problems had always been her MO. Back when her fiancé left her for another woman, I'd taken her out for drinks. Of course, her ex was an asshat of epic proportions and the bar we went to was Cohen's, so it had all worked out well in the end. "I guess some things do change."

Hen gestured toward the kitchen. "They sure do. How are you feeling about him?" she whispered.

"It feels... different," I admitted. "I've never had a guy take care of me like he does without expecting anything in return."

Birdie nodded. "Jonas really is a great guy."

"I agree," Hen said.

I smiled. "Me too. We're officially boyfriend and girl-friend now."

My friends' mouths fell open, and they quietly squealed so the guys wouldn't overhear us.

"No freaking way!" Birdie whisper-yelled.

Hen shook my shoulder. "I'm so happy for you!"

Jonas and Cohen came out of the kitchen carrying plates full of breakfast food, from chocolate chip pancakes to eggs, bacon, and buttery slices of toast.

"Who's ready for breakfast?" Jonas asked.

My friends piped up their agreement, but I went to Jonas, hugging him tight as soon as he set the plates on the table. "Thank you," I said into his ear. "For thinking to invite them over."

HE HELD ME BACK, his strong arms wrapping around my waist. "I thought you might want some friends around."

I pulled back, smiling at him before kissing him on the lips. I forgot my friends were around as I said, "I love you, Jonas."

He grinned back and said, "I love you too."

We celebrated my first I-love-you with all of our friends and way too much breakfast food. It might not have been happily ever after, but it felt damn close.

39

JONAS

The girls decided to spend the day at the beach, and Cohen had to check in at Collie's, so I went into the office to make up for the work I'd missed the day before. There were countless emails and even a voicemail from Mr. Rusk I'd been avoiding, but I had to face it. And besides, there was plenty left to do.

Since it was tax season, I definitely wasn't the only person in the office. People dressed in jeans and T-shirts filled half the cubicles and all the offices.

If I was being honest, I'd slacked a little these last few weeks, choosing to spend time with Mara instead of extra time at the office, but now that we were on steadier ground, I could recommit to work.

I nodded at a few people as I walked past them and went in my office, closing the door so I could buckle down and focus. Mara had mentioned stargazing later that night, and I'd be damned if I missed out because of work.

The first thing I did was sit down at my chair and call the CEO of SeatonMade, who I'd run out on the day before. It felt like so much longer than one day, but a million things had changed in twenty-four hours.

Mara had confessed to sleeping with another man.

She'd committed to me.

She'd said she loved me.

The client answered the phone, and I said, "Hey, Sarah, it's Jonas Moore from ESR Accounting. I'm so sorry I had to run out yesterday. I had a family emergency."

"Oh, that's totally fine. Mr. Rusk came in and helped finish things up, so we're all good."

"Mr. Rusk?" I said, my stomach sinking. Part of me had been hoping one of my staff accountants would take over and Mr. Rusk wouldn't know at all.

"Yes, he was fabulous. But I do hope everything is okay on your end."

"It is now," I said.

"Good deal. See you again next tax season!"

I smiled. "See you again next year."

Almost as soon as I hung up the phone, a knock sounded on the door. Through the rectangular window, I saw Ernest Stanford Rusk, the man who single-handedly grew this practice to what it was.

I quickly got up, wishing I'd worn more formal clothing, and answered the door. "Mr. Rusk. Great to see you. Thanks for handling that client yesterday, by the way. I really appreciate it."

He was all business, not a hint of a smile on his face. "Can I speak with you?"

My spine straightened, and I tried not to clench my jaw too hard. Those words were just as bad as "we need

to talk" coming from a girlfriend. "Of course. Come in."
I stepped back, letting him walk past me.

Mr. Rusk wasn't a big man, but he commanded a
presence. In fact, my office felt too small to hold him. He
took a seat at my desk, his tailored pants raising just
enough to show plain black dress socks. "Have a seat," he
said. He'd offered me a seat in my own office. Although, I
supposed, technically it was his.

I sat down across from him, waiting for him to speak.

"What happened yesterday?" he asked.

"My girlfriend's been getting stalked by her abusive
father," I said. "Things sort of came to a head yesterday."

"In the middle of a client meeting?" His eyes were
calculating, curious, but not at all concerned.

I sat up straighter, bristling at his dismissal of Mara
and her predicament. "Yes, that's when she called me. I
was worried for her life, Mr. Rusk."

He cleared his throat. "She called you? Shouldn't she
have called 911 if her life was in danger?"

I blinked, not sure where he was going with this. Was
he seriously suggesting my loved ones *shouldn't* call me in
the event of an emergency?

"How long have you been at this, Jonas? Eight years?"

He knew damn well how long I'd been working here.
"Ten," I answered anyway.

"I opened this firm thirty years ago, had worked in
public accounting for seven years before that. I've had
employees go on to work in C-suite level positions at the
Big Four. I've had people move across the country and
start firms of their own. And I've seen people crash and
burn and lose everything they worked for."

I nodded, still watching him, wondering where this was going. Wondering if he was threatening me.

He spun the thick gold ring on his finger. "The successful people? Some of them were smart as a whip. Others, I had to wonder how they got their shoes tied every day. You know, being an accountant isn't all that difficult. You just have to show up. Eight to eight on weekdays, maybe fill in a few hours on the weekends, for a few months out of the year."

I nodded. Anyone who worked in public accounting understood the rigorous schedule. But the benefits were great too—a secure job, good pay, plenty of benefits especially during tax season, and connections with amazing people.

"The ones who failed?" Ernie said. "They had something in common. They quit showing up like they were supposed to."

I held my breath.

He let out a sigh. "It's easier to show up to work when you're single, which you've been for as long as I've known you. It's harder when you have a girl. Even harder when you're married with children."

Without giving me a chance to respond, he stood up and walked toward the door. With his hand on the knob, he said, "I'd hate to see you fail when you're so close to getting what you say you want."

Ernie shut the door behind him, but I stared at it, stunned. Was he really threatening my promotion because of one day? I'd been working at this very firm for years! I never called in sick. Never took an early afternoon. Certainly never walked out on a client. Even when my mom was starting dialysis, I worked remotely from my laptop!

I got up and paced my office, trying to work off some of the indignant anger pumping through all of my veins.

Fuck being chained to my desk. If Mara needed me, she needed me, and that was that.

Accounting wasn't fucking brain surgery. No one's life depended on me sitting in my office day in and day out.

I'd always done my best to stay out of office politics, and like Mr. Rusk said, people had come and gone over the years, leaving when the job was hard on their family, but I never imagined me being one of those people to leave. Not even close. I knew my mom and sister would help out my future wife with our children if I needed late hours, and I was willing to get up early or stay up late to put in some extra time working from home if need be.

But here I was, feeling like my job was on faltering ground.

My pacing wasn't helping, so I got out my phone and called Cohen.

"What's up?" he said, music playing in the background.

"Can we talk?"

"Sure. What's going on?"

I told him about my encounter with my boss, and when I was finished, he let out a big sigh.

"You know those old guys," he said. "They think things are still in the 'good old days' where they could go off to work and come home with the kids in bed and a hot meal on the table. It's not like that anymore. He's retiring soon, right?"

"As soon as he promotes someone to run the place. I

was hoping it would be me, but I don't know if I can do business like that."

"So, hang in there and run it different," Cohen said. "He'll be in Cabo raking in a paycheck and won't give two shits if his employees are being treated like actual human beings."

I nodded. I could do that. Hang in there for just a couple more months until he left and I could run things my own way. "Thanks, Cohen."

"Sure thing."

I was about to hang up when he said, "And, hey, for what it's worth, I think you did the right thing by being there for Mara. It's how you showed her she could trust you. And you both seem happier than you've ever been."

I smiled for the first time since getting off the phone with my client. "I am," I said. I just hoped it could stay that way.

40

MARA

Confession: I write about badass women, but sometimes... I'm worried I'm not one of them.

JONAS STAYED at work until it was almost dark, so I went by the grocery store and picked up a fruit and vegetable tray and then a meat and cheese tray to take with us to the beach.

By the water was my favorite place to be, and I couldn't wait to share it with him. In fact, I almost couldn't believe we hadn't spent time on the sand already. But I was excited for tonight, mostly just to spend some time with him and show him how incredibly thankful I was for him and all he'd done for me the last couple days.

I went by his office to pick him up and looked around the parking lot. I'd figured his car would be the lone one there, but it was almost completely full of vehicles. Were all these people seriously working this late on a Saturday night?

I called his number and said, "Hey, I'm out here."

"Out where?"

"In the parking lot!" I said cheerfully. "Standing by my pickup like some teenage boy in an eighties romance movie."

He chuckled, but it sounded strained. "I need to wrap some things up, but I'll be out there in fifteen?"

I frowned over at the trays of food in my center console, but forced a smile on my face so I'd sound happy on the phone. "Sure thing. I'll see you in a bit."

I got on social media, commenting on as many posts from my readers as I could before Jonas came out. But when I glanced at my clock again, it had already been twenty minutes. I didn't want to be needy, since he was only five minutes late, but it bugged me...

It was past seven on a Saturday night. Was he really that tied to work that he couldn't come to the beach with his new girlfriend?

I took a deep breath, remembering all he'd done for me. Telling myself that I wasn't pathetic to sit here and wait for him. Relationships required compromise, and I'd certainly gotten so much more from him than I could ever give.

I got back to my phone, focusing on social media again. I was so engrossed in it, that when a knock sounded on the passenger door, I jumped.

Jonas smiled at me, and I glanced from him to the clock on my phone. It had been more than thirty minutes.

As soon as I unlocked the door and he got in, he said, "I'm so sorry. I was finishing a return and lost track of time." He leaned across and kissed me.

"Lost track of time?" I said. How could he do that?

"Yeah, don't you ever do that when you're working on a book?"

"I mean, not when my brand-new girlfriend is waiting on me."

He frowned and took my hands. "I'm really sorry." He kissed my cheek, then moved his lips to my ear. "I can think of a way to make it up to you." He flicked his tongue over my earlobe to prove it.

The tickle of his tongue mixed with that sexy promise sent heat to my center. "Fuck, Jonas. No fair."

He chuckled, pulling back, then looked at the grocery bag in the center console. "What's this?"

"Supper," I said, backing out of the parking lot. "I'm not as great of a cook as you, but I'm an excellent shopper."

He laughed. "Anything involving meat and cheese, and I'm in."

I drove away from ESR Accounting, my annoyance quickly melting away. Jonas was fun to spend time with. And I could ignore one flaw, right? Especially knowing I had plenty of my own.

"How was your day today?" Jonas asked.

"You mean before or after a bunch of frat boys made fun of the girls and me for being 'beached whales'?"

He seemed horrified. "They did *what?*"

I rolled my eyes. "It happens sometimes. Apparently 'how not to be an asshole' isn't included in a high school or college curriculum."

He let out a quick laugh, but his eyes were still concerned. "Are you okay?"

"I'm fine." I frowned. "I think Hen took it pretty hard. They were talking about how no one would want to date us. Birdie's married, and I'm with you, but Hen's never really dated anyone."

"Never?" he asked, stunned. "She's beautiful though."

"I know. But her confidence... I just wish she could see how worthy she is. Unfortunately, that's not the kind of thing you can teach someone."

He reached across the console and grazed his fingers over my thigh. "Have I mentioned you're incredible?"

I smiled. "Doesn't hurt to hear it twice."

We drew closer to the beach near Brentwood, and I pulled to a stop in the nearly empty parking lot. They didn't allow bonfires here, so it wasn't as highly trafficked at night like the beach by Seaton Pier. In fact, it almost looked like we'd be the only ones here.

We got out of the pickup, and I reached into the toolbox in the back, pulling out instead of tools, a thick blanket, a throw blanket and a couple of pillows.

"You came prepared," Jonas commented, the grocery bags looped over his fingers.

"Sure did," I replied.

We walked through the thick sand until we got closer to the waves. It was so dark out here, the only source of light the moon reflecting off the water and a few deck lights from the houses behind us.

When I got to a spot that I was sure wouldn't get hit by the tide, I rolled the blanket out and dropped the pillows on top of it, then I sat down, spreading the other blanket over my lap. Nothing cut through you as much as a salty sea breeze.

Jonas sat beside me opening the box of cheese crackers and meat and began making a sandwich for himself. We began eating while listening to the calming sound of the waves. I took in a deep breath, loving the smell of the beach. I really did love it here. Maybe someday I would be able to afford one of the houses behind us, overlooking the water.

But for now, I was in the present, sitting next to a man who'd been so solidly there for me, the last few days especially. I wanted to connect with him, and not just sexually. "So, tell me about work," I said. "What did you do today? Taxes?"

He continued chewing, giving me an annoyed smile.

"I know it sounds bad, but I still don't really understand what accountants do all day," I admitted. "I just give mine my bank statements and let him run with it."

Jonas laughed this time. "You and ninety-nine percent of the population. That's why we get to charge so much."

"So that's the secret," I said.

He nodded. "Work was okay. A little annoyed with my boss, but it's not a big deal."

A guilty feeling spread in my stomach. "Was he mad at you for leaving early?"

"Don't worry about it," he said. Which definitely meant yes, his boss was mad. "Are you having a good time?"

I nodded. Despite the guilty feeling, I was loving being out here with him. "It's different for me. Dating someone who I can actually see a future with."

"What kind of future?" he asked, the limited light dancing in his eyes.

My cheeks grew hot. I so wasn't used to discussing this kind of thing. "You know, the mushy gushy kind?"

He laughed. "Have you named our future children yet?"

I shook my head. "I don't really see myself as a mom," I admitted.

His eyebrows drew together. "What do you mean? You don't think about the future like that?"

I shivered, pulling the blanket more tightly around me. "I mean, being a kid wasn't exactly easy for me, and I wouldn't want to screw up another human being."

He gave me a confused look. "Why would you screw them up?"

I raised my eyebrows in return. Was he being serious? "It's not like I have a million great examples to look to."

"You can always learn though," he said with all the confidence in the world. "There are classes and podcasts, and you know my parents are great."

"I'm supposed to learn how to be my best self with the crying baby on my hip? Can you really picture me with child, listening to podcasts about how to not be a fucked-up human being?" It was laughable if it wasn't so damn sad.

"You're not giving yourself enough credit."

I let out a sigh, sandwiching together more crackers and cheese and meat. "Maybe not, but I've had a lot of time to think about whether I want to be a parent. And I like my life. I like working when I feel like it and going out with friends when I feel like it. I *like* being able to focus on me and becoming the kind of person I could have been if I hadn't grown up the way that I did."

"But what about later?" he asked. "What about when you're older?"

"What about it? It's not fair to put the weight of your retirement on children who didn't ask to be here, and I'm sure there will be friends to make in the nursing home."

He shook his head slowly. "I... I always pictured myself being a father."

He said it so quietly I almost didn't hear him, but the second his words registered, my chest constricted. This was the deal-breaker. The thing that wasn't good enough about me for him. And it made me want to get up and run as far away as I could. Even though the last time I ran was probably in an elementary school gym class. I didn't want to take away from him what he so desperately desired. But I also had to wonder why wasn't I enough? Why weren't we enough? Wasn't love supposed to conquer all?

"Hey," he said gently, lowering his head to meet my eyes. "What are you thinking in there?"

I quickly looked away, bracing myself for the worst. "I'm not going to change my mind about this, Jonas."

"But you changed your mind about relationships. You're dating me," he said. "You told me you loved me."

"I can't imagine changing my mind about putting a whole extra person in my control or even just putting my body through childbirth. I already have mental health issues. What happens when I have PPD so bad I can't get out of bed? And what happens if we are one of those fifty percent of people who divorce? We'll be shuttling a child back and forth who never asked to be here. Your parents would hate me, and I'd really be on my own on top of learning how to be a good parent. It doesn't make sense to me. It's not what I want, even under the best of circumstances. That's why I got an IUD that lasts seven years, and when the seven years is over, I'm probably just going to go with an even more permanent option."

"More permanent than seven years?"

"I want to get my tubes tied," I said.

He blinked, stunned. I hated that he looked that way, like he couldn't see where I was coming from. All he said was, "You're right. It's probably too soon to talk about this." He put the lid back on the meat and cheese tray and scooted closer to me.

But I scooted away. I could feel our relationship slipping away before it even began.

"Mara," he said, looking hurt. "I didn't mean to upset you."

"You did," I replied.

"Can't we move past it? We've only been official for a day."

"It doesn't matter. I now know that for us to continue our relationship, one of us isn't getting what we want."

We were quiet for a long moment as the waves continued lapping over the shore, oblivious to the nerves and the pain racing through my heart.

"Maybe it's for the best," he said.

I turned to him. "For the best?"

"Well, part of my conversation with my boss today was him telling me that if I'm going to become partner, I need to stay dedicated to the firm. If I had a family, I couldn't do that."

"Why would he say something like that?" Indignation spread through me for him. Why would an employer say something like to Jonas? It should be illegal.

"Because I left yesterday. I put you first, and he didn't like that."

Guilt rocked through me. I had threatened Jonas's promotion and upset his future in a matter of minutes. "I'm having a hard time right now," I admitted.

He shook his head. "You didn't do anything wrong."

"No, I am," I said. "I don't want to be the person who takes you away from your dreams."

His eyes connected with mine, taking me in. "What if *you* are my dream?"

41

JONAS

Mara and I had sex that night, but it didn't feel right like it had before. It was like there was a wedge between us. A baby-sized bomb that would go off if we got too close. I felt dumb for bringing it up. Because really, she was right. We'd only been together for a short period of time, but in a lot of ways it felt like I had known her so much longer, and I wasn't the kind of guy to mess around. When I was ready to jump, I was ready to jump.

But I couldn't keep thinking about that. Because any time I pictured a future without Mara, it was wrong. But the idea of giving up the kind of family I'd grown up with… that didn't feel great either.

So I tried to keep my mind off it by going into the office on Sunday while Mara spent the day reading and writing. Monday morning, I got up to go to work, Mara got up to help Mom with her dialysis, and we gave each other a chaste kiss goodbye.

The entire time she was at Mom's, I wondered what they were talking about. If my mom had somehow convinced her that having children wasn't the scary thing she thought it was. Or if Mom would be upset because I knew she wanted to be a grandma someday.

Around eleven, Mom texted me and asked if I could come over to the house for lunch. Dread immediately took over as I imagined being chastised in front of Mara.

I said sure but reminded her I couldn't stay too long because Mr. Rusk definitely had his eyes on me, whether they were his or someone else's. So at lunch, I got into my car and drove to the house.

When I arrived, I noticed Tess's car was in the driveway too. My stomach sank. The last time Mom had us all over on a weekday was her telling us she was going into kidney failure, and that no matter how many times we offered, she would not be accepting a kidney from Tess or me.

My body was stiff as I walked into the house, bracing for the worst, but when I walked through the door, everyone greeted me, smiling. If something was wrong, no one had been told yet.

Mom held up a bag from Flanagans. "Got your favorite," she said, "a Reuben with extra sauerkraut."

Mara laughed. "Can't wait to kiss you later."

My family cracked up, but I couldn't find it in myself to laugh. I just wanted her to hold me and tell me I hadn't messed everything up. I sat at the table with the rest of my family as the food was divvied up. Despite the amicable conversation, I felt in my gut like something was going on, but no one was saying anything.

"I'm dying over here," I said. "Why are we here?"

Mom smiled across the table at my sister. "Tess just

said she wanted some time with our family before the wedding planning got too busy."

I looked to Tess for confirmation, but she wasn't meeting my eyes. Instead, she and Derek were exchanging glances.

"Well," she said, "that's not exactly true."

Derek nodded. "We have some news for you."

My mouth fell open. "You're breaking up?" I knew wedding planning could be stressful, but the way they met was stressful. "Are you sure you can't work it out?"

Tess and Derek laughed.

Mom got out of her seat and screamed, "YOU'RE PREGNANT!"

My mouth fell open as I looked between Tess and Derek to see who had guessed correctly.

Tess had a sour look. "How could you tell? I'm only eight weeks along!"

Mom said, "You've been moody on the phone, you didn't come over for breakfast on Saturday because you didn't feel well, and I can totally tell your boobs are bigger."

Derek laughed at her assessment. "We just found out last week and had our eight-week sonogram."

Tess reached into her purse hanging over the back of her chair and pulled out a black-and-white picture of something that almost looked like a little bean. My jaw dropped. That little bean was my niece or nephew.

"Oh my gosh, Tess, that's amazing!" I said, getting up to go hug them. Tess had been waiting for this her whole life. "You're going to be amazing parents."

Dad wiped his eyes. "I'm going to be a grandpa?"

Tess nodded, tearing up herself. "The best grandpa in the world."

I glanced next to me and saw the forced smile on Mara's face. Underneath the veneer, I knew what she was thinking. She was thinking back to her childhood when she was a little baby not being taken care of the way she deserved. And she was thinking of me and wondering if the kind of life she would give me would be enough.

To be honest, I was too.

"This calls for champagne," Mom said. She got up and walked toward the kitchen, and Dad said, "Do we even have some?"

"Of course." She got on her hands and knees and pulled a dusty bottle from the cupboard. Dust billowed as she blew on it. "I always keep one on hand for exciting news." She came back into the dining area and gave Mara and me a look. "I figured I'd be using it on you two, but this is just as good."

She set the bottle on the table, then grabbed a massive butcher knife from the drawers. After ripping off the gold foil, she swung the knife forcefully at the cork. A loud pop sounded as the cork flew across the room and hit the wall, sending Oaklynn skittering after it.

Mara laughed. "Best party trick ever."

Tess and Derek laughed, and Mom poured champagne into coffee mugs for everyone since they weren't big drinkers and didn't have champagne glasses. They just did their best when there was a special occasion.

I drained the liquid after toasting with everyone in reach. Tess, of course, drank her lemonade from Flanagans, which still might have been better than the room-temperature fizz the rest of us were downing.

My phone went off, and I noticed it was a call from one of my staff accountants. I silenced the call. He could wait an hour for me to have lunch with my family.

But as soon as that call ended, a new call started, this time from Mr. Rusk himself. I swore under my breath. "I've got to take this," I said. "Sorry. My boss has been riding my ass lately."

"Go ahead," Mom said.

I stepped outside, leaving everyone chattering behind me as I answered the call. "Mr. Rusk."

"Another 'emergency'?" he asked brusquely.

"Lunch break. I do believe we're allowed to eat."

"That's how employees think. They take all their free time and use it to the hilt. Bosses stick around, eat at their desks, make themselves available for the people who need them."

"I had a family thing," I explained. "My sister just announced that she's pregnant."

"And Jenkins's daughter has a dance recital. They're filming it; he'll catch it later."

I ground my teeth. How had I never noticed what an ass Mr. Rusk was before? Or was he just upset with me now that I actually had a life? It wasn't like I was skimping out on my work. It was all getting done.

"Can I be honest with you?" he said.

You haven't been? was my first thought. "Of course," I said instead.

"I've always been partial to you over Jenkins. You're a little younger, but you've always put work first. I'd hate to see it all slip away come crunch time."

"I won't let you down," I said. He was right. I'd worked too damn hard the last ten years to let it slip through my fingers now. Especially when I knew I could manage people with more humanity than Mr. Rusk ever had or Jenkins ever would.

"Glad to hear it." He hung up, and I went back inside. I gave Tess and Derek a big hug, congratulating them again, and then said goodbye to Mom and Dad, promising to see them again later in the week.

Mara stood and said, "I'll walk you outside."

We went to the door together, but she didn't say a word. She walked beside me, quietly trailing the toes of her sandals over the sidewalk.

"That was work?" she said.

"Yeah."

She twisted her mouth to the side. "Exciting news, becoming an uncle."

"Yeah, I'm really happy for them." We reached my car and stopped by the driver's side door. I knew I should be getting to work, but I couldn't leave her when she was looking so completely defeated despite her best efforts to be happy for me.

"Are you sure this is what you want?" she asked. "Me? Will I be enough?" She looked to the ground for a moment, then braved looking me in the eyes.

"I'm not going to lie to you, Mara. I have always wanted a family. I always thought I would have children." Her eyes fell to the ground again, but I cupped her cheek, drawing her gaze back to me. "But it was more of a thing I thought I *should* do. I liked my life growing up so much that I wanted to live like my parents. But it doesn't *have* to be that way. I can try something new."

"Try?" She stepped away from me, leaving me to slowly lower my hand by my side. "But what if you regret it? I don't want to get ten, twenty years down the road and have you resent me because you didn't get what you wanted out of life."

I stepped forward again, put my hands on each side of her face, looking into her deep brown eyes. "I'm thirty-two years old, Mara. If I wanted a family as much as I thought I did, I probably would have done it by now."

"What if..." She bit her lip, her eyes glazing with tears. "What if you haven't met the right person yet?"

The way she said it fucking tore me in two. "Mara, you are the right person. You're kind and funny and you go after what you want and you hold boundaries like no one else I've ever met, but you also forgive. I admire the hell out of you, and I know you make me a better person."

"But a child—"

"I can't give up on an incredible woman, on an incredible relationship, for a child I've never met. What if it's an asshole?"

She finally cracked a smile. "You know it won't be. Any child of yours would be amazing."

I brushed her hair back behind her ear, hoping she would see that I thought she was incredible. "Sometimes we don't get what we want; we get what we need. And I needed you before I ever knew it."

Her lips trembled. "I needed you, Jonas. I never wanted to rely on anyone, but fuck, the thought of losing you? It's eating me alive."

"Don't let it." I kissed her deeply. "I love you, and I'm not going anywhere."

"Then neither am I."

42

MARA

Confession: Life is perfect... almost.

THE NEXT COUPLE months were a whirlwind of writing, editing, heading to the Moores' house to help Mariah with dialysis, and Jonas staying plenty busy with tax season. He would get up and leave for the office at seven and be home at eight or nine at night. He said he was getting closer and closer to his promotion, and I wanted that for him, more than anything, I wanted him to have what he wanted.

At night, we would sometimes make love and sometimes we would just pass time together, watching movies, joking about the tropes that he was now learning to recognize. On Fridays, I drove to LA and spent half an hour with my dad. Sometimes we talked about his treatment. He asked me about my career, and I asked him what he was planning to do when he was released from rehab in another month's time. We weren't close—would never be—but my anger was subsiding. I was learning that he was a person who hadn't faced his demons until he'd been forced to. But at least he was now. At least I didn't have an ache for a person he could never be. I was coming to accept him as he was, dropping my forbidden hopes, and becoming more satisfied with life overall.

On the weekend afternoons when Jonas wasn't working, we went out to eat with his parents or helped Tess and Derek with wedding (and now baby) preparation. Spending time with my friends and laying out on the beach fit somewhere in between.

Charlotte was having me go on more and more podcasts, plenty of talking points in hand to make sure I didn't have another fiasco like the one before, and I was getting better and better all the time. It was all going great, really, which surprised no one more than me.

To top it off, my movie was less than a month away, and I could not wait to sit in those velvety red chairs and see my name come on the screen with the line *based on a book by Mara Taylor.*

I'd been putting off dress shopping until closer to the premiere, but today was the day; I could feel it. Henrietta, Birdie, and I all had the day off. Jonas and Cohen were working. And now if I wore the dress every day until the premier I wouldn't completely ruin it.

The three of us met at Vestido, a dress store in Emerson Shoppes. They had some of the best dresses, and I wanted to shop local for the movie premiere. Since my friends were coming with me to the premiere, they had to be red-carpet ready as well.

We sat in the corner of the shop around an empty podium, drinking glasses of cheap champagne while a saleswoman mingled through their admittedly smaller plus-size section. She said she was confident she'd find a great fit for all of us. I hoped she was right.

"Are you getting so excited?" Henrietta asked.

"I am," I said with a smile. "It's almost like my life is so perfect I can't believe it. Well... mostly perfect."

Birdie's lips pursed. "What do you mean? Is everything okay with Jonas?"

"He's great." I set down my empty champagne glass and spread my hands over my lap. "It's just something he said, and I haven't been able to get it out of my head."

Henrietta leaned forward, setting her glass down too. "You two look so happy together. What's going on?"

I let out a sigh. "He mentioned a while back that he's always seen himself as becoming a father someday, and I told him I'm not going to give him that. He says he's okay with it now and that he's happy with it just being the two of us, but I keep worrying that it won't be enough." I turned to Birdie. "How did you and Cohen come to the decision not to have children?"

She tilted her head to the side, studying me for a moment. "It was a little easier for us since Cohen already had Ollie. So we do have a child. Technically, I know he is not mine. I have to share him. But I also feel like my calling in life is to be a guidance counselor and to work with those kids. And sometimes when you have children of your own, it's hard to give them everything they need while working in a service role. I know it can be done, but I'd rather give all I have to hundreds of kids through the years."

"Was Cohen okay with that?" I asked.

She nodded. "He was open to having another baby

with me, but starting over after sixteen years wasn't exactly something that was calling his name."

I nodded slowly.

Birdie said, "It's probably different for Jonas since he's a good ten years younger than Cohen, and he hasn't had that fatherhood experience yet."

I hadn't meant for this day to be all about me and my worries, but now I felt like I was about to cry. "So much of my life is perfect, but how can I accept my happiness when it came at the cost of someone I loved?"

Henrietta drew her eyebrows together. "Am I missing something? Did he say that being child-free was a deal-breaker?"

"No, he said that he couldn't give me up for a child he didn't know. But I don't want him to resent me down the road, you know?"

Birdie nodded. "I could see why you'd be afraid of that, but that's *his* decision. If he decides to stay with you, he knows what the cost is going to be."

"But why does it have to be *his* cost?" I asked. "Why does he have to be the one to sacrifice all the time? I feel like I'm taking so much away from him. He could have had this perfect girl like Tracey who has nice parents and is best friends with his sister and probably wants to have a dozen kids, and here he is with me and all of my trauma and my alcoholic dad in rehab." I let out a mix between a sob and laugh. Because if I didn't laugh, I would break down at the unfairness of it all. I loved Jonas, but all I had to give him was me. "I want better for him."

"But he gets to choose that," Henrietta said. "He gets to choose what he wants for himself. And it sounds like he's choosing you."

The saleswoman came back with armfuls of gowns made from all different materials. "I have a few for you gals to try on. I can't wait to see how you look in them!"

I stood up ready to move on from this conversation. "Let's go try them on," I said with a smile.

Birdie gave me a concerned look, but I shook my head. "This is a happy time," I said. "The first and last time we'll ever be able to shop for my first movie deal."

Henrietta put an arm around me. "Well then we better enjoy it."

43

JONAS

I shut my computer down at eight and cleaned off my desk. It was a habit I learned from a mentor back in my first internship. Clearing your desk was like clearing away all the problems from your day and giving yourself a fresh start.

I shrugged on my suit jacket, turned off the light, and locked my office door before nearly walking into Mr. Rusk.

"Sorry about that," I said, straightening my lapels. "How are you doing?"

"Great. Mind if I walk you out?" he said.

"Not at all." My nerves were already on edge. We hadn't spoken much since Tess announced her pregnancy, so I assumed that meant I hadn't fucked anything up in his eyes, but I already felt guilty.

The office was nearly empty as we made our way past the cubicles and toward the front entrance.

"I've been noticing you doubling down on your hours, Jonas. Our clients are happy, and that makes me happy."

"Thank you, sir," I said, grateful for the acknowledgement. I really had been breaking my back, wanting more than ever to take over. Before, work had been all about a stable income, providing for a family, but now I knew if I got into a leadership role, I could truly change the lives of people here at the firm.

We reached the door to the parking lot, and he paused. "I like where your priorities are." He smiled, deepening all the lines on his face. "If you keep this up for the next month and a half, I see great things happening for you. Better wear your best to our end-of-season party. People are going to be looking at you."

He held the door open, and I walked into the darkening parking lot, grinning. I was so close to this promotion; I could taste it.

I waved goodbye and got into my car to meet Cohen and Dad at a tux fitting for Mara's movie premiere. This was a big deal for her, and it was exciting to know we'd be spending the night with her, watching alongside the dozens of people who'd worked on the film.

A quick drive later and I pulled into the parking lot and parked next to Dad's old truck. Through the big front windows, I could see him and Cohen already inside, standing by the front counter. The bell rang over the door as I walked in, and they turned to greet me.

Dad put his hand on my shoulder. "I never thought I'd be fitted for so many suits in such a short amount of time," he said. "First Tess's wedding and then this premiere... I didn't even wear a tux to my own wedding."

I chuckled. Dad was definitely a jeans-and-work-shirt kind of guy, not into anything fancy.

A sales guy dressed in a suit came up to the desk and said, "We're ready. Follow me, gents."

Cohen nudged my elbow, mouthing, *Gents.*

I smiled at him, glad he was along for this too. Even though Mara didn't have blood family she was close to, it felt like he was her family just as much as he was my friend, him and Birdie and Henrietta. And I had better get used to it since we weren't going to make a family in the traditional way.

The sales guy (his name tag said Jarrette) had us sit on some chairs around a podium while he went to get the tailor. They were modern chairs without backs, and Dad cringed as he sat down.

I worried about him. How his body would hold up in his line of labor. It made me want to make more money to take the pressure off of him and Mom that much more. They'd given me and Tess the best life a kid could ask for—I owed them that much.

Cohen said, "How are you and Mara doing? I know you've been busy with tax season, but I haven't heard much from you since the big disagreement you told me about a couple months back."

"What disagreement?" Dad asked. "You better be treating our girl right."

Cohen laughed. "They've already got a new favorite."

Dad didn't deny it. "What happened, son?"

I gave him the abbreviated version. "We were talking about kids, and she said she doesn't want to have any. I tried to tell her she'd be a great mom, but..." I let out a sigh.

Dad sucked in a breath through his teeth. "How'd that go over?"

"Like a lead balloon," I replied. "I don't know. I always pictured myself having kids."

Dad and Cohen nodded, listening.

"But Mara, you know how she grew up. She said she doesn't want any children she could possibly mess up."

Dad frowned. "Mara would be an amazing mother. I can already tell by the way she takes care of your mom."

Cohen shook his head, explaining, "It's not about that. When you grow up like she did, you spend your whole life knowing that the worst-case scenario could come true."

Dad and I exchanged a glance. We just didn't understand. Not in the same way Mara and Cohen did. Sometimes, I felt jealous of how Cohen inherently understood her. But I knew I wouldn't trade my upbringing for his. Not in a million years.

"Is that something you could get past?" Dad asked. "That's a pretty permanent decision, not having kids."

"It's a pretty permanent decision to break up with Mara for kids I don't even know I can have," I said, looking across the room at all the suits. The thought of making a decision that would change my entire life was scary, but not having Mara in my life, that seemed just as outrageous. Each day with her got better than the last. She was always having fun, working toward something, talking about characters that existed only in her mind and on the pages of her books. I loved my life with her and knew I would love it more when I wasn't so busy with work.

Dad thought for a moment, then put his hand on my shoulder. "Every time we say yes to something, we're saying no to something else. If you're saying yes to her, make sure you're okay with the no as well."

The tailor approached, holding a floppy pink measuring tape. "Let's get you gents set up for this premiere!"

44

MARA

Confession: Mariah is the mom I always wanted.

MY HANDS WERE SHAKING SO MUCH I couldn't even apply my mascara. "Help please," I said to no one specific.

Henrietta took over, holding the brush and telling me when to blink. She and Birdie had come over to Jonas's to get ready for the premiere. The guys were all hanging out at Jonas's parents', watching some baseball game. They'd probably put their suits on five minutes before it was time to leave and be just fine. No fair.

"I'm sorry," I said. "I'm just so damn nervous! What if everyone hates the movie?"

Birdie shook her head at me in the mirror. "No one's going to hate it... unless they're stupid. It's an amazing book, and the movie is just as good."

I couldn't tell. I'd only seen clips from the trailer. Which, yeah, looked good, but that didn't keep me from panicking. I'd seen plenty of good trailers that turned out to be shitty movies.

Henrietta capped the mascara and said, "Honey, you're nervous. It's totally normal. Millions of people are about to watch something you inspired—I'd be worried if you *weren't* nervous."

That actually calmed me down a little bit. But maybe I wasn't worried about millions of people. "What if Jonas doesn't like it?"

Henrietta laughed out loud. "That boy thinks you hung the moon and every star."

I smiled. It was crazy to think I'd gone from the occasional hookup with random guys to a committed relationship, all in six months. "He's amazing. I can't wait for tax season to be over so we can spend more time together."

Birdie nodded. "I totally get it. Cohen and I have all these fun plans for the summer. We're going to fly to Mexico again where we had our honeymoon, and this time Ollie is coming and he's even bringing his new boyfriend!"

"Ollie has a new boyfriend?" I asked, excited. His last boyfriend had been a real dick. And I know it's not okay to talk about kids like that, but still. He was a dick.

Birdie grinned. "Technically Ollie has a they/them-friend. They met at this horticultural convention in Santa Monica and totally hit it off. They're the cutest kid."

"That's amazing," Henrietta said. "I love how supportive you both are of him. My parents would have blown a gasket if I dated a girl, let alone someone in transition."

"There's no other way to be. It's either love and

accept him or lose our kid," Birdie said. "Loving's always the better choice."

I smiled. "You sound like a character in one of my romance novels."

"Obviously, you write brilliant characters," Birdie teased.

I knew she'd said the compliment offhandedly, but it touched my heart. Soon, thousands of people would be getting to know my characters too. My eyes were already tearing, and I grabbed a tissue to help dab at the corners. "I should have worn waterproof mascara today."

"Aw, honey, why are you crying?" Henrietta asked.

I looked between her and Birdie, reaching for their hands. They slipped their fingers through mine, and I squeezed. "This is just such a big dream for me, and I can't tell you how much it means to me that you're here to experience it with me."

Birdie hugged me. "Remember when you were waiting tables at that dive bar and you saved up singles to pay for a used Apple computer? That's when I knew you were going to be big someday. You've always done whatever it took to succeed."

I'd almost forgotten that. It felt like eons ago. "Life is so different now."

Henrietta nodded. "I've only known you two for a year and a half, but it feels like forever. You're the best friends a girl could ask for."

The lump in my throat grew even larger, and I waved my hand at my watering eyes. "Okay, we have to stop." I let out a laugh. "I don't want to be a blubbering mess in front of all those famous people."

Birdie took my hand, pulling me to stand. "All smiles from here on out."

Henrietta nodded. "All you need is your dress."

We went from Jonas's big bathroom to the guest room, where I was hiding my dress in the closet. Jonas still hadn't seen it, and I couldn't wait to see the way he would react to me wearing it.

I pulled it from the tan garment bag and stared at the shimmery fabric. I could already picture the way the gold sequins would catch the lights of the paparazzi and how chic I'd look next to Jonas in his neat black tux.

The girls got their own garment bags from the closet, and we all began slipping into our gowns, helping each other zip the backs and tuck the hanger straps in. Soon, we were all in our red-carpet attire, staring at each other.

I covered my mouth with my hands. "I know I said no more crying, but..."

"But this is a whole damn moment," Henrietta said, staring at herself in the full-length mirror affixed to the back of the door. She drew her thick bronze leg out the slit of her aqua-green dress, obviously admiring the look.

"That dress was made for you," I said.

Birdie hugged her from behind, her own bright yellow dress with a poufy skirt flaring around Henrietta. "You're gorgeous, Hen."

I nodded in agreement. "We all are."

Birdie held both of our hands. "Are we ready to go pick up the guys?"

I nodded. We finished packing our clutch bags with the essentials and walked out the front door, down the sidewalk and toward the waiting limo like the queens we were.

The driver opened the door to let us in, and as soon as we were settled, I reached into the fridge, grabbed a bottle of champagne, and popped the cork. "No need to wait for the guys when we can start the party now." I poured them each a glass and passed them to Birdie.

Birdie smiled, taking the drinks from me and passing one to Hen. "It's too bad Jonas's mom isn't coming. I thought she really loved your books."

"She does," I said, frowning, "but she didn't want the headlines the day after the premiere to be about how she looks. I just wish she knew I don't care about things like that. I'd love to have her with us."

They nodded solemnly. Each one of us knew what it looked like to hide our bodies from the world and to face judgement in a way not many did. It wasn't the same as having scars from a fire, but it wasn't exactly the opposite either.

A short drive later, the limo stopped in the Moores' driveway. I peered out the tinted window, wanting to catch a glimpse of the guys stepping out of the house.

Jonas's dad looked so suave in his suit. I almost didn't recognize him outside of his work clothes. And Jonas was a handsome, younger version of his father. He looked damn good in that tux, but that was no surprise. I already knew he would look amazing.

Cohen looked debonair too, his graying hair contrasting his black suit perfectly. But then someone walked out the door behind them.

I covered my mouth with my hand, seeing Mariah in a cream-colored, long-sleeved dress. "Oh my gosh," I breathed. She was coming. She was facing her fears. And she was going to be there for me.

Tears streamed down my cheeks, and I got out of the limo, running to her. "You look beautiful, Riah," I breathed, taking her in up-close.

She smiled and looked down, color staining her cheeks. "I couldn't miss your big day."

45

JONAS

I'd never seen Mara look more beautiful than she did when she was hugging my mom. The love in her eyes for the woman who raised me did things to my heart I'd never felt before.

When she and Mom parted, she smiled at me, tears in her eyes matching my own. I kissed her deeply and pulled back just enough to whisper against her lips, "I love you, Mara Taylor."

I felt her smile against my mouth. "I love you, Jonas Moore."

I hugged her tight, then pulled back to take her in. The dress she wore was perfection on her. It dipped low, showing her sexy cleavage, and the material caught all the light, illuminating her face. "You look absolutely stunning."

"Thank you." She smiled, fluttering her lashes in the most adorable way. "You don't look so bad yourself."

"I specifically requested a red-carpet look," I said. I didn't tell her that I'd done a considerable amount of googling, not wanting to embarrass her during the moment she'd been working toward her entire life.

"It's very suave," she replied.

I laced my fingers through hers and followed my family into the limo. As soon as we were settled, she cuddled close to me, still holding my hand. It was sheer perfection, only made better by the glasses of champagne Birdie was filling and passing around.

Dad's voice cut through all the noise, and he said, "I think it's time we have a toast for Miss Mara."

Cohen put a champagne glass in my hand, and I held it up, waiting for Dad's toast.

His eyes crinkled as he smiled at the woman I loved. "Mara, when we met you six months ago, we knew you were special, but we had no idea how important you'd become to our family. I've watched you care for my wife with all the love she deserves. I've watched you push my son to open up and be the man he was made to be. And I've watched you bravely step beyond your past and move into your future. I can't wait to see the movie you inspired, but mostly, I can't wait to see what you do after. All signs point to something incredible."

"Cheers," I said emphatically, matching all our friends.

Mara wiped fruitlessly at the tears streaming down her cheeks. "I have a toast for you too." She sniffled, trying to regain composure.

We all quieted, waiting for her to speak.

Her chest rose and fell with a deep breath. "When I ran away from home at sixteen years old, I thought I was leaving my family behind... I just didn't know that I hadn't found my true family yet." Mara sniffed again, her face full of pain, and I put my hand on her lap to soothe her. She covered my hand with her free one and smiled. "I'm so thankful for every one of you in this limo, and I'm so damn lucky to call you my family."

Everyone cheered and drank, but I kissed Mara's cheek. "We're damn lucky to have you, babe."

She smiled, then placed a kiss on my lips full of love and passion and a promise of what was to come tonight.

Soon the driver lowered the window between the front and back seats and said, "We're almost there. Are you ready?"

We all looked to Mara to respond. She took a deep breath and answered, "I am."

Out the windows, we could see the busy LA streets and extremely crowded sidewalks. It soon became obvious where all the commotion was coming from. There was a red carpet lined with photographers and fans.

The limo slowed until we were right in front of it. "Mara's up first," the driver said. "The rest of you give her a good fifteen feet and then follow."

"Sounds great," she replied. She took my hand and scooted closer to the door.

"Are you sure?" I asked. "I don't want to take up all your pictures."

She placed her hand gently on my cheek. "I want to celebrate with the person I love most at my side."

My chest swelled, and I kissed her deeply. "We'll all be watching you shine."

The limo stopped, and soon the driver was opening the door and Mara and I were stepping out into a completely different world than any I was used to.

Cameras flashed all around us. People yelling, "Is that

Mara?" And then another one saying, "That's the author of the book!"

They shouted questions at her and shoved microphones in her face with such force I didn't know how she stayed standing. She responded with grace and ease like she was always meant to be here.

"Mara," one of the paparazzi called. "Are you excited to see your book in this movie?"

She smiled, easily replying, "It's been a lifelong dream," and continued walking with me.

We didn't make it two feet before someone else asked, "Things still going well with your beau?"

She replied, "He's more than that." She smiled at me, her eyes holding so much love and light. "He's the love of my life."

I couldn't help the dopey grin I wore after that. And I could only imagine the number of photos and tabloids that would have my goofy face next to Mara's beautiful one, front and center.

Charlotte and Jenny stood at the end of the red carpet, and Charlotte took Mara's hand, leading both of us to a big canvas with the title of the movie printed on it in repeating patterns with the studio logo.

"Stand here for some photos," Charlotte said. We were posed over and over again. The both of us, then Mara and Jenny, then Mara and Charlotte, then Mara with the director and members of the cast.

It was amazing watching her shine, seeing her interact so easily with all these successful and influential people. She was in her element and having the time of her life, and I was just lucky to be along for the ride.

I glanced around, wondering where our friends and

family had gone. We hadn't really discussed our game plan or meeting place, so I got out my phone and saw a text from Birdie.

Birdie: We're waiting inside.

Jonas: Perfect. We'll come in when Mara's done with pictures.

A few minutes later, my eyes were stinging from all the camera flashes, but Mara took my arm.

"How was that?" I asked.

She shook her head, still grinning. "My cheeks hurt from smiling so much."

I laughed. "Better get used to it. I'm pretty sure you're going to have the most ripped cheeks by the end of the night."

She laughed. "Well, at least one part of me will be ripped."

We walked inside through the revolving doors, and there was a line for concessions being paraded up an escalator to a movie theater. There were signs everywhere for the premiere, posters with the actors' pictures or shots of the book cover.

Birdie called out to us, already holding armfuls of popcorn containers. We took a couple from her to lighten the load and went up the escalator with our friends. We gave our tickets to security at the door and went to a long row of seats reserved for Mara.

She sat between Birdie and me, holding my hand with one of hers and her buttery popcorn in the other.

Mom sat on the other side of me, both of her hands holding tightly onto her own popcorn. I could tell how happy she was but also how nervous by the pinch to her lips. Being here was a huge deal for my mom. For Mara and me. Not only had she gone out in public, but to be around so many people and so many cameras... My mom really thought Mara was special. And so did I.

I leaned over to Mara and whispered in her ear. "Am I going to have to do the whole yawn and stretch thing, or will you let me put my arm around you?"

She gave me a wicked smile. "I was already planning on making out like teenagers."

I laughed, giving her a deep kiss.

The loud sound of the credits starting over the speaker system quickly broke us apart.

Mara's eyes went wide as she looked at the screen. "They're playing the movie. They're playing *my* movie."

And then her name appeared on the screen.

46

MARA

Confession: This is the best day of my life.

Based on the book written by Mara Taylor.

I STARED at the words on the screen, tears forming in my eyes. This had been a lifelong dream, and here I was, watching it come true.

Everyone had told me when I was younger that I wouldn't amount to anything. They'd said that dropping out of high school would be the end of my life, that I'd be a single mom by the age of eighteen, living in a trailer house. (As if that was anything to be ashamed of.)

But they were wrong. Here I was, living the life of my dreams, having the career of my dreams, loving the guy of my dreams—without a high school degree. Without the support of my parents.

I had done it on my own.

I had gotten here.

314 OF MY LIFE.

I had reached my dreams.

My name was gone as soon as it appeared, but I sat enraptured by the movie, seeing the characters interact so flawlessly with each other, listening to the score as if the songs had been written specifically for the story.

As a writer, usually I put my book into the world, and I never really got to see or hear from readers until they were done with it, if they chose to reach out at all. But now, watching everyone respond in the moment, was incredible. At every good moment, Birdie would squeeze my hand. And at the sad moments, I looked around and saw people with their eyes wide, completely engaging with the characters. It was more, better, than I ever imagined it could be. Of course, some things had been changed from the book, but that didn't matter. It was a process. My work was growing, taking on a life of its own, becoming something completely outside of myself. And the fact that so many people would be able to take part in it was beautiful. And I got to experience the story that I've written in a completely new way.

I laughed with the other people in the audience. I cried quietly with them, and I squeezed Jonas's hand when a particularly loving part happened on screen. The characters were getting their own happily ever after, and I was letting myself have the same. *Finally.*

As the end credits rolled over the screen and my name appeared again, Jonas and Birdie ushered me to my feet, and everyone clapped. I would remember this moment, this feeling of creating something so tangible, for the rest of my life.

I couldn't wait to see what this had done for my book sales. The movie had been done so perfectly, it couldn't be a flop. It would be the perfect movie to eat ice cream to before Jonas and I fell asleep.

When the credits went blank and the blooper reels had finished, everyone in the theater began shuffling out. And as soon as we had some time, my friends and family were hugging me and telling me how amazing the film was. Charlotte even pulled me aside and told me that we had several interviews scheduled for the next week to help promote the movie and its sequel.

Down in the atrium, Mariah and Cade both gave me a big hug. Cade said, "I'm proud of you, kid."

Then Mariah hugged me tight. "I'm so happy for you, Mara. Tonight was a fairytale."

"I know it was because my fairy godmother came," I said with a smile. "You are the most beautiful woman I know, Riah. I mean it."

She wiped at her eyes. "I love you, honey."

She held my hand for a moment before leaving. They took a cab to stay at a hotel for the night, and the rest of us got into the limo to ride to the after-party.

It was at this kitschy club not too far away from the theater. I couldn't help but wonder how many people had stood in the same spot, and I was now a part of the building's history. I didn't have much time to reflect though, because the after-party was a huge whirlwind of being pulled between different people, getting introduced to actors and writers and producers and change makers I'd never in my entire life imagined I would be hanging out with. And then Charlotte said, "I have someone you *have* to meet."

"Who is it?" I asked. I'd already met actors I'd only fantasized about on screen. Plus, I wanted a chance to catch my breath. To dance with Jonas and thank him for being by my side through it all.

A twinkle gleamed in Charlotte's eyes. "It's a surprise."

I excused myself from Jonas and the rest of my friends and went with Charlotte to see an attractive guy standing by the bar. Even from behind, I could tell he was *rich*, with the cut of his suit to the shimmering watch on his wrist.

But when Charlotte walked up to him and said, "Hello," my mouth went slack.

"Mara," she said, "I'd like for you to meet Bradley Mason."

My eyes were wide as I looked between him and Charlotte. "Bradley Mason. The famous showrunner Bradley Mason. The guy who created *Buy Me Chocolate Not Love* and Book Club Conquest. That Bradley Mason?" I knew I was being a fangirl, but I couldn't help myself. I *was* a fangirl.

He smiled easily, showing off bright white teeth and dimples through his carefully trimmed scruff. "That would be me."

"I'm a huge fan," I blurted, as though that weren't incredibly obvious by my embarrassing read of his resume.

He took a drink of his scotch on the rocks, and the ice tinkled against the glass. "I have to say I'm a fan of your work as well. Do me the honor of having a drink with me?"

"If you want me to die and go to heaven," I replied.

Bradley grinned over at Charlotte. "Is she always this charming?"

"Absolutely," Charlotte said with a grin.

Bradley held up his hand, easily commanding the busy bartender's attention. He sized me up. "You look like a martini girl. Dirty."

And damn if I didn't blush. "That's right."

Soon the three of us were sipping from drinks, and Charlotte said, "Bradley actually came to me with an interesting opportunity for you."

My lips parted. Just meeting him was opportunity enough. I looked to him, wondering what could possibly be better than this?

He smiled and said, "I actually have a show coming out late next year, and we are set to begin working on the story next week. There is a plus-sized main character, and I don't yet have anyone on my writing team that can handle it quite like you did in *Swipe Right*."

My brain short-circuited. "I didn't write the script for the movie. I mean, I looked over it, but that genius wasn't mine."

"I meant the book."

My eyes widened. "You read *Swipe Right*?"

"Of course I did. It was sexy and funny and incredibly powerful. Just like what I'm trying to accomplish with this show."

"How strong was that vodka?" I asked, staring at my drink. "You really want *me* to help you write your TV show?"

He nodded.

"Me, with no GED and raunchy sex in my books?"

He chuckled again, saying to Charlotte, "She's adorable."

"Absolutely," Charlotte said.

He continued, taking my hands in his. "I think you'd be an *excellent* fit."

I nodded enthusiastically. "Yes."

"You haven't heard the terms yet," he replied.

"Yes."

He laughed. "We can go over numbers more formally on Monday, but it looks something like $30k an episode. We have twelve episodes planned for the first season and hopefully plenty more after that."

Dollar signs flashed in my eyes.

"Now, it is being filmed in Atlanta, but I can arrange a temporary apartment for you each season."

My mouth was completely on the floor. "Yes! I accept. Yes!"

He smiled. "You're in? Just like that?"

I said, "Absolutely. Writing TV has been a dream of mine forever."

"And there's no one for you to talk it over with? A boyfriend perhaps?" I could see the flirtatious smile on his lips.

"This is not an opportunity I'm going to miss," I said. Jonas would understand. In fact, I couldn't wait to tell him and see how happy he was for me.

"Great," he said. "Charlotte gave me your contact information. We'll be in touch." He took a sip of his scotch. "If you'll excuse me, I see someone I need to make an appearance with."

I nodded and said goodbye. And then I made sure I was out of earshot before I started screaming.

47

JONAS

Mara and Charlotte ran up to us, squealing with excitement.

I laughed. "What happened? Did you meet Channing Tatum? I think I saw him around somewhere."

"Better!" she cried, hugging me and then reaching for Birdie's hand. "I got invited to write for a TV show with BRADLEY MASON!"

Birdie squealed just like Mara was. "WHAT?!"

Who was Bradley Mason? I wondered. Clearly Birdie knew, though, and it was a *big* deal.

Mara nodded, bouncing up and down on her feet. "Storyboarding starts next week in Atlanta. He said he'd have an apartment for me and everything. And they're paying me $30,000 AN EPISODE! Can you believe that? I made less than that a YEAR when I was a waitress."

My heart had stopped working. Mara was moving to Atlanta in a week?

"I'm going to miss you, but that's incredible!" Birdie said.

"Yeah," Cohen agreed. "Congratulations! Just don't forget about the little people when you go."

I had a feeling she already had.

Mara turned to me, expecting me to be excited for her. I could see it on her face. But forcing a smile for her was the hardest thing I'd ever had to do. "Congratulations."

A worried look crossed her face. Clearly, I hadn't been that convincing. "What's wrong?" she asked. "I thought you'd be happy for me."

Suddenly, everyone was staring at us, and I felt like I'd been shoved into a fishbowl without any gills to breathe the limited water.

"I need some air," I said. "Come outside with me?"

A crease formed between her eyebrows, but she nodded and followed me toward the stairs that led to a rooftop terrace. It was full of people, but we found a spot at a standing table near the corner. From here, we could see glittering city lights and a twenty-foot drop to the dirty streets below.

I couldn't help but feel like my heart was teetering between the beautiful expanse of happily ever after with Mara and getting run over by a trash truck and smashed to pieces on the ground.

"What's going on?" Mara asked. "I thought you'd be happy for me."

"I didn't even know that there was anything to be happy for aside from the movie until two minutes ago," I said. "I think I'm a little caught off guard. What's going on?"

She shook her head as if annoyed. "Charlotte just took

me aside and introduced me to Bradley Mason, you know, as in the showrunner for half of the shows that we watch before bed, and he invited me to write on a new TV show that he's doing. They haven't even named it yet. But if it's Bradley Mason, I know it's going to be amazing."

"And you've committed to it?" I asked. How had she made such a life-altering plan in a matter of minutes, without even consulting me?

"Of course I did! Why would I want to turn that down?"

I shook my head, trying not to feel betrayed or left behind. "I just figured that it would at least be a conversation between the two of us before you decided to up and move across the country for nine months!"

"A conversation about what?" Mara asked. "About me doing something completely incredible and amazing? Tonight, seeing my book turned into a movie, it was better than anything I've experienced in my life. Why wouldn't I want to chase that feeling with a television show?"

Pain edged its way through my chest, making it hard to breathe. "You didn't think about us?" I asked. I knew it sounded needy and whiny and pathetic, but I couldn't help asking the question. I almost blew a promotion I'd worked toward for years to support her in her time of need, and now she was going to move across the country without so much as a second thought of how it would affect me?

Mara shook her head. "Jonas, if I'm making that kind of money, I can fly back every weekend if I want to. I can fly you to come and visit me. And it's not like I'll be in

Atlanta full time for the rest of my life. Honestly, I don't see why this is such a big deal."

"A big deal?" I asked. "We fall asleep together every night, and now you're telling me that I'm supposed to *maybe* see you on the weekends? And what about Tess's wedding coming up? Are you going to miss that?"

All her features were pinched as if she thought I was being insane, which only made me more frustrated.

"You know I wouldn't miss that," she said. "But I don't know *why* you're trying to guilt me about this. You've been working *insane* hours lately. I hardly ever see you at night before you go to bed, and then when you do, you're obviously tired from the day, so all we do is watch a little TV and go to bed. Are you saying it's okay for you to do and not for me?"

I shook my head. She wasn't understanding this at all. "Tax season is *temporary*, Mara. It's a few months out of the year. You're talking about a television series where you're going to be gone for nine months at a time! The show could go on for years if it does well!"

A few people were looking at us now. Mara kept her voice low, talking just loud enough for me to hear her over the music. "Jonas, it's just nine months. You're borrowing trouble."

"If Bradley Mason is as amazing as you say he is, you know damn well anything he touches is going to be out for at least six seasons."

"Okay... so we make it work. We can do video calls and phone calls and letters like old times."

I shook my head. Why hadn't she thought this through? "What about my mom? She's just going to go back to doing dialysis in a public place until she dies or gets a kidney?"

"*Jonas*," she said harshly. "Don't even talk about me like I would just write her off. I'll be making $30,000 *an episode*. I think I can afford to have someone come and give your mom dialysis."

"But it won't be you. You know how she is about strangers." I was grasping at straws, but I knew Mom would miss her just as much as I would.

"Strangers only stay strangers for so long," she said.

"Is there a contract?" I asked. "Anything other than just some rich guy talking to you in a club?"

She raised her eyebrows. "So you're jealous?"

"No, that's not it," I said, flustered, frustrated, everything in between.

"Then what is it?" she snapped. "Because, honestly, Jonas, I got the best news for my career that I've gotten since finding out I had a movie deal, and you've said nothing positive about it. I would expect more from someone who *says* he loves me."

I took a deep breath, closing my eyes. "Mara, of course I'm happy for you."

She shook her head, tears sliding down her cheeks. "It doesn't feel like it."

"What am I supposed to do?" I asked. "Jump up and down that you're going to be away from me for the unforeseeable future? I had to practically beg you to commit to me, even as a girlfriend, and now you're just going to run off for some show in a new town with a new guy? Are you that eager to be away from me?"

"It's not about you!" she yelled, now ignoring the people staring. "Why are you making it about you?"

"No, it's about us," I said. "It's about you finding any chance you can to run away from something real. If *we* mattered so much, if—if an *us* mattered, you would have thought about it. You would have hesitated for a second at least, but you just came over so thrilled at the chance of leaving me." God, I felt like shit now. The best thing in my life was leaving, and I didn't know what it would mean long term.

"It's not at the chance of leaving you. It's a chance of chasing a dream."

"A dream I didn't even know you had," I said. "I thought you were just happy writing novels."

Her lips trembled. "And raising kids. Right?" She shook her head and looked away before drawing her eyes back to me. "That's what this is about, right?" She didn't even give me time to answer before saying, "I don't want the kind of life that you want to have, and now you're punishing me for it."

"That's not it at all. I—"

"This is *exactly* why I didn't want a relationship. I didn't want someone who would be holding me back."

The venom in her voice, her words, her posture, it felt worse than a punch to the gut. "I don't want to hold you back either," I said. She was quiet for a moment, and I swallowed down the lump in my throat. "If that's what you think I'm doing, then maybe we shouldn't be doing this."

Her lips parted, fear shooting through her eyes. "You're breaking up with me?"

It was the last damn thing I wanted. But the girl in front of me.... this was supposed to be the best night of her life and I was ruining it. And she was right. I didn't want her to go to Georgia. How selfish could I be? So I said the words I needed to say. "If all I'm doing is holding you back, then I don't see a reason for you to be with me."

She shook her head, picked up the hem of her dress, and ran away from me, and I realized I'd known all along where this thing with Mara would end. I just hadn't realized how soon.

48

MARA

Confession: Maybe I didn't believe in happily ever after. But I sure as hell believed in heartbreak.

TEARS STREAMED DOWN my cheeks as I ran downstairs, toward the place in the club where I'd left Birdie and Cohen. Instead of lounging around the sides and talking like we'd all been doing earlier, the two of them were dancing together, so lost in each other the rest of the world had clearly faded away.

The sight of two people being in the kind of love I so desperately wanted to have with Jonas ripped me apart. I couldn't interrupt them, couldn't add more drama, so I left. I walked out the front doors to the curb where several cabs were waiting and got in one.

"Can you take me to Emerson?" I asked the driver.

"That's an hour away," he replied, looking at me like I was insane. "It'd be hundreds of dollars."

"I know," I said. "I don't care how much it is."

He nodded, pushing the button to start the meter, and then drove away from the club. I looked out the window at the rooftop terrace. I could see people dancing, talking, so small from down here. But I couldn't see Jonas. I couldn't see the man who'd promised me a future I could never take part in.

Tears streamed down my cheeks as we drove away from LA. Away from what should have been the best night of my life. Away from the man I loved.

The truth was, I hadn't hesitated when I'd made the decision to go to Atlanta. I'd been so confident in us, no matter how far apart we were, that I thought it would be okay. I'd expected him to pick me up and spin me around and brag to have a girl-friend who was writing for a TV show with Bradley Mason. I'd had more faith in our relationship than he had.

Instead of celebrating with me, he'd been disappointed. Upset even, that I hadn't talked to him before accepting something I should obviously say yes to. And maybe he was right. Maybe I should have consulted with him. But to what end?

I was taking this job opportunity, no matter what anyone said.

Did that make me selfish?

Did that make me unfit for a relationship?

Probably.

I'd lived so much of my life alone that I didn't even know how to factor people in when it came to big things like this. And if I'd had kids in school, what would I do? Pull them so I could write for TV? Drag a baby along with me to the writers' room?

This was exactly why I hadn't wanted a serious relationship. Exactly why I didn't want children.

I'd been so wrong to think I could have been anyone different than this exact version of myself. And now it wasn't just me who would be getting hurt. Jonas was hurt. His parents would be hurt.

Mariah. I nearly choked on a sob. I promised myself I'd find the perfect person to do dialysis with her. I wanted her to feel comfortable and loved by anyone who walked into their home, especially with all she'd done for me. Mariah had been more of a mom to me in the last several months than my own mom had in years. She'd healed me in ways she'd never understand.

And Tess and Derek.

A fresh wave of tears came at the realization that I'd miss their wedding.

She was going to be such a beautiful bride.

But that was the life I was made for. The life I'd inherited from my parents and generational cycles of trauma and abuse. People didn't stay in my world. They left, which was exactly what I was doing.

The sun was beginning to rise out the window, and I said, "Take me to the beach?"

"Sure," he said. He pulled over to adjust his map and then started again. Within minutes, we were pulling up to the parking lot at the beach near Brentwood Marina. Even if Jonas and I had broken up on the rooftop, this is really where it all started falling apart. This is where I knew we wanted different things, and I couldn't be the girl he wanted. The woman he deserved.

I got out of the car, giving the driver what cash was left in my clutch for a tip, and walked toward the water.

Something about the ocean felt like home. It was always there. The waves never stopped, never went away.

I hit the sand and slipped out of my heels, holding the straps in the crook of my fingers. Then I walked over the cool sand that hadn't yet been warmed by the sun, sitting as close to the water as I could without getting my dress wet.

The orange rays coming from the sunrise hit my dress, lighting me up despite the darkness of my world.

I stared at the horizon, thinking about all I had lost. The things I had been crazy to think I could count on, when really there was only one: myself, and I was right here for me.

I watched the sunrise, trying desperately to convince myself that I was enough. Because once upon a time, I had been, until Jonas turned my world upside down and showed me how incredible it could be to be half of a pair with him instead of a whole on my own.

I loved him with all my heart, but that didn't mean happily ever after was waiting for us. And if it hurt this much to love him for six months, how much would it hurt after a year? A decade?

Maybe I didn't believe in happily ever after. But I sure as hell believed in heartbreak.

I could feel it, and it took all I had to hold myself together and hope a better future was waiting for me in Atlanta than the one I was leaving behind.

With the weak morning sun rising behind the horizon and people beginning to jog along the beach, I realized how crazy I must look in my evening gown and makeup streaming down my face. I reached into my gold clutch and retrieved my phone, turning it on. It had been off since before the movie, and now it was full of notifications from Jonas and Birdie and Henrietta and even Cohen.

I ignored them and called a ride share to drive me the couple miles home. But when the driver stopped along the curb at my house, I saw Jonas's car in the driveway.

49

JONAS

After trying and failing to find Mara at the club, I enlisted the help of Cohen, Birdie, and Henrietta, because I didn't know what else to do. I told them about our conversation and admitted that I fucked up, but even with their help, we couldn't find Mara.

So, we took the limo back to Birdie and Cohen's, and I stayed at their place, hoping that Mara would come by to see Birdie and then I could sort it all out. When it was clear she wasn't doing that, I just went to her house.

All the lights were off, and my mind immediately went to the worst thought. She had found someone else. I had driven her into someone else's arms.

But I stayed, I waited, determined to apologize. To undo the mess I had made. Around seven, I saw a car pulling up, and I prayed to God that it wouldn't be another guy riding with her. Another guy taking her home to take away the pain I'd given her.

Leaning against the outside of my car, I watched it pull to a stop. There was a guy in the driver's seat, but thank fuck there was also a sticker saying he drove for a rideshare company. I let out a deep breath, but the relief only lasted so long.

She got out of the car, still wearing her dress from the night before. It shimmered in the morning light, but the curls in her hair had fallen, and the makeup that had looked so perfect earlier formed dark streaks down her face. She looked miserable, and I nearly doubled over with pain, realizing that I had caused it. I messed up worse than I ever had, and I wanted to tell her how sorry I was. I wanted to do everything over again and tell her exactly how excited I was for her. I just hoped it wasn't too late.

She stopped a few feet away from me, letting her skirt fall from her fingers and trail over the cement. "What are you doing here?" she asked, not quite meeting my eyes.

I shook my head remorsefully. "I came to say how sorry I am. What I did earlier was not okay. And I need you to know that." The words kept coming fast because I felt like Mara could run away at any moment, and I wanted—*needed*—to get it all out. "I know that writing and stories are a huge part of who you are and a huge part of how you made it through everything you've been through, and the fact that I was anything but supportive was a huge slap in the face to you. Especially after you've been so supportive with me working all these extra hours at the firm." I swallowed hard. "I want a do-over, Mara. I want you to come to me and tell me that Bradley Mason wants you to write on a show. And I want to pick you up and spin you in a circle and tell you how proud I am to be your man and how much you're going to kill it in the writers' room. And it doesn't matter that you've never written for a TV show before, because I know you're going to step in there and you're going to be amazing, because you understand people and you see things in a way that no one else does. And I think that's what TV needs. I think that's what made your movie so amazing. And I wish I could go back and punch myself in the face for thinking anything else and for being selfish, because the truth was I was going to miss you and I didn't want to miss you."

Her eyes were still on the ground, and I somehow found it in me to stop talking, although I could have stayed there all day and all night to convince her how sorry I really was.

She slowly looked up at me, her eyes red from crying. Her lips trembled, and my heart broke. I felt the words before she ever said them out loud.

"It's too late," she said.

"Too late for what?" I asked anyway.

She shook her head. "Jonas, I've been crying on the beach for hours, the day after my movie premiere."

I closed my eyes against the pain and regret washing over every inch of my body. "It was a mistake, Mara. A snap judgement after a long day. I *promise* it will not happen again."

Her expression didn't change. Didn't soften. "I can't do this. I can't be the girl who cries about what a guy thinks of her on the most successful night of her life. I can't be the girl who turns down an opportunity like this or even thinks twice about something so incredible." She took a deep breath. "I'm not going to have children, Jonas. My books, the movie, the television show... that is my legacy that I get to leave to every girl who's ever felt the way I've felt."

I looked at her, met her eyes, silently begging for her to say something else, to change what I knew would happen.

"And I love you so much, that for a moment there, when I was on the beach, I thought maybe I should just cancel this Atlanta thing and be together." She chewed on her lip, tears streaming down her cheeks again. "I'll always love you, Jonas, always love your family for all that they've done for me, but I *have* to love myself more. Because there's never been anyone in my life who put me first. I have to do that for myself."

My stomach churned with regret, because she was right. I'd had a chance to put her first. And I hadn't. I had put my own selfish wants above her dreams. And if this is what she was saying she wanted, if this career was what she wanted and she thought that I could get in the way, then I had to let her go. I had to respect what she wanted. What she'd told me from the very beginning. I had been selfish, arrogant to think that she could want anything else than what she told me right up front.

"I'm so sorry," I said, my voice shaking. "I'll never be able to tell you how much."

She looked me in the eyes, breaking down every last part of me, and said, "Me too."

50

MARA

Confession: I walked away from the love of my life.

I WALKED INSIDE, tears hot on my eyes, and closed the door behind me.

I'd just walked away from the love of my life; I could feel it.

But I couldn't go back. Couldn't live a life I wasn't meant for.

I had dedicated my entire adult life to creating stories, and that's what they were. Fiction. And no matter how much I wished my own life story could end with a neatly wrapped bow in the form of an HEA, this was real life. It didn't work like that—not where I was concerned. And certainly not in the way it looked in the movies.

In real life, love required sacrifice, and there were some sacrifices I wasn't willing to make. So I let him go, no matter how much it fucking hurt. My version of happily ever after was making something of my life after the hand I'd been dealt, showing other women that no matter what hell life had put them through, they could always reach for their dreams.

Writing, creating, that was my dream. And I'd soon have a ticket to Atlanta to do just that.

In my living room that felt much less like home than Jonas's did, I slipped out of my dress and walked to my bedroom, peeling off the sticky backless bra I'd worn to the premiere and then slipped out of my thong as well.

I stepped into the shower, rinsing the lingering sand and salt from my body, then got out, twisting my hair up in a messy bun. In my room, I flipped through my closet, seeing only leggings and big T-shirts, a couple dresses, and one pair of jeans that probably didn't fit anymore.

I needed to better than this. I couldn't dress like a slouch in front of professional writers. And okay, maybe I needed a distraction, so I decided to go shopping.

I grabbed my purse and left the house, going to the closest department store that actually carried my size. It had been forever since I'd worn something that didn't have a stretchy waist, so I grabbed a heap of jeans and brought them to the dressing room to discover what size I actually wore.

In the fluorescent light, surrounded by four gray walls, I realized how much of a mess I looked. There were dark, puffy circles under my eyes. I hadn't brushed my hair, so my bun was particularly tangled and askew. But more than that, the perpetual smile was missing from my lips. There was no light in my face.

I'd left it with Jonas when I walked away.

I turned away from the mirror. This version of me

would fade, like all the skins I'd shed to become the woman I was today.

I finally found my size—or the closest thing to it—and emotionlessly noted the digits. Twenty-four, although that would probably change brand to brand. I waited for the old shame about my size to come back, but it didn't. I was actually okay with myself, okay with my body that had carried me this far.

I hung all the pairs back up so the attendant wouldn't have to do it and went in search of business-casual clothing, loading my cart with jeans and skirts and tops that would go with them. Each one I found was a little boost of endorphins, dulling the sharp edge of my loss for a moment or two before I moved on to the next.

I even got a few dress shoes (mostly flats) that were cute and comfortable enough to go with the clothes, and hell, while I was at it, I got a few necklaces and a cute hardback rolling bag for the plane too.

The person at the register looked at my cart in shock and then got to checking. She didn't even ask me if I found everything I came for (which is a silly question anyway, if you ask me). Six hundred and ninety-seven dollars later, I was back in my truck, driving toward my house, wishing I could stop at Jonas's instead.

I spent the day cleaning, packing, tearing tags off new clothes and running them through the washer before adding them to the bag.

My heart hurt the entire time.

But it broke when I stopped.

So I didn't stop.

Not until the doorbell rang.

338 HELLO FAKE BOYFRIEND

I went to it, halfway fearing Jonas had sent something by delivery. It was his move, the way he showed he cared.

But instead of a delivery person, it was Birdie and Henrietta holding a bottle of Cupcake wine and a gallon of gourmet ice cream.

Birdie took me in her arms, hugging me tight. "Jonas told me what happened."

Henrietta wrapped her arms around the both of us. "He thought you might need your family."

This was it, I realized. His last delivery. Because even though he believed in forever, that didn't mean he believed in forever with me.

My friends and I sat in my living room, eating ice cream and drinking wine from oversized glasses Birdie had gotten me as a joke for one of my birthdays. It wasn't a joke right now, though. This size felt appropriate for what I was going through.

Birdie held up her own glass, swirling around the pink moscato. "If this would have happened a year ago, we'd be at the bar, drinking shots of something a lot harder than this."

"*This* wouldn't have happened a year ago," I replied. I never would have let someone close enough to hurt me, much less break my heart.

Hen nodded. "I knew it would take a special guy to make you fall in love, but I never saw Jonas coming."

"Me neither," I agreed. A year ago, it would have taken a literal Viking with muscled thighs, a sexy armored skirt, and a powerful weapon to have even close to a chance at becoming more than a casual hookup. Maybe that's why Jonas was able to get under my skin. I'd never expected an accountant in a suit to be the one to sweep me off my feet. But he had, with his quiet confidence, unassuming tenderness, and generosity.

I set my glass down and shoved a spoon into my melting bowl of ice cream. "This sucks."

"Mhmm," Hen agreed.

"And I'm so stressed about leaving Mariah. I'd pay for someone to come to their house for dialysis, but I have no idea who would do it..."

Birdie and Henrietta both looked deep in thought.

Hen said, "Don't Jonas or Tess have friends who work from home or something?"

That would be the dream. Someone Mariah already knew and trusted... Someone who made their living online, perhaps as a virtual assistant. "Let me text Tess real quick."

Mara: Hey, I'm going to be out of town for a few months for work, but I want to make sure your mom is covered while I'm gone... Do you think we could pay Tracey to stay with her?

I let out a breath, and we were all quiet as we waited a few minutes for her to reply. Either way, I knew the answer would break my heart. One way, we'd have to keep searching for the perfect fit. Another way, I'd be leading Jonas right into another woman's arms.

Jonas had asked Tracey out before me. She'd told me herself she wished she'd given him a chance. What if me leaving was the thing that finally brought them together? Could I live with myself if it was? If it wasn't?

Tess: Tracey's in. She said she'd do it for free. She offered as a backup a couple weeks after you started.

My mouth dropped right along with my heart.

"What?" Hen asked.

I flipped the screen, and they both came closer to read the words.

"What?!" Birdie cried. "They could have had someone else handle it this entire time and Jonas had you doing it?"

My eyes were feeling hot with tears again. "Why would he do that?"

Birdie shook her head in confusion.

"Maybe because he thought you would be the best," Hen said.

I wiped at my eyes. "Joke's on him."

Hen tilted her head sympathetically, and Birdie sat on the arm of my chair to rub my back. As she made slow circles with her hand, she said, "He loved you. That wasn't fake."

"It would be easier if it was," I said. "Then I wouldn't feel like such a villain for being myself."

Henrietta opened her mouth to argue, but my text tone went off again, and we all huddled around my phone to see what Tess had said.

Tess: How long are you going to be out of town? Tracey wants to know how long she should pencil it in.

Mara: Nine months.

Tess: That's so long!!! Why nine months?

Mara: I got a deal to write for a TV show!

It was good news, even if it didn't totally feel like it.

Tess: !!! That's so exciting! Congratulations! Make sure you take time off for the wedding. ;)

Mara: Thanks, girl. <3

Looking over my shoulder, Birdie said, "Nine months? Have you gotten any other details?"

I nodded, swallowing my bite of ice cream. "My

agent called me today, and we went over the contract. My flight leaves tomorrow morning, and I meet the other writers on Tuesday."

Hen said, "I had no idea it took that long to write a show. Do you think you'll rent out your house here while you're gone? You could make some good money."

"I don't think the initial script takes nine months, but we have to be there during filming to weigh in on the script and how things play out. I haven't even thought of renting my place..." I wondered how much else I hadn't thought of. For the first time, I was feeling overwhelmed.

I'd be making enough money that I wouldn't need to rent out the house, but I didn't like the idea of it sitting empty either.

"No pressure," Hen said. "I just know someone who might be interested."

I raised my eyebrows. "Please say it's you?"

She laughed. "Still saving for my own house and it doesn't get much better than free. The promotion should help speed things up though."

Birdie and I both gave Hen a surprised look. "What?" Birdie asked. "You got a promotion?"

Henrietta looked a little bashful. "They asked me to manage the build for the new apartments! I get a raise and a year of free rent on a two-bedroom in the new building!"

My smile grew wide—I knew how long she'd been wanting this. "Hen, that's amazing!" I stood up with my giant wine glass. "We have to celebrate!"

She gave me a look. "It's okay. You have your own thing going on."

"Which means I get to do what I want," I retorted.

"Hear, hear," Birdie said.

I grinned, pulling Henrietta up. "To us."

Henrietta clinked her glass to mine. "To us."

Birdie followed suit and said, "To us. Best friends forever."

My smile faltered, but only for a second, as I clinked my glass to hers.

I drank deeply, finishing the rest of my wine, and for the first time, I wondered if having only friends, if missing out on lasting, lifetime love, was enough.

51

JONAS

I spent the day at the office, throwing myself into the only thing that I could think of to distract me, because when I'd gone home, all I saw was Mara. Everything there reminded me of her after months of her practically living with me.

It still had most of her touches, like how she put her cups away with the tops down instead of up. All the towels were folded a certain way because of her time as a maid. Even the pantry had her favorite snacks, carefully clipped at the top for maximum freshness. Her favorite fleece blanket was over the reading chair, and her bobby pins were on the vanity.

Unlike the last time she'd left me, this time had been unplanned and completely my fault. There wasn't time for her to pack her things or erase every last trace of herself from my life, and there would be no replacing her from my heart.

So, I stayed busy. When my eyes began crossing from

staring at balance sheets for too long, I got out my phone and called Tess.

"Hey!" she chirped into the phone, her happiness a stark contrast to my misery. "How was the premiere? Mom and Dad said the movie was amazing."

"The movie was really good," I said, not ready to lie to my sister, but also not ready to tell her the truth. "Hey, I was wondering if you could be there for Mom's dialysis on Monday?"

"Mara already texted me..." She paused for a moment. "Didn't she tell you?"

"Oh, I'm at the office. I haven't checked my texts in a while." Lie. Half a lie, at least.

"Work?" I could hear the frown in Tess's voice. "It's a Sunday! You should be spending time with your girl! She's about to go out of town for months!"

I couldn't even find it in me to smile at her teasing tone. I should have been spending time with Mara, but I'd ruined it. There was no going back. "So it's taken care of?"

"Tracey's going to start doing Mom's dialysis with her, at least until Mara comes back."

My eyes felt hot as I blinked. Mara had made sure my mom was taken care of, before she even left. "I'll talk to you soon," I said over the lump in my throat. "Love you." Before she could ask any more questions, I hung up. My family loved Mara too, and I wasn't anywhere near ready to tell them how colossally I'd messed up with the best woman I'd ever met.

I refocused on work for the next few hours until Birdie's name came across my screen. I answered, desperate to have her tell me that Mara had come around, that she would forgive me and give me another chance. Instead, I heard sadness in her voice. "Hey, Jonas. Is it okay if I swing by your house to get some of Mara's things? Her agent called and said that the job starts in Atlanta on Tuesday, so she has a flight tomorrow that she needs to pack for."

It was like one punch after another, directly in the gut. Mara's stuff was leaving my house. She was leaving Emerson tomorrow. "When are you getting her things?" I asked.

She was quiet for a moment. "Tonight if that's okay."

It wasn't. "There's a key under the planter by the door. Be sure to grab her bag of Cheetos from the pantry. I don't need those."

"I will," she promised. After a quiet moment, she asked, "How are you holding up?"

"Hanging in there."

She sounded skeptical. "Are you hanging in there?"

"By a thread," I replied. "How is she?"

"Exactly the same."

We hung up, and I stayed at the office well past midnight so I could be sure Birdie had taken everything of Mara's from my house. And when I walked in, I was prepared this time. Every trace with her things had been removed except for the cups. And the towels.

I tore through the cupboards, flipping them over as fast as I could, as if I could rid myself of the guilt, of her memory. I mussed up the towels, leaving them in haphazard piles that she never would have approved of.

And then I changed into my pajamas, wanting nothing more than to fall into an oblivious, heavy sleep without dreams of the woman I'd loved and lost.

But as soon as I lay in my bed, I could smell her on the sheets. I couldn't fucking handle it. Couldn't face the *constant* reminder of how badly I messed up. So I worked the sheets off the bed, threw them in the washer, and then went to the guest room, lying in that bed with sheets that still smelled like detergent.

But that only reminded me of the first night when I'd set it all up because I was so turned on by her I couldn't control myself. And then I thought about sleeping on the couch, but I couldn't do that either because we all knew that was Mara's place.

I wished I hadn't sold the first couch. It may have been uncomfortable, but not as uncomfortable as this visual reminder of all the ways Mara had changed my life. Or the way I was wrecked by her absence.

52

MARA

Confession: If Jonas couldn't convince me to stay, his parents could.

I COULDN'T LEAVE for Atlanta without saying goodbye to Mariah and Cade. I wasn't sure what Jonas had told them about my departure or our breakup, but that didn't really matter. Over the last months, I'd come to love and care for them. My relationship, or lack thereof, with Jonas wouldn't change that.

So I got up early enough to make it there before Tracey arrived. And this time, I took my truck. I was tired of the lies, of covering up who I truly was. I felt just as much shame for that as anything else.

Hayden's place passed out my window as I drew closer to the Moores' house. My time spent with him felt like so long ago... almost like it had happened to another person in another life. Maybe it had. I felt like a different woman than the one who had lain next to him for comfort, for fun.

I parked in front of the Moores' house, and a fresh wave of pain came over me. I loved these people with all I had.

Cade's truck was still in the driveway, and I could see them moving about the living room through the big picture window. They were so sweet together, the perfect complements to each other. Cade was strong and steady while Mariah was deep and feeling. I'd miss their example of once-in-a-lifetime love.

I turned off Bertha and walked toward the front door, taking deep breaths despite the aching in my chest.

I wasn't sure what Jonas had told them or how I'd handle it. I was better at talking on paper, but I crossed my fingers and knocked on the door.

Cade answered it, welcoming me with one of those big, warm smiles I'd miss like hell. "Mara! I'm so happy I caught you. Do you want some breakfast with us?"

Breakfast. I almost collapsed into a puddle right there. "Actually, I needed to talk to you two..."

His face fell, and I could see Mariah walking toward us with a worried look.

"Come inside," she said. "What's going on? Jonas told us you weren't feeling well."

Cade let me pass, and I walked into their living room, not sitting. Just standing there trying to memorize every tiny detail of the home, from the original hardwood floors to the stacks of books to all the pictures on the wall and Oaklynn's permanent indentation on the couch.

"I..." I took a deep breath, which only made them look more concerned. "I got a job writing for a TV show in Atlanta. I'll be gone for at least nine months."

The wrinkles in Cade's forehead deepened. "Nine months?"

I nodded.

Mariah was quiet, her eyes drifting out the window as they so often did. Then her eyebrows drew together, and she looked closer at their driveway. "What is that truck doing here? It's always parked at that Hayden boy's place."

"That's part of why I needed to talk to you," I said, looking between them despite every cell in my body telling me to run and leave the pain in the past like I had so many times before.

Mariah studied me, looking confused. "What's going on, Mara?"

"Jonas and I didn't start dating out of love or attraction. My career was slipping through my fingertips, and being the good son he is.... he agreed to save my reputation if I helped you with dialysis here."

They didn't have the surprise I expected, and when I looked to them for an explanation, Mariah said, "It was obvious, honey, when you had that news interview. But we've seen the love you two have for each other grow over these last few months." She took my hand in hers. "It doesn't matter to us how it started, only that you and Jonas are happy."

I shook my head, stepping away from Mariah's touch. From her comfort. This was so much harder than I thought it would be. I didn't want to see the love in their eyes fade away. But I had to. They had to know the truth before I left, and I had to stop hiding behind the lies. "I'm not the good girl you think I am. I slept around, with Hayden a lot, and Jonas had me buy a new car to drive here so you wouldn't know that was me. But it's time to stop pretending that I'm the kind of person who can make a long-term relationship work. I never have before."

A tear slipped over the tight skin on Mariah's cheek. "You're leaving him because of old mistakes? I know that's not you anymore. I know *you*."

Cade wrapped his arm around her shoulder, saying, "We all have a past, Mara. That doesn't take away from who you are now."

I couldn't let them comfort me, couldn't let them say one more word that would convince me to stay. "Your son, he's the most incredible man, and he deserves someone so much better than me. Someone who can give him babies and a life like the one you two have." My throat got tight. "It's so beautiful. And I wish—more than anything I wish I could be the person to give that to him. But it's just not me, and I can't keep pretending to be something I'm not. It's hurting all of us."

Mariah and I were both crying, and even Cade's eyes were red.

"I wish you'd stay," he said.

I shook my head. "If I were to ever get married, you would be exactly the in-laws I'd want. If I were to have dream parents, you would be them." But my dad was an alcoholic in state-mandated rehab, my mom was dead, and I was... me. An equal split of them both, who lived more in the pages of a book than I ever had in real life.

I reached for Mariah's hands, and she held mine tight. "I'm sorry, for everything. And I hope you know I'll never stop loving you. I'll always appreciate the time we had."

Mariah pulled me closer, hugging me tightly, and then

Cade wrapped his arms around both of us, holding us close.

We stayed like that for as long as we could, crying, wishing, knowing that this would be our last time holding each other like this, being in the same room... like a family.

"I love you," I said, stepping back.

Cade nodded, his jaw clenched too tightly to speak.

Mariah touched my shoulder with her scarred hand. "Wherever you go, I hope you know we love every version of you, even the ones you're trying so hard to run away from."

I blinked back another flood of tears and swallowed hard before walking out the door and driving away from my family. Away from home.

53

JONAS

My mom called me right before I got to work. "Why didn't you tell us?" she asked before I could even say hello.

I let out a sigh, taking my time to park before giving my mom my full attention. "You talked to Mara?"

"She came to say goodbye. She said she's leaving for Atlanta and will be gone nine months? And you're not together? What happened between the premiere and today? You two were so happy together!"

"It was a fake relationship—"

"Don't give me that nonsense. We all know it started fake, but the way you looked at her... you can't make up those kinds of feelings."

"I love her, Mom, I do, but Mara wants to be a career woman who can pick up and leave without a moment's notice."

"And?" Mom demanded.

"And, I wanted to be factored in," I admitted. "I

wanted her to maybe hesitate to leave me for nine whole months! Is that so horrible?"

"Maybe the reason she didn't hesitate was because she believed in the two of you. She knew you'd be there for her when she came home."

I shook my head, even though she couldn't see. "It's a moot point now. I went to apologize, and she told me this isn't the kind of life she wants." My throat got tight, and I cleared it, wishing I could just sleep away the ache of losing her. But I couldn't. I'd slept like shit the night before and had a full day of work ahead of me.

Mom was silent for a long moment. "What are you going to do?"

I gazed toward the roof of my car. "Nothing, Mom. Mara doesn't do anything she doesn't want to do, and I can't change her mind."

A sigh came through the phone, and she said. "I love you, son. But I love her too."

I rubbed my hand over my face trying to stop the tears. "I do too."

54

MARA

Confession: I still love my dad.

MY FRIENDS and I met at Waldo's Diner for our last pancake breakfast for the next nine months. Birdie's grandpa even came to say goodbye.

The four of us sat at his usual booth, drank coffee with plenty of cream and sugar, and talked about life. We shared what we'd miss about each other, what I'd miss about Emerson, and how excited they were to come and see Atlanta once I'd settled in.

But there was a sadness about the table too. For as long as I could remember, it had been Birdie and me against the world, and for the last year, Henrietta had been a part of that too. And no matter what happened, no matter how shit of a day we'd had, we knew we could go to Waldo's Diner, have some great food, and see Grandpa Chester's smiling face.

But that was going to be gone soon. Even if I'd be

back after nine months, I knew it wouldn't be the same. Life would go on without me, and I'd miss them all like hell.

My phone alarm went off, letting me know it was time to go.

"So this is it?" Birdie asked as I quieted my phone.

I only nodded, not trusting myself to speak.

Chester opened his arms in the seat next to me. "Come here, kid. I need a hug."

I hugged him, breathing in the smell of coffee and diner food on his clothes. "I'm going to miss this place."

"It'll miss you too," he said. "And so will I."

I smiled tearfully, wishing I could just bring them all with me. But since I couldn't, I got out of the booth and hugged Birdie tight. She whispered in my ear, "I'm only a phone call away."

I nodded. "You better answer, even though I'll be on Eastern time."

She smiled, using her thumbs to wipe away my tears. "I'd answer if you were on the moon's time zone."

Henrietta hugged me next and said, "You're going to kill it out there. I know it."

"Thank you," I breathed, hugging her close. "And when I get back, I expect you to have a new house and some man candy."

Hen laughed. "I can promise one of those things, but I won't say which."

I smirked. "I love a good surprise."

Then Birdie and Hen put their arms around each other, watching as I walked away from the table. Away from my family. Away from the people I knew would be there for me no matter what.

The tears came as I drove out of Emerson, taking in everything one last time. I'd miss it all, but I had to be excited for this new adventure, for the opportunity to reach so many more people through my words. They were powerful, and so were my choices.

Life was always a series of forks in the road. Whether you turned left or right, you had to accept it because there was no going back. There was no undoing what had been done. All you could do is make peace with your past and choose better in the future.

Just like my dad was choosing better with his life out of rehab. He'd gotten out a couple weeks ago and let me know he had an apartment and a job.

And I had a gift for him, something to help him make the right turn, if that's what he chose to do. I didn't need my car anymore, the one we'd used to fool Jonas's parents, and my dad would be eligible for a license soon. I already had a mechanic scheduled to come and install a breathalyzer on the car that day.

An hour after leaving Emerson, I reached a set of shabby apartments near the airport and stopped in the parking lot. I looked up and saw my dad standing near the apartment entrance, a thick jacket wrapped around him. He looked older than the man I knew growing up. Softer.

I got out and said, "Hey." I still couldn't call him Dad out loud. I held out the keys. "She's all yours."

"You sure you want to do this?" he asked, looking between the car and me. "I can keep walking to the bus stop."

"It's a mile from here. It takes you two hours to get to work," I said, pushing the keys into his hand.

He shook his head, looking between me and the newer vehicle. "I don't deserve it."

"No," I agreed. "You don't."

He finally met my eyes, his a murky brown reflection of my own. "Thank you."

He hugged me. It was awkward but healing at the same time. He wasn't ever the dad I wanted and certainly never the dad I needed. But he was the dad I had. I wasn't raised by the Moores. My story didn't have a cute garden in the backyard or summers spent playing on the beach.

But this story was mine, and I deserved my own kind of happy ending. That involved knowing that the man who contributed to my DNA had the best chance possible at turning his life around and making however much was left of it count.

"Have fun in Atlanta," he said.

I nodded. "I hope you make this count."

"I will," he promised.

I got my suitcases out of the trunk and walked out of the parking lot, toward the crossroads where a cab driver was supposed to meet me.

It was time to embrace my future, whatever and whoever it held.

55

JONAS

The guys and I sat around a poker table, drinking beers and very carefully avoiding the topic of Mara and my broken heart.

Well, at least Steve and Cohen were avoiding it. I didn't care if we talked about it or not. I'd feel like shit either way. I'd miss her either way. I'd still be losing this fucking game either way.

After the third conversation about the weather, I set my hand down and said, "We can talk about it, you know?"

Cohen and Steve exchanged a look.

"Talk about what?" Cohen said.

"Yeah," Steve added, "I have no idea what you're talking about."

I stared them down, giving them a *cut the bullshit* look. I hated the way they felt like they had to tiptoe around me. I was fine. I mean, I wasn't, but I would be eventually. I hoped.

Steve caved first, saying, "Back when my wife and I

were dating, my grandpa told me if it's meant to be, it'll be."

I nodded. I believed similarly to his grandpa. "I just never thought there would be a world where it wasn't meant to be."

Cohen said, "Maybe it's a sign that you should be a dad someday? You know, you need to date someone who's willing to have children. A family. Be a stay-at-home mom so you can keep pushing forward in your career."

I nodded, not quite convinced. "I just hope I won't spend forever comparing whoever she is to Mara."

Steve nodded. "It wouldn't be fair to her."

"I agree." My phone rang, and I saw Tracey's name on the screen. "Hey, sorry, I have to take this," I said. "She's gonna be the person doing my mom's dialysis from now on."

"Go," Cohen replied.

"Yeah," Steve said. "It's not like you're beating us anyway."

I flipped him the bird and stepped out of the garage, walking on the driveway. "Hey, Tracey," I answered. "How's it going?"

"Hey," Tracey replied. "Tess said that I should call you."

"Yeah, I wanted to talk to you about Mom's dialysis and what you were thinking for pay. We can't do a lot, but we want to do enough to keep you."

"Don't be silly. Mariah is like another mom to me. I can always work from home those mornings anyway."

"Wow." I stood still, stunned by her offer. Was she really willing to spend twelve or more hours a week with my mom for nothing in return? "That's amazing, Tracey. Thank you."

"Of course."

We were quiet for a moment, and then she said, "Actually, I did want to talk to you about something else too."

"Yeah?" I asked. I could feel the guys staring at me, but I turned my back to them, ignoring them completely.

"Well, I kept thinking about the question you asked me before you and Mara got together. And I was kind of wondering if we can revisit it?"

I raised my eyebrows. The question she was talking about was that I'd asked her to go out with me before Mara came up with this whole fake dating thing. Why would she want to talk about it now?

"I was actually about to call you and take you up on your offer before I found out about you two," she admitted.

I scrubbed my hand over my jaw. That was about the last thing I'd been expecting Tracey to say. "Really?"

"Yeah," she said softly, almost like she was shy. "You're a great guy, and you're career-focused. Plus, you're my best friend's brother, which is the ultimate fantasy, you know? When you asked me before, I was just so worried about messing up my relationship with Tess if things didn't go well with us."

I shook my head. "Impossible. Tess would be more mad at me if things went off the rails than she would ever be with you."

Tracey laughed. "You might be on to something."

"I know." I replied. I was still waiting on Tess to let into me for what happened with Mara.

"So," she said, "are you still interested? I know it's soon, probably too soon, but I didn't want to miss my chance again."

I glanced back to the garage where Cohen and Steve were playing, and they quickly looked back at their cards. *Eavesdroppers*. But Steve's words ran through my mind. *If it's meant to be, it'll be.* There had to be a reason Tracey called today and asked me out, right?

"Yeah, Tracey, I'm interested," I said. My stomach sank, already knowing I'd miss Mara like hell, but she didn't want me. And I had to find a way to move on, one way or another.

"Great," she said, clearly smiling big. "How does La Belle sound?"

I closed my eyes against the memories. It was time to cover them up with some new ones. "I'll pick you up on Friday at six?"

"Sounds perfect," she replied.

To me, it sounded anything but.

56

MARA

Confession: If I couldn't have forever with Jonas, I wanted to have forever with something.

I PICKED up my leased car after arriving in Atlanta and went to the address that Bradley Mason's assistant had sent to me. When I pulled up to a bougie apartment complex with palm trees out front and a massive pool, my mouth fell wide open.

This was probably one of the nicest places I'd ever been. And I had to double-check the address to make sure I was in the right place. Holy shit, it was the right address.

I followed the directions in the email and walked inside to the front desk. (Yeah, they had someone manning a front desk full time at an apartment building too.)

"Hi," I said to the girl behind the desk dressed in all black. "My name is Mara. I'm here for unit 1420, but I'm not sure I'm in the right place... Is there maybe a smaller apartment complex behind this one that doesn't have a giant pool or a twenty-four-hour doorman?"

She laughed politely and spoke in the sweetest southern drawl. "You're in the right spot, Mara. We've been expecting you." She handed me a set of keys along with a parking pass and a brochure that listed all the amenities. (The list took up THREE SIDES!)

"It's great to have you here," she said.

"It's great to be here," I replied, and I meant it. This felt like a fresh start I needed, away from all the pain and loss I'd left in Emerson. Embracing the newness of it, I went back outside to park my car in the multi-level parking garage and used a baggage cart to bring all my bags upstairs. I was on the fourteenth floor out of twenty, and I couldn't wait to see the view and what was inside the apartment.

I pushed my key into the lock, twisted it, and pushed the door open. My eyes wide as saucers, I looked around, completely stunned. If twenty-year-old waitress Mara could see me now, she'd know all the struggle, all the extra shifts and late nights in front of a used computer were more than worth it.

There were floor-to-ceiling windows on one side along with a balcony, giving a panoramic view of the Atlanta city lights. They twinkled as a backdrop to the smooth stone floors and all the modern furniture that looked both beautiful and functional. There were two bedrooms, one with a desk in it, which I assumed would be my office space in case I needed to work from home, and then the other had a huge king bed. A fluffy white comforter topped it off and so many pillows that I... I pushed the baggage cart fully inside and ran to the bed, jumping in it like a little kid.

This was just confirmation that I was *exactly* where I needed to be.

My phone began ringing, and I had to get out of the bed to pull it from my pocket and answer it. I didn't recognize the number, but when I swiped and said, "Hello?" Bradley Mason's smooth-as-butter voice came from the other end.

"What do you think of the apartment?" he asked.

I smiled so wide my cheeks hurt. "It's beyond perfect. Are you sure this is mine?"

He chuckled. "I like to treat my writers well, and money goes a hell of a lot further here than it does in LA."

"Well, I feel like I'm sitting in the lap of luxury."

He chuckled. "That's the goal. So how about you come out with me tonight, and I'll show you around the city?"

"I'd love that," I replied. I'd never been to Atlanta before, and it would be good to get my bearings.

"Great. I'll come by and pick you up for dinner in an hour. Sound good?"

"Perfect," I said.

As soon as we got off the phone, I called Birdie and Henrietta on a conference call and showed them around my apartment.

At the end of the virtual tour, Henrietta laughed and said, "I might be coming to live with you."

"I have an extra bed," I replied. "But that's not even the best part. Bradley. Freaking. Mason is showing me around town tonight."

For a second, I thought the phone had frozen until I heard Birdie's excited cheer come through the line.

"That's amazing!" Hen said.

"I'm so excited. Knowing someone like Bradley could be *huge* for my career, take my life in an entirely new, different direction." It already had. I was in a place that I'd never been before, in a new apartment, with a new car, in a city full of new people.

"As long as it doesn't take your life so away from us," Birdie said.

I winked at her. "You know you girls are my besties for the resties."

Hen chuckled. "You're going to have so much fun."

I nodded. "I better go get ready for dinner!"

We said our goodbyes, and then I showered and did my hair, curling it just the way I liked. I got one of my new outfits from the bag, ripped the tags, and put it on. I felt good. Damn good.

When Bradley Mason came to the door, it was like an entirely different version of me answered. Because this was my new life. The new me who wasn't pining over her ex-boyfriend. Who was confident in her choice to be here and chase this dream.

He looked me up and down, slowly studying my body in a sexy, appreciative way. It made my heart hurt, made me miss Jonas like crazy.

"Are you ready, beautiful?" Bradley asked.

I nodded, shoving down all my feelings about Jonas. They would go away eventually, fade over time. But I needed to be patient.

I clutched my purse around my shoulder and said, "Let's go."

We rode the elevator down, making small talk about my flight and the apartments, then walked out front to a car that was idling in the circle drive. Instead of getting in the driver's seat, though, he sat in the back and I did too. He had a personal driver, which was just a level of rich that I had never completely comprehended. But here I was, living a new life, going down this fork in the road.

The driver took us to a fancy restaurant that outmatched even La Belle. I was excited to try the food, but mostly I kept my eye out for the dessert cart. When the waiter came to take our orders, I immediately pointed at the dessert cart at the next table. "I want one of those chocolate things, and then I'll have the steak and mashed potatoes."

"Do you want me to bring the dessert afterwards?" the waiter asked.

"First," I replied.

Bradley asked with a teasing grin, "Won't eating dessert first spoil your dinner?"

I had déjà vu to Jonas sitting with me at Waldo's Diner, asking me the same question about a dessert named after my favorite waitress.

I looked back at Bradley, only seeing Jonas's face, and smiled. "You need to have the sweet stuff first."

"I like it."

The waiter actually pulled the dessert I wanted directly off the dessert cart and set it in front of me before going away to put in the rest of our order. I dipped my spoon through the cake and drew it to my mouth, savoring a decadent chocolate.

Bradley said, "Now I feel like I've made a mistake by starting with the salad course."

I laughed. "It's never too late to change your ways."

He flagged down a different waiter and ordered another dessert. After a couple bites, he said, "So tell me about yourself. What does *the* Mara Taylor want out of her life, out of her career?"

I slowly pulled the chocolate off my spoon, my eyes growing unfocused. What *did* I want? I used to be so confident in my expectations for my life, but so much had changed in the last six months. I'd gone from happily writing books to having one adapted into a movie and wanting to write for television. I'd gone from shunning away all serious romantic relationships to falling for the love of my life and breaking both our hearts.

The answer fell off my lips, and the moment I spoke it, I knew it was true. "I want to do something that lasts." Because even if I couldn't have forever with Jonas, I wanted to have forever with *something*.

He nodded slowly. "One thing I've learned from working in this industry is that the only limits are your creativity."

It was an interesting take. One I'd never heard before. "What makes you say that?"

As we continued our meal, Bradley told me about growing up in LA with a dad as an actor and how he always felt overshadowed by his dad's accomplishments. He said he didn't act because he didn't want to be compared to his dad. So, he turned to writing and creating shows and eventually got to where he was today through creating one opportunity at a time for himself.

It was fascinating, hearing the twists and turns of his life. So similar to the ones that I'd taken.

Before I knew it, all of our food was gone from our

plates, and I already had dessert. He paid, leaving a hundred-dollar bill for a tip, and then we got back into his car. He sat on one side while I sat on the other, and he had the driver show me around town. They showed me the closest stores to the apartment complex, took me by where we would be working the next day, and even drove down the main downtown street where so many tourists filled the sidewalks.

It was late when we got back to the apartment complex, and my eyelids were heavy from the length and the emotion of the day.

"I'll walk you up to your door," Bradley said, "just to be safe."

I smiled. "I appreciate it." I was in a new town, and no matter how brave and bold I pretended to be, I'd gotten so used to staying with Jonas and feeling protected by him that it was nice to have someone else looking out for me.

We rode the elevator alone up to my place, and when we got to my door, he stood in the door frame. With a sultry smile, he said, "You know, if you'd feel more comfortable, I could stay the night here."

I could see the spark and desire in his eyes. Any other time, I would have thrown caution to the wind and taken him up on the offer, seen what a fox Bradley Mason was in bed, if only for the story. But instead I said, "I need to be fresh for tomorrow."

He gave me a close-lipped smile, assessing me with a wistfulness I completely understood. "I'll see you at work tomorrow, Mara Taylor."

I returned the smile. "Goodnight, Bradley Mason."

He turned away, and I shut the door on the night, on

his offer, and on my time being consoled by another person. No matter how hard it was for me, I was on my own.

I walked back to my room, washed my face in the bathroom sink, and stripped down to my underwear before sliding into bed.

Surrounded by pillows and covered by plush blankets that didn't smell like home, I wished more than anything that Jonas could be beside me.

57

JONAS

I stood in the mirror in my bathroom, straightening my tie. This would be my first date since Mara and I agreed to fake date. I'd grown so used to being myself around Mara that I wondered what Tracey would see in me.

Would she notice my teeth, which my parents paid way too much money to straighten with braces? My tailored clothes that Mara always liked so much? Or maybe the subtle wave to my dark brown hair?

Would she like what she saw long-term?

Would I like what I saw in her?

Tracey used to be everything I wanted. She was slender, shorter than me, standing at about shoulder height. She had honey-blonde hair and big blue eyes and full lips that I used to imagine kissing. But she just wasn't Mara.

I shook my head, trying to clear myself of the thought, because it wasn't fair. The whole reason I was going on this date was because Mara did not want me. She didn't want a long-term commitment. She wanted to live her own life alone instead. So, I had to find a way to live my life without her, no matter how fucking hard it was to imagine.

I sprayed on some cologne and left my house, making a mental note to get rid of the furniture Mara had helped me pick out. I didn't care if I even made a fourth of my money back on it and if I had to buy something from the thrift shop to replace it. I just couldn't handle looking at it anymore. I needed a fresh start, in my home and in my love life.

I got in my car and drove to Tracey's house, which was just ten minutes away from mine. It was a cute town-home, and she had one of those big wreaths on her front door like Tess did at her apartment. I walked up, feeling not nervous, not excited. But... numb.

Trying to muster excitement, or anything really, I pressed my finger on the doorbell and heard a chime inside the house.

"Coming!" came Tracey's muffled voice. Seconds later, she opened the door, greeting me with a smile. I took in her tight dress and high heels. "You look great," I said.

"Thanks, you too," she replied. She flicked a blonde curl over her shoulder and said, "Ready to go?"

I nodded, walking beside her to my car, opening the passenger door for her. She didn't argue, just smiled at me and said a demure, "Thank you."

It was such a strong contrast to Mara, who had argued with me, saying that she didn't need me to do that for her. Obviously, I'd known she didn't need me to do it. I wanted to.

I walked around to my side of the car, got in and pushed the start button. The radio began playing the country station I had on earlier, and I asked, "What do you like to listen to?"

"This is fine," she said.

"Great." It was easy, sitting here with her. No arguing. No worrying. Just *being*.

I drove to La Belle, where a valet took my car. We walked inside, taking our seats, and it was *normal*. The waiter who was not Tracey's ex; he only asked what we'd like to eat. Tracey ordered a perfectly respectable meal, not getting dessert first. I did the same. We ate our food, talking pleasantly about our families or friends, our careers. It was *easy*. There was no tension. No worry. No feeling like all of it was about to slip through my fingertips at any moment.

And then when the date was over and I walked her to her door, she fumbled with her keys just long enough to let me know she wanted me to give her a kiss goodnight. And she smiled up at me, giving me the perfect opening. Her red lipstick still flawlessly in place, she said, "I had a great night, Jonas. I can't believe it took me this long to take you up on a date."

"Me too. Thanks for coming out with me." I smiled, bending down and pressing a quick kiss on her lips because I knew it was what she wanted. And it felt *fine*. No sparks, but no drama either. No crossed wires or miscommunication.

"Goodnight," I said.

"Call me," she replied.

"I will," I promised, and as I walked toward the car, I realized maybe that's how my life was supposed to be. It wasn't supposed to be full of fireworks or feeling like I was walking on the tightrope or worrying about turning the water too hot. It was supposed to feel *comfortable*. It was supposed to feel *fine*. And I just hoped someday I could find a way to believe that.

58

MARA

Confession: I missed Jonas so much it hurt.

MY PHONE WENT off with a calendar reminder.

Tess's rehearsal dinner.

I stumbled into my living room chair, trying to catch my bearings. How was it already the night of her rehearsal dinner?

The last few weeks were a complete blur. I've never worked so hard or so collaboratively on something. Along with three other writers, I spent twelve-hour days in the writing room, throwing out ideas that would get shot down, but also having suggestions that were heard and respected.

When my book had been adapted to a movie, I'd been able to weigh in on the script for consistency, but they didn't have to listen to me. Here, my feedback actively changed the story we were all shaping. I loved the energized way I felt working with other people instead of by myself, even if I did feel completely worn down at the end of the day.

In fact, my book writing took a complete backseat to the show. At night, I'd write a few hundred words in Reid and Liza's love story. It wasn't perfect, but it was progress.

Over time, I made friends with the people in the writers' room and even some of the people on the crew. We went out together on weekends, and when I wasn't working or spending time with my new friends, I video called my old ones. I couldn't wait for work to slow down so I could invite them here and show them the new life I was building day by day, minute by minute.

I was busy. I was lonely, but I was free. For the most part.

Thoughts of Jonas stuck in the back of my mind. I missed talking to him, missed falling asleep beside him, missed spending slow mornings with Mariah in the sunroom and eating Cade's homemade breakfasts on the weekends.

And now I would be missing Tess's wedding too.

It was tomorrow, and I'd have to celebrate from afar. I'd already picked up her card and written a check to send in the mail, but my heart ached that I wouldn't see her walking down the aisle.

I wondered if she was showing now. If they'd had to pick out a new dress to accommodate her growing bump. Even though I didn't want children of my own, I had looked forward to spoiling her baby with Jonas. Being an auntie would be so much fun.

I shook my head as if I could shake away the thought.

I needed to accept that this was *my* life; I had made my choices. There was no going back, no matter how much I may have wanted to.

No matter how much I missed them.

So, I dialed the people from home that I *could* call. Henrietta and Birdie, the loves of my life.

Henrietta answered first, a big smile on her face. "How's my favorite writer doing?"

"Missing you guys. Tell me about home," I said.

She sat down on a couch, getting comfortable. "Still busy at work, getting ready for the construction crews to come in. Taking my grandma for her weekly pedicure. You know, the usual."

Birdie answered the call, her face appearing on the screen. "My favorite people! I miss you, Mara."

I smiled. "I miss you too. How's everyone doing there?" I asked, not quite wanting to bring up Jonas's name. But from the quiet on the other end of the phone, they could tell what information I was hoping for.

Birdie's face was serious as she said, "Honey, I have some news."

My stomach dropped. Had Tess and Derek split up? What about the baby? God, if anything happened to that baby... "What kind of news?" I finally asked.

"Jonas is seeing someone," she said.

It felt like a piece of my heart had been hollowed out. Like whatever small candle of hope I'd been holding on to had dimmed.

"Mara?" she said. "Did you freeze?"

"I'm still here," I said, trying not to show how much it hurt that Jonas had already moved on. I hadn't been able to come close. A few people had asked me out, including

Bradley Mason himself, and I'd always said no. Being with anyone else felt... wrong.

"Who is it?" I asked, closing my eyes against the answer I already knew.

"Tracey," Birdie confirmed.

I nodded. Of course it was her. The girl with a thin waist and perfect hair. The girl who always looked adorable and put-together. The girl he deserved.

"Is it serious?" I asked, only torturing myself more. The thought of her living in the house with him, sitting on the furniture we'd picked out together... It fucking gutted me. But maybe that pain was what I needed to move on. To commit to my new life.

Birdie frowned. "I've seen her around a few times at the bar and things like that."

Another punch to the gut. "Good for him," I said, I lied. "Hey, I think there's someone at the door. I've got to go."

"Mara—" Henrietta began, but I hung up. I didn't want my friends to see me cry. I didn't want them to hear how much I missed Jonas and how much I just wished we could be together again.

But he was living his new life with Tracey, and that's what he wanted before I ever came along. She'd be the perfect girl for him—one who wouldn't push him away or take away the possibility of children. One who could be his forever happily ever after.

59

JONAS

I couldn't believe Tess and Derek's rehearsal dinner was here or that I was going with Tracey instead of Mara. We were all in a nice restaurant near Tess's boutique, surrounded by Tess and Derek's closest friends and family.

The two families sat on opposite sides of the table, not intermingling. Things were awkward between Derek's family and our own, and I suspected they still wished that he would have sued my sister.

But the two of them... they were perfect together. Even from several seats away I could feel the love and happiness between them that they had found their person.

Part of me wondered if this could be Tracey and me in a few years. We'd been going out a few times a week since our first date, and there had yet to be a fight, yet to be anything other than amicable conversation. We hadn't slept together, but things were easy, and that's probably where it was going. Maybe even after the wedding.

She wasn't Mara, but then again, no one was, and I had to let it go. I had to let her go. As far as I'd heard from Cohen and Birdie, Mara was having a great time and fitting right in with her colleagues. Making waves in the writers' room and making Atlanta a good temporary home.

The show she was working on was supposed to air a year from now, and I knew when it came time, I would watch it. Even keep it on during all the credits, just to see her name. She was a part of my past, part of my heart, but not a part of my future.

Tracey, the girl next to me, could be that future. Even if I wasn't excited about it yet.

Toward the end of the dinner, Tess stood up, held her nearly empty champagne glass that had been filled with orange juice, and tapped her knife against it.

It burst into shards.

Everyone watched with amusement (or annoyance in Derek's family's case) as a waiter cleaned up the pieces.

"Sorry," she said, when the commotion was finally over. "I'm not the most graceful person." A polite chuckle came from our side of the table. We knew Tess the Mess all too well.

She looked around the table and said, "I know it's uncommon for the bride to give a speech, but I'd like to make a toast to Derek."

Derek smiled up at her, all the love in the world in his eyes. I imagined that's how I used to look at Mara. How she looked at me.

"Back when I first met Derek, love was the last thing to cross my mind. More like, 'Oh shit,' which was probably what he was thinking too."

Everyone around the table chuckled, even his family, if uneasily.

"But," Tess continued, "the more I got to know him, the more I understood what love was. I used to think it was all fireworks and kisses in the rain. But now I know that there's so much more to it. It's looking at your partner and seeing the best version of yourself reflected back. It's knowing that they're going to challenge you to be better for the rest of your life. It's knowing that no matter what compromises you have to make, you'll still love them just as much. And it's knowing that in a thousand lifetimes, you could meet them over and over again and still choose them every single time."

She smiled, lifting her glass. "So here's to Derek, the love of my life and a thousand others."

Everyone around the table lifted their glasses, some wiping their eyes, and we all toasted to them. Their love story was beautiful, no matter how it started. And as I looked to Tracey next to me, saw the pride in her eyes for her friends, I realized I didn't feel that way about her. I didn't feel the fireworks or even that I'd choose her over and over again.

Maybe Mara had been right all along. Maybe the people who got those feelings and had them forever were just the lottery winners. They weren't like everyone else.

It was a fucking miserable thought. Because I'd felt that for Mara, and now she was gone. I'd both won and lost the cosmic lottery in less than a year.

I downed the rest of my drink and ate the rest of my meal and tried not to think about all that I had lost. Feeling down, I decided to duck out early, thinking no one would miss me on the way to my car.

Halfway through the parking lot, Tess yelled after me. "Jonas!"

I turned, waiting for her to reach me. "What are you doing? You're supposed to be in your party!"

"No, what the hell are you doing?" she demanded.

Frowning, I glanced toward my car. "I'm going home. It's going to be a long day tomorrow, and I want to be ready to help."

"That's not what I meant," she said, a crease between her eyebrows just like the one Dad had when he was upset. "What the hell are you doing with Tracey?"

My spine stiffened. "Shit, I forgot to tell her I was leaving."

She shook her head, disappointment clear in all of her features. "You don't love her."

"We've been dating for a month," I replied.

"You and Mara had been fake dating for a day when I knew she was the one for you."

I let out a heavy sigh. "Remember what you said in your toast? Both people have to choose each other, and she didn't choose me."

"Mara didn't say that she didn't choose you. She said she wanted to choose herself. You can choose both when you're in love."

I shook my head, growing frustrated. "Tess, you got lucky. Don't you understand that? There are not many guys who could walk out of a store with a chair leg up their ass and propose to the girl a year later."

She glared at me. "You're just scared! She's scared. You both need to get over it."

"No," I said.

"No?"

382 HELLO FAKE BOYFRIEND

"No! I'm dating Tracey. It's *comfortable* and *easy* and I don't have to wonder where she's going to be the next day or what I'm going to do that'll set her off. Love shouldn't be scary."

"It's always scary, Jonas!" Tess cried. "You can't put your heart in someone else's hands without being scared."

I looked down at the asphalt parking lot and then back up at my sister. "I'm happy for you and Derek; I really am. You're going to have a beautiful life together."

She tilted her head, looking concerned. She was about to speak, but I saw Tracey approaching behind her.

"Hey, Tracey," I said, lifting my hand.

"Derek said I might find you two out here," she said, wrapping her shawl around herself.

"I was just getting some fresh air, but I think I'm ready to go," I said, lifting my arm so Tracey could slip underneath.

Tess's eyebrows pulled together in annoyance, but she masked it as soon as Tracey looked at her. "I'll see you both tomorrow?"

"Bright and early," Tracey said.

My sister leaned forward, kissing us both on the cheek. Tracey hugged my sister and said, "I just can't believe you're getting married tomorrow!"

"Me neither," Tess said. Over her friend's shoulder, she gave me a meaningful look and then pulled away.

Tracey and I said goodbye, then walked the rest of the way to my car. I held the door open for her, more out of habit than anything, then got in and began driving toward her house.

Squeezing my leg, Tracey said, "So I was *thinking* you could stay over if you wanted to."

The meaning behind her words was clear. She was ready to move forward with me. And I needed to move forward with her instead of hanging on to the past. "That's a good thought," I said with a forced smile.

"Oh, I forgot. I wanted to talk to you about this." She let go of my leg and reached into her purse, pulling out an envelope. "This is yours."

I glanced at it, trying to make out what it was in the light cast by the dash and streetlights outside. "What is it?"

"All that money you sent me in the mail. I've told you a million times that you guys don't need to pay me to help your mom with dialysis. She's practically a second mother to me. I'm happy to help."

Confused, I pulled over alongside the road. "Tracey, I didn't pay you, and I know Tess and Dad don't have the money to pay you either."

"Well it came from somewhere," she said, opening the envelope and pulling out a notecard tucked amongst the cash. "The heart was a nice touch."

My eyebrows drew together, and I reached out to tilt the card toward me. My eyes blurred as I recognized the writing.

Thank you for everything you've done for the best mom ever.

60

JONAS

I studied the note for longer than I needed to, realizing Mara's fingers had been on this page. Realizing that even though she was gone, she was still there for my family. For me.

I set the note on my lap and looked across the car at the woman I knew wasn't right for me. "Tracey..." I took her hands. "I can't do this with you."

"Do what?" she asked, concern clear in her voice.

"What Tess said earlier in her toast was right. You deserve someone who feels that way about you, the way she and Derek feel for each other." *The way I feel for Mara.*

Her eyes shined in the dim lighting. "You don't feel that way about me." It was a statement. And we both knew it was true.

"I don't want to take the love of a lifetime away from you."

She looked down at her lap, at the ring she was twisting around her index finger. Tears spilled over her cheeks. "It's her, isn't it? Mara?"

I nodded, needing her to know the truth.

"What is it about her?" she asked, looking back at me.

I studied Tracey, wondering where the question was coming from, but I had to be honest. "Seven months ago, you were exactly the kind of woman I wanted to be with. You're kind and beautiful and driven... I never saw her coming, but she turned my world upside down in the best possible way. It wasn't fireworks—it was a feeling. And it hasn't gone away."

Tracey nodded. "I can't say I understand, but I hope I do someday."

I hung my head, feeling like the biggest piece of shit for causing her pain. For stringing her along when I always knew that Mara was the one for me. "I'm really sorry."

She shook her head. "I should have said yes sooner." She gave me a tearful smile. "There was a window, and I missed it."

I didn't tell her that I was glad she had. Instead, I said, "Let me take you home."

She agreed, and I drove the rest of the way to her house. But this time, I didn't get out of the car. I just unlocked the door and said goodbye, knowing that the next time we saw each other, it would only be as friends. And hopefully, it would be with Mara at my side.

As soon as she got inside her door, I started driving toward LA. I needed to find a plane; I needed to be with Mara.

I needed to know that I would choose her in a thousand lifetimes. I just hoped in this lifetime, she would choose me too.

61

MARA

I couldn't sleep the night before Tess's wedding, knowing that I was going to miss it. So I stayed up writing on my novel instead. I was getting so close to the end, to the part where the characters got out of their own way and accepted the love they deserved.

How the hell didn't I see it before?

That's exactly what I was doing with Jonas. I was choosing my fear and my wound over him. He had tried to apologize, to change his ways and be more supportive, but I'd ran away for one transgression.

I rocked back from the computer, putting my head in my hands. I'd made the biggest mistake of my life, lost the best thing that ever happened to me. Because I got fucking scared.

And now it was too late. There were already pictures online of him and Tracey sitting next to each other at the engagement party and looking like a couple straight out of *GQ*. No way would I storm back in and fuck that up for him.

I had missed my chance to have my once-in-a-lifetime love, and my realization that it didn't have to be one or the other had come too late. It doesn't have to be love *or* career. Love *and* pain. But my own pull-your-head-out-of-your-ass moment had come too late, and I couldn't edit the story to fix my mistakes.

Tess and Derek would get married without me in the room. Mariah and Jonas would watch, holding each other as Cade walked his daughter down the aisle. Tracey would stand next to Tess as a bridesmaid, and as Tess and Derek spoke their vows, their truth, I would be here. I would be staying out of the way of Jonas's happiness.

I couldn't give him everything he said he wanted, but I could give him space to create a family, a future, with Tracey.

So maybe it *was* better this way.

Maybe my happily ever after was knowing that Jonas could have his.

I put my fingers to the keyboard again, tears streaming down my cheeks as I wrote the final words in Liza and Reid's story. It was so much more powerful now that I knew love wasn't just something I wrote about in books. It was something *real*. I'd felt it with Jonas, and maybe someday, I'd feel it again.

A knock sounded on my door, and I jumped because I'd been so in the flow. I wiped at my cheeks as I got up to see who it was. I'd probably ordered something on Amazon and forgotten about it like usual.

But when I opened the door, it wasn't a delivery person or a package. It was *Jonas*.

I stared at him in his charcoal suit and plum-colored shirt that I'd seen in photos from the rehearsal dinner.

Was I that tired, that delusional, that I'd hallucinated him here?

"What are you doing here?" I asked, despite the very real possibility that I'd imagined it all.

"Mara, my sister's getting married today," he said, reached for my hands. His touch was a balm to my soul, healing to my fractured heart. "I can't watch her and Derek tie their lives together without the woman I love by my side. *You* are my family. And I want you there with me. While my sister gets married. When I get this promotion. When we watch this TV series come out. I want you there with me when I become an uncle, and fuck, I want you there with me when I retire. And I want you there with me when I'm blushing about everything that you write in romance novels. I want you there with me in person, on the phone, however you'd have me, every day for the rest of my life."

I covered my mouth with my hand, a fresh stream of tears falling down my cheeks. "Jonas..."

"I need to get this out, Mara." He didn't even take time to come into my place, laying his heart bare, right there in the hall. "I was afraid when you said you were leaving for Atlanta. I was afraid it meant that you were leaving me, but I realize now that you weren't leaving me. You were chasing a dream, and I want to support every dream you have, no matter how big or small. I promise if you choose me, if you are with me, that you'll get nothing but my love and support, no matter how hard it is. And every time you run away, I promise I will chase you. I'll never stop chasing you for the rest of my life. *Please* just say yes." His voice broke. "Just say yes."

I leaned against the door frame, pretty sure it was the

only thing keeping me upright. "These last few weeks without you have been the most amazing of my life. And the most horrible at the same time. I've missed you like I've never missed any other person. I've cried for you like I've never cried for another man. And I've hoped for you to have your happily ever after, even if it wasn't with me. I never believed a love like that was true until I met you. And I don't want to take your heart, the kind of future you want, away from you because I'm too selfish to let you be with Tracey."

Jonas shook his head, cupping my cheek in his hand. "I thought if you and I weren't meant to be, then maybe Tracey and I were, but it was over before it even began. I was sitting back in my life. I wasn't taking control of my life like you do." He smiled. "You've taught me so much just by asking for what you want. You've made me see that I need to ask for what I want too."

"You deserve the best," I breathed, still not quite believing it could be me.

"Then I deserve you."

I shook my head. "Jonas, you deserve so much better than me. I can't give you children. I can't give you the traditional life you want."

"What if that's not what I want anymore?"

"What if that's just you settling?"

"I could never settle with you. Not when all I've been thinking of every day since you left is lying next to you at night, hearing your voice on the phone during the day, and making love to you for the rest of our lives."

I was done fighting, done resisting, done thinking that our picture of happily ever after couldn't be the same. I took him in, with his five o'clock shadow and his outfit that he'd worn since the night before on his way to me. This was the love of my life. And I was finally, *finally*, getting out of my own way.

I took that face in my hands, and I pressed my lips to his, pouring every ounce of my love for him into the kiss.

"Does this mean you'll be with me?" he asked against my lips, already breathless.

I smiled into our kiss. "For the rest of our lives."

62

JONAS

I picked her up and carried her to the bedroom, desperate to feel her, to touch her, to show her just how much I loved her. I laid her back on the bed and kissed her face, her cheeks, her neck, and then I pulled back her robe, kissing every part of her I'd missed so much.

Her hands roved over my shoulders and back, savoring me just as I was doing with her. Our bodies responded to each other, and I could feel the damp heat through her underwear. I tugged them aside and slipped two fingers inside, feeling and stretching her.

She whimpered. "Jonas."

"I know, baby," I said, curling my fingers to touch her sensitive spot, then pulling them out and circling her clit.

Her hips bucked. "Jonas, I missed you. Please."

I knew I wouldn't last long. Not with her body, not with all the emotions building me up and breaking me apart. I'd almost lost this. Almost lost her. I promised myself I'd never be so stupid again.

"Please," she said.

"I won't last long."

"I don't care," she gasped, reaching for my pants, fumbling for the button.

I gently moved her hands aside, sliding my zipper down and freeing my cock, which had been straining against my pants.

She took it in her hands for a moment before lying back and pulling me down.

Desperately, I moved my tip against her entrance, pressing once, twice, before sliding all the way inside her as close as I could.

I couldn't hold back, not now, not with Mara, not after missing her for so damn long. I pumped inside her, going fast.

Tears streamed down her cheeks as she took me, wrapping her thick legs around my waist. "I love you," she sobbed. "I love you so fucking much."

"I love you forever," I said back, savoring the words as they melded between us, as our bodies pushed and pulled, saying everything that we'd missed in the time we'd been apart.

"I'm getting close," I warned. I didn't want our first time to be about me, so I pulled back to pleasure her first, but she wrapped her legs tighter around me, holding me in and not letting me go.

The motion was enough to push me over the edge. I came into her, dropping my face into her shoulder and sobbing with all the pain I'd held in. With all the hopes I'd thought I'd lost.

"I love you," I cried.

She held my head to her chest and cried right along with me.

63

MARA

Confession: I crashed a wedding.

I WISHED airplane seats were more comfortable. And that cars didn't have center consoles.

As we made our way back to Emerson for Tess's wedding, I just wanted to be near him, to hold him and make up for all the time we'd lost. But instead, we held hands, we kissed. He told me about the weeks leading up to Tess's wedding, and I told him about how much I loved writing for TV.

And when my eyelids grew too heavy to continue speaking, he held me against his chest and let me sleep. I only woke when the airplane had landed and he gently kissed me awake.

We hurried through the airport and went to his car he'd left in short-term parking. I'd worn a dress since we wouldn't have time to stop at my house and get ready, so we drove straight to the clubhouse at Emerson Trails. It

394 HELLO FAKE BOYFRIEND

was situated at the edge of the woods that walking trails wound through and was so beautiful with floor-to-ceiling windows framed by dark wood.

He pushed open the door, and I gasped at the sight inside. It had been decorated with poppy mallows and daisies. The combination of fuchsia, white and yellow was so stunning yet understated, just like what I knew of Tess and Derek. People milled about, finding their seats for the wedding, but Jonas pulled me down a hallway at the back of the building, toward the dressing rooms.

His dad stood at the end of the hall, probably getting ready to take his daughter down the aisle.

Jonas called, "Dad!"

Cade turned, a frustrated look on his face. "Where the hell have you—" His jaw dropped open. "Mara?"

I grinned, running toward him and hugging him tight. "Sorry I held up your son!"

He laughed, holding me back. "You hold him up all you'd like, sweetheart." He pulled back, taking me in. "We missed you like hell. Please tell me you're back together?"

I looked at Jonas, who seemed just as happy as me and his dad. "We are."

Cade hugged us both. "I swear this is the best day of my life."

"Mine too," Jonas and I said at the same time.

The dressing room door opened, and Tess and her mom came out.

They both looked between the two of us, and Tess started screaming. "OH MY FREAKING GOD, YOU DID IT, JONAS!!!"

I grinned at her, jumping up and down. That was exactly how I felt.

Mariah, who looked absolutely beautiful in her mint-green dress, came and took me in her arms, just like her husband had. "I knew you'd be back. You two were meant for each other."

Tears streamed down my cheeks as I held her. "We all were."

The five of us were teary eyed as I stepped back and said, "I'm so sorry, Tess. This is supposed to be your day."

She shook her head. "It's all of ours. It's a celebration of love."

A woman in a deep plum pantsuit came closer and said, "I'm sorry, but we need to get down the aisle. The groom's getting a little nervous."

Tess giggled. "We have forever together. He can wait a few minutes." She hugged me tight again and said, "Save me a dance at the reception?"

I laughed. "Of course."

Jonas extended his arms for his mom and me, and we took them, walking toward the ceremony space. As we walked in, I saw Birdie and Cohen sitting a few rows back from the front. When she saw Jonas and me together, her mouth fell wide open.

"Talk later," I mouthed. We'd have so much to cover at the reception.

But the great part, just like Tess said, was that we had forever.

64

JONAS

Dropping Mara off at the airport after such an incredible weekend was the hardest thing I'd ever had to do. But today was the last day of tax season, and I had to be there. We'd finish strong, and then I would get the promotion I'd been working toward my entire career. Mr. Rusk had made that much clear.

I went into the office, trying to focus on my work instead of how much I missed Mara. After a month apart, I didn't want to be away from her again, but I had work to do. As soon as I sat at my desk, Mr. Rusk knocked on my door.

I wondered what he was there for, but he only said, "Come with me." He had an unreadable expression on his face as he walked me toward the conference room.

"What's going on? Did I forget a meeting?" I asked. But then he opened the door, and I saw everyone inside with party decorations and a giant cake in the middle of the table that said, "HOWDY, PARTNER."

"Congratulations!" everyone yelled, and while I was

still speechless, Mr. Rusk said, "We've made it through another tax season, and I'm sad—happy, nervous—to say it will be my last of taking such an active role in the firm! We're promoting Jonas Moore to partner, and he'll be the man in charge next year!"

Everyone clapped for me, and Mr. Rusk said, "Jonas, would you like to tell them a little of what you have planned?"

I nodded, wondering why this didn't feel like a massive success. It was. I could see on Jenkins's face the gutted, disappointed look. He'd worked so hard for this. I was only thirty-two, and I was already partner. Plenty of people worked twenty years or more to get to this point. But I had been given the honor, and I wanted to let them know I wouldn't take it for granted.

"Working at this firm for the last ten years has taught me so much. I've learned what I love about accounting, and of course, some things I'd like to change. One of the biggest changes I see coming in the next year is the ability to work remotely. Jenkins, I want you to go to your daughter's dance recital and be able to work from home the rest of the day. Karen, I want you to work from home in case you need to keep an eye on your grandkids after school. I—"

Mr. Rusk cleared his throat, and I looked to see him shaking his head. He wore an uncomfortable smile as he said, "All changes are going to be approved by me, and we've never been one of those work-from-home firms. Face to face means a lot."

I drew my eyebrows together, confused. We had all these people here, all my colleagues he was allegedly placing me in charge of. "So what does this promotion mean?"

He lowered his voice. "More pay, more hours, and more responsibility. I'm still the owner of the firm, Jonas."

I blinked slowly, realizing everything I'd been working toward had been in the wrong direction. I didn't want to run a business like Mr. Rusk did. I wanted my employees to have a life and the kind of love I was experiencing. But he didn't want me to have that.

I missed Mara like hell, and I couldn't imagine even more hours away from her. And then I realized I didn't fucking have to.

We got to write our story, and I was done writing my part away from her.

"Thank you so much for the opportunity, Mr. Rusk," I said, speaking just as much to him as everyone else. "I've spent the last ten years at this firm. I've made great friends, I love working with our clients, and the money hasn't been bad either."

My coworkers gave a polite chuckle.

"I'm so honored to be recognized this way, but unfortunately, I'm going to have to respectfully decline and resign, effective immediately."

Murmurs broke out around the room, but I kept going.

"See, I met this girl." I couldn't help the dopey smile on my face. "And I miss her. I know I might be making less money and an opportunity like this might not come along again, but this girl is once in a thousand lifetimes. Stay in touch."

As the murmuring continued, I walked out of the conference room, already on my way to my office to get my things and go. I wasn't sure how I'd pay for my house, but I'd figure it out. Everyone needed an accountant, and I could do client work while Mara was busy writing.

I just missed her. I wanted to do life with her. And I knew, after this weekend, she wanted to do life with me too.

A heavy hand fell on my shoulder, and I turned to see Mr. Rusk with a murderous expression on his face.

"What the hell are you doing?" he asked. "You're throwing away the best opportunity of your life for some pussy?"

I stepped back, shrugging his hand off my shoulder. "I'll pretend you didn't say that because I'm thankful for the work you've given me, but I'm done letting this firm run my life."

Mr. Rusk sputtered, his face growing redder, but I didn't wait for him to say anymore.

I was packing up my things, and I was going to the place I belonged.

As soon as my box was packed, I went to the parking lot, opened my trunk and put it in my car. But when I shut my trunk, someone else was there.

"Jenkins, what the hell? You scared me."

He gave me a sheepish smile. "Sorry about that."

I looked around, wondering what he was doing here. "I'm guessing Mr. Rusk gave you the promotion. Congratulations."

Jenkins shook his head. "He offered it to me. But I said no."

My jaw scraped the ground. "You're kidding me."

"Not one bit. I listened to what you said in there, and you're fucking right. I've missed a lot of shit, and I'm a dumbass if I think I had to. I liked your idea about working remote, and between the two of us, we've got thirty years in this business. What do you say we make something that works for the both of us?" He extended his hand.

I grinned, looking between him and his hand. "You've got yourself a deal."

65

MARA

Confession: He made my dreams come true.

I WAS DISTRACTED ALL MORNING. The other writers knew it. I knew it.

I just missed Jonas so damn much.

I knew I'd said video calls and weekend visits would be enough, but I hated the idea of going home to an empty apartment tonight. It was like my life was in two places. Here in Atlanta and back with Jonas.

I stepped out of the writers' room and called his number. But when he answered, I heard his voice twice.

"Jonas, I think there's an echo," I said.

He laughed, twice again, and then he said, "Turn around."

Still holding my phone to my ear, I turned, seeing him standing in the studio hallway. My mouth fell into a surprised grin, and I ran to him, jumping in his arms. "Jonas! What are you doing here?"

He spun me, then set me down. "I quit my job."

My eyebrows flew up. "You *what?*"

"They offered me partner, but Mr. Rusk told me I couldn't change things as much as I thought I could. All I was able to think about was the extra hours I'd be away from you. I quit, and Jenkins quit with me. We're starting a fully-remote firm together." He took a quick breath. "I get it now, why you didn't need to talk this opportunity over with me. Because the second I had the opportunity, I knew it would be good, for me, for us, and I knew you'd be in my corner. I knew I couldn't keep working at the job and be away from you. Because when you find out who you want to be with, tomorrow isn't soon enough, and forever doesn't feel like enough time."

I smiled, shaking my head, then hugged him again. "Have I mentioned I love you?"

He grinned. "I love you too."

66

MARA

Confession: I believe in forever.

SIX MONTHS LATER

WE ALL SAT in the living room of Jonas's house to watch the first season premiere of the show I'd written for, *Big Plans*. It was about a plus-size woman who was planning weddings for her three roommates but had never been in love herself, and it was the cutest damn thing I'd ever seen.

I couldn't wait to show it to all of our friends and Jonas's family.

We'd decided to go with a silver-dollar pancake bar for the party, so there were containers of syrup set out, along with little trays of pancakes and all the toppings you could imagine.

A knock sounded on the door, and I went to see who

404 HELLO FAKE BOYFRIEND

it was while Jonas finished setting up the last of the food and drinks.

When I opened it, I saw Tess with her adorable baby bump and her husband, who looked happy as always.

"Hey, you two!" I said, hugging Tess first. Her bump pressed into my stomach, and then she stepped back, saying, "Did you feel that? She kicked!"

I grinned, letting her put my hand to her stomach. "I felt it! She must be excited for pancakes."

"Or to see Aunty Mara," Derek said.

I smiled at him. He was such a sweetheart. "I can't believe we only have to wait a couple more weeks to meet her in person!"

Tess smiled, holding up her crossed fingers.

I stepped back so they could both go inside and then saw Birdie, Cohen, and Henrietta coming up the sidewalk. I hugged each of them, then let them in.

Jonas's parents came next, both of them dressed up in the show's colors for the event. It was so damn sweet my teeth hurt.

Soon, everyone was inside, sitting on our *comfortable* furniture, and Jonas was running the remote to access the right channel.

As soon as the opening credits played with *written by Mara Taylor, Grayson Jones, and Fredricka Martin,* our friends cheered loudly, patting me on the back and grinning at me. I felt just as famous as I had at the premiere for *Swipe Right*.

We watched through the episode, laughing at the jokes I had written, gasping at the surprises, and swooning over the love interest that had been cast so perfectly. Bradley Mason was a genius, and so were us writers, if I did say so myself.

But when the end credits should have been rolling, a video played in front of the text. Bradley Mason stood in front of the camera, saying, "We have a special surprise for one of our writers! Check this out." The imaged changed to Jonas.

"What is this?" I asked him, but he pointed to the TV, where he was kneeling on the screen.

"Mara Taylor, you're an incredible writer and an even better woman. I'd like to know if you'll write the rest of your future with me as your husband."

Tears stung my eyes, and I turned to Jonas, who was now kneeling across the coffee table from me, holding an open ring box in his hands. Inside was a gold band with carefully hewn details and a green stone in the center.

I covered my heart with my hands. "Jonas... are you sure? I'm with you forever either way."

He grinned. "I've never been surer of anything in my life."

It felt like the whole room was holding its breath, waiting for my answer, including me. Fear ripped through me. Fear of messing it up. Of being less than Jonas deserved. But then I looked into his eyes, and I remembered that I believed in happily ever after. I believed in him.

Most importantly, I believed in *us*.

And I said yes. Because the best love stories had no end.

EPILOGUE
HENRIETTA

You know how they say when you find someone you want to spend forever with, forever can't start soon enough?

That was Mara and Jonas.

Just a week after Jonas's grand proposal, Mara had a date set for less than a year away. Two weeks after the proposal, Mara, Birdie, Tess, and I were in Vestido looking at wedding gowns.

This store had a bigger plus-size section than most, and it was so fun sifting through the gowns, thinking which one would look best on our friend. Unlike me, Mara had all the confidence in the world, so we weren't limited by styles she would feel comfortable in.

Between the four of us, and a saleswoman named Venetia, we had multiple dresses for Mara to try on in every style and color the store had available.

While Mara went to the changing room to try on the first gown, Venetia passed out glass flutes and filled them to the brim with bubbling champagne. I took a sip, loving the way to the sweet fizz felt on my tongue. It had this warming effect that settled my nerves.

I was happy for Mara, I was, but there was this terror in the pit of my stomach too. What if I never had this moment for myself. What if I'd never be the one to walk down the aisle in the fancy dress as the love of my life stared back at me and then promised me forever?

"There she is," Birdie said, setting down her wine glass.

I snapped out of my thoughts and stared at the hall-ways from the dressing rooms. Mara walked toward us in a mermaid style dress that clung to her hips. The sweet-heart neckline accentuated her chest. With her dark hair down, contrasting the stark white color, she was a vision.

"You look incredible," I said.

Mara smiled back at me. "Thanks babe."

Venitia walked toward Mara, a veil in her hand. "Let's try this." She slipped the veil into Mara's hair and adjusted the tulle so it cascaded down her back.

Tess's jaw dropped open. "Oh my gosh, Mara! This is stunning on you! My brother is going to love it."

Mara's face contorted with tears, and she wiped at her eyes. "I can't be crying already!"

Birdie laughed. "Let it out. Weddings always come with waterworks." She spoke like a wise woman, one who had been there before—because she had.

In fact, all three of them had been married—or were at least engaged. And here I was. Perpetually single, not a boyfriend or even casual fling in sight.

Mara spun, looking at herself in the tri-fold mirror. "What do we think of the color? Am I allowed to wear white, considering..."

Birdie laughed. "I don't think anyone's policing that."

"If they were, I'd be in black," Mara joked.

Tess laughed. "I think a little blush pink was perfect for me on my big day."

"Cream for me," Birdie replied, a sweet smile on her face.

They looked at me, like they were waiting. My cheeks warmed because I had a secret I hadn't told them yet. One I was too embarrassed to say out loud.

"White," I admitted. Snow white. Without a hint of color.

Because me?

I wasn't just the funny fat friend. I was a twenty-eight-year old virgin with no prospects in sight.

But I made a promise to myself right then and there: I was going to lose my virginity, once and for all.

♥⸱♥⸱♥⸱♥

WANT to read Henrietta's happily ever after? Grab your copy of Hello Temptation today! Or get the rest of the Hello Series Bundle here!

Want to catch up with Mara, her friends, and get a spicy cameo from Jonas? Read "Girls Trip" today!

Start reading Hen's story in Hello Temptation.

Get the series bundle!

Get the bonus content!

ALSO BY KELSIE HOSS

The Hello Series

Hello Single Dad

Hello Fake Boyfriend

Hello Temptation

Hello Billionaire

Hello Doctor

Hello Heartbreaker

Hello Tease

JOIN THE PARTY

Want to talk about Hello Fake Boyfriend? Join Hoss's Hussies today!

Join here: https://www.facebook.com/groups/hossshussies

AUTHOR'S NOTE

Dreaming big dreams is scary as fuck.

What if you fail?

What if you get hurt?

... What if they never come true?

Mara was a person, who, by all intents and purposes had no business chasing her dream of being a successful writer. She had a rough childhood, and abusive, alcoholic father, a mother who ran away, and no one to ever lean on and tell her what she was worth. She dropped out of high school, not even getting her GED.

But she did it anyway.

She objectively had no business being in a long-term relationship. She had no good examples, had been single for all her life, and had a career to focus on.

But she did it anyway.

This is the part where most people point out that Mara's story is fictional... but is it? I bet you know people who have accomplished incredible things despite over-whelming odds. I bet there have been times in your life when you've done something that someone else said was impossible.

I certainly have.

I've had people in my life tell me I'd never accomplish what I said I wanted to. When I got married at nineteen, I was told I'd never finish college. I got a master's degree. When I said I wanted to change the world, I was told I had no chance. I get messages every day from women who say they love themselves for the first time, because of my books.

I did it anyway.

And I'm not anyone who's any more special than you are. I grew up in western Kansas on a farm. My graduating class had nine people in it. There was domestic violence, addiction, and so much pain in my home. But I dreamed my way out of it.

Whatever you're suffering from, whatever big goal you're reaching toward, I know change is possible for you.

The best thing we can do for ourselves is allow our minds to dream those big scary impossible dreams. Mara almost missed out on the love of a lifetime because she couldn't picture herself having that kind of love. She almost missed out on a relationship with her father because she couldn't imagine anything between love and hate.

What have you missed out on because you didn't allow yourself to dream?

What can you start dreaming today?

I know it might feel impossible, silly, scary as fuck. But those are the best kinds of dreams, especially when they come true. <3

ACKNOWLEDGEMENTS

I've always been an introvert and had trouble delegating, but the older I get, the more I know how much I need help to succeed! (Especially when doing something new and different like writing a *smutty* romance book.)

Some of my best supporters are my family, who give me the love and space I need to get these stories written. They have so much faith in me to provide for us, and it is the biggest honor and privilege.

My bestie for the restie, Sally Henson, is a great cheerleader, friend, and sounding board. I love knowing that she's always a phone call or text message away.

Sarah Madelin is a new writer friend, who invited me on a fun retreat where I was able to finish this story! Knowing her is such a treasure, as was that extra time spent with this story.

My editor, Tricia Harden, has been with me for so many books now, I've lost count. But whether I'm writing sweet high school romance or steamy books with heart, she gives the best, most thoughtful feedback. My books are better for having her in my corner.

My cover designer, Najla Qamber, has been so fun to work with! I love how she made these covers so unique and fun, and I can't wait to share the next one.

To my readers in Hoss's Hussies, thank you for being

so fun and supportive. I love our group and getting to chat with you every day!

And to the person reading this, you're my favorite kind of person. One who gets lost in a story and supports creatives. It means the world to me that you've spent time with my words, and I hope you enjoyed every single second.

ABOUT THE AUTHOR

Kelsie Hoss writes sexy romantic comedies with plus size leads. Her favorite dessert is ice cream, her favorite food is chocolate chip pancakes, and... now she's hungry.

You can find her enjoying one of the aforementioned treats, soaking up some sunshine like an emotional house plant, or loving on her three sweet boys.

Her alter ego, Kelsie Stelting, writes sweet, body positive romance for young adults. You can learn more (and even grab some special merch) at kelsiehoss.com.

facebook.com/authorkelsiehoss
instagram.com/kelsiehoss